Out of Bounds

A Best Friend's Brother Sports Romance

Julia Connors

To all the girls who've ever watched their plans go up in flames,
I hope you also get to watch a better life rise up from the ashes.

Chapter One

SIERRA

I hold up the two ties I've purchased against the white dress shirt with the French cuffs that I know Peter prefers. I have a clear favorite—the rose gold tie that matches the color of my bridesmaid dress. But because I can guess how Peter is going to react to the color, I bought the tie in black too, as a backup.

My suitcase is already zipped up and sitting in front of the closet door. Sure, we're not leaving for thirty-six hours, but I like to be prepared. Peter's in Seattle for work and doesn't get back to Park City until tomorrow night, so I figured it'd take some of the stress off if I packed for him too.

But I'm not sure which tie to bring. Normally I wait for him to call me when he's on business trips so I don't interrupt work, but it's late enough that he might be done. I shoot him a quick text.

SIERRA

Hey, are you free for a quick question?

PETER

Sure, I've got a couple minutes, what's up?

I know he had a big dinner with clients tonight, so I'm surprised his reply is instantaneous. I hit the button to video call him, knowing that I have a better chance of getting him to wear the tie if he sees that it's not too pink. If I describe it, he'll veto it on principle.

"Hey," he says, as he sinks into a chair in his hotel room. His voice is quiet but rough, and his eyes are weary. Behind him, I can see the lights of Seattle twinkling through the enormous wall-to-wall windows. He runs his hand through his thick black hair, a sure sign that he's stressed. *How long has it been since I've run my hands through that hair?* It feels like maybe it's been forever. Peter is always tired from work or from working out, the two things he prioritizes these days. "What's up?"

I glance around our bedroom. It kind of looks like a bomb went off with all the clothes I have strewn about—the ones that didn't make the cut for the trip. "I'm just trying to get everything ready for Jackson and Nate's wedding. I bought you a tie, and I wanted to show it to you and make sure you like it," I tell him, and I flip the camera so he's looking at the tie draped over the neck of the white shirt hanging off the handle of the chest of drawers in our bedroom. I reach out and run my hand over the silk printed fabric, admiring the way my engagement ring sparkles and wondering if that will ever get old. "It's the same color as my bridesmaid dress."

"Pink," he says and then sighs, while running his hand along the stubble that's already covering his face—he always has a five o'clock shadow by the end of the day.

"It's not pink, it's rose gold. It's like if rosé and champagne had a baby," I say, the smile evident in my voice. But the way his face contorts into more of a grimace makes it clear that my description didn't help soften him to the color. I flip the camera back toward me so he can see my big brown eyes, the ones he always says he can't resist. "It'd be really nice if we coordinated, you know?"

He sighs again. I feel like there have been a lot more sighs this past year and a half that we've been engaged and living together, compared to the two years we were dating before that. I assume it's just because of the stress of his job, but he never seems to want to talk about it. I know he likes to keep work at the office, but I wish I could do more to support him when he gets home. That's hard when he travels so much and won't let me in on what's causing the stress.

"Should I add it to your suitcase?"

"My suitcase," he says, his brows furrowing, "is here with me."

"I mean the one I packed for you for our trip. I wanted to make things easy when you got home since we're leaving again like twelve hours later."

"Jesus, Sierra," he says, his eyes rolling to the ceiling. "I can pack my own damn suitcase."

"Fine," I say, my eyes narrowing at his ridiculous response. "I was just trying to be helpful."

"The thing is," he says, but then I hear a door open and a woman calls his name. His eyes go a little wide as he looks up, past the phone, and says, "Just a second, I'm on a call." Then he's back looking at me. "It's Jane. She stopped by with some paperwork for me to sign."

"Oh," I say, the word reflecting how deflated I feel that his administrative assistant seems to get so much more of his attention than I do, and apparently she even has a key to his hotel room.

Wait, why does she have a key to his room?

Then in the glass behind him I catch her reflection as she leans casually against the doorframe of the bathroom with one hand on her hip and her legs crossed at the ankle. It's not a super clear image, but it looks like she's wearing a black bra and panty set, with a black lace garter belt and thigh-high stockings leading to black stilettos.

"*Oh,*" I repeat, but this time it's the sound of a woman who knows she's just become the jilted fiancée. "Here's the thing, Peter." My voice is angry, and I can tell by the look in his eyes that he's surprised. I'm never angry. "I can see Jane's reflection in the window behind you, and there's not a piece of fucking paperwork in sight."

In the reflection, I see Jane dash back into the bathroom, and Peter's eyes are wide. I can't tell if he's surprised by my response, or just surprised to have been caught cheating.

"I was going to tell you," he says quickly.

"Oh yeah?" My voice, like my anger level, is rising quickly. "When, exactly? At Jackson's wedding?" I'm doing nothing to hide my anger and I know I sound practically hysterical.

Maybe this explains why he's been incapable of committing to a wedding date for us, even though we were engaged well before Jackson and her fiancé, Nate.

"No. Tomorrow, actually." He takes a deep breath. "I'm not coming home, and I won't be going to Jackson's wedding. I need to go to San Francisco for work."

"That's right you're not coming home!" I'm so mad I can't

even look at him. "I can't believe you, Peter. Sleeping with your admin. How fucking cliché."

I have the sinking realization that I'm Jackson's maid of honor, and I sure as hell was not planning to show up back in my hometown without my fiancé. Marrying Peter was going to be my proof that I'm not my mother, that I'll never be like her.

"Sierra, don't make this harder than it has to be," he says, his hand running through his hair again. I thought that was a signal he was stressed, but maybe instead he does it when he's guilty. For all the times he got home from work long after dinnertime, I now have to wonder if it was because he was with her instead. "Things haven't been good with us for a long time."

"Yeah," I say, "maybe because instead of working on *us*, you've been banging *her*."

"I'm sorry I've hurt you, but I'm not sorry about Jane," he says.

"You are an asshole," I tell Peter as I bring my fingers to my throat like I can hold back the bile rising up there. "I hope she gives you syphilis!"

"I'll be back in ten days," he says, his voice eerily calm despite my reaction. "That should give you time to move out after you're back from the wedding."

I throw the phone on the bed when he hangs up on me. Then, I pick up one of the pillows, cover my face with it, and let out the scream that's been building since I first saw Jane's reflection in the window.

———

"You're going to be fine," Petra insists as she pours some vodka into the plastic cup of orange juice and sets it on the tray table in front of me. I watch it bounce as our plane hits a little turbulence, but I don't reach out to steady it. I've never consumed alcohol for breakfast, but Petra insists it'll help me "calm the fuck down" about my life imploding. "In fact, you are going to be so much better off without that wanker."

I snort out a laugh at her Briticism. Petra looks like a Russian princess and she speaks four languages. She went to a British international school in Austria until her junior year of high school, and periodically these British phrases sneak into her English.

"My fiancé just left me for a younger woman who looks like a freaking underwear model. The bitch has a flat stomach and the tits of a twenty-year-old. No offense," I say, because Petra's original reason for moving to the States was her modeling contract, and I basically just described her body.

"None taken." She shrugs.

"I am *such* an idiot. There were so many signs," I say, because now that I've had a day to think about it, I'm ashamed I didn't see that he was cheating sooner. Always showering the minute he got home from work or the gym, business trips that lasted through the weekend, lack of interest in having sex with me—I should have recognized those signs for what they were.

"And you ignored them?"

"Ignorance is bliss, you know?" In response to my question, Petra shakes her head. I can imagine what she's thinking—poor pitiful Sierra, knowing something wasn't right and choosing to look the other way. "I wanted so badly for us to work. I kept telling myself I was being ridiculous and that there was no reason not to trust him."

"Had he ever given you a reason not to trust him?"

My eyebrows dip as I consider her question. "No. I mean, obviously he *wasn't* trustworthy, but I'd never caught him doing anything that made me think I shouldn't trust him."

"Then stop beating yourself up about it," Petra says. "What he did, that's on him. It's easy to see the signs in hindsight, but don't feel bad that you didn't see it sooner."

Don't feel bad? Right, like it would be possible *not* to feel bad about this.

"And now not only am I down one fiancé, I'm also going to be homeless."

"Let's not exaggerate about your housing situation," she says. "You can always stay with me until you find a new place. Or why don't you just ask Jackson if you can stay in her old condo until you find a new place? Her renters just moved out, right?"

I didn't realize the couple who were renting her Park City condo had moved out, and it irks me a tiny bit that Petra knew this, but I didn't. It's another reminder of how hard it is to have your lifelong best friend up and move across the country.

We both worked for the National Ski Team in Park City and for years I lived in Jackson's condo with her. When I got engaged a year and a half ago, I moved into Peter's place. Then a year ago Jackson reunited with her boyfriend from high school and together they moved to my hometown of Blackstone, NH—where I first met Jackson skiing, and where she, her fiancé Nate, and I all raced when we were in high school. Now they own the mountain and are ridiculously busy managing its growth. She's walking down the aisle in two days, and it feels like she lives a whole lot more than 2,000 miles away.

"Hmm," I say to Petra, "that idea has merit. I wouldn't want to take advantage, though. I'm sure they could rent that condo out weekly and make a killing, like Nate does with all his other properties."

"The last thing they need is another rental property. I'm sure she'd be happy to have you there."

One of Petra's special talents is expecting that the world will just bow to her, which it always does. She'd never think twice about something like this, never stop to consider if it might be an imposition. She's so upfront about everything, and I think sometimes she assumes everyone else is too. Like if Jackson and Nate didn't want to rent me their condo, they'd say so. But the truth is, Jackson would do anything to help me —just like I would for her—so she wouldn't say no if I asked. And I never want to take advantage of her like that.

"Maybe I'll float the idea when we see her at that cocktail reception thing tonight."

"I can't wait to see this place!" she says.

Nate and Jackson have built a new hotel at the base of the backside of Blackstone Mountain, and everyone attending their wedding is staying there. The hotel doesn't open for another three weeks, so this wedding is a trial run of sorts for them. Jackson has sent us pictures, but I have a feeling it'll be even more beautiful in person.

"Me too." With this early flight followed by the two hour drive from Boston's Logan Airport north to Blackstone, I'm sure all I'll want to do once we get there is crawl into my comfy hotel room bed and take a nap before tonight's event. Unfortunately, instead I'll be dropping Petra off at the hotel and then heading to my mom's place because she insisted on seeing me when I'm in town, and I refuse to give her any of my time tomorrow or the following day, which are all booked up with wedding plans.

I'm in Blackstone for Jackson, not for my mom's drama.

"You haven't even taken a sip yet," Petra says, eyeing the glass still sitting in front of me. Then she raises her own glass and says, "To being young and single and free!"

I raise my plastic cup and clink it with hers, even though thirty doesn't feel young and I don't want to be single or free.

I take a sip as Petra says, "We're going to find you the hottest guy at this wedding and you're going to have some no-strings-attached sex."

I almost choke on my drink, because everything Petra just said is consistently how she operates, but the complete opposite of my personality.

"I don't go for hot guys who want one-night stands," I say once I've successfully swallowed my drink. "I go for steady, stable guys who are looking for long-term commitments."

"Yeah, and that got you, Peter," she says, glancing out the window of the plane. "So maybe for once you can just let your hair down and have some fun."

"Is there any problem you don't think can be solved with sex?"

"Not that I've ever encountered."

————

"I don't know what you want from me, I really don't," I say to my mother. My back is to her as I stand at her small kitchen sink washing the takeout containers from the late lunch I picked up on my way here, but I can see her in the plastic-framed mirror hung above the faucet. She's sitting at the square kitchen table that takes up most of the floor space in her kitchen, chain-smoking cigarettes as she berates me for my life choices.

"Just want you to stop acting like you're so high and mighty. You're the queen of *nothing*"—she practically spits out the word—"and your gravy train just left the station with a new conductor."

I'm not sure that mixed metaphor works quite as well as she wants it to, but it stings just as she'd intended.

"Peter wasn't my gravy train, Ma, he was my fiancé. My partner. The person I was building a life with."

"Only reason a man goes looking elsewhere is if he ain't gettin' what he needs at home. Like your dad. Once you were born, I couldn't pay as much attention to him as he needed, so he went looking elsewhere." She inhales her cigarette so hard it's like she's trying to drink it.

I close my eyes so she can't see them roll back in my head, and I take a deep breath. I was raised on this story, this line of thinking. And when I was younger, I actually believed it. I spent the first decade of my life certain that I was the cause of my dad leaving. It wasn't until I saw other mothers in healthy relationships with their spouses, raising children they loved, that I understood the problem was actually my mother.

"The twins' dad too," she says, referring to the man who lived with us long enough to knock my mom up with my younger sisters and be gone before they turned one. "You think servicing your man is hard when it's just the two of you? Try it with a whiny-ass toddler and two babies."

I don't know which fallacy to address first. I wasn't a toddler when my sisters were born, I was six years old. Old enough to know the best places to hide when he started smacking my mom around, and too smart to attract attention to myself by whining. But there's no point in reminding her of this. Ma remembers things how she remembers them, and only a fool tries to convince her that she's wrong.

I turn and rest my lower back against the Formica countertop, locking eyes with her.

"The only problem with our sex life was how infrequently he was home." That, and the man had zero sense of how the female body worked. I literally had to teach him how to give me an orgasm, a skill he never *quite* mastered. "He worked long hours and had to travel a lot for work," I add, because apparently I feel the need to justify why I didn't know he was cheating. I really did think he was working all the time. I believed him when he said he was doing it for us, so we could have a comfortable life, buy a nice house, settle down, and have kids. Looking back, I was so naive not to suspect his lies.

"Yeah, well," she says, stubbing the end of her cigarette into the ashtray, "I think now we know that 'work' was really an excuse for fucking someone else." A look comes over her face, it's something like empathy which would make sense if my mom wasn't a sociopath.

Okay, maybe that's not a clinical diagnosis. But I can still remember sitting in Psychology 101 my freshman year of college and learning about antisocial personality disorder, or ASP, and feeling like everything finally made sense. My mom checked all the characteristics of a sociopath: her inability to think of anyone other than herself, the way she twists and manipulates people and situations, her complete lack of empathy, how often she lies to get her own way, and how she's never had a healthy relationship in her life—not with her friends, boyfriends, or even her children.

"Well," I say, crossing my arms across my chest. "At least I found out before we were married."

"You were never going to marry him," she says, then laughs like it is the most ludicrous suggestion in the world. Cue my internal groan, because here we go with her batshit crazy theories of curses and conspiracies. "The Lemieux women do . . . not . . . marry. As far back as our family tree goes, there's not a single marriage."

It's true that as far back as we *know* our family's history, at least the last four generations, Lemieux women have not married, and they've only had female children, all of whom have carried on the family name. But it's hard to know if that's choice or circumstance, and I think it's safe to say it's not the freaking curse my mom has always insisted it is.

It's a story her mom told her when she was young, before my grandmother died and my mom went to live with her aunt, who raised her with her own daughters. Her aunt believed in the curse, too, preached it like it was gospel. It's hard to know where the story originated—did my grandmother and great-aunt start telling that story, or had it been passed down from previous generations, told so frequently that it became a self-fulfilling prophecy?

"I'll be happy to be the first to break the curse, Ma."

"Oh yeah, like your sister Lydia did?"

Lydia was engaged, too, but got pregnant and then her

fiancé disappeared. No goodbye, no note, no car left behind, and no trail to follow. He just didn't come home from work one day, and no one has heard from him in the three years since. Lydia swears it was the curse, and I can see why it's comforting to believe that. Much easier than having to admit to yourself that your fiancé didn't have the balls to tell you he didn't want to marry you and raise your kid together. Lydia's a lot like Ma—difficult.

I'll admit that the experience did give me pause. Every single woman in my family has followed a similar pattern— got pregnant before marriage, then never got married. As far as I know, Lydia's is the only case of a disappearing fiancé. Ma was never engaged to my dad or the twins' dad and as far as she knows, neither her mom nor her aunt were ever engaged either.

Still, I may have visited my gynecologist and gotten an IUD a few years ago when Lydia's fiancé disappeared. Because even though I think the idea of a family curse is ridiculous, I also don't want to tempt fate by accidentally getting pregnant before I get married. Better safe than sorry, always.

"Don't bring Lydia into this," I say and press at the space between my eyebrows. It's hard to know if it's the smoke or the conversation, but this headache is coming on strong. I wish Sydney was here with me. My other little sister is my ally in this crazy family but, like me, she moved away as soon as she could. Now she lives in Boston with her boyfriend. Maybe she'll be the first to break this curse?

Stop it. There is no freaking curse. There's just a family full of dysfunction and difficult women.

"Whatever," my mom says, pausing to light up another cigarette. I wonder when she started chain-smoking? When I still lived at home, she was a casual social smoker and she never smoked in the house. "I'm just trying to help you set reasonable expectations. You've always been too much of a dreamer, envisioning yourself as so much better than the rest of us."

My eyes dart around Ma's trailer. As far as mobile homes go, it's a fairly nice one, but the windows are coated in a hazy layer of grime from all the cigarette smoke, the TV is always on even if the volume is off, and every horizontal surface is covered in knickknacks and mail and junk.

"I don't think I'm better than anyone else." This life my mother leads isn't for me and it never has been, but I can't say that to her. I was the straight A student who never got in trouble at school. I turned down some great colleges and instead got a full-ride to a state school nearby to stay close to my sisters, to protect them from Ma's crazy as much as I could. But when I graduated from college, I'd had enough.

By then, Sydney and Lydia were halfway through high school, and mostly self-sufficient. I spent a few years in Boston working at a startup and running their very successful marketing campaign, then I started my own company as a social networking adviser. Companies hired me to help them develop their social media marketing strategy, their branding, and their online aesthetic. Once Jackson started working at the Elite Training Center, which houses the offices and training facilities for the National Ski Team, in Park City, UT, she suggested I apply for a marketing job there. I haven't regretted that move for a day, not even when my best friend moved back to Blackstone.

"You can run your fancy ass all the way to Park City," Ma says, "but you can't outrun the curse. Admit it, baby girl, you're just like your mama and her mama and her mama before her."

I push myself away from the countertop, walk over to my mom, give her a kiss on her cheek, and say, "It was nice seeing you, Ma."

She coughs out a laugh, knowing how not nice the last two hours were for me. Still, I did my daughterly duty and visited my mom while I was in town.

Now, I can get on with my weekend, celebrating my best friend as she takes her walk down the aisle that my mom insists I'll never take.

Chapter Two

BEAU

I'm being watched.

I'm sitting on one of the large leather club chairs angled toward the two-story fieldstone fireplace in the lobby of the hotel when my neck starts tingling with the uncomfortable feeling of being watched. Maybe my sister is finally here, ten minutes late.

I glance to my left, toward the registration desk, and sure enough, the sweetest brown eyes stare back at me behind a piece of long blond hair that's fallen over her forehead. Definitely not my sister. She glances down at the key card in her hand, like she's embarrassed I caught her staring, then she glances back up at me. I'm surprised by what I see in that look and the shy smile she gives me. It's the look you give a guy across the bar when you want him to come talk to you, not the look you give someone you've known since they were in kindergarten.

She doesn't recognize me, I think with an internal chuckle. It's both a relief—given how things ended the last time I saw her—and some sort of poetic justice wrapped into one.

My lips curve into a smile, the one I've perfected. My smile is my secret weapon—it gets me into exclusive clubs when I'm not on the VIP list, and into the underwear of more women than I can count. She glances down at the suitcase that stands next to her, then lifts her eyes to look at me through her thick eyelashes. Is she trying to decide whether she should head for the elevator or come talk to me?

I'm about to make the decision for her, because honestly, Sierra realizing she's attracted to me before realizing who I am . . . this could be the most fun I've had in a while. But as I lean forward to stand, she turns and rushes toward the elevators. I'm so stunned I don't move, I just stay hunched forward and rest my elbows on my knees while I consider that she just ran away from me. Because shit like that doesn't happen—when I head toward women, they don't head in the other direction. Then again, Sierra has never been normal when it comes to my charms.

A few seconds later, Jackson rushes up, calling my name, and I'm forced to turn toward her. I stand and give her a quick, awkward hug over the back of the chair.

"Hi." She exhales. "Did you get it?"

"I did." I reach in my pocket and hand her the ring box I just retrieved at the jeweler thirty minutes away. "How did you manage to forget to pick this up?"

She shoves it in her jacket pocket as quickly as possible. "I've been a tad busy, Beau."

Be nice to your sister, my mother's words run through my brain as if she was standing right here speaking to me. "How's it going?"

"The wedding planning? Or opening a new hotel?"

"Both," I say, without mentioning how stupid I think she is for scheduling the two things so close together.

"It's . . . well, it's going. It's way more stressful than I want it to be. I'm not really sure what we were thinking."

"You could have picked a less busy weekend, or a different location," I suggest.

She looks at me like I'm an idiot. "New Year's Eve is our anniversary," she says, and it pulls at memories I've had no reason to think of in a long time. Pretty sure they first got together on New Year's Eve back in high school, and they definitely started dating again on the same date last year. "And," she continues, "it made sense to host it in the hotel and have you all stay here as a trial run before we open. But I wish someone else was in charge of all of it, you know?"

"Don't you guys have a general manager for the hotel who's handling all the details this weekend?" I mean, that's what Mom has told me, anyway.

"Yes, but we still have to . . ." She sighs. "Never mind. I wouldn't expect you to understand."

Don't let her get to you. Jackson's specialty is reminding me of all the ways I don't measure up. She's like a miniature version of my dad in that way. Instead of engaging, I look over my shoulder to see if Sierra is still in the lobby, but she's disappeared.

"I thought I just saw Sierra," I tell her. "How come she's getting here so late?"

"She had to go visit her mom." Jackson's voice is low and grim.

"Oh," I say, understanding immediately. From the time she was fourteen to eighteen, Sierra lived with us every weekend during the winters. She and Jackson were on the ski team together, and it was part of the agreement my dad, who was then the president of the ski team's Board of Directors, made with her mom—Sierra could ski if she paid for it herself and her mom didn't have to bring her to practices or races. I've had minimal interactions with Sierra's mom, but from what I've heard from everyone who knows her, she's quite a piece of work. So different from her very sweet oldest daughter.

"Listen, I have a favor to ask," I tell Jackson, eager to change the subject from Sierra. I don't know why I brought her up in the first place. Sierra was my first and longest-lasting crush, and Jackson always teased me mercilessly when I was a kid. Given that I was in middle school and she was in high school, it was stupidly optimistic of me to think our five-year age difference wasn't going to matter. And it still mattered, even when we were older, a painful lesson I learned before I even became an adult.

"Yeah?" she asks, glancing at her watch.

"You still have that condo in Park City?"

She eyes me suspiciously, then sweeps her hair over her shoulder. "Yeah, why?"

"Any chance I could stay in it for a few weeks in January?"

She assesses me with her bright green eyes. "You're going to be in Park City?"

"We're snowboarding there in preparation for the X Games, but my accommodations fell through."

"Fell through? How?" Her dark eyebrows dip as she tries to read into this situation.

"I was supposed to be staying with this girl, but things got complicated . . ." I don't bother finishing the sentence. She can make of it whatever she wants.

"Ohh," she teases, "did she want more than a one-weekend commitment?"

"Not exactly," I tell her.

"Well, as it turns out, you're in luck. We had renters who just moved out, and we're about to start remodeling the primary bathroom. You're welcome to stay there if you can be the point of contact for the contractors. Let them in every morning, make sure they're doing quality work."

"Sure." I shrug. "I can manage that."

"All right," she says, "I'll text you the code for the keypad and let the condo association know you'll be staying there. Just text me the dates when you have a minute."

"You're the best," I say on autopilot. Jackson is the best at a lot of things, but being my big sister isn't one of them.

She looks like she wants to say something in return, but she sighs instead. "I've got to go get ready for the cocktail reception. Thanks so much for picking up the ring for me. See you in a couple hours."

With my one wedding-related responsibility complete, I head out to my car. I promised Mom that I'd come over for an early dinner before tonight's party, and right now I will take every moment with her that I can have. Even if Dad is going to be there.

———

"So," Dad says as soon as my mom is done serving up the lasagna, "how is snowboarding going?"

"It's great," I tell him.

"You actually competing, or just partying?"

Whereas Dad was never anything but supportive of Jackson's skiing, he's always been skeptical of my snowboarding. I try to remind myself that he just doesn't understand the culture like he does skiing, but it's also hard not to be frustrated by his lack of willingness to try.

"Here," I say as I whip out my phone and open to a video a friend took of me four days ago, "watch." I hand it to my dad, and my mom gets up and comes to stand behind him before he presses play.

As I take a few bites of lasagna, I study their faces as they watch me do what I love. I can tell exactly what's happening in the video by Mom's face. It's full of worry as I approach the first jump, and she pulls her head back like she's watching a car accident as I enter a backside rodeo, then breathes a sigh of relief when I complete the one and a half rotations and land. It's like Mom's face is on a loop, repeating the same look each time I approach a jump and complete a trick. Dad's face remains stonily impassive.

"Wow," my mom says when the video ends. "I don't know how you do that."

"Lots of practice," I tell her.

"Good," my dad says before shoving a bite of lasagna in his mouth and chewing it aggressively.

"The X Games are coming up," I tell them, and my mom smiles at me like the sun shines out my ass while my dad just grunts in response. At least Mom loves me enough for the both of them, or she tries anyway. "We're training in Park City for a few weeks, then heading to Aspen."

"Who's we?" my dad asks. Does he really not know, or is he feigning ignorance?

"Same as always. Drew, Lance, and me." They've been my

best friends since college and we've traveled together ever since.

"What's after the X Games?" Mom asks.

"We might be going up to Whistler. Not sure, though, we might head back to Switzerland. I have to be in Austria a few weeks after that."

"You ever get tired of being a nomad?" Dad asks.

"Not really." I shrug and take a bite of Mom's lasagna. I chew for a second before I say, "It suits me."

Mom laughs, her dark face lighting up in delight, the polar opposite of Dad's scowl. My mom is a first generation Italian American and has the dark Southern Italian complexion to prove it. Until recently, her long hair was brown, so dark it was almost black. Now it's a soft gray. Dad, on the other hand, grew up in Ireland. He's fair-skinned with hair that was mostly red when I was younger but has deepened to an auburn. Jackson is like a fairer version of Mom and I'm a darker version of Dad.

"You'll get tired of it eventually," Dad says, so sure that he knows me better than I do.

"We'll see." It's an old argument, and there's no point in engaging. In the end, it's inevitable that he'll be right—I'm sure I won't want to do this *forever*. But I'd be stupid not to hold out as long as I can.

———

I glance around the cocktail reception, then give my mom a kiss on the cheek and tell her, "I'll be back in a bit." Mom's sister just sat down next to her, and I want to give them time to catch up. Like the rest of her family, Aunt Marianna still lives in Brooklyn. With Mom finally in remission after her second recurrence of cancer, they haven't seen each other in person recently.

I mean, maybe I'm also giving them space because I want to do a lap around this room to see if I can spot Sierra. I want to see her reaction the moment she recognizes me, because I can promise it's going to be priceless.

I'm walking toward the bar when a large hand reaches out of the crowd and grabs the back of my neck, pulling me toward him. "Asshole," I mutter when I glance up, fists already formed, and see Nate grinning at me. "You don't grab a guy from behind like that unless you want to get punched."

"Someone's a little high-strung tonight," Nate says as we step aside to let a waitress with a tray full of empty glasses pass by. She has some kick-ass legs, and the fact that Nate doesn't even look at them makes me feel better about him marrying my sister. Not that I ever had any doubts they'd end up married. Even during the years they spent apart, when Jackson was sure Nate had left her for good, I figured there must be more to the story. Turns out I was right.

"Sorry," I mumble. "Not my favorite place, not my favorite people."

"Don't be a dick. This is your family, and this is my home."

I don't relish being the black sheep of my family, despite the fact that I play the role well.

"You really didn't have anyone else who was willing to be your best man?"

"Don't make this awkward," Nate says, and shifts his weight while shoving his hands in the pockets of his expensively tailored pants.

"Awkward like having to wear a fucking tux?" I ask. Seriously, who invented those ridiculous monkey suits? There is just no need for a suit with a vest and a dress shirt with tiny buttons and a stiff collar, and don't even get me started on the stupidity of a tie.

"No, I mean awkward, like having to tell you about the sexual seduction your sister engaged in to convince me to ask you."

It's a good thing I'm not taking a swig of my beer, because hearing those words would have had me spitting it out all over Nate. Somehow, he manages this with a straight face.

"Yeah, because when you asked me and she yelled 'don't fuck this up, Beau' in the background, that really seemed like she wanted me standing up next to you at her wedding."

Nate cracks a smile and reaches out to clasp my shoulder. "Let's face it, you *do* kind of have a way of fucking things up."

"Not everyone can be the perfect golden boy like you." Even though Jackson and I have a tenuous relationship on a good day, and he's been dating my sister most of my life, I've always liked Nate. I guess in some ways, he's been the supportive older brother I needed when my dad refused to be the father I wanted him to be.

"Hey," Nate says, "I fucked things up once too. But I owned it and made up for it, and look where we are now." I watch as his eyes immediately track Jackson as she moves across the room, talking to guests.

I'm tempted to ask him if the ball and chain ever hurts, but instead I just say, "Yeah, congrats."

You could not pay me enough to trade places with him. The guy walked away from his spot on the National Ski Team after a stellar first year back on the ski racing scene, all so he could move to Blackstone and marry Jackson. Traveling the world doing what you love versus living in a tiny ski town in Nowhere, New Hampshire—not exactly the choice I would have made. My boots are made for walking, and so far they've walked on four continents, and I'm determined to make it to all of them, eventually.

I mean, Nate did also buy a ski mountain, and they built this really beautiful hotel. So it's business that brought him back here too, not just my sister. But still. I could not imagine being tied down like this. Under any circumstances. Ever.

Nate takes one look at my face and says, "You seem like maybe you could use something stronger than that beer."

"You might be right about that. Have fun tonight," I tell him as I head toward the bar.

Chapter Three

SIERRA

It takes a long shower and a glass of wine while getting ready, but I finally feel like myself again. The grimy feeling from my visit with my mother has been washed away. My long blond hair is curled into the loose beachy waves I prefer. My makeup is simple: minimal eyeliner, some mascara, and red lips.

The red lipstick is courtesy of Petra, who handed it to me at the airport this morning, assuring me that a bold red is just what I need to feel confident about my new life. Looking at myself in the mirror, I think that maybe she was right.

Peter doesn't know what he's missing, I tell myself—but my throat tightens and my eyes water as I think back to seeing Jane's reflection in his hotel room. Did he go running to her because I wasn't good enough, or was there something so tempting about her that he strayed, even though he didn't want to?

I grab my clutch and head for the door to my hotel room so I can't dwell on losing Peter. I spent too damn long on my makeup to ruin it with more tears.

Maybe Petra's right about a rebound this weekend. That guy I saw in the lobby this afternoon was so hot I almost couldn't look at him. Those chiseled cheekbones, the strong jaw covered in a few days of stubble, the brown hair shot through with strands of auburn, those piercing eyes so dark they were almost black. I'm flushed just thinking about him.

Obviously, it's someone Jackson and Nate know. He looked slightly familiar, but even though I've been thinking about him since I got up to my room, I still can't figure out how I know him. Earlier in the lobby, I couldn't get away fast enough because, after traveling and being at my mom's, I was a frumpy, smelly mess—in no state to meet someone that hot. Maybe I'll bump into him tonight, and hopefully he won't recognize me as the disheveled girl he saw earlier.

I'm in the elevator when Petra's text comes in.

PETRA

You're more than fashionably late.

SIERRA

I know. I'm heading down now. Where are you?

PETRA

With Jackson at a table by the fireplace.

SIERRA

Be there in a sec.

The elevators are tucked into a mirrored vestibule off the lobby, so when the doors open and I step out, I'm greeted by about twenty visions of myself. And for the first time in a long time, I feel confident. The black lace dress I'm wearing has a plunging neckline and hugs every curve but also hits my knee, so it feels sexy but sophisticated. The three pieces of black ribbon that circle the waist make me look like I have more of an hourglass figure than I really do.

Jackson and Petra are great friends, but sometimes going out with them, I feel like the awkward sidekick to two super-models. It was better before Lauren had her babies, because then there were four of us. And Lauren is as normal as I am in that she's never graced a billboard or a magazine cover. But now she mostly stays home with her girls, and I'm always with Petra.

I weave through the crowd and wonder how I could be at my best friend's wedding and still know almost no one here, then find Jackson and Petra standing at a cocktail table near the fireplace, just where Petra said they'd be.

When I approach, Jackson puts both her hands on my shoulders and holds me at a distance. "Wow, Sierra, you look gorgeous tonight."

"Thanks," I say as she pulls me in for a hug. "I'm sorry I couldn't get here any earlier. My freaking mom." I sigh. "Put me to work tomorrow . . . anything I can do to help, just let me know."

"Don't be ridiculous," Jackson says. "Tomorrow we relax. We'll get massages and mani-pedis at the spa, and then we have the rehearsal."

"The spa is already open?" Petra asks.

"Just for us. Gotta test it out and make sure everything's up to snuff before real guests start booking appointments. And Lauren will be here in time to join us. She and Josh are taking the same early flight tomorrow as you girls did today. And my mom, but that's it. Oh, and there will be champagne, of course." Jackson's green eyes gleam against her gold eyeshadow, which is subtle but matches her dress. With her wavy brown hair falling halfway down her back, and her dramatic pouty lips, she looks amazing.

I tell her as much and she rolls her eyes. "You can't even imagine how *not* glamorous my life is right now. I'm up to my eyeballs in meetings, and planning, and business negotiations, and decorating."

"Well, it paid off," I tell her. "Everything about this hotel is perfection. I think you have a little bit of your mom's interior design blood in you, after all."

"It's true," Petra says. "You have amazing taste. I can't believe you did all this! And with Nate still racing for part of it." Petra shakes her head. Those months at the beginning of this project where Nate was still in Europe racing and Jackson was here managing the project were tough on her.

"I swear I've spent the last few months in a hard hat and steel toe boots," she says with a small laugh, "hoping this place turns out as beautifully as Nate and I envisioned. It's nice to get dressed up and feel pretty for a change."

"We are gorgeous," Petra purrs. "Let's get a photo before we mess up our lipstick with drinks." She props her phone up on the table and sets the timer and somehow we manage to take a great photo, which she sends to me immediately. "Post this, so Peter sees it and knows what he's missing."

"Oh my God, Sierra," Jackson says. "How are you holding up? I'm so sorry, I should have asked sooner. You just looked so amazing when you walked in, like there was no way you were pining away over *him.*"

"I'll be fine," I say, glancing away. I'm not lying, I will be. "Eventually." It's hard to admit that I'm more upset about not seeing his betrayal sooner than I am about never seeing him again.

"I told her she should just find someone this weekend and have some rebound sex," Petra says, her throaty voice booming loud enough that I feel like people are looking at us.

"Seriously, Petra, could you not announce this to the whole room?" I say under my breath.

"I fully support that plan. Several of Nate's college friends are still single." Jackson wiggles her eyebrows.

"We'll see. I'm still trying to forget that Peter could have been so perfect."

"You can't love people for who they could be, you have to love them for who they are," Petra says, her eyes distant in a way that makes me wonder who she's thinking about.

"You read that somewhere?" I give her a wink to let her know I'm at least partially kidding. According to Petra, she's never been in love—but sometimes I wonder.

"I love you guys with all my heart. There's no room for anyone else," Petra insists. "Hey," she says to me, "weren't you going to ask Jackson something?"

The only reason I don't kick her is because I'm an adult. Or trying to be one, anyway. I thought by thirty I'd have this shit all figured out, instead I'm asking my friends if I can crash at their place.

"So, Petra mentioned that you don't have renters at your condo anymore. Do you have new renters moving in?"

"No, not yet. Why?"

"Well, Peter gave me ten days to get my stuff packed and move out." I bite my lower lip because I can feel it trembling and I will not cry. Not tonight.

"Oh, sweetie," Jackson says, putting her arm around my

shoulders and pulling me to her side. "That asshole. Stay at my place. For as long as you want."

"I *really* don't want to intrude."

"We probably won't rent it until after ski season because we're hoping to slip away at some point in the early spring for a long weekend in Park City. Honestly, stay as long as you'd like." Jackson gives my left shoulder a squeeze and rests her head on my right one.

"Thank you." I'm beyond relieved to at least have some time to find a new place. Petra's great, but with the string of men who parade through her bedroom, couch surfing at her place would have been awkward.

"Oh, shit," Jackson says, her head popping up off my shoulder.

"What?" Petra and I ask at the same time.

"Shit," Jackson repeats, scrunching her eyebrows together. We just stare at her, waiting for her revelation. "I forgot that I already told Beau he can stay there for a few weeks."

"Beau is going to be in Park City?" I ask. My stomach is flipping over in a way that's hard to ignore. I've never told Jackson about the last time I saw her little brother—first because I didn't want her to think less of him, then because by the time I'd finally worked up the nerve to say something, it felt like I'd already kept it from her for too long.

"Yeah, I guess they're training for the X Games before heading to Aspen," she says. "I'm not sure how long he'll be there. He's supposed to text me the dates."

"Okay, no worries," I tell her. "Petra already offered up her couch, which will be fine. It's only until I find a new place anyway. How long can that take?"

"During ski season?" Jackson rolls her eyes. "Could take months."

She's right. People who aren't living in their condos rent them out on a weekly basis to out-of-town skiers unless, like Nate and Jackson, they don't need the money.

I glance at Petra, who shrugs. "You're welcome to my couch as long as you need it."

"No," Jackson says, "that's ridiculous. Why would you sleep on Petra's couch when I have two bedrooms in my place? You and Beau can easily stay there at the same time. And he's not even going to be there for that long."

My stomach ties into a knot when I think about coming face-to-face with Beau. Thanks to our Maid of Honor and Best Man duties, I know we'll have to spend some time together this weekend. And I've been praying he's forgotten all about the last time we saw each other almost ten years ago. If he looks at me with the same hurt in his eyes, I'll feel like I need to apologize all over again and that'll be way more awkward than just pretending like it never happened.

"I really don't want to impose," I tell Jackson.

Petra groans. "Stop with the 'I don't want to impose' shit," she says, her husky voice like a growl. "You are our friend, and it's not an imposition to help you. For either of us. You'd do the same for one of us in a heartbeat. So stay at Jackson's or stay at my place, but stop feeling bad about it."

"Maybe I don't want to impose *on Beau*. I assume he isn't planning on having a roommate?"

Jackson sweeps her hand through the air like she's brushing away my argument. "I didn't promise him the whole place to himself. Besides, you used to live there. In fact, your bed and dresser are still in the spare bedroom." I hadn't taken those with me when I moved into Peter's apartment after we got engaged because he had a one-bedroom place that was already furnished and there was no room for my furniture.

"Why don't you check with him and make sure he's okay with me staying there too?" I suggest.

"If he's not," she says, "he can find somewhere else to stay. There's no way I'm leaving my best friend homeless so Beau can crash there for a few weeks. Nope. The place is yours, Sierra, and he can stay too if he wants." She tilts her drink back and takes a sip.

"Just talk to him, okay? I assume he's here?"

"Yeah, I saw him earlier today, but haven't seen him yet tonight," she says. "He actually went and picked up Nate's ring for me. Would you believe I almost forgot to pick it up from the jeweler after having it engraved?"

"You're juggling a lot," I remind her. "It's a miracle you haven't dropped anything big yet."

"At this point, I just can't wait to get married," Jackson says. "I think everything is in place. Now I just want to enjoy the next couple days."

"Cheers to that," Petra says, raising her glass. Jackson raises hers to the toast, but I'm empty handed. "How do you not have a drink?" Petra says, a distinct ring of disappointment in her voice.

"I don't know, I just came right to you two when I got down here. I didn't stop at the bar."

"Go get a drink," Jackson says, smiling at me. "We'll be here all night."

———

The bar's a little busy when I arrive, which is to say that the one bartender is having trouble keeping up with the twenty or so people who all want drinks at the same time. I give her a sympathetic smile as she deals with a group of older men who are shamelessly flirting with her. *Who are these people?*

I grab one of the cocktail plates sitting on the bar and collect some hors d'oeuvres from the passing servers. After the late lunch with my mom that left my stomach turning sour, I wasn't in the mood for dinner. But I'm already feeling that one glass of wine I had in my hotel room and know that if I don't put food in me now, the alcohol will hit me hard. I don't need to add a hangover to the list of reasons this weekend already sucks for me. Nope, it's only up from here.

Think about how far you've come, I remind myself. *Think about the job you love and the life you've built for yourself. The wonderful life you'll continue to build without Peter, because fuck him.* I spear an olive with my toothpick, wishing it was Peter's heart.

I'm furious at myself for not seeing the signs. I'm embarrassed and ashamed that I let someone deceive me like Peter did. But, I'm not heartbroken. Maybe that part comes later, after the anger fades?

Another bartender comes through the swinging door behind the bar with a fresh rack of glasses. After setting them on the bar, he turns his attention to me.

"What can I get you?" he asks.

"Prosecco?" I could really use something bubbly.

He pops the cork out of the already open bottle and gives

me a heavy pour. "Have a great night," he says as he slides the glass over to me.

I thank him and shove the last of my hors d'oeuvres, a goat cheese stuffed fig, in my mouth so I don't have to carry my plate back to our table. I realize—too late—that I really should have taken smaller bites. It's so large I can hardly chew it.

"Hey," I hear from beside me. The voice is smooth and rich, deep without being raspy. I glance up, and *holy shit*, he's even more gorgeous up close. The eyes that looked almost black from across the lobby this afternoon are a dark brown with flecks of amber around the pupil. His skin is pale with olive undertones, and if the thick scruff on his face is any indication, it's been a few days since he's shaven. I didn't think I liked facial hair, but man was I wrong. And he's so close— sitting on the barstool right next to me—though I have no idea how he got there. Was he there the whole time? Or was I so lost in my own thoughts that I didn't even notice when he sat down?

I give him a closed-mouth smile, then point to my mouth as I start chewing. This is humiliating. Why can't I just be normal and not have shoved a huge fig in my mouth before the hottest guy in the place started talking to me?

He takes a sip of his drink. "I hope it's good," he says as I chew.

I lift one eyebrow and nod. I can feel myself turning red from the embarrassment. But after I swallow about half of my bite, I recover with "Oh, *it's good*."

His resulting smile is blinding. Seriously. And the seductive laugh that follows is like a hit of adrenaline to my system. After I finally swallow the rest of my food, I take a sip of my Prosecco, set my elbow on the bar, and rest my chin on my palm as I lean toward him. "I highly recommend the stuffed figs."

"Interesting choice," he says, and his eyes track from my face down my body.

"Why is that?" I ask, analyzing his face closely. There's something so familiar about him, but I can't figure out how I know him.

"Well, figs have a long history of being linked to human sexuality."

"*Do* they, now?" Clearly I'm skeptical.

"In the Western world, fig leaves are often used in art to cover, or represent, men's and women's"—he glances down where my dress folds in my lap—"genitals. According to several ancient texts, Adam and Eve gained their knowledge of good and evil from a fig tree in the Garden of Eden—thus the fig is the 'forbidden fruit.' And in some Eastern religions, the fig represents feminine sexuality. They're often used to symbolize the *yoni*, which in Hinduism is a symbol of the divine procreative energy and is a representation of the goddess Shakti."

"You know an awful lot about"—without even meaning to, I lean toward him like he's a magnet—"figs." I try not to laugh. He's got to be making this up.

"You don't believe me," he says, but his voice is teasing. He's not offended in the least.

"Do you specialize in figs?" I tease as I pull a lock of my hair back behind my ear.

"Not exactly," he says.

I tilt my head to the side like I'm considering his story. "Is knowing about figs part of your job?"

"Not really." The hint of a smile plays at his lips.

"Do you grow figs?"

"Can't say that I do." His low voice is somehow familiar, an eerie yet comforting sound.

"So why would I believe you?"

"Care to place a little wager on this?" he asks as he moves his hand so it rests on the back of my barstool. I've never felt more comfortable being boxed in by a man.

I take another sip of my Prosecco and the glass is nearly empty. *When and how did that happen?* My brain reminds me that he wouldn't want to wager on this unless he actually did know a thing or two about the topic. If he was blatantly making shit up, he wouldn't offer up a bet. Unless he's bluffing?

"What do you have in mind?" I ask, eyeing him over the rim of my glass.

"If I'm right, you have to *really* try to catch the bouquet at the wedding."

I roll my eyes right in his face. "No, thanks."

"Why not?" His face is only a foot from mine, and I don't remember how we got quite so close.

"I don't want to catch it."

"Fair enough," he says, sitting back in his seat. "But look into figs when you have a minute, just so you'll know if I was making all that up."

"Were you?"

"I guess you'll find out." He shrugs.

I take my last sip of the Prosecco and set my empty glass on the bar, hoping the bartender will notice I need a refill. "So, do you live around here, or are you in town for the wedding?"

"Just in town for the wedding," he says, but the way his lips curve up on one side makes it seem like there's more to his words than I'm understanding.

"So, how to do you know Jackson and Nate?"

A silent laugh makes his shoulders shake. A fact that barely registers because I can't stop looking at his ridiculously gorgeous smile and those full lips surrounded by closely trimmed facial hair. They are stupidly kissable, and that's all I can think about as I gaze at them. "I've known the Shanahans my whole life."

"Then why haven't we met before?"

"What makes you think we haven't?"

Is he fucking with me? "I think I'd remember if we'd met."

"And why's that?" he asks, a mischievous sparkle in his eyes.

Fishing for compliments, I see. Obviously, I'm not going to tell him he's too hot to have forgotten about. "I have a good memory."

He starts to lean toward me again, but then there's a hand on his shoulder and one on mine, and I turn to find Jackson literally in my face.

"I'm so glad you two found each other," she says. Which probably means that this hottie is one of Nate's single college friends she mentioned earlier. She turns toward him and says, "I've been looking for you. Did Sierra already catch you up on the roommate situation?"

Roommate situation? My brain must be a little fuzzy from the Prosecco, because I thought her little brother was going to be my . . .

Oh.

Holy.

Crap.

They both look at me expectantly, but it's like my tongue is paralyzed inside my mouth. My brain is too busy trying to convince my lungs not to hyperventilate, it can't focus on forming words anyway.

"The roommate situation?" he says.

"Yeah," Jackson says when I don't respond. "Sierra needs a place to stay while she looks for a new apartment, so I told her she could have one of the bedrooms in my condo. I hope you'll be a good roommate," she says to him, but the way she says it, she might as well have said *don't be a dick to my best friend.*

"Probably time we set some roommate ground rules then," Beau says, and gives me a wicked grin. "Talk to you later, Jax."

Jackson bristles, as she always does when anyone but Nate calls her by that nickname, but she doesn't move. She looks at me like she's trying to figure out if I want to stay and have this conversation or if I need her to help me escape.

"I'll be over in a minute," I tell her. She nods, and as she walks away, I suddenly wish I'd just gotten up and gone with her. Why the hell did I stay here with Beau?

"So," he says before his top teeth sink into that lower lip. "I guess you didn't recognize me."

"Obviously." My mind is spinning, and a million questions are bouncing around in there. *Has he grown a foot and gained forty pounds of muscle since I last saw him? How could a shorter haircut and facial hair so completely change someone's look? Oh shit, does flirting with my best friend's little brother make me the sleaziest maid of honor ever? I can't take my eyes off him, how am I going to live with him?*

That last thought is the one that's got my stomach turning over, because I can't convince myself that this delicious man sitting in front of me—so confident and powerful and large—is the scrappy little brother I used to hang out with every weekend growing up. The boy I knew was just that—a boy—and he looked and sounded nothing like this man. Even the last time I saw him, when he was still in high school, he hadn't lost the baby fat in his face, was barely taller than me, and probably outweighed me by all of twenty pounds.

Still, how could I not have known? I wonder. I guess because I expected Beau to look like a grown-up version of that boy, and he's changed a lot. I try to remember the last time I saw a picture of him when he didn't have ski goggles and a helmet on, and I can't think of a time.

"I feel like you're having a moment right now," he says, his eyes sweeping over my face before he turns toward the bar and orders us both more drinks.

I watch him talk to the bartender, and I realize that I had actually bought into Petra's plan for rebound sex, and I'd been hoping it would be with him. *No, no, no.*

Why does he have to be so easy to talk to? Why does he have to be so good looking? Why does he have to be so much younger than me, and share DNA with my best friend?

"Here you go," he says as he hands me the champagne flute filled with another glass of bubbly. I stare at the glass in my hand like I've forgotten what to do with it.

"I can't be your roommate," I blurt out.

I cringe at this new reality, where I am officially the most awkward person in human history.

Beau raises an eyebrow at me, and says, "Take a breath, and a drink."

"Don't patronize me, Beau."

"Why are you looking for a new place to live?"

"My old living arrangement fell through." I take a drink just to break the eye contact, then glance at the mirror above the bar. He's still staring at me, but he doesn't press me for more details, which I appreciate.

"So why can't we be roommates, exactly?"

"I . . ." I don't know what to say. "I don't really want to live with a guy."

"But you knew what the roommate situation was, and you agreed to it. Until you realized exactly who *I* was." He puts a hand on his chest and I realize the trap he's placed me in. I was okay living with Beau when I thought it was Jackson's little brother who I had zero interest in. But this gorgeous man bantering with me, the one I'm stupidly attracted to but could never touch because of who he is—*him* I don't think I can live with. "You afraid you won't be able to keep your hands off me if we're roommates, Sierra?"

The sound of my name on his tongue might be the sexiest thing I've ever heard, and it has me flushing. The heat travels up my chest and my neck as I mumble, "Don't be ridiculous."

"Then it's settled, Roomie. On one condition."

"I haven't even agreed to live with you and you think you're setting conditions?"

"Believe me, you'll be okay with this one." He pauses. "You have to take Jackson's old bedroom."

"Why? The spare bedroom is still filled with my furniture from when I lived there."

"Because honestly, I can't stay in a room and sleep in a bed that I know Nate was fucking my sister in."

For reasons I don't understand, I'm turned-on by the word *fucking* coming out of his mouth. It's the way his teeth press into his lip before the word rolls off his tongue and the slow way he enunciates it. It's actually a sensual word to watch someone say—not that I've noticed before now. But once again my eyes are glued to his lips, and when his tongue darts out to wet them, I feel the familiar pull of attraction right between my legs.

I need to get out of here, away from him.

"Fine," I say as I push my barstool back and stand. I should have thought about the close proximity that'd put us in before I did it though, because suddenly his face and mine are only inches apart and I'm standing between his legs. "I'll take Jackson's old room."

I grab my drink off the bar and turn, pushing past his knee in my rush to get away. And as I walk back toward Jackson and Petra, I'm trying to figure out if the sound I hear is him laughing at me, or if it's all in my imagination.

Chapter Four

BEAU

"You okay?" I ask Nate as I approach him. He's staring out the window, seemingly oblivious to the obnoxiousness going on around him. His best friend from childhood, Brian St. Cyr, started passing around a flask half an hour ago. Nate's the only one of us who isn't buzzing right now.

"Yeah," Nate says, tugging at the knot of his tie where it meets his shirt collar. His voice has a dreamy quality to it that I'm only used to hearing from chicks.

"What's up, then? You seem . . ." I don't know how to describe him right now. Nervous? Anxious? He's about to get married, so I have no idea how he might be feeling.

He takes a deep breath. "I'm ready to watch her walk down the aisle already, that's all."

"You're so fucking whipped," I say as I knock shoulders with him. He glances over at me, a weary side-eye if I've ever seen one. I spent so much of my life looking up to Nate, both literally and figuratively, that it's still disconcerting to look him in the eye.

"Do you remember when we ran into each other a few years ago? Where were we, Lake Louise?"

"Hell if I know." The mountains all start to blend together when you travel as much as I do. "But yeah, I remember. You were a mess."

"I don't drink, and you got me drunk—asshole."

Nate's only got one kidney and as a preventive measure he abstains from alcohol. He's also a vegan or some crazy shit, but given that the dude doesn't have an ounce of fat on his body, I guess it works okay for him.

"If I'd known you were going to get all sappy about my sister, I'd never have given you alcohol." Nate and Jackson were still broken up at that point. Dude was definitely not over her, though.

"That was the lowest I'd ever been. It had been like four years without her, and I thought for sure we'd be back together by then, but she'd just started dating Marco."

"Is that what finally lit a fire under your ass?" I ask. Less than a year after that, Nate managed to snag a spot on the National Ski Team, seemingly out of the blue, and landed Jackson as his physical therapist. The rest, as they say, is history.

"That's when I realized that it was now or never with her. You can't even imagine what it's like to spend five years without the person you love more than anyone or anything in the world." He pauses, and I don't respond because he's right. I can't imagine. I wouldn't even want to know what that feels like. "Sometimes I still can't believe that I managed to get her to marry me."

"Maybe you should be looking at this a little differently.

Like maybe she's lucky to have you," I say. I was always on Nate's side, even when he left her.

Nate coughs out a laugh. "I'm the lucky one, man." His voice is reverent and sincere, and I'm not used to seeing him vulnerable like this. So I do what I always do—I give him shit.

"You sure? Because if you're having second thoughts, my car is outside. I can get us to the closest airport in like thirty minutes."

He lets out a real laugh this time. "Not going to happen. Dude, nothing's stopping me from getting to the altar today." He's quiet for a moment, then says, "You think Sierra is making the same offer to Jax right now?"

"That's not her style." Sierra is far too sweet to make that suggestion. Then again, if memory serves, she's also a fierce friend—so if it's what Jackson needed, I don't doubt she'd drive the getaway car.

"Still hanging on to that crush?" Nate asks, folding his arms over his chest without looking at me. I glance out the window to see what's got him so transfixed, but he's just looking at the woods that surround this place.

"That's not *my* style."

"Yeah, she's not a fuck-and-forget kind of girl, is she?"

"I wouldn't know." I shrug.

"Don't go there, okay?" he says, and I can't read the tone of his voice.

"What are you saying, man?"

"I hear you're going to be living together. Don't fuck with her, Beau. She's a good person and my future wife's best friend." He turns toward me to say, "Messing things up with Sierra would permanently damage your relationship with your family."

"Thanks for the vote of confidence," I mutter, crossing my arms over my chest, unintentionally mimicking his stance. Nate's just confirmed what I already knew—in my family's eyes, I rank below Sierra.

"I'm telling you this because I've always thought of you like a younger brother. But I know that you've always had a crush on her, and I also know your reputation with women."

"Can't help it if women crawl into my bed left and right."

Nate grunts in response but doesn't say anything.

"So you're saying she deserves better than me?"

"I'm saying that she deserves better than what you'll *offer* her, which is a short-lived fling before you rush off to a new adventure."

Nothing he's saying is wrong, but it still pisses me off.

"Don't worry, man. I'm not looking for an older woman. That shit's fun when you're a teenager with a crush on your older sister's best friend, but she's in her thirties now." Five years is still a big age difference, even at twenty-five. "Besides, she's not my type."

Everything I'm saying is true, which means I can't explain why I can't get her out of my head. I had fully planned on giving her the brush-off when I saw her. If necessary, I was going to be a dick to her. Make her feel like she'd made me feel all those years ago. I didn't expect her to be so genuinely sweet, with a smile that did strange things to my chest. I didn't mean to flirt with her, it was like my brain was giving my body directions it was making up on the fly, instead of the directions I'd planned out ahead of time.

"Good," Nate says, slinging an arm over my shoulders. "What is taking so fucking long?" he asks, nodding over his shoulder toward the door that leads into the room where the ceremony will be held.

"I'll find out," I tell him. I turn toward the door, but the wedding planner saves me the trouble of having to find her by walking right through it.

"All right, guys," she says, "time to roll."

She gets us in order, with me behind Nate, followed by his friend Jeff from the ski team, and his friend St. Cyr from high school. We walk out and stand at the front of the room, just like we practiced at last night's rehearsal. The one where Sierra wouldn't even look at me. I'd tried to talk to her at the rehearsal dinner afterward, but she was stuck like glue to one friend or another's side all night, clearly trying to ensure she wouldn't be alone with me. Childish and immature don't strike me as her style, but maybe I'm wrong about her.

I glance around the room, wondering how long we have to stand up here in front of everyone in these monkey suits. Did we really need a vest under the tux jacket? And really, pink ties? Jackson called them rose gold, but I'm not fooled. In front of us, people chat, seated on white spindle chairs, surrounded by the potted fir trees with white twinkling lights that border the entire room.

The huge arched wooden doors at the end of the aisle finally sweep open, and everyone stands. Next to me Nate takes a deep breath but I think he forgets to exhale, so I elbow him and whisper, "Relax."

Jackson's friends come slowly down the aisle—first the redhead whose name I've never bothered learning, then Petra who is gorgeous but unobtainable, and then beyond her I spot the top of Sierra's head. She moves down the aisle, one careful step at a time, and I can finally see all of her once she passes most of the guests.

She's a fucking angel, which is not a cliché I've ever used. It's a good thing angelic girls are not my type. Her blond hair falls well past her shoulders in loose curls, and pieces from the front of her hair are braided into some sort of intricate pattern that looks like a loose crown around her head. Her skin glows and her lips are a shade of pink that's so fucking kissable I forget that I don't even like her. One shoulder is entirely bare as the rose gold fabric sweeps over her other shoulder, and the dress hugs her waist and the curve of her hips before flaring out at the bottom.

Nate elbows me and whispers, "Relax." In my head, I call him an asshole, but I don't dare say it out loud because one of the videographers is standing right on the other side of him.

As Sierra gets to the end of the aisle, she glances over, her eyes skimming past Nate and landing on me. She holds my gaze for about two-hundredths of a second before she glances down at the huge bouquet she carries and steps up to stand next to Petra.

I'd been so focused on Sierra I hadn't even noticed those wooden doors shut, but suddenly they are flung open again and my dad and sister step through them. I can practically feel the emotions rolling off Nate, buzzing like an electrical current next to me. Even after all these years, his love for her is still growing. I wonder what that must be like, and how long it'll be until it consumes him—until he's not him anymore, but just an extension of her. At least, that's what love has always seemed like to me: a surefire way to lose your independence, to get your balls shackled up so tight they eventually fall off.

My dad gives Jackson away, and she takes Nate's hand and steps up next to him. Words are said and vows are exchanged, but I hardly notice it because—except for when Nate turns to me to get Jackson's wedding ring—I can't take my eyes off Sierra. And it's like she can feel me watching her, because she keeps glancing at me, then glancing over at Nate and Jackson like she's reminding me that I should be paying attention to them.

Finally, the justice of the peace tells Nate he can kiss his bride, and the entire room bursts into applause, which shakes me out of my Sierra-induced trance. Sierra hands Jackson the bouquet she's been holding for her, and my sister walks down the aisle holding Nate's hand. Then Sierra steps forward and I offer her my arm.

"Can't avoid me forever," I say quietly as she slips her hand into the curve of my elbow.

"What makes you think I'm avoiding you?" she asks, her lips barely moving through the smile plastered on her face. I'd forgotten she and Jackson used to do that all the time when we were kids. They could carry on entire conversations without looking like they were talking at all, which was infuriating for a little kid who just wanted to know if they were talking about him.

I nod to my parents as we pass them, then tip my chin down close to Sierra's ear. "Well, let's see. You were all flirty on Thursday night until you realized it was me you were talking to, and you haven't said a word to me since."

"Maybe I just don't have anything to say to you." Her tone is dismissive, but the way her body is leaning into mine—with her fingertips digging into the crook of my elbow and her breast pressing against my tricep—is anything but.

Oh, this will be fun. "Keep telling yourself that if it makes you feel better, sweetheart."

"I'm not your sweetheart," she says with a hiss.

My smile is wide and genuine now as I glance down at her, but her face is pinched.

"Ah, does someone have a weakness for guys calling her sweetheart?" I tease.

"Someone has a right hook reserved for guys who call her sweetheart. Keep testing me and I might just use it," she says, glancing up at me as we walk through the doors. Immediately she pulls away, telling me, "I'm going to go help Jackson." And then she rushes off across the room to where Jackson and Nate stand, throwing her arms around my sister before stepping back and fluffing her veil. My parents and Nate's dad approach as they form their receiving line.

Across the room, Nate's eyes meet mine and he gives me a small shake of his head, sending me a clear message: *Don't go there.*

———

"I just want to see you settled, you know?" Mom says, giving my arm a squeeze as we stand at the edge of the dance floor together.

I managed to get through my best man speech pretty well, but it paled in comparison to Sierra's maid of honor speech. Thankfully, I went first. I would not have wanted to follow her very personal anecdotes about Jackson and Nate's journey together—a story she was part of every step of the way, while it's more obvious than ever that I've always been on the outside of my own family.

I watched as Jackson and my dad shared their father-daughter dance, and Nate pulled my mom onto the dance floor for the second half of it. Then he delivered her to me, and she's worn out from just the two minutes of dancing. But she refuses to sit, saying she's not an invalid, and instead insisting on questioning my life's direction.

"I know, Mom. And eventually I will settle down. But wouldn't I be stupid not to snowboard down every mountain I can, for as long as people are willing to pay me to do it?"

She smiles and pats my cheek. "For as long as it makes you *happy*, yes. You're very talented, and as long as you love the nomadic life you're living, then do it. But the minute it stops being fulfilling, the minute you want more than all the partying and snowboarding—move away from it. I know you're having fun, but I want you to find that thing in life that you can't live without. I want you to chase whatever you *really* love, and right now, I feel like you've just been filling the time."

The thing I love is photography. Snowboarding lets me travel to places where I can take amazing photos. And you'd think Mom would know that from all the pictures I send her, even if I haven't said it out loud.

"I am happy, Mom," I say as I put my arm around her shoulder and kiss her temple.

"If you say so," she says, putting her hand on my chest. "Oh, Sierra!" Mom says and reaches her arm across me.

There, the flash of sparkling rose gold stops short. Was she trying to get by without me noticing her? With my head turned toward my mom, it would have worked if Mom hadn't spotted her.

"Mrs. Shanahan," Sierra says warmly as she reaches out her hand and gives my mom's arm a loving squeeze.

"Sierra, I thought we discussed this at the spa yesterday. You must call me Cat, or even Catarina, if you don't like nicknames. I've known you far too long for this *Mrs.* business."

"Sorry." Sierra lets out a little laugh. "Old habits die hard." There is so much affection in her voice and her eyes as she talks to my mom, who was a bonus mom to Sierra when we were younger.

"I meant to tell you yesterday, dear. I'm so sorry about Peter."

Sierra's easy smile falters for a moment before it's back. "Thanks. It's better this way, though."

Interesting. I'm not sure who Peter is, but I can guess he's her ex. I wonder what happened, and if she really means that things are better without him? And then I wonder why I care. As a rule, I don't get involved in other people's personal lives.

"So you and Beau are going to be roommates for a bit," Mom says, then glances at me as she tells Sierra, "I hope you'll keep this one in line. I hear he can be a bit wild."

Sierra opens her mouth to respond, but I cut her off. "I'm sure Sierra's plenty busy keeping herself in line. It's always the good girls you have to worry about."

"Beau," Mom says as she slaps my chest, then rolls her eyes in Sierra's direction as if to say, *There's no controlling this one.* She's not wrong.

Sierra makes her excuses and continues on her way, obviously flustered by my teasing. Interesting.

Mom wraps her free hand around the back of me, so she's encircling my waist. I feel like I might actually be holding her up at this point, which is the only reason I don't say anything about her comments to Sierra. Luckily, she doesn't comment on my contribution to the conversation either.

I take my mom back to her table, where I know others will want to visit with her, then spend most of the reception catching up with people I haven't seen in years—like Jackson's friends from high school and the Blackstone ski team.

Shortly before midnight, the upbeat song a huge group of us are dancing to fades and a slow song replaces it. I see Jackson's high school friend Ava heading toward me, and spin away to head in the opposite direction. I've already danced with her three times, and heard ad nauseam about how much she misses her husband and newborn. Girls normally only cry on my shoulder before they climb into my bed. If I'm not getting some from Ava—which I'm definitely not—I don't need to hear about her problems.

But as I turn, my foot catches someone else's and suddenly a body slams into my side on a collision course with the floor. I catch her by her waist and pull her to her feet. Her arms come up to my chest as she takes a few deep breaths, leaning against me before looking up to meet my eyes. Those beautiful brown eyes get even bigger as she takes me in.

"I mean, if you insist on throwing yourself into my arms, I guess we can dance," I tell her as I unwrap one of my arms from her waist and take her hand. Her mouth is still hanging open as we begin to move.

"You—" she stutters, "you can dance. Like, we're not just awkwardly swaying back and forth here."

"Try to keep up," I say as I spin us toward the center of the dance floor.

Sierra doesn't say anything, and keeps her head tilted down. It's hard to know what she's looking at—that hollow area where my neck meets my chest, which is visible because I've unbuttoned the top button of my dress shirt and unloosened the tie, maybe?—or if she's just trying to avoid looking at me.

Finally, she glances up at me, rearranges her features into a mask of disapproval, then asks, "Why did you come talk to me the other night? At the bar?"

"You sat down next to *me*. It would have been rude to ignore you." I wonder at what point I should worry about how easily these lies come to me? I definitely sat down next to her when her attention was focused down at the other end of the bar.

"But why did you flirt with me?" she asks, her voice a little small for my liking. She should be far more confident, and if this has something to do with that asshole Peter, then I'll castrate him. Men who go around breaking down women's self-esteem are the lowest form of asshole.

"What makes you think I was flirting?" I ask, but I give her enough of a smile that she knows I'm teasing. Or I think she does, anyway. "Did you look into the figs?"

She nods.

"And?" I prompt.

"And it's all a bit ambiguous. I think maybe you were exaggerating a little." She glances up at me again—her eyes travel across my chin, linger on my lips, glide up my nose, and finally meet my eyes.

"I think you need to do more research." I wink, then I spin her away from me before pulling her back against my body.

"You mentioned setting some roommate ground rules the other night—"

"Before you ran away?" I interrupt.

She shakes her head, then continues. "What would be on your list of ground rules?"

I pause for a minute, thinking. "Honestly, this is a three week living arrangement. Maybe less if you find an apartment sooner, right? So I think we can just agree not to be assholes to each other and call that our roommate agreement."

"I feel like maybe we need a bit more in the way of . . . parameters," she says, her eyebrows dipping down until they almost touch her long lashes.

I open my mouth to respond, but then Petra is there, literally pulling us apart. She grasps each of our hands in one of hers and pulls us to the center of the dance floor. "Come on," she yells over the music, "it's almost midnight!"

Waiters are descending on the room with trays of champagne flutes and someone hands one to each of us as we approach Jackson and Nate, who are staring into each other's eyes like they can't wait to get back to their room. The thought has a chill running down my spine, because, *ew*, that shit's not cool when it's your sister.

"Hey," I say, handing my glass to Sierra. "Could you hold this for a second?"

She takes the glass and I slip my camera out of my pocket. It's small but powerful, and it's the one I have on me at all times. I snap a few pictures of the newlyweds, then check the LCD panel to make sure they came out okay. They are better than okay.

"I hate you so much right now." Sierra's lips are so close to my ear that I can feel her warm breath across my cheek, and a shiver of longing unexpectedly travels down my spine.

"Why's that?" I ask, not daring to turn my head. If I did, I couldn't be held responsible for my actions, or hers.

"Because Jackson made me promise that I wouldn't take any pictures tonight, insisted that I enjoy the night and not think about running her social media accounts. And you just captured some amazing shots that should have been mine. You even have my camera."

"You mean you have my camera," I say, glancing at her from where she stands next to me with her face resting against my bicep as she glances down at the LCD screen in my hands.

"Will you get some shots of them right at the New Year?" she asks.

"Obviously." I slide the camera back in my pocket so I can take my champagne flute from her.

"And will you send them to me so that I can post them for her tomorrow?"

"Sure," I say, reaching into my other pocket for my phone. "Give me your number and I'll text them to you later on."

She finishes putting her number into my phone right as the DJ announces the countdown. Everyone's screaming out the numbers, but I'm fumbling to get my phone back in one pocket, hand my glass to Sierra, and get my camera out of the other pocket in time.

"Four . . . three . . ." I start snapping photos nonstop, hoping that the low light and movement don't result in blurry photos. There's only so much I can do with limited time to prevent that, so I focus in on Jackson and Nate, trying to get them crystal clear. "Two . . . one!"

I snap a couple more photos, then Sierra leans in to look. "You get them?"

"Of course I did," I say, and I don't care if I have to stay up half the night editing them until they're perfect, I will be sending her flawless pictures in the morning.

Then I turn the camera around in my hand, pull her in with my other arm, point the camera at us, and whisper, "Smile."

That one is just for me.

Chapter Five

SIERRA

"Where should we put this one?" Petra asks as she carries a box labeled *Dishes* into my bedroom.

"It can go in the back of my closet too."

She laughs, a deep throaty sound that's distinctly unfeminine yet works so well for her. "I can't believe you really took all the dishes."

"And the silverware," I remind her. I'd bought it all after moving in with Peter, and we'd gotten rid of his mismatched pieces. "I hope he has fun with his breakfast tomorrow."

"You brought all the food with you too."

"Oh yeah." I feign forgetfulness. "I hope he starves."

"This is the best version of you I've ever seen." Petra smiles, then turns and sets the box on top of another at the back of the walk-in closet.

"Angry and vindictive?" I roll my eyes at her back.

"No, badass bitch. You are rocking the whole jilted ex-lover thing. Now we just need to find you some rebound sex with someone much hotter than Peter. Whatever happened to that hottie you said you saw at the hotel when you arrived at the wedding?"

I'd made the mistake of texting Petra about him after check-in, but obviously I could never tell her that the hottie turned out to be Beau. That was a week ago, and it hasn't come up, so I thought she'd forgotten about it by now.

"Don't know." I shrug. "Didn't see him again."

"That's weird though, right? Since everyone who was at the hotel was a wedding guest?"

"Who knows," I say, shoving a hanger into the neck of another sweater.

"Too bad," she says as she takes the stack of clothing on hangers that's piled on my bed, ready to be hung, and walks into the closet with them. "He sounded entirely fuckable."

That's not a word I *ever* thought I'd use to describe my best friend's little brother. And yet, here we are.

"It doesn't matter." I shrug. "I don't need rebound sex anyway. I'm probably better off alone for a while."

"I'm not asking you to commit to someone new," Petra says as she returns to the bed for more items. "Just to have some fun for a change."

"I've never been any good at one-night stands."

"No one said it has to just be one night, but don't discount it either. And don't get caught up in another relationship right away. Those seem like a lot of work." She brushes her hand through the air like she's sweeping away the idea of a relationship.

"They *seem* like a lot of work? Petra, have you never actually been in a relationship?"

Petra was always Jackson's friend. We hung out a lot, but never got close until Jackson moved away a year ago. And in all the years I've known her, I don't think she's dated someone seriously.

"Define relationship," she says, and her pouty lips purse together.

"I don't know. Dating one person monogamously for, like, a month?"

"Nope, can't say that I have," she says, eyebrows raised and a triumphant look on her face. I'm not sure I believe her, though. "Why would I commit to just one guy when there are so many out there to be had?"

I laugh, then tell her, "I envy your approach to sex. I've never managed not to have feelings for a guy if I sleep with him."

"Hmm," she says as she starts taking items out of my suitcase and putting them on hangers for me. "That sounds complicated. What if the guy's a dick?"

"Why would I sleep with him if he's a dick?"

"Ohh," she says. "You're one of *those*."

"What the hell does that mean?" I ask, not even trying to hide how insulted I am.

"Sierra," she says, with the condescending voice of someone who feels sorry for me. "Sex isn't about emotional feelings, it's about physical ones. Confusing the two is a mistake."

"Why can't it be about both?"

"Because that just complicates things. Seriously. You should try having sex with someone you have no feelings for, aside from attraction, and see what that gets you. Honestly, if the only purpose for being together is to make each other feel good, think about how . . . rewarding that could be."

I take a stack of T-shirts from my suitcase and carry them

over to the dresser, so I have a moment to think about what she's saying. I mean, I've never had really great sex except with my vibrator. And I've only had sex with people I was in a relationship with. Could Petra be right? Could letting my feelings decide who I have sex with be committing me to mediocre sex?

Behind me, Petra lets out a low whistle. "What the hell is this?" She laughs and I spin around to find her holding up one of my sexiest sets of lingerie. "I would never have pegged you as someone who . . . Good girls don't wear underwear like this."

"Right, because underwear like that is reserved for gorgeous and unattached girls like you?" You know, the kind of girl who doesn't get cheated on by their fiancé.

"That's not what I meant, and you know it."

"Well, it's still insulting," I say as I turn back to the dresser and tuck my stack of T-shirts into a drawer.

"Why is it insulting?"

"Because it means you pegged me as the kind of girl who wore boring, bland underwear."

"You just told me about how you only have committed, monogamous sex. Of course I didn't think you'd be walking around wearing freaky lingerie."

"There's nothing freaky about those bras, Petra," I say as I walk over and take them from her. "They're just pretty."

"The last time I saw that much lace, I was walking through the red-light district in Amsterdam," she says, her throaty laugh bursting out of her. "So here's what we're going to do. You're going to shower and get dressed up, maybe even put one of these sexy bras on, and we're going out. There's no way you're sitting home feeling sorry for yourself and unpacking on your first night in your new place."

"Aren't you exhausted?" I ask her. I know I am, and she was at my old place yesterday helping me finish up my packing, then she, Lauren, and Josh helped me move everything over here this morning. She came back again tonight to help me unpack.

"Life's too short to not go out, even when you're tired," she insists. "Come on, let's go get a few drinks. And if you happen to pick up a guy and bring him home with you tonight, so be it."

"Petra, I'm too tired to go out. And I can't bring a guy back here. I don't even know when Beau is arriving." I thought about texting him to find out, but I can already envision the return texts laced with innuendo. It's safer not to open that door with him. "What if they ran into each other?"

"Why would that matter?" Petra rolls her eyes. "Unless you've slept with Beau?"

I try to contain the laugh, so it comes out more like a snort. "No, I haven't slept with Beau." I'm tempted to tell her about our history, just so she'll understand why this whole thing is so awkward. But I can't do that, not when I never told Jackson.

"It's too bad he's Jackson's brother. When I first saw him talking to you over at the bar during that the cocktail reception, I was certain you'd be in his bed that night. You two seemed like you had chemistry."

"Beau and I? Chemistry? No." I shake my head emphatically. "Definitely not. He's like a little brother to me." That would have been the truth before last weekend, but it's better if she believes that what she saw was just two people who know each other really well hanging out.

"Like I said, it's too bad because he's seriously hot."

Just thinking about Beau has me hot and bothered. I both can't wait and am dreading his arrival . . . whenever that happens. This is bad. So very bad.

"You know what," I tell Petra, "it's Saturday night. Maybe we should go out after all."

————

"I had a really good time tonight," Jared says as he reaches across the elevator and puts a hand on my shoulder.

I glance down at the hand, wishing it was sending chills of anticipation through me. Instead, it's the light touch of dread. It was nice of him to give me a ride home from the bar, but I have no idea why I agreed to him seeing me to my door. The thought of having to keep up the pretense that I'm fine and that it was fun going out tonight is exhausting. It's like swimming against the tide for hours and ending up in the same place—still a little too far from shore, with too little energy left to keep swimming. I want to crawl into bed and sleep until Monday morning, not make conversation with some guy I just met.

He gives my shoulder a little squeeze and I realize that I've waited a tad bit too long to reply. "Me too." I spit out quickly, knowing that's the expected response. I give him a quick smile as the elevator doors open.

The deep, pounding beat of the electric drum assaults me the minute we step into the hallway. *Where the hell is that noise coming from?* I know from two years of living with Jackson before I moved in with Peter that most of the neighbors are either older folks or families with kids. One of the things Jackson loved about this building was how quiet it was: a haven where she could escape from her crazy, hectic life.

"Someone's having a party," Jared says. "Maybe we should crash it?"

"Maybe another time," I say as we approach my door. "I'm really tired."

"Oh, sure," he says, but the tone of his voice is unclear, like he could be saying *Oh sure, let's do that* or *Oh, sure you're tired.*

I'm standing in front of my door when two realizations hit me at once. The music is coming from my place, and the reason it's so loud is that the door isn't shut all the way. *What. The. Hell?*

I think I might have said that out loud because Jared gives me a classic *I don't know what's going on* shrug as I reach out and push open my front door.

The scene before me is . . . confusing. The emerald green velvet couch that normally faces the fireplace has been turned at an angle to better face the TV on the adjacent wall, and combined with the two armchairs that usually flank the coffee table, a triangle-shaped gaming station has been set up. Three fairly enormous men are centered around the coffee table, tipping back beers and shouting to be heard over the music, while their game is paused on the TV.

Who are these people and where is that music even coming from? As I look at this scene, I swear my eye twitches. I finally locate a portable speaker on the sofa table that used to be behind the couch but is now floating in between the entryway and living room. I pull Jared along with me, suddenly thrilled I'm not facing these three giants alone.

When I hit power on the speaker, everyone's heads snap toward me. And there's one face I recognize. A face I'd like to shred into pieces at this point. I leave Jared behind, taking slow steps around the couch as I head toward Beau with murder in my eyes.

Behind me, I can sense Jared backing away, but I still move forward.

Beau doesn't break eye contact, I'll give him that much. "What. The. Fuck. Is. This?" I ask as I take in the takeout food spewed across the coffee table and even on the rug. The game controllers lying around haphazardly, sweatshirts discarded over the backs of the furniture, a pint of ice cream sitting half-melted on a plate.

"Well, hello to you too, sweetheart," he drawls, and I have to wonder for a minute who this fool is. This is not the same guy I hung out with at Jackson's wedding. It's like I'm witnessing Performance Beau. Or maybe this is who he really is and the side I saw of him last weekend was the performance. The anger unfurls inside me, seeping out and spreading through me like smoke.

I reach out and grab the fabric of his hoodie at the base of his neck, pulling up swiftly so that, in his surprise, he stands. Which maybe was a mistake, because now he's inches away, looking down at me with heat in his eyes and I can't discern whether it's anger or something else. *Is he enjoying this?*

"First of all, don't call me sweetheart. It's demeaning and disrespectful. And second, when I wanted roommate ground rules, you said the only one we needed was: don't be assholes. Well, guess what, asshole, you already broke your one and only rule." I push him backward onto the couch, where he lands with a thud. "Pick your shit up and keep the music down because we have neighbors with little kids."

"It's Saturday night," the idiot on Beau's right says, and as I turn toward him I see Beau shake his head back and forth. "Never mind . . ." he mutters, but I swear I hear a whispered *grandma* at the end.

When I glance up, I see Jared hovering halfway between the couch and the front door. I walk back to him, surprised he stuck around for all this. Behind me, the music starts up again at a very low volume, barely loud enough to be heard.

"You okay?" he asks me quietly while I take off my jacket and hang it on one of the wall hooks that line the top of the board-and-batten trim in the small entryway.

"Yeah. That's my best friend's little brother, and he's staying here for a few weeks. Just moved in tonight while I was out. I wasn't expecting this . . . scene . . . when I got back."

"I can tell," he says and reaches out, placing his hand lightly on my hip. "Can I do anything to help you relax?"

I breathe in sharply, not expecting the tenderness in his voice or the obvious sexual advance given the room full of guys behind me. I shouldn't be surprised, I guess. We flirted tonight at the bar, and I let him drive me home. He probably assumed that when I said he could walk me to my door, that was code for *let's fuck*. After Peter, who I didn't sleep with until our fifth date, this feels really fast. I hardly know this guy, and I'm definitely not in the mood. The need to get him out of my apartment comes on suddenly.

"I think I just need to be alone tonight," I tell him. "But thank you so much for the ride home."

"Another time, then," he says, and holds out his hand.

"Here, give me your phone so I can send myself a text from your number."

When I glance over into the living room, Beau is watching me carefully. It's all the encouragement I need to unlock my phone and hand it to Jared. He seems nice enough, I guess it couldn't hurt to see him again.

He types his number in, saves the contact, and then sends himself a very long text. I stand there a little uncomfortably, waiting to find out what the hell he's writing.

When he hands me back the phone, I can't help but laugh at his message.

SIERRA

> Hi Jared, it's Sierra. Long blond hair, sweet brown eyes, big pouty lips. I'm the one who couldn't get enough of your sense of humor tonight. I'd love to see you again. Maybe we can go out next weekend?

By the time I'm done reading the message, he's already got his phone out and has sent a reply.

JARED

> Sure, how about next Saturday?

I smile at my phone and he steps closer.

He leans down and says quietly in my ear, "This is when you say 'Saturday is perfect, I can't wait.'"

Instead, I raise an eyebrow in his direction, then glance down at my phone and type out my reply.

SIERRA

> I can probably fit you in on Saturday ;-)

His laugh is soft as he reaches up and takes a lock of my

hair between his fingers. "I'm willing to be squeezed in if that's what it takes to get more time with you."

I glance up at him and his eyes are locked on my lips. As he starts to lean in, a deafening roar goes up behind us that has me spinning around in surprise. One of Beau's friends is on his feet and one is on his knees on the ground.

"What the hell, dickwad," one of them says as he reaches over and swats at Beau, who's facing me and not the TV. "You just got all of us killed."

"All right," I say, turning to Jared. "We'd probably better say good night. I'll see you Saturday."

"Yeah," Jared says, taking a step back toward the still-open door. "I'll text you later."

I shut the door behind him, grab my water bottle off the countertop that divides the kitchen and living room, and head for my bedroom.

Thirty minutes later, I'm in my pajamas, have washed my face and brushed my teeth, and am ready to crawl into bed after an emotionally draining day. Except, I'm hungry. And as the pleasant fuzziness of tonight's margaritas have worn off, I'm also left with a bit of a headache.

I stare longingly at my bed, wanting to crawl into it, but also knowing that in my world, a pre-bedtime snack is practically a prerequisite for a good night of sleep.

I crack open my bedroom door. It's quiet out in the living room, and I'm guessing that Beau's friends—and maybe him as well—left while I was in my bathroom getting ready for bed. Thankfully, we're not sharing a bathroom, at least!

I start down the hall and am surprised to find the door to my old room, his room now, is open, and it's dark inside. Does he sleep with the door open, or did he go out?

I'm two steps into the living room before I notice Beau sitting on the couch with his bare feet up on the coffee table and his laptop on his thighs.

"You scared the crap out of me!" I say, pressing a hand to my chest as a shot of adrenaline goes through my system.

He looks up and throws one arm across the back of the couch, putting his bare chest on display. "I'm literally just sitting here. How could I have scared you?"

"I didn't think you were here. I thought you'd gone back out."

"It's almost one in the morning. Is anything even open at this time?"

"No, not here." Park City was referred to as Sin City during the mining era, but what qualifies as "Sin City" in Utah is a bit different from other parts of the country. Most bars close at midnight or 1:00 a.m., even on weekends.

We stare at each other for a minute before I ask, "Why aren't you wearing a shirt?"

"Because I'm relaxing at home and it's freaking hot in here."

It is warm in here, but you don't see me stripping. "How would you feel if I was walking around with no shirt on?"

"You really don't want me to answer that." He smirks as he eyes my chest.

I cross my arms over my breasts, realizing too late that I'm wearing a thin T-shirt and no bra. "Is this going to be a frequent occurrence, you walking around only partially dressed?"

"Why? Do you like it?" He raises his eyebrows in a challenge. His laptop is blocking his abdomen, but if the way his arms, shoulders, and pecs are sculpted is any indication, I'm sure he has impressive abs as well.

"Quite the opposite," I tell him. "I'm going to have to bleach my eyes now."

He grins, baring his teeth like a wolf about to eat its prey. "Too bad bleaching your eyes won't get this image out of your mind."

Ugh, the arrogance of him!

I spin and head to the kitchen before he can see how easily his ego and immaturity piss me off. I grab a cereal bar out of the box I'd unpacked into a cabinet earlier this afternoon, refill my water bottle, and head back to my room.

I go into the bathroom and splash water on my hot face, hoping it will help wash away the picture of a shirtless Beau in gray sweatpants out of my head. Spoiler alert: it doesn't work, and I'm left feeling like a voyeuristic cougar.

Chapter Six

SIERRA

My eyes fly open when the banging starts. The alarm clock on my nightstand says it's 7:20 a.m., ten minutes before my alarm is set to go off. What is that banging?

I fly out of bed when it happens again, because the sound of someone's fist hitting wood over and over—that's happening against my bedroom door. I'm fully aware that my sleep shorts and T-shirt with no bra aren't really appropriate to answer the door, so instead of opening it I just ask, "Yeah?"

"Ahh . . . it's Ed. The contractor?"

"The contractor?"

"Yeah." His gruff and decidedly annoyed voice carries through the door. "The one redoing your bathroom."

I reach over and grab a cowl neck sweatshirt that I left sitting on top of my dresser and drag it over my head before I open the door a crack.

"I'm sorry, redoing my bathroom?"

"Yeah, we're scheduled to start demo today."

"On the primary bathroom?"

He sighs and puts his hands on his hips, along the waist-band of his paint-splattered work pants. "Yes. I get the sense you have no idea what I'm talking about."

"You're absolutely right."

"Listen, Beau just let us in. He knew we were coming, and he said just to go ahead and knock on the door and you'd show us to the bathroom."

I haven't had coffee yet, so I can't be responsible for the fact that it is taking my brain a little longer than normal to catch up.

The bathroom in this bedroom is getting remodeled.

And Beau knew about it, but didn't tell me.

And he insisted I take this bedroom, where all the construction will be.

"Okay, sorry, this is obviously all news to me. So you're starting demo on my bathroom now, but also I'm just learning about this, which means the bathroom isn't ready to demo. I just moved in a few days ago and, not knowing this was happening, I unpacked all my stuff into the bathroom."

Ed looks at me like, *What do you want me to do about this?* "I got a crew showing up here in about half an hour. Think you can have your stuff outta there by then?"

Deep breaths. It's not like I was about to hop in the shower and then get off to work or anything. Sure, why not just drop everything and pack up the bathroom first?

"Of course." It's not like I have *that* many toiletries. "If you're doing demo today, how are you going to prevent the rest of my bedroom from filling with dust?"

"Can I step into the room and show you?" he asks. He's an older guy, probably early fifties. Seems like a decent human being, and apparently he's here for legitimate reasons.

"Sure," I say, taking a step back into the bedroom so he can enter.

He takes a look at the bathroom, then eyes my rumpled bed across from the bathroom door. "We'll put up a zip wall right here," he says, pointing from the left side of my room to the right. It leaves a couple feet between the bathroom wall and my bed for them to get from the bedroom door to the bathroom. He explains how the plastic sheeting will completely wall off the rest of my bedroom and I will use a zipper to get in and out.

Great, just great. "How long will this whole remodel take?"

"It should be done in a week, two tops. We're not moving anything, just redoing all the tile, paint, and putting in a new vanity and new fixtures," he says as he shoves his hands into the pockets of his Carhartt sweatshirt.

"All right, I should get to packing this bathroom up," I tell him.

"Right," he says. "I'll go grab a cup of coffee and be back to meet my guys at eight."

"Thanks," I say, then walk him to the door and lock him out.

Thirty minutes to pack up my whole bathroom and shower before they get back here. Okay, I can manage this. I run to my bathroom and grab my stuff out of the shower, moving it to the bathroom off the hallway. The one I'm now apparently sharing with Beau. Two more trips and I've got my stuff moved into the hall bathroom. Luckily, Beau has hardly anything in the bathroom, aside from little trimmed beard hairs all over the sink and counter. I roll my eyes at what an inconsiderate little shit he is for pulling this whole *you take Jackson's old bedroom* stunt when he knew about this bathroom reno and I didn't. The only thing he's accomplished is pushing me to look for my own apartment even more quickly than I would have.

———

It's past 7:00 p.m. when I get back to my apartment that night. I spent my lunch break scouring various websites, looking for potential apartments to rent, and went to see two after work. I'm starving and still pissed at Beau about this morning. I can hear him banging around inside the apartment and I am half dreading facing him when I open the front door.

After pausing and taking a few breaths, I crack the door open. The smell hits me before I'm even inside—it's garlic and cheese and bacon-scented in here.

"Hey," Beau says when I walk in from the entryway, looking up from where he stands at the kitchen counter. "I just made dinner. Want some?"

I'm tempted to say no because I'm still furious about this morning and don't want to even have to talk to him, but the loud rumble of my stupid stomach answers for me. He just laughs and grabs another of the big flat bowls out of the cabinet and loads a heaping portion of pasta into it. Then he grates some fresh parmesan on top.

"What is this amazingness?" I ask as I approach the peninsula that divides the kitchen from the open living room and dining room combination.

"Carbonara," he says as he slides my bowl toward the barstool closest to me and pushes his bowl toward the other seat. He opens two of the drawers closest to him and pulls out napkins and silverware and slides them over to me. "What do you want to drink?" he asks as I grab the utensils to place them at our seats.

"Water's fine." I shrug.

"You don't want wine or something?" he asks, gesturing to the several bottles I have sitting on the counter. I took literally every item of food and drink from my old apartment, even though it was petty. But it brings me just a little bit of satisfaction to exact that tiny revenge on Peter, because *fuck him.*

"Nah," I say, "that wine will taste like bitterness anyway." I don't plan to drink it. I just didn't want Peter to have it because they were all bottles he'd chosen. He was a much bigger wine drinker than I ever was.

Beau laughs, and the sound dissipates some of the tension I'm feeling. "Why's that?" he asks as he grabs two glasses and fills them at the water dispenser on the refrigerator door.

"They were my ex-fiancé's, and I took them when I moved out."

"But you're not planning on drinking them." It's a statement, not a question. But I feel the need to respond anyway.

"I haven't decided."

He nods as he walks around the counter and sits next to me, placing my glass at my place setting. "Fair enough," he says.

It's strange having Beau sitting on the barstool to my left again. Though the arrangement is the same, it's not the easy, flirtatious feeling I had sitting next to him at the cocktail reception. Thank goodness. But it's also not the hate-filled rage I expected to feel when I saw him tonight after the stunt he pulled this morning.

"I'm sorry about this morning," he says, as if he can read my mind. "The contractor told me what happened. I didn't realize that you didn't know. Jackson told me about the bathroom reno when I asked to crash here, so I assumed she told you too."

"So you didn't ask me to take the primary bedroom just so you didn't have to deal with the mess and inconvenience?" I ask as I wind my first bit of pasta on my fork, my skepticism clear in my voice.

"I told you why I didn't want that room," he says, "and it had nothing to do with the bathroom."

"You know, it's not exactly like the bed you're sleeping in hasn't been christened as well."

A look passes over his face, but he quickly raises his glass of water to his lips so I can't quite tell what it was. "At least not by my sister, though, right?"

"I mean, not that I know of, but I wasn't living here anymore when she and Nate got back together. So, no promises." I take my first bite of the pasta carbonara and a small moan involuntarily escapes. "This is delicious," I say, even though my mouth is full. This is quite possibly the best pasta I've ever tasted.

"Thanks," he says and takes a bite as well.

"Do you always cook amazing food like this?" I ask. I absolutely hate to cook.

"Eh, this is deceptively easy to make. But yeah, I do okay in the kitchen."

"How'd you learn?" I ask. I'm always surprised by people who have this skill that I seem to lack no matter how hard I try.

"I usually travel with my two best friends. We spent years eating crappy food or ordering out before I decided I should just learn to cook. I followed a bunch of food bloggers on Instagram and watched a bunch of tutorials on YouTube. It's much easier to follow a recipe when you've watched someone do it before. And then, I guess, it just became more natural over time."

Ah yes, the travel. This is Jackson's primary issue with her brother: he's never around. He didn't even come home last winter when his mom was going through chemo for the third time. Instead of spending that time with his family, he was snowboarding all over the globe. I don't think Jackson expected him to give up his career and move home like she did, but she's definitely been holding a grudge that he couldn't be bothered to even come home when his mom was really sick. But of course, it's not my place to bring that up, so instead I focus on the food.

"I can't imagine cooking something like this," I say as I wind more pasta on my fork. "I love baking, hate cooking."

"Isn't baking cooking?" he asks, a small smile playing on his lips.

"Baking's an exact science," I say. "You follow a recipe to a T and it comes out as it should. As long as your measurements are correct and the heat's right and you cook it for the right amount of time, it always comes out. I feel like with cooking there are way more variables, and you have to have this innate sense of when to turn the heat up or down, or when to add more seasonings or more liquid or whatever. Every time I cook, it either comes out blah, or it's totally unrecognizable from what I intended to make."

Beau laughs, and insists, "It can't be that bad."

"It is," I assure him as I shove another bite of pasta into my mouth.

"So how have you survived adulthood as an anti-cook?" he asks.

"I've mostly been lucky that my roommates—Jill in Boston, then Jackson here—have been better cooks than me. But I can feed myself. It's just more Kraft Mac & Cheese, and less"—I gesture to the remaining pasta in my bowl—"this."

"And after you stopped living with Jackson?" he asks. "Who cooked then?"

I really do not want to talk about Peter, but there's really not any choice. "My ex-fiancé was actually a really good cook. But he made a terrible mess in the kitchen and it always pissed me off to have to clean up after him. Like really, I swear he used every single pan and cooking utensil, every single time he made a meal."

"You gotta clean as you go," Beau says. "It's the only way to not leave a huge mess."

"Someone should have taught Peter that hack."

Beau gets up and takes his bowl into the kitchen for a refill. He's wearing low-slung gray sweats again, but at least he's got a shirt on this time. It's tight enough that it highlights his strong shoulders and his outstanding biceps, a fact I can ignore a whole lot more easily when he has a shirt on.

"So what did this asshole do to break it off?" Beau asks as he reaches into the pot and pulls out a piece of bacon between his fingertips, popping it into his mouth.

I think of all the things that Peter did—the lying and cheating, the duplicitous behavior he must have engaged in for months, if not years, before I found out. I think of all the moments where he said one thing, and I now wonder if he meant something else. He left me wondering how I can truly know myself if I didn't even know his love wasn't real. "He cheated."

Beau looks over at me from where he stands in front of the stove. "What a dick."

I do that thing I sometimes do, where I raise my eyebrows and shrug, because what else is there to say. Internally, though, I have a whole lot to say and most of it is self-deprecating. How could it not be, when I was so wholly and truly blind to what was happening right in front of me?

"Hey," Beau says as he takes in whatever look has crossed my face. "What he did was about him, not you. Okay? Don't internalize it."

"Sure." I glance down at my plate. It's a kind and well-intended comment, but honestly, how does he expect me to not internalize my fiancé deciding to stick his dick elsewhere?

"So, how come you got home so late today?" he asks as he walks back to his seat with his pasta replenished. "Or is this what time you normally get home?"

"No, I'm normally home between five and six, but tonight I went and saw two apartments."

"By yourself?"

Is that worry I hear in his voice?

"I can handle myself," I tell him, "but I brought Josh with me just in case." I mean, I'm not stupid.

"Josh is . . .?"

"Lauren's husband."

His face is still blank, like he has no idea who she is.

"Lauren . . ." I prompt, but there is no recognition there, "the bridesmaid with red hair."

"Ohh," he says as he pops another bite of pasta into his

mouth, chews a few times, and says through a mouthful of pasta, "the married one."

I take a second to process what he's saying. "Wait, did you not know her name because you just thought of her as 'the married one'?"

He raises his shoulders, like it's not an issue that he obviously viewed her as a commodity who, since she wasn't available to him, wasn't worth knowing.

"Oh my God, you really are an asshole." I can't help but laugh a bit as I draw my conclusion out loud.

Another shoulder shrug.

"Anyway, Josh was the skier Jackson trained before Nate—"

"Oh, *that* Josh. Yeah, I know who he is."

"Well, his wife, Lauren, is one of our best friends."

"Got it," he says. "So you already went to see apartments, like two days after you moved in here?"

I feel silly mentioning that finding out about the bathroom reno this morning and feeling like he set me up with that was a big motivator for me to get out of here.

Instead, I confirm that yes, I am already looking at apartments.

He leans toward me, something that I've noticed he does a lot in conversation. "You just left your cheating fiancé and moved out of his place. How can you already be ready to commit to a new place?" His eyes scrunch up and his cheeks pull back as he says the last few words, like he's tasted something unexpectedly bitter. I wonder what gave him that look, and figure it was probably having to use the word *commit*.

"I just like to be settled," I say, meeting his eyes with my own defiant look. Who is he to judge? I don't think he's ever committed to a person or a place in his life.

"What's so great about being settled?" He looks away as he asks the question.

Images of my mom, the dozens of apartments and mobile homes we lived in throughout my childhood, the men who came in and out of her bedroom, the impossibility of finding a quiet place to do my homework, having to raise my two siblings because my mom wasn't capable of loving them—it all flashes through my mind.

"I just like things, *and people*, to be constant. Dependable. Steady."

"Yeah," he says, leaning in even further. "What'd that get you so far?"

Ooh, gloves off, I see. "Well, I'm the social media manager for one of the largest sports organizations in the country."

"And?" he prompts.

And my best friend moved away and got married, I have no family and only a couple close friends in Park City, my fiancé left me, and I'm crashing at my best friend's place because I'm essentially homeless.

But I refuse to sit around feeling sorry for myself. I have a good life—a life I created. It could be so much worse.

"Thanks for dinner," I tell him, standing and taking my almost-empty bowl to the sink.

His voice is placating when he says, "Sierra—"

"I'll take care of the dishes in a bit," I cut him off. I don't need his pity or his criticism. I'm giving him no power to make me feel bad about my life or my decisions.

I storm into my room in the dark, only to run into a wall of plastic with a big red zipper down the center. This sends one of the poles holding the plastic sheeting crashing down onto my bed. The plastic that was taped to the ceiling rips away, and the sheet sails to the ground. And now there's construction dust everywhere. This day just keeps getting better.

———

Two hours later, I've cleaned up as much of the bedroom mess as possible, then cuddled in the big chair in the corner of my room and, wrapped in a warm blanket, finished the latest romance novel I'm reading. It was exactly the escape I needed.

Now those dishes I said I'd do are calling my name, even though I really don't want to go out there and face Beau.

Don't be ridiculous, I tell myself. *This is just what Beau does. He pushes people's buttons. You know this about him. Jackson warned you.*

Despite the years of listening to her complain about what an asshole her brother had become, I guess I could never quite rectify her version of Beau with the sweet kid I grew up thinking of as a younger brother. According to Jackson, it was like something flipped when he was in high school and he became moody, sarcastic, self-righteous, and angry. But by then, she and I were both away at college, so I had very little interaction with him until that time I stayed with their family overnight years ago.

And when you flirted with him at Jackson's wedding.

I lean my head back on the top of the chair and groan, thinking about how close I came to making an absolute fool of myself. I can only imagine he was flirting with me to prove a point—that I am attracted to him—so he could turn me down and cause me the same kind of embarrassment he probably felt last time I saw him.

It's a good reminder that I should keep my physical distance, which is no easy feat now that we live together. At least it's only for a few weeks.

I set my book on the blanket as I get up to go do the dishes I promised to do. When I come out my door at the end of the hallway, Beau is doing pull-ups in the doorway of his bedroom. I shift to the right to move around him, using the open doorframe of the bathroom across the hall to get by without getting too near him. With his back to me as I pass, I take a split-second to admire the way every muscle in his shoulders and back ripple with the effort of something that appears effortless from afar. There are peaks and valleys of muscle groups I didn't even realize could be cut like this, and the muscles of his lower back end in a sexy V as they enter his pants. In the books I read, the hero always has unbelievable abs that end in a V above his man parts, which, based on my own personal experience, always seemed like a fantasy. Until now, I didn't even realize that a back could be just as unbelievably sexy. In fact, I think backs may be the unsung hero of the male anatomy. Beau's muscles glisten with a thin sheen of sweat, the only indication that this isn't as easy as he makes it look.

I look away the second I'm past him so he won't know I was staring, and then I cross the living room toward the kitchen. I'm just passing the peninsula when I notice his laptop is sitting open, with a gallery of edited photos in Photoshop on screen. I pause and glance at the photos, but my breath is taken away by their beauty. Both the stunning photography and also the skilled editing.

I try not to stiffen when I feel him behind me, but it's impossible—his breath is on my bare neck and his proximity has me on edge. He reaches his right arm around me and taps on one of the photos and it fills the screen.

In the foreground of the shot are snow-covered trees with a crystalline blue-green lake beyond. Snow-covered rocky peaks line the far side of the lake.

"What do you see in this one?" he asks.

"The composition is perfect. The angle and the light, the shadows. The way the orange clouds of sunrise are reflected across half the lake. It's a perfect shot."

"Hmm," he mumbles approvingly.

"I used to take pictures like this," I mutter under my breath, but there's no way he doesn't hear me.

"I remember how much you always loved photography," he says and my stomach drops at the mention of him noticing my passion even when I was a teenager. "Maybe you ought to be using your talent for more than just photographing my sister."

I turn my head over my shoulder to give him the nasty look he deserves. Instead, my eyes act of their own accord, traveling down his body, over the planes of his chest and abs, where every muscle in his torso is sharply defined under a light layer of chest hair, down to where his low-slung gray sweatpants hug his muscular legs and, from what I can tell, a pretty impressive package of his male bits as well.

Okay, eye contact only from now on.

"I don't *only* photograph your sister," I tell him, looking back up, though it's true that for years a large majority of the photos I took were of her. Running her social media when she was ski racing and until she married Nate was my almost full-time side hustle. But I was such a natural at it and she hated managing her social media and sponsorships, so it was a great fit for two best friends. "I live and breathe photography and videography at work too."

"Is sports photography your passion?" he asks. His eyes are locked on mine now and his face looks sincere as he questions me, but his tone informs me that he already knows the answer.

"Photography's not really a big part of my job anymore. What I do is more about social media engagement."

"Con-grat-u-lations," he drawls. "You get people to like more photos."

"No, I help people get to know our athletes, to care about them, to passionately root for them." I love that part of my job, the way social media lets these athletes who spend most of the year training in small groups get to show their fans what their day-to-day is like, lets their fans get to know them. "Skiing used to be something that people cared about every four years when the Winter Olympics rolled around. What I do helps people stay connected to the sport and realize that it's a nearly year-round endeavor every single year."

"And what reward do you get out of it, besides a paycheck?" On each side of the flat bridge of his nose, his nostrils flare.

Is he looking for a fight?

"It's a job, Beau," I say as I step away, reminding myself that I don't have to attend every fight I'm invited to. "What kind of reward do I need besides the satisfaction of doing it well, and a paycheck?"

"Don't know," he says, as I walk toward the sink. "I'm not exactly an expert in the whole job department. But I guess I'd want to use my skills to do something fulfilling that I felt made a difference."

"Like you do with snowboarding?" He doesn't compete often enough that he's a household name like Shaun White or Chloe Kim, but if you follow professional snowboarding, there's no way you wouldn't know him. Especially if you're on social media, because now that I've really looked into it, he's all over every social channel—usually without a shirt.

Even so, he's not "making a difference."

I turn the water on full blast so if he responds I don't hear it, and get to work cleaning the dried carbonara off the dishes before loading them into the dishwasher. I don't turn to see if he's gone, but I assume he has—leaving just his words to haunt me. *What reward do I get out of my work? Where does my fulfillment come from? And is the fact that I don't know actually the problem?*

I think back to high school, when I got ahold of my first digital camera—a hand-me-down from a friend's mom after we had a long conversation about photography. I took every photography class my college offered, and in the early days of working in social media marketing, I spent countless hours each day setting up and getting the perfect photo. But engagement is where the money is, and I always had a sixth sense for knowing how to engage an audience online.

I've had a great career over the past ten years and don't regret it. But I did love photography, especially nature photography, and I don't remember why I dropped something I loved so much. Why I let work and relationships take precedence over something I was truly passionate about. Or maybe I wasn't passionate enough?

As I load the last dish into the dishwasher, I wonder if there's a way I could use photography to help people. Not like I helped Jackson build her brand on social media, but like *really* help people. Maybe there's some type of photography volunteer work I could do? Lord knows I could use something to distract me from thinking about my failed relationship with Peter, and the roommate who seems intent on getting under my skin.

I dry my hands off on the dishtowel, and as I hang it neatly across the handle of the dishwasher to dry, I'm resolved to spend a little time this week seeing if volunteer photography work is a thing. Hopefully it is, and bonus points if it gets me out of being home with Beau.

Chapter Seven

BEAU

"Look who finally decided to fucking show up and practice," Lance says when I meet up with them at the base of the mountain. "I mean, it's only fifty thousand dollars of prize money on the line." He says it as if I have a shot of taking first place, which he believes I do, but I think is a pretty big stretch. Last year I earned a second place finish in Slopestyle and a fourth place finish in Big Air. I'm better now than I was then, but the competition keeps getting younger and better. I've also spent less time training this year, and more time working on my photography business that not even my best friends know about.

I drop my board on the ground at my feet. "Been busy." I bend down to strap my right foot in the binding on my snowboard.

"Busy with that hot roommate of yours?" Drew asks. From my bent over position, I give him the side-eye, but I don't think he sees it.

"Yeah, I bet you haven't left the bedroom for the past three days. Now we know why you aren't crashing with us," Lance adds.

"I was never staying with you assholes," I remind them.

"Oh, right, because Annalise was going to hook you up with a sweet pad." Drew rolls his eyes.

Lance coughs out a laugh. "Pad. That chick belongs in a padded cell."

He's not wrong. I'd let her good looks and the amazing sex lead me straight down the Main Street of her Crazy Town. I ignored the signs that she was unstable all because she was hot, and I suffered the consequences when I tried to pull away and she told me I couldn't stay in her uncle's one-bedroom downtown condo with her in Park City.

Drew elbows Lance, before saying, "And only a couple weeks later he's already shacking up with another hot blonde. What do I need to do to attract some ass like that?"

"Start with"—my voice comes out harsh—"not talking about women like they are something you deserve and start acting like they're something you earn." My friends look at me like they're trying to figure out if I've been possessed by someone else, which only pisses me off more. "And then, shave that hideous porn star mustache."

Drew rubs his light brown mustache with his thumb and forefinger like he's some sleazebag from the seventies. "That what you did? Used that silver tongue of yours to talk your roommate right into your bed?"

"That's my sister's best friend," I tell them as we all push off toward the lift line.

"You've always liked older women," Lance calls after me.

It's midweek and all the lifts are rolling so there's virtually no one in line and we push straight up to the loading area of the 3 Kings lift. As soon as we're seated and heading up the mountain, I attempt to rectify their misconception. "Sierra and I are *not* shacking up. We both just happen to be staying at my sister's condo. Repeat after me: older sister's best friend. That shit's never going to happen."

"You don't think she's hot?" Lance asks.

"Obviously she's cute." Hot isn't the right word for Sierra. She doesn't exude sexiness in that way that women often do when they're trying too hard. Like Annalise was. Instead, Sierra is sexy without trying—a combination of being cute with a smokin' body that has curves in all the right places, and seemingly little idea of how attractive she is. "But we practically grew up together. She's like another sister to me."

God, I wish I believed half the shit coming out of my own mouth right now. It'd be a hell of a lot easier if I weren't still attracted to her.

Nate's warning traipses through my head. *Messing things up with Sierra would permanently damage your relationship with your family.* There is no possible happy ending for Sierra and me. She's a settle down and get married kind of girl, and I'm always plotting where I'll go next. I'm never with anyone for more than a few weeks—usually it's more like a night or two —which suits my lifestyle, my need for constant change, and my appetite for sex just fine.

Because my relationship with my family is already fucked up, I don't for a second doubt that Jackson and Dad would choose Sierra over me if it came down to it. And I would never want to put my mom in the position of having to choose. She loves Sierra, but I know she'd choose me and it would cause even more tension with my family.

"You sure?" Drew asks me. "Because the other night she

looked at you like you were a cheeseburger and she was starving."

A laugh bursts out of me, for the first time in . . . fuck, too long. "That's a disturbing analogy. But you're wrong. She looked like she wanted to kill me."

"If you say so, dude."

Less than five minutes later, we're standing at the top of the terrain park. Lance and Drew explain the layout to me since they've been here practicing for the last two days while I was stuck in endless phone meetings with a huge sponsor for my photography business. I have a big giveaway coming up, and the lead up to it has been a bit more work than I anticipated. The payout and additional visibility for my site are going to be worth it, but it's meant I couldn't get on the mountain until now. Which is fine, I still have a few weeks to get ready for Aspen. It's just hard to explain to my friends because they have no idea that I have millions of followers for my photography account. What started out as a pet project based on my two passions—travel and photography—has turned into a full-time job, on top of snowboarding. And I've never told a single soul about it.

On our first trip down the terrain park, I take it easy, practicing a couple tricks on the rails and getting in a double cork, an inverted aerial spin with two full rotations, on the last jump. On the second and third runs, I manage to pull out triple corks on that jump. It's funny, a few years ago you could win the X Games and even the Olympics with a triple cork and now it's pretty standard. I'll need to land a quad cork, a full 1440 degree spin, or something equally impressive later this month if I have any shot of placing in the top of the Big Air competition. And I'm working to up my game in

Slopestyle—my favorite event—by throwing together a string of impressive tricks I've been working on since the summer.

"Your head in the right place?" Lance asks me when I come to a stop at the end of the terrain park after our fourth or fifth trip down.

"Yeah, why?"

"You said you were going to do the quad cork that time, and you pulled out after the triple. Again."

"I just wasn't feeling it." I pull my goggles up onto my helmet and wipe the sweat off my face.

"You haven't been feeling it since Switzerland," Drew says, playing bad cop to Lance's good cop. They like to keep me accountable, but it's not like I need a reminder right now. "Was there magic snow or some shit over there?"

I was on fire this summer in Switzerland, but now even these triples are making me feel like I'm kind of rusty.

I shrug, not wanting to get into it. "I need food. Let's grab lunch."

———

I don't know what the hell is happening, but it sounds like a whiny toddler is trying to break down my front door. I'd go investigate, but I'm trying to shred this chicken before I overcook it.

Suddenly I hear the door jerk open and Sierra's ever-patient voice says, "Whoa there." She sounds unsure, and it's so unlike her that I turn off the stove and come around the corner to the entryway.

There, with his big feet running in place against the slick wood floor while Sierra holds the leash tight and attempts to shut the door behind her is an adorable chocolate lab puppy struggling to break free. He looks like he is about ready to overpower her despite their differing sizes.

"What's this?" I ask, finding it impossible to keep the amusement out of my voice. I'm laughing at her and she knows it.

She holds her head up defiantly. "I'm fostering this guy for a few weeks."

"How the hell did this happen?"

"Funny story," she says, looking both mortified and amused at once. "So, you know the other night when we were talking about photography and my job, and wanting to do something fulfilling that would make a difference?" she asks as she struggles to juggle the leash between her two hands while also getting her coat off.

I reach out and take the leash from her as the dog jumps up on my legs, then slides down. As my sweatpants slip down my hips a couple inches, I'm thankful for the drawstrings. Something flashes in Sierra's eyes as she takes in the sweats and my bare chest, a look I've seen a few times from her over the last few days but am not sure exactly what it means. I'm not used to having to decipher a woman's looks. The women I spend time with are open with their emotions. And because I'm always honest about my intentions, there's rarely ever anything but desire for me to see. I don't do relationships and I don't stick around. Since we're living together, I've already spent more time with Sierra than I've spent with any of the women I've slept with since college.

"I remember," I say causally, even though my mind is running through the entire experience again, remembering how close I was to her that night, only a thin veil of air between our bodies. If she'd even leaned back the slightest bit, I'd have cradled her body in mine. But she didn't, and it's a good reminder that she doesn't see me that way. Which is perfect, because I don't date chicks like Sierra.

"Well," she says as she hangs her coat on a wall hook, then turns to me and holds out her hand for the leash. "It got me thinking . . ." She pauses for a minute when I hand her the leash and my fingers accidentally glide across the silky skin of her inner wrist. I feel that touch everywhere, like a spark between us that sends lightning through my veins. Given her inability to form the next words, maybe she feels it too?

"It got you thinking . . ."

She shakes her head slightly. "It got me thinking that maybe I could use my photography skills to help people. So I started looking for some volunteer opportunities, and there was an animal shelter looking for someone to come in and take good photos of their pets to be used on their website. They were hoping better photos would lead more people to come in wanting to adopt pets."

She lets the brown ball of energy at the end of the leash lead her into the kitchen, where he sniffs around the base of every cabinet. I move to the stove and turn the burner back on, letting the sauce the chicken is cooking in come back up to a simmer.

"So you went there intending to take photos and left with a puppy?"

"Well, this guy was going to be put down this weekend if someone didn't take him!" Her voice is passionate and defensive.

"He's adorable, and obviously adorable puppies get adopted," I remind her. "What's wrong with him?"

"According to the shelter, he has a lot of energy. The first family that adopted him had a toddler, and this guy was constantly playing rough with him, knocking the kid down, asserting his dominance, that kind of stuff. The second family that adopted him apparently wanted someone who was already housebroken and didn't want to put in the work to train him. They brought him back after he ate the wife's Louboutins."

"Louboutins?" I ask.

She looks at me like I was raised in a jungle by apes. "You know, those heels with red soles that are a total status symbol. Needless to say, that lady was pissed and apparently didn't want a dog who was going to eat her thousand-dollar shoes. Why anyone would leave those sitting around where a puppy could get them is beyond me." She rolls her eyes as she sinks to the kitchen floor and lets the puppy come over and sniff her.

He is adorable, I'll admit that. But I have a feeling that she has no idea what she's in for. Puppies are like babies, they need constant care.

"So what are you going to do with this guy during the day, while you're at work?"

"What do you mean?" she asks.

"I mean, you're not going to let a puppy wander around the apartment when no one is home, chewing on whatever he can get his mouth on, right? Pillows, shoes, the legs of chairs . . . puppies will chew on anything, especially if they're teething."

"They told me he was crate trained."

"Did they give you a crate?" I ask. She certainly didn't come in with one.

"Yeah, it's still in the back of my car. He rode over here in it. I didn't trust him not to run wild in my car and get us into an accident."

She runs her hand down the fur on his back as the puppy rubs the top of his head under her chin. Her other hand comes up to stroke his belly, and fuck, I have to turn away before I start imagining those hands running themselves all over me. It's obviously been too long since I've gotten laid, because what the hell is wrong with me?

I grab two forks and resume shredding the chicken in the pan with a bit more vigor. There's something cathartic about quickly slashing the tines through the meat, ripping it apart. It's a good way to take out my sexual frustration.

"So what's your plan for how long he'll spend in the crate versus out of it?"

"I—" she stumbles over her words, "I haven't really thought about that."

"You don't strike me as the type to do anything without a plan."

"Yeah, well, I'll develop a plan." She looks back down at the puppy and continues petting him as if that will manifest a plan for her.

"Good, because you're on your own with that thing," I tell her. Dogs are a commitment, and I don't do those. In fact, I think that the only reason a single woman would get a dog is because she wants to settle down. In the absence of a significant other, Sierra's probably trying to fill that void with a dog. She might think she got this puppy to save him, but I bet it's more about wanting something to love now that Peter left her.

"I didn't ask for your help," she says.

I glance down, expecting to see pain in her eyes because I know that was an insensitive thing to say. I assumed she'd need help and my policy is always honesty before all else, so I wanted her to know that I'm not here to be her dog trainer.

Instead of those gorgeous brown eyes reflecting hurt, I see nothing but defiance.

Good. Independent and strong. I like that in a woman.

Nope, I have to remind myself, *not thinking of Sierra like that.*

"You interested in chicken tacos for dinner?" I ask.

"I'm going to forget how to feed myself if you keep making me dinner," she says.

"Well, we can't have you starving in the future. Guess I'll just have to eat these all myself." The resulting look on her face has me laughing. "Kidding! I would never deny you tacos."

"Thank God." She sighs. "Honestly, I don't even think I could let go of this guy long enough to cook something. Who knows what he'd tear apart while my back was turned?"

I glance down at the little monster, who's currently cuddled up in her lap, his body surrounded on all sides by her folded legs. His eyes are drooping shut, like all the excitement of coming home has worn him out.

"I think he's falling asleep," I tell her, because I know she can't see his face.

"Oh, great, so if I want any peace, I'm probably stuck here while he naps." She strokes his back gently.

"Do you have a dog bed for him?" I ask as I start plating our tacos.

"No. The crate has some bedding in it and they said he

should sleep in it at night, but I guess it'd be good to have a dog bed for when one of us is home."

I don't correct her assumption that I'll be letting her dog out when she's not home.

"You really didn't think this through before bringing him home, huh?"

"Saying I'd foster him wasn't exactly a premeditated moment for me. I just saw his adorable face, so full of love and curiosity, and there was no other choice."

It's hard not to admire her intentions, even though I disagree with her decision.

"What do you want on these tacos?" I ask, then list out the options. "Salsa? Sour cream? Lettuce? Guacamole?"

"Yes."

"Yes to which?"

"All of it. I'm starving and it smells amazing in here. I want *all* the tacos and *all* the toppings."

"I like the way you think," I tell her as I build us identical plates of tacos, then bring the plates over to the corner where she's sitting with a sleeping puppy in her lap. I hand her a plate and sink down next to her with my back against a cabinet. It's not the most comfortable way to eat dinner, and I should probably let her sit here alone, so she realizes how stupid it was to get a dog—how tied down she'll be—but whatever. I'm not *that* much of a dick.

"You don't have to eat on the floor just because I got myself into this mess," she says.

I glance over at her. Her blond hair is held back in a low ponytail with loose pieces framing her practically makeup-free face. She looks sweet and wholesome, completely at ease sitting on the floor with a dog napping in her lap. Her innocence tugs at a thought that's been forming in the back of my mind.

"How long were you at that shelter before they told you about this puppy?"

"I don't know, not long. He was one of the first dogs I photographed," she says.

"If he was being put down this weekend, why would they have you take pictures to advertise that he's available for adoption?"

The hand that was reaching for her taco stills in midair, hanging above her plate. "Uh . . . I don't know."

I give her a half smile, one that's more *you'll laugh about this someday* than *I'm laughing at you.*

"They totally pulled one over on you!" I can't help but laugh.

"Crap," she says, then looks down at the dog. Her voice changes so that it's almost like she's talking to a baby when she says, "We'll just have to make you the best damn dog ever. People will be lining up to adopt you!"

Warmth spreads through my chest. Normally someone speaking babytalk to their pet would be a hard pass, but there's something about the way she does it, as though helping this dog find a loving home is a big fuck you to the world. And that's something I can get behind.

"You should start a social media account for him. Take all the cute photos and videos you'll inevitably take of him, and post them there. Build up a little following, and then when he's ready for adoption I bet tons of people will want him. They'll be tagging friends left and right, being like 'this is the perfect dog for you!'"

She gives me a small but hopeful smile. "That's actually not a bad idea."

"Thanks. I do know a thing or two about social media. But I'll leave this to the expert."

"You want to help?" she asks. "I can create the account and give you the password so you can post photos too."

"I'm not really the kind of guy to sit around taking pictures of a dog, but thanks for the offer."

She finally picks up her first taco and takes a bite, and a moan escapes her mouth while her eyes roll back in her head. *I wonder if that's the same look and sound she makes when she comes?* Before I even realize what's happening, I'm envisioning my face between her legs and the sounds I could draw out of her. The thought has my body reacting in all the appropriate ways, which are so inappropriate given the circumstances. I set my plate across my thighs to cover the growing bulge between them, but the plate won't sit straight, so I have to balance it with my hand.

Sierra gives me a look, probably wondering why I practically threw my plate onto my lap. "These are amazing."

"You have quite the reaction to my cooking."

"What do you mean?" she asks.

I shrug, because even though I want to make a smart-ass comment about her orgasmic response to my food, I don't want to risk her storming off like she so often does because then she'd wake the dog up.

"I like that you enjoy the food I make you."

We sit in companionable silence while she finishes two of her three tacos. Then she sets her plate on the floor next to her and says, "I ate those too fast. I need to slow down."

She tilts her head back against the cabinet and closes her eyes for a second. In the time it takes for me to look at her and notice how her eyebrows are a light brown, a couple shades darker than her hair, the puppy has not only woken up, but has bounded off Sierra's lap and gotten ahold of her remaining taco.

He whips his head back and forth, like it's a toy he's playing with, and the contents of the taco start flying all over the kitchen. Before I even have time to reach across Sierra and grab his collar, there are drops of the red adobo sauce and a smear of guacamole on the cabinets, chicken and lettuce mixed with sour cream coat the floor under the dog's paws, and Sierra has both guacamole and sour cream on her face and half the contents of the taco in her lap. Even my arm wasn't spared from the chicken taco massacre, despite Sierra being between the dog and me.

Once I've got him by the collar, he immediately sits, hanging his head like he knows he did something wrong. "Winston," Sierra coos, "you bad boy." She takes the empty tortilla out of his mouth.

"You can't talk to him like he's a good boy when he's done something wrong."

"What do you mean? I said he was a bad boy."

"He doesn't speak English." My voice comes out sounding as exasperated as I feel. She obviously knows nothing about dogs. "You have to use a tone of voice appropriate to his actions. When he's been bad, you need to be firm and reprimand him. You can't coddle him and expect him to behave, *you* have to be the alpha in this relationship, or he will be. Try again."

She looks at me like she wants to smack me, but instead turns toward the dog. "Winston," she says, the word like a sharp, reprimanding crack. "Bad!"

He sinks down to the ground and puts his head between his front paws, looking up at her with the saddest puppy dog eyes I've ever seen. I press my lips between my teeth to keep from laughing, and she turns her head away from him, tucking it between her shoulder and mine. I can feel her laughter before she whispers, "Oh, man, I'm in so much trouble with this one."

I pull back, hoping Winston doesn't make a run for it when I let go of his collar. "Stay," I tell him, my voice low and the word slow. I don't take my eyes off him when I say, "Why don't you go get cleaned up. I'll take care of this mess and then we can find a pet store and get him some chew toys and a bed."

"We?" she asks without moving.

"Does this dog seem like a one-person job?"

"I'll appreciate any help I can get," she says, putting her hand on my thigh as she pushes herself up to a standing position.

Winston's eyes follow her, but I put my hand on his back and repeat "Stay." Amazingly, he listens and I think perhaps he's going to turn out all right after all.

Chapter Eight

SIERRA

"I'll have that to you by the end of the day," I tell Heather as I gather my laptop and notebook up. On the opposite side of the table she looks up, surprised at my abruptness. While I'm normally happy to hang out and *kibitz* (as Petra would say) with my boss, I'm also desperate to know why my phone has been buzzing away in the pocket of my down vest for the last hour of that three hour marathon meeting I've been stuck in.

I turn away quickly and make a beeline for the door, slipping through it and into the hall before anyone can talk to me. I pull my phone out and check the screen as I walk through the Elite Training Center to my office. Not only have Petra and Lauren been texting on our group chat but also I have four texts from Beau. *What the hell?* He hasn't texted me once since New Year's Eve, so four texts in an hour has me a little worried. Did he injure himself training or something? But even if he did, why would he contact me about that?

When I get to my office, I shut the door behind me and unlock my phone.

The group chat is open on my screen, so I scan that and see Petra and Lauren are trying to convince Jackson to FaceTime with us tonight while we're out for our girls' dinner. That can wait, so I hop over to Beau's texts. When I open that thread, picture after picture of the puppy fills my screen. Winston licking peanut butter out of the rubber KONG we got him last night. Winston laying on the living room rug with his big paws in the air, clearly enjoying a belly rub. Winston outside in midair as he tries to catch a snowball with his mouth. Winston wrapped up in a sherpa blanket like a burrito.

SIERRA

Why are you home playing with the puppy?

BEAU

Oh NOW she responds!

SIERRA

I was stuck in a meeting. Aren't you supposed to be training?

BEAU

It's snowing faster than they can groom the terrain park. Awesome powder out there, so we did some runs for fun instead, then I came home early.

SIERRA

So how's my baby doing?

BEAU

The contractors started laying the tile today, and the sound of the wet saw had him pretty freaked out.

SIERRA

Oh shit, I didn't even think about how the
contractors being there would affect him.

The bubble pops up, indicating that Beau's typing, then it disappears. My stomach plummets as I imagine he was about to say *Of course you didn't* or *That's because you don't know anything about dogs.* Finally, the bubble pops up again and he responds.

BEAU

It's fine, I took him outside to play in the snow
for a while. They were done with the tile saw
by the time we came back in.

SIERRA

Thanks for taking him out. And for the cute
pictures of him.

Not for the first time in the last twenty-four hours, I wonder if I made a mistake agreeing to foster Winston. I work a fair amount. Is it okay to leave him home like that? The shelter said he'd be fine crated while I'm at work, but maybe that's not fair to him. Some days, I can probably get away at lunch and take him for a quick walk to get some exercise. I wish there was a way I could bring him to work with me.

BEAU

No problem. You should post them on the
social media account you created last night.
You've only got the one picture up there.

SIERRA

Because I'm working! And I don't have any
other pictures of him.

BEAU

Which is why I just sent you some.

SIERRA

Will you please post them? I don't have time.
I'll share the login info with you.

BEAU

Fine. He's basically decided we're best
friends. Now he's conked out on top of me
and I'm afraid to move.

SIERRA

LOL, now that I'd like to see.

A picture of Winston snuggled on the couch with a shirt-less Beau appears on my screen. The top half of Winston is laying across Beau's stomach, right above those damn sweat-pants he always wears that leave *nothing* to the imagination. His pecs and shoulders are perfect—he's unbelievably ripped —and he's giving me a stupid grin. At first glance, his dark eyes appear amused, but it's like there's something beneath that look that I can't quite pick up despite zooming in on his face and squinting at my phone.

"You doing okay?"

The question comes out of nowhere, and even though I recognize Heather's voice, it still scares the crap out of me and I fumble my phone. It lands upside down on my desk and I glance up at her, standing in my doorway.

"You scared me! I didn't even hear the door open."

"It wasn't shut," she says, even though I could swear it was. Then again, I was in a hurry to check my texts, so maybe I didn't push it closed all the way. "But are you okay? You seemed off at the end of the meeting, then you hightailed it out of there like you couldn't get away from us quickly enough. Just wanted to make sure all is well."

"No, I'm fine. My phone was blowing up at the end of the meeting, and I just wanted to make sure nothing was wrong. Turns out it was just my roommate sending me pictures of my new puppy."

Heather takes a few steps toward my desk and pulls up the chair across from me. "Okay, rewind. Roommate? Puppy?"

I sigh. "Yeah, Peter and I broke up—"

"Oh my gosh, why didn't you say anything?"

"Because it's fine," I say. At least, it's fine when I don't think about it, when I don't fixate on his betrayal. "So now I'm living back at Jackson's place and her brother is staying there too."

"Beau Shanahan is your roommate?" she asks, her eyes wide. She looks like I just told her I live with Ryan Gosling. Why do all women seem to have this reaction to him—even my boss?

Heather's six years older than me and has been here since before I started. She pretty naturally stepped into the role of big sister as well as boss, but she's like the big sister who's significantly older and you don't actually know that well because you're at different points in your life and don't have a ton in common. She'll look out for you, but you don't exactly swap secrets.

"Yeah, it's just a short-term thing. He's training for the X Games, and he'll be off to Aspen in a few weeks. Why is this such a big deal?"

"Sierra, he's a professional snowboarder. I know you're more into skiing, but you *do* know where you work, right?" she says, reaching forward and tapping the desk between us.

Her light brown hair falls forward over her shoulder, and she gathers it into a low ponytail as she sits back in the chair. "I know your job is only to cover social media for the alpine ski teams, but you do realize that this organization supports the national snowboarding, cross-country, aerial, and mogul teams too, right?"

I roll my eyes at her sarcasm and smile. "Of course, but that doesn't mean I follow those teams as closely. Just the men's and women's alpine teams, competing in five different disciplines with races all over the world—that keeps me pretty busy. I let Kevin handle snowboarding, which is his job. Besides, it's not like Beau's on the National Snowboard Team."

"He should have been," she says.

"What do you mean?" This is news to me. I've always thought of this organization as Jackson's thing, first as a member of the women's alpine race team, then as a physical therapist for the men's team. I didn't realize Beau had any connection to the organization.

"He's certainly good enough. Hey, I have to run to my next meeting, but can I see a puppy picture before I go?"

"Of course." I unlock my phone and scroll back to the third picture Beau sent, of Winston jumping in the air, trying to catch a snowball. It's a great shot, and the one that shows so much of his rambunctious personality. "Here you go." I hand her the phone. "The next one's cute too."

"Oh my goodness," she gushes. "Who's such a good boy?"

I want to point out that he can't hear her, but I'm pretty sure I said the same thing, in the same tone, in my head when I first saw the picture.

"What's his name?" she asks as she swipes to the next photo.

"Winston."

"I love it when people give dogs old man names. It just, like, suits them, you know?" She smiles down at the photo of Winston wrapped in the sherpa blanket that I'm one hundred percent sure Jackson didn't buy with the intention of wrapping a dog in it. Cue the internal realization that I haven't told my best friend that I have a dog living at her condo, and I'm not actually sure how she'll react. Maybe I don't need to tell her? I mean, it's short term. I'm sure we'll find someone to adopt him soon, especially if Beau's right about using social media to attract attention to Winston.

I'm so lost in my thoughts debating if not telling Jackson about the dog is still lying that I'm caught off guard when Heather sucks in a breath, then laughs and says, "Roommates, huh?"

"What?" I glance up to find her holding my phone with two fingers like she's stumbled upon something dirty. She turns the phone to face me and from this vantage point I can see it as she sees it: my roommate sending me half-naked pictures of himself with my puppy.

"He refuses to wear shirts inside." I roll my eyes. "It's maddening."

"Maybe he's trying to catch your attention with his"—she gives a little nod toward the photo as she glances down at it before saying—"impressive physique."

"Actually, I think he's just clueless. He's never lived with a woman before, and I don't think it has even crossed his mind that while it might be okay to walk around in nothing but sweatpants with the guys, it's less okay in this circumstance."

"Have you said anything?" Heather asks, but she still hasn't taken her eyes off the photo.

I let go of an uncomfortable laugh. "He's Jackson's little brother. I feel like if I said something, he'd think I was checking him out, and that would be really uncomfortable."

A flashback of him flirting with me at Jackson's wedding is closely followed by the vision of him standing behind me as we dissected his photograph a few nights ago, and I wonder at the truth of my words. Yes, it would absolutely be uncomfortable to have that conversation with him. But part of me knows that in saying something to him, he'd know that part of the issue is that I'm trying *hard* not to be attracted to him.

It's a physical response I can't really help, it's not a choice I'm making—the choice very much has been to keep my distance because he's my best friend's little brother.

Not to mention that Beau is a classic bad boy—the kind of guy my mother could never resist. He'll give you everything you need for a couple days, just long enough for you to hope it'll last, then he'll be off on his next adventure and in the bed of a different woman.

I'm looking for someone responsible to settle down with, someone who'll make a good husband and a good father.

"I mean, obviously he wants you to check him out or he wouldn't be sending you pictures like this. If you don't want to receive them, you need to speak up."

"Good point," I agree as I hold my hand out for my phone.

"I have to leave or I'll be late for my next meeting. Let me know how the conversation goes with him, okay?" she says as she backs away toward the door.

"Sure thing," I say, but I regret it instantly. Because this is not a conversation I'm going to have with Beau. I don't care why he walks around without a shirt on or why he sent me that picture. He's here for a couple more weeks and that's it. I'm going to keep my head down and ignore him as best I can.

I have every intention of doing just that as I shove my phone back in my pocket and sit down at my desk to bang out this last project so I can get home, take Winston out for a walk, and get ready for dinner with my girlfriends.

————

Beau's not there when I get home, and wherever he is, he must have Winston with him.

I stop in the kitchen to grab a drink before I get ready to meet my friends. As I stand at the counter pouring myself a glass of wine from a bottle I bought this week, I eye the bottles of Peter's wine still sitting on the counter. I haven't heard a word from him since I moved out. I'm not sure that I expected to, but I guess I hoped he'd at least send me an angry text about taking every last item of food and drink, and everything you could use to eat or drink with. But it's been radio silence, which I've taken to mean that even if I riled up some emotion in him, he didn't care enough to tell me he was mad.

It was a childish, petty thing to do—I know that. I wanted to piss him off even if it didn't compare to what he did to me. But there's no glory in it unless I know it had the desired effect, and I will never know.

I glance down at my glass, which I filled far more than I intended as I stood there looking at Peter's wine bottles. I take a sip, wondering what he's doing now. Are he and Jane fucking in his office every chance they get?

I shake my head to get those visuals out of my mind. When I start imaging my ex having sex with his admin, I have to acknowledge that Petra's probably right, I need to have some amazing sex of my own. The kind that will help me forget the very disappointing sexual relationship I had with Peter.

Petra's voice fills my head as I remind myself: *At least you're not committed to mediocre sex for the rest of your life.*

I take my wineglass into the bathroom and enjoy the extra time I have to get ready for dinner with my friends. I'd planned on taking Winston out for a quick walk when I got home, playing with him for a bit, then rushing to get dressed to go out. I never appreciated how luxurious it was to get ready without having to be responsible for another living being until right now. I've only been a dog mom for twenty-four hours, and most of that time Winston has been with Beau —who insisted he wanted nothing to do with the puppy, and yet they are off somewhere after spending the whole after-noon together. He swaddled the puppy like a freaking baby and if it wasn't the cutest thing I've ever seen, I'm not sure what is.

Once I've curled my hair and refreshed my makeup, I send Beau a text.

SIERRA

Where are you guys? I've been home for almost an hour. I thought at least Winston would be here.

BEAU

So cute that you're missing us. We're almost home.

I don't correct him, because why bother? Instead, I head to my bedroom, change into an ivory turtleneck sweater dress, pull a pair of matching sweater socks up over my knees, and then pull on a pair of thigh high rust colored suede boots that I love and will find any occasion to wear. I'm tightening up the laces along the back of the boots when I hear Beau and Winston return.

It sounds like there's a tussle in the entryway, and I hear Beau's firm voice telling Winston to sit, so I head out there to see them. As soon as I enter the living room, Beau glances up and Winston bolts toward me, but Beau's still holding his collar and is literally pulled over by the effort of holding him back.

"Shit, Sierra!"

Now that he's laying sideways on the ground holding onto Winston, all I can see is his beanie covering his head and his jacket.

"Go back to your room," he growls as Winston continues running in place, with Beau's vice grip around his collar.

What the fuck?

"Excuse me?" I say, taking on a haughty tone I reserve for men who boss women around like that.

"Can you—" He pauses with a deep exhale. "—give me a second with him? Just go back to your room so he can't see you."

"Fine." Though it's anything but fine that he's here in my space, telling me what to do like he's in charge of me.

I've paced around my room for a few minutes when he knocks.

"What?" I spit out as I swing open the door and glare at him. *Why do you let him piss you off?* I ask myself. He makes me feel like an irrational toddler—angry one minute and overly excited the next. I'm more mad at myself than at him about that, but it's easier to take it out on him.

"Sorry," he says, looking at the ground as he runs his large hand through his unruly dark hair. It's both matted down and sticking up, clearly just freed from the confines of a winter hat. "I didn't mean to snap to you like that. But Winston was muddy from being outside in the sidewalk snow and slush, and you're all . . ." He pauses and gestures his hand up and down toward my body while looking at me with his lips pursed together. "And I didn't want him to come jump all over you and get you filthy. He has zero self-control. He'll learn eventually."

I soften a tiny bit because I would have been really upset if I had to change, or if Winston ruined my dress or suede boots by smearing his muddy paw prints all over them. And the fact that Beau's first reaction was to protect me from that . . . I'll have to think about what that means later.

"Thanks for explaining," I say. "Is he clean now?"

"I wiped him down with a wet towel and dried him off as best I could. He's clean, and he's in his crate calming down. You want to come see him? Or are you on your way out?"

"I'm just going to dinner with Petra and Lauren, I'm not leaving for another half hour or so. Where were you, anyway?"

"I needed to pick up a few things at the store, so we walked over to the market together."

"They let dogs in there?"

"No one said anything to me about him being there. I kept him on a *very* short leash," Beau says with one of his half smiles, "literally."

"Thanks for taking him out," I say and take a step forward to slip past him into the hallway. He barely moves out of the way in time, and my shoulder and arm drag along his chest and I imagine that my hand barely misses brushing against a very important part of his anatomy. The thought has my stomach tumbling over itself and a longing sensation—the need to fill the hollow area in me—pulses through my core.

I can feel him behind me as we walk down the hall toward the living room. His presence has its own energy, and I am pulled toward it like a magnet. Part of me wants to stop, so he runs into me, just to see what he'd do with that full body contact. But then I remember it's Beau, and I think about all the adjectives Jackson has used to describe him: wanderer, womanizer, selfish, partier, lost. So even if he wasn't my best friend's younger brother, even if I hadn't known him since he was a child, he'd still be the wrong guy for me.

He doesn't have to be the perfect guy to settle down with. Sex doesn't have to be a relationship. It's like my inner voice keeps getting co-opted by Petra's.

I am not, under any circumstances, having sex with Beau, I insist to myself because apparently I need the reminder. If I'm this starved for sex, there's always tomorrow night's date with Jared.

The second I step into the living room, Winston starts jumping around ecstatically, his tail thwacking the metal edges of the crate in a rhythmic pattern. I approach slowly so as to not get him even more excited, but it doesn't seem to work. He's now running in circles in the small, confined space.

"Do you want some unsolicited advice?" Beau asks gently as he steps up beside me.

"About Winston?" I clarify, because I'm all for advice about this dog if it's going to help me get him trained and adopted.

He chuckles as he glances over at me. The heat in his gaze has warmth flowing through me. "Yeah, about Winston."

I glance down and Winston is still running in circles in his crate. "If you know what you're talking about, then yes."

"I know what I'm talking about," he says quietly. "You need to show him you're not playing, or he'll never take commands from you." He sees something in my reaction, because he puts his hand on my lower back and his voice is low and level as he continues, "I'm not saying you can't love on him and play with him. But when you tell him to do something, there has to be clarity. He has to know what you want him to do, and that you mean it. He's still so young, he is absolutely trainable. But you can train them to have bad habits more easily than good ones. So it's important that you're consistent."

I glance over at him and we lock eyes. I feel like I'm swallowing a golf ball as I stare into those dark brown eyes with their flecks of amber scattered around the pupils. Suddenly, my mouth feels extremely dry, and I instinctively lick my lips. His eyes shoot down to my mouth.

"Show me?" I ask, and the way he looks at me makes me forget there's a crazy dog running in circles in a crate at my feet, or that I'm headed out to dinner with my friends. It makes me want to stay in, spend more time with him, maybe get naked with him.

Luckily, that train of thought is broken when he squats down and says, "Winston, stay."

The puppy stops running in circles and looks up at him, his tail wagging so fast I can't believe he doesn't fall over. "Stay," Beau says, his voice a warning tone as he reaches over for the crate door.

I can see how tightly wound Winston is, how much effort

he's putting into staying in one place. And I'm curious to see if he bolts the minute Beau opens that door. I'm not sure how I'll contain my laughter if he does.

Beau reaches his hand through the bars on the crate and rubs Winston's little brown head, right where his floppy ears meet his skull. "Stay," Beau says, his words still slow, like a warning.

He reaches out and slowly unlocks the crate. To his credit, Winston doesn't move except for the tail wagging, even as Beau slowly opens the crate door.

The care and patience Beau has when dealing with Winston has me questioning some of the things I thought I knew about him.

"Come," Beau says, and Winston quirks his head at him, not knowing what to do. Beau reaches in and grabs Winston's collar and repeats himself as he leads Winston out of the crate. "Do you want to try?" he asks me.

"Sure. What should I do?" I ask, feeling incredibly out of my league.

Beau nods toward the couch. "Why don't you sit down and then use the same commands I just used."

I take a few steps over to the couch and when I'm seated, I tell Winston to stay using the same tone Beau just did. Beau slowly lets go of Winston's collar and when he stays in place, I am so proud of him that I can't help grinning. I give it a second before I say "Come" and the second I do, Winston bounds toward my outstretched arms. He jumps right up with his front paws on my lap, and I spread my knees and bend down to kiss his head as he dances around on his hind legs. The force of his tail wagging would probably knock him over if he wasn't being supported on both sides by my knees.

I reach down and pick him up, cradling him in my arms like a baby and talking to him like he's one too. I can't help it, it just happens. And in a way, it's a relief. After seeing how my mom raised me and after practically having to raise my own siblings, I've always wondered if I'd ever want kids. I kept waiting for those instincts to kick in—I've always *known* I wanted kids, but I've never *felt* the need for them. It had me questioning whether I have those motherly instincts. But I feel them now, as I cradle this bundle of energy in my arms. I know he's a puppy, not a human, but I imagine that this desire I have to love and protect and help him is similar to how I'd feel if I were holding a human baby.

Winston quickly wiggles out of my arms and onto the sofa, so I pick him up and set him on the rug, where he runs around the coffee table and right to Beau, who is still kneeling on the ground next to the crate. Beau takes some of the dog toys out of the crate and I go sit on the floor with them and we marvel at Winston as we try to teach him how to fetch his toys by name.

Eventually, I glance up at the clock on the wall and realize that we've been playing with Winston far longer than I thought, and I was supposed to leave about ten minutes ago. The thought of being late has my skin itchy, like an allergic reaction.

I ask Beau if he wants me to crate Winston before I leave, but he says, "Nah, I'll put him in the crate before I go out later."

I look away, trying to ignore how badly I want to ask him what he's doing tonight, and who he's doing it with. It's none of my business, and if he'd wanted me to know, he'd have volunteered the information. So before I can press him for that information, I turn and head for my bedroom to grab my purse.

"Sierra?" he says from behind me.

"Yeah," I call over my shoulder as I head down the hall.

"What's wrong?"

I both hate and love that he's so perceptive. I think he'll be a good partner to someone someday—once he's ready to settle down. And I hate how uncomfortable it feels knowing that he'll make someone else happy someday. What the hell is wrong with me? Is this all it takes for me to start thinking of a guy as marriage material—he just has to be nice to my dog? Who isn't even really my dog, just the dog that I'm fostering but already starting to think of as my own?

"Nothing's wrong," I call out, "I just realized I'm running late, and I think you know how I feel about being late."

———

"Okay, I've got to go for real." Jackson laughs. "My husband is literally dragging me to bed." She holds her phone behind her so we can see Nate pulling her up off the couch. He must scoop her into his arms once she's standing because the camera is jostled all over the place before she brings it up and focuses it on their faces.

"You've had her long enough," Nate says into the camera. His lips curve up in amusement, but when he glances at Jackson, the look is suddenly full of heat. "Good night, ladies."

We don't even get a chance to say our goodbyes before the call is disconnected.

"They are so freaking cute I can't stand it, and I think I might cry because these stupid postnatal hormones are no joke!" Lauren says tearfully as she wraps her napkin around her finger and dabs at her eyes.

"Darling, your pregnancy convinced me that I never want to have children," Petra purrs at Lauren.

Lauren's eyes go wide and fully fill up with tears. "Well, that's a shitty thing to say," she tells Petra.

I reach over and grab Lauren's hand, giving her a supportive squeeze while I look over at Petra with my eyes as wide as I can possibly make them. *What the hell?* I mouth. Petra just shrugs and takes a sip of her martini.

"Hey," I say softly, turning back toward Lauren. "These hormones are making you feel all these really big feelings, and you know how Petra is about emotions. Besides, she was never planning to have kids anyway."

Lauren gives me a small smile before she looks over at Petra, who's got one arm resting up along the curved back of the banquette as she takes another sip of her martini. Her long curly hair flows around her shoulders like tendrils of black smoke. Her eyes are cast somewhere across the bar, most likely staking out tonight's conquest.

I reach over and nudge her foot with mine.

"What?" she asks, the question is defensive as she slides those perfectly made-up eyes my way.

"You know what."

Petra looks over at Lauren. "Sorry, sweetie. Sierra's right, I don't want kids and it wasn't your pregnancy that turned me off to the idea. But even if I hadn't already decided against having children, seeing someone go through a difficult pregnancy like you did would make me second-guess my choices."

"Wow." I sigh. "You *almost* managed an apology."

"I'm not sorry that I don't enjoy other people's misery.

Would it be better if I'd said it was wonderful watching Lauren puke every day and lose all that weight and have to go to the hospital once a week for an IV just to make sure she got enough fluids?"

"It wasn't *that* bad," Lauren speaks up.

"Honey, you couldn't keep anything down for months, and when you finally could, all you ate were canned peaches and those fresh cheese ravioli drowned in butter. And you had those purple circles under your eyes because you were so dehydrated from throwing up all the time. And then your belly got as big as your whole body."

"Well, when you put it that way . . ." Lauren smiles. "But even as crappy as I felt, I was elated that Josh and I had finally managed to start our family after trying for so long."

The two of them had gone through over a year of infertility treatments before conceiving their twins.

"I'm happy for you that you finally got what you wanted," Petra says. "And I will be the best auntie ever—just wait till you see how I spoil those little girls when they're older. But motherhood is just not for me."

I wonder sometimes what Petra's childhood was like. She never talks about it and evades questions when they are asked. I know the bare minimum: her American mother and Russian father met and married in Russia, and settled down in Austria where she grew up. Her mother and older brother died in a tragic accident when she was thirteen. I know a ton about her years skiing on the World Cup circuit, which is where she met and became good friends with Jackson. But I wonder who she was before she became this Wonder Woman-like goddess who is fiercely protective of her friends, yet doesn't really know how to show us she loves us.

"Oh God." Lauren sighs. "You really will spoil them, won't you? You'll probably come over and do their makeup, and take them out to fancy restaurants, and make them have these big dreams about what they can do in life."

"Pretty much," Petra says and takes another sip of her martini. "And Sierra will be the one they come to when they need advice, or when they're mad at their parents and need a sympathetic ear. And we should let her take them shopping for all their bras and panties, because did you know the girl has a lingerie collection to rival a Victoria's Secret model?"

"Really?" Lauren says, one eyebrow arched as she looks at me with amusement. "Do tell."

"There's nothing to tell. I just like pretty underwear. So I collect it." I don't really know why they don't know this about me, it's not like it's a secret. "Why is it such a big deal?" I ask Petra.

"You're like the quintessential good girl. The girl next door. The *good* one," she emphasizes.

"You are repeating yourself," I inform her. She's using the word *good* like it's a bad quality.

"You just . . ." Petra looks to Lauren for backup.

"I think you already made your point," Lauren says, but she doesn't disagree with Petra.

"So let me get this straight," I say, grabbing my cocktail. "You think I'm too much of a Goody Two-shoes to have a collection of sexy lingerie?"

"I don't even know what a Goody Two-shoes is," Petra says and I'm pretty sure she's playing up her accent, "but if it means you seem too virtuous and well-behaved to also strut around in sexy underwear, then yes."

I give Lauren a questioning look.

"I mean, I'm a little surprised too. But more power to you," she says, raising her glass and clinking it with mine.

"Now let's use that sexy lingerie collection to get you properly fucked," Petra says, bringing her glass up to join ours. "Are you going to see that guy you met last weekend again?"

"Yeah, we have a date tomorrow. He's taking me to dinner."

"Good," Petra says, the word rolling off her tongue like a purr.

"How are you feeling about dating again?" Lauren asks as she brushes her long red hair behind her shoulder, her voice gentle because she understands that this is hard. Unlike Petra, she knows what it's like to get your heart broken.

"Honestly, I don't even know. I'm still so angry about what Peter did to me. I was so blindsided by it, I just don't know how I could trust anyone again. I don't really think I can even trust myself."

"Did you really love him?" Lauren asks, and when my head spins toward her in surprise, she rushes on with, "Hear me out. You were engaged to the man for over a year, but neither of you seemed in a hurry to set a wedding date. And when he cheated on you, you were, and still are, rightfully pissed. But never once have you expressed that you were certain Peter was *the one*, or that you don't know how you'll live without him. You don't seem heartbroken."

"I don't know why we didn't set a date," I tell my friends. "I felt like every time I brought it up, Peter had a good reason for not settling on a specific time. And I was afraid if I pushed too hard . . ." I haven't told my friends about my mom's family's ridiculous curse. Jackson is the only other person in my life who knows. How do I explain this without explaining that I was afraid I'd cause it to come true for me too?

To my right, Petra perks up. "Hon, if you were afraid that insisting on setting a date over a year after getting engaged was going to result in you and Peter breaking it off, then that marriage was never meant to happen."

I take a drink of my margarita and let the combination of the sweetness and saltiness wash down my protests that it was just the curse I was afraid of. Because if our relationship *was* strong enough in the first place, I wouldn't have had to worry about some stupid family curse that I don't even believe in, right?

"Well, I think going out with Jared tomorrow night's a good first step in walking away from that relationship," I tell my friends.

They both agree that this is the right attitude, and I only wish that I believed my date with Jared would somehow help anything. That little text exchange we shared in the entryway before he left was cute—the kind of thing that the old me would have run through her mind over and over, seeing it as a hopeful sign that he was really into me. But I've hardly heard from him since—just a quick text telling me (not asking) what time he was going to pick me up on Saturday. I don't quite feel like I can trust him. Or anyone, for that matter.

Chapter Nine

BEAU

I glance at my alarm clock, wondering why I'm up at 5:00 a.m. on a Saturday. Then I hear the whining and scratching sound coming from the living room, and I know why. It's because Sierra just can't help herself, and got talked into fostering a puppy who's part demonic monster and part lovable as shit.

I pull the covers back and grab the sweatpants lying on the end of my bed. My bare feet pad across the carpet to the door, but the hardwood floor of the hallway is cold when I step onto it. The heat isn't on yet and the cool air and floor send a shiver up my back and my muscles contract. I'm about to turn around to find my slippers or a shirt, but Winston lets out another whine, louder this time.

I head into the living room and turn on the overhead light to the dimmest setting.

"Hey, bud," I whisper as I kneel down next to his crate, hoping not to wake Sierra up. If there's one thing I've definitely learned about her, it's that she is *not* a morning person. "What's going on?"

125

Winston lets out a bark and paws at the door to his crate. *Shit.* Now I'm going to have to let him out or he's going to start barking, and it's too early to wake up our neighbors. I reach for the latch to the crate door, and as soon as it's unlocked, Winston barrels through and jumps on me. His paws are on my shoulders, nails digging into my skin, as he licks my face. I manage to calm him down enough that all four of his paws are on the floor, but he dances around, waving his butt in the air. It's more than just his typical tail wagging.

"Guess you have to go to the bathroom, huh?" I say to him.

"That's what I figured," Sierra says from behind me. I turn to find her in thick leggings with ski socks pulled over the top, and a thick fleece zipped up to her chin. "I'm taking him out. Sorry he woke you up, you can go back to bed." Her voice is full of apology, but also frustration.

"I know you don't really do mornings," I tell her. "Want me to take him out?"

She sweeps her eyes over me lazily, obviously too tired to pretend she isn't checking me out. Sierra looking at me like this is the beginning of pretty much all my teenage fantasies. "I'm already dressed," she says when her eyes land on my face. "And per usual, you aren't."

So this is what desire looks like on her. I like it.

"I can get dressed and take him out to go to the bathroom if you want to go back to bed," I say, then wonder who has taken over my brain because these are not the kinds of favors I do for people.

"Don't be ridiculous," she says, gesturing down at her clothes. "I'll take him out. You go back to bed. One of us should get some sleep." She heads to the entryway and pulls on all her winter gear. The minute she pulls the leash off the hook by the door, Winston goes bounding across the floor so quickly he loses his balance and crashes into her feet face-first, then he hops up and dances around anxiously as Sierra tries unsuccessfully to get his leash attached to his collar.

"Here," I say as I walk over to them, "let me hold him in place for you." I sink back to my knees and wrap him in both my arms. I dip my head down and use some of the commands we've been practicing to get him to stay still for her. "Okay," I say, glancing back up to tell her to try again. But she's holding her phone out in front of her with a small smile on her face.

"What do you think?" she asks as she turns her phone toward me. "Should we post this on Winston's social media?"

In the picture, Winston is looking up at her from my bare arms, which I'll admit look pretty damn cut with the way they're circled around him like a cage. My sweats are slung low on my hips and my hair is kind of a bed head mess, but at this angle it doesn't really matter because it covers most everything but the side of my face and my jawline.

"Okay. And make sure you say that getting him ready to go to the bathroom at five in the morning is a two-person job. No false advertising if he's going to find his forever home."

"That's almost word for word what I was planning on saying. He's adorable, but he's a puppy and he's a handful. Whoever adopts him has to be ready for that." Then she looks at Winston and says "Stay" as she bends down and clips his leash to his collar.

Her hair swings forward and I inhale the scent of her shampoo or conditioner, marveling at how sweet she smells, like a tropical drink that I can't quite remember the name of—something with strawberries in it. I sit back on my heels, wondering when the hell I became the kind of guy that goes around sniffing girls' hair and filing the scent away for future reference? *You DON'T do that*, I remind myself.

I think about all the little things I know about her from living together for the last week. Hates to cook but loves to bake, likes to sleep in, takes her coffee extra light, still hurting from that dickwad of an ex-fiancé, huge heart that always wants to help, likes her job but misses the creative element photography provided, hyper-organized and easily frustrated when things don't go how she planned . . . I could keep going through the list of small details I've cataloged. But I don't because she's turning and leading Winston out the door. I close and lock it behind them.

I glance at the clock on the wall. Even though I don't need to leave here to head to the mountain for another couple hours, I'm awake now. So I head to the coffee maker and turn it on, glad that I'm the kind of guy who sets it up at night.

I grab my phone while I wait for the coffee to brew and the heat to kick on, I scroll through my unread texts from last night. I headed home earlier than my friends would have liked, as evidenced by all their messages calling me a pussy and telling me they hoped I was getting my beauty sleep while they were busy picking up hot chicks. There are texts from two different girls I met last night, each of them highly suggestive. On any other weekend, in any other town, I'd have gone home with one of those girls. We'd have had a good time for a night or maybe two, and then I'd have moved on to the next girl in the next ski town.

Instead, I came home early, hoping to spend a little time with Sierra when she got back from dinner with her friends. But she was already home and in her bedroom with the door shut, so I didn't even see her. The idea of calling up one of those girls from the bar and inviting them over did cross my mind for .02 seconds before I realized that I didn't even want to.

The only person I really wanted to see was on the other side of that bedroom door. I'd gone to my own room for the night, both sexually frustrated and pissed off that I seemed to be having all these confusing emotions.

By the time the coffee maker is beeping to let me know it's done brewing, Sierra is already walking back through that door. And she looks like she's about to cry.

"What's wrong?" My voice is filled with concern—again, who the fuck am I?

"I forgot a baggie and so now I have to go back out and clean up his poop. And it's like negative five degrees out there right now."

"Here," I say, reaching down and grabbing a bag from the roll we keep on the small table in the entryway. I hand it to her and say, "I'll get his feet wiped off while you run back down and take care of this. Just think, if it's really that cold out, it'll already be frozen, so it'll be easier to pick up."

She rolls her eyes. "Picking up poop was not what I envisioned when I agreed to foster him."

She hands me the leash and heads back out the door. I have Winston's feet wiped off and am sitting on one of the chairs in the living room with my cup of coffee in my hand and him curled up at my feet when she returns.

"Well, aren't you the picture of domesticity," she says after she takes her coat, hat, mittens, and boots off.

I can't help but bark out a laugh. "Yeah, you've really nailed the essence of me."

She gives me a wry smile in return. "You're not going back to sleep, I take it?"

"No, once I'm up, I'm generally up for the day, no matter how early it is."

She comes into the living room, takes a deep breath, inhaling the scent of the coffee. "That smells so good, but I feel like if I don't go back to sleep, I probably won't be able to stay awake for my date tonight."

"Oh? You have a date tonight?" My voice is teasing, which covers up the pang of jealousy that shoots through me. I can't remember the last time I was jealous like this. I've set my life up just how I like it, with no time or energy for jealousy or regrets.

"Yeah. That guy who was with me last weekend when you moved in. He's . . . sweet, I think."

"You sound *really* excited about him," I say and take a drink of my coffee.

"I don't really know him, so it's hard to be too excited. I'm only going out with him because my friends insist that I'll get over Peter quicker if I see other people."

"You don't seem like you're hung up on your ex," I say.

"No, I'm just angry."

"You have every right to be angry, and anyone who wants you to move on so you let go of that anger isn't looking out for your best interest."

"Petra and Lauren don't want me to move on so that I'm less angry," she says through a yawn, "they just think I need to . . . how did Petra put it? Get properly fucked—" her brown eyes widen. "And I'm so tired that my filter has malfunctioned and I've said too much. Going back to bed now," she says, her words tumbling out quickly as she stands and takes a few steps backward. She trips over a basket of blankets, but rights herself quickly, spins around, and rushes toward her bedroom.

I try not to laugh, but I can't help it. The look on her face when she said she needed to get properly fucked was priceless. Now my imagination is going crazy and I need to get these images out of my head.

I get up and head into the kitchen to make myself some peanut butter toast, and Winston follows closely on my heels. As I stand there waiting for my bread to finish toasting, I squat down to pet Winston and he rolls onto his back with his legs in the air.

"Damn, you do love a belly rub, don't you," I say, but my mind's not really on the dog. Instead, I'm thinking about how the guy Sierra's going out with tonight isn't right for her.

I watched them carefully last weekend when they were saying goodbye, and there's nothing there. In his eyes, Sierra could have been any random girl—there was nothing to indicate he was particularly into her in any way beyond getting in her pants. And Sierra . . . I saw this morning how she looks at a guy when she's attracted to him, and I certainly didn't see that when she was looking at him.

They don't have to be that into each other to fuck, that annoying voice inside my head reminds me. I've certainly slept with plenty of girls I wasn't into. I've never felt like emotions had to be involved. Attraction, definitely. But emotions make everything murky—they confuse what should be clear-cut, they make the rational irrational. But for the first time in as long as I can remember, I'm wondering if maybe the *right* emotions could make sex even better.

The toaster dings to let me know it's done, and the sound

is like a bell alerting me that I got the right answer on a game show.

But that doesn't even make sense because how could emotions—which have such a tendency to mess things up—possibly make me better at something I've already mastered?

I spread peanut putter onto my toast as I consider this line of thinking. I'm pretty sure that the idea of emotions having any impact on how good sex is between two people is just ridiculous. Attraction and skill. That's what makes for good sex.

At my feet, Winston whines as he puts his nose in the air and sniffs.

"You want some peanut butter, buddy?" I ask him. I know he doesn't understand me, but he can clearly smell it and he loved it when I gave him some yesterday. I dip a spoon into the jar, and hold it out so he can lick it off while I stand there at the counter eating my toast and wondering if I'll be thinking about Sierra and her date all day.

———

I can smell the richness of the chocolate and the creamy roasted scent of the peanut butter as I approach the front door. Sierra must be baking, and whatever she's making already has me salivating.

When I open the door, the scent hits me full force, and it's enough to have my eyes rolling back in my head. I trained hard today, and about half the time it felt like the mountain was winning. I'm sore in a way that makes me feel old. This shit never used to happen, and it makes me wonder if the best years of my professional career are behind me. That's a sobering thought for a twenty-five-year-old.

I grabbed a burger and a few beers with Lance and Drew after practice, and even though whatever Sierra's making smells amazing, I'm still uncomfortably full. That's another thing that never used to happen. I'm like a fucking old man already. I make a mental note to ask Nate for pointers navigating this new phase of my life.

In my head I'm already crafting the snarky text I'll send him while I hang my coat on a hook in the entryway, right next to Sierra's coat and ski pants. I wonder if she went skiing today? She was still asleep when I left for the mountain this morning, but maybe she got a few runs in.

"Honey, I'm home," I call out in a singsong voice, hoping to hear her laugh.

"Oh, good," she says, materializing in the living room in nothing but a sweatshirt that hits mid-thigh and a pair of sheepskin slippers. I force my eyes away from the smooth curve of her thighs and make myself look her in the eye. "I made you something," she says, sounding so damn pleased with herself.

"Yeah? Is it whatever is making this place smell like a bakery?"

She laughs, and the sound is such a delight it makes my throat feel thick and my skin feel hot. Maybe I'm getting sick. "I made dark chocolate peanut butter cup brownies. I'm taking them out of the oven now," she says as she breezes past me, grabs pot holders, and pulls the brownies from the oven. Then she reaches into an upper cabinet and pulls out a small jar of flaky pink salt that she sprinkles over the top of the brownies.

I take a few steps into the kitchen so I can get a better look at them. "You can make brownies that look and smell like this and you've been holding out on me? After how many times I cooked you dinner this week?"

She looks over at me and grins, and I pretend not to notice how her sweatshirt got caught on the curve of one of her thighs when she reached up into the cabinet to get the salt, and how I can now see the sheen of her soft leg nearly to where it meets her hip.

"I know," she says, "I feel like I haven't been home enough and you've been so awesome, making me dinner and helping with the dog. And I just wanted to say thank you. With chocolate and peanut butter, because I know how much you like your peanut butter."

I know it's just brownies, but I don't think anyone has ever made me dessert to thank me for anything. I wonder for a moment if it's because I don't normally do things for people that require a thank you.

I open my mouth to tell her I appreciate the gesture, but somehow the words don't come and I'm standing there with my mouth open. She's looking at me like she's expecting me to say something, and the only thing I can think of is how my dad used to love to surprise me and Jackson when we were kids so that he could tap us under our chins when our mouths fell open in shock and say, in his thick Irish brogue, "Don't let the flies in."

Sierra's huge brown eyes are lined with smoky eyeliner and her eyelashes are coated with mascara. They're the eyes of a woman who's getting ready for a date, the eyes of a woman who may well be looking at another man tonight with naked lust. But right now, they are looking at me with concern, the unspoken "Are you okay?" hangs between our gaze, but I don't even know the right answer to that. What's wrong with me?

I glance down just to break eye contact with her, which is a mistake because my eyes land on the revealed curve of her thigh that's got her sweatshirt bunched up around it. Instinctively, I reach out and push the sweatshirt down, making sure I don't touch her skin when I do. I'm afraid that my fingers dragging along her thigh might actually make me combust. "Geez, Sierra, put some clothes on maybe?" I say. I need her away from me, she's taking up all the oxygen in the room and I feel like I'm going to pass out.

"Oh?" she says, but I can hear the teasing in her voice. "The guy who walks around flaunting his abs is afraid of seeing a little thigh action? Lucky for you," she says as she picks the pan of brownies up off the stove and sets them on the wire cooling rack setting on the counter, "I'm going to get dressed right now. If Jared arrives before I'm back out, can you *please* entertain him for a minute? I'm totally late because these brownies took longer to put together than I thought."

"Sure," I say as she slips past me where I stand in the opening of the kitchen. As she turns sideways to pass me, her ass lightly brushes my crotch. I'm almost positive it's an accident because Sierra doesn't do shit like that on purpose, especially not to her best friend's little brother.

"Oh," she throws over her shoulder as she walks toward the hallway to the bedrooms, "and save me a brownie too, okay?"

"Like I'd eat the whole pan myself."

She pauses in the hallway and turns, letting out a little laugh. "I seem to remember a time you did just that."

Oh God, I did do that once when I was like ten. Spent half

the night throwing up. "You remember the most flattering things about me," I say dryly.

"Someone's gotta know the real you—bring your international playboy-slash-snowboarding god status down a notch."

I actually bark out a laugh at that one. International playboy? Snowboarding god? She obviously has a much different perception of me than I do of myself. I'm just a guy trying to live life to the fullest, but feeling like the only thing I do well these days is take pictures. I think I like her assessment of me better.

She turns and heads down the hall again, and once she's safely ensconced in her room, I feel like I can breathe. Maybe I need to see a doctor, because this tightness in my throat, shortness of breath, heat in my chest—none of this is normal. I must be getting sick.

I don't even make it to my bedroom to take off my snowboarding pants before the buzzer rings, so I press the button to let Sierra's date into our building. I call out to let her know he's on his way up and hear her let out a string of curses before she calls out that she needs five minutes.

I briefly consider chasing him off before she's ready, but even though I know he's not right for her, that's just not the kind of thing I do. It doesn't stop me from wanting to, though, and that's a first for me.

"You must be Jared," I say when I open the door after he knocks.

He's definitely taken aback by my presence and gives me the quick once-over, sizing me up. He hasn't done anything but look at me and already I want to kick his ass. He's a few inches shorter than me, and just smaller all around—I could take him.

"Yeah," he says. "And you are?"

"Beau Shanahan," I say, and hold my hand out to shake his. "Sierra's roommate."

"Oh, shit," he says on an exhale as he reaches his hand out. "I know who you are. Huge fan." He shakes my hand enthusiastically.

"You a snowboarder too?"

"Yeah," he says as I step aside and he walks into our condo. "But just as a hobby on the weekends, nothing like what you can do."

Good. Sierra can't stand snowboarders—hates the whole culture around snowboarding—so this doesn't bode well for Jared. When I don't say anything, Jared glances around and says "Nice place you've got here" as if he's forgotten that I just moved in last weekend and he was here for it.

"It's my sister's place, actually. Jackson lives in New Hampshire now, and I'm just crashing here for a couple weeks until I head to Aspen for the X Games."

"Oh, shit," he says again. "I forgot Jackson Shanahan was your sister. Man, she's hot. I used to have a poster of her in that tight-assed white race suit above my bed when I was a teenager." He gives me that conspiratorial look that a guy might give his wingman before he hits on a girl at a bar, because obviously I know the only reason why a guy puts a poster of a hot chick above his bed. And the thought of him whacking off to visions of my sister is enough to make me almost throw up in my mouth.

"Dude, she's my *sister*." I shudder. "And Sierra is her best friend, so maybe don't mention that fact to her." Why the hell am I giving this asshole advice?

"Sorry, man," he says, but he doesn't sound sorry in the least. He sounds like a lecherous asshole, which is not the kind of guy Sierra is looking for. I should send him on his way before she even comes out of her bedroom. She'd be pissed, but I'd be doing her a favor.

Again, for the folks in the back (which apparently includes me): *That's not who I am. I'm the guy who doesn't get involved.*

If she wants someone to settle down with, she may have to kiss a few frogs before she finds her prince, or whatever that stupid analogy is.

"Where are you taking her tonight?" I ask, trying to sound casual, even though I feel like this is the exact question my dad would have asked Nate when he came to pick Jackson up for a date when they were teenagers.

"Got us a table at Equis," he says, and glances at his watch. "I hear they make strong drinks and I like a girl who doesn't put up a fight at the end of the night." He winks at me and every muscle in my body tenses.

I open my mouth to respond and even though I can't find the right words, my fists are itching to deliver the message. It's not like I haven't heard guys say shit like that before, but this is about Sierra. Even if she wasn't my roommate, she's my sister's best friend. I have to get involved here, don't I?

Then I hear Winston bounding across the living room behind me, and I turn toward him just as he barrels into my legs. I bend down to pick him up, because he's still small enough that I can hold him, even when he's squirmy.

As I stand up with Winston in my arms, I notice Sierra following behind him. And she's a fucking vision. She's taken her hair out of the bun it was in while she was getting ready, and it's falling in waves over her shoulders and down her back. She's put on lipstick, which she almost never wears, and her mouth looks luscious. I'm overwhelmed with the desire to know what those lips taste like, what they feel like on several different parts of my anatomy. I'm pretty sure I flush in response, so I glance over at Jared to see why he hasn't said anything to his date yet, but his eyes are locked on her body.

She's wearing another sweater dress. It's not as short as the one she wore last night, but it's even sexier. It's black and has a low-cut V-neck that shows off her cleavage, and there's a gold zipper that runs from that crease between her breasts— which holy shit, how did I not notice she's totally stacked?— and down her stomach to the hem above her knees. There's no way you can look at her in that dress and not envision unzipping that zipper.

I glance back at Jared, who's finally uttered "Wow" and follows it up with "You look amazing, Sierra."

It pisses me off immensely that he sounds so reverent when he speaks to her, after just sounding like a complete sleazeball. I'm quite confident this is the act and I actually saw his true colors before she walked in. But maybe I'm wrong and this is who he really is, and he was just talking to me the way he thinks guys talk to each other?

Shit, I don't know.

I watch helplessly as they make casual conversation and he helps her slip into her coat, then I feel awkward as hell lurking so I step out of the entryway—which is crowded with three of us in there—and head into the living room with Winston on my heels.

"Do you mind crating Winston before you head out,

Beau?" Sierra asks. I glance up at her, and she must see the conflicting feelings I'm having because she rushes on. "Or I can do it now, if you want?"

"No, it's fine, I can crate him if I go out."

She gives me a questioning look, surprised by my *if*. After all, I *always* go out.

"Okay," she says softly, like she's trying to figure out what this look is on my face. Hell, I'm trying to figure it out too.

She turns back toward Jared, who wraps his arm around her shoulders as he leads her through the door. She gives me a quick glance over her shoulder, her eyebrows dipping in a look that combines confusion and concern.

Five minutes later, I've paced a hundred laps around the living room and dining room, and feel like I'm going to crawl out of my own skin. What if that asshole really does get her drunk and tries to take advantage of her?

She's a big girl, she can stand up for herself. But what if she can't?

My chest feels itchy. My fingers are curling and uncurling into fists. My thoughts are racing through my head too fast to hold on to a single one of them. My heartbeat is erratic.

I know this feeling. It's adrenaline mixed with anxiety, and based on previous experience, the only way out of it is through exercise. So I head to my room, strip off my sweaty snowboarding clothes, throw on a pair of shorts, and start the workout sequence I do every night—a combination of high-intensity cardio, body-weight exercises, and pull-ups.

Winston gets bored with this quickly and wanders out of my bedroom, probably to take a nap. I'm envious, I wish I could go to sleep right now and stop picturing Sierra on her date with that asshole.

The exercise helps and an hour later my heartbeat is normal. I can think more clearly. I hop into the shower, and when I get out, I decide that the best thing to do is to contact Sierra. I'm weighing the benefits of just texting her a warning about Jared, versus calling her with a fabricated emergency, as I walk back into the living room in nothing but my towel.

"What the fuck?" I utter out loud, even though there's no one to hear me. I sprint across the living room to where Winston lies on the kitchen counter. He's panting even though he's hardly moving. I place my hand over his chest, and his heartbeat is so fast. I look down at the brownies spread all over the counter. The chocolate. All that chocolate, which he ate who knows how long ago?

"Oh, shit, NO!"

Chapter Ten

SIERRA

We've been at the restaurant for going on two hours, and I've been plotting my escape for at least seventy-five percent of that time. I've ruled out excusing myself to go to the bathroom then bolting instead, because it wouldn't make any sense for me to take my jacket to the bathroom and I'm certainly not leaving it behind. I've thought about faking a stomach ailment, but Jared has ordered dessert, and it feels unfair to not let him eat it when the end of our date is already so close.

I could text Petra. We have a plan for situations like this. If either one of us texts the other an "X" and nothing else, it means we're in a situation we need help getting out of. The person receiving the "X" text message will call the sender and explain a fake emergency that the sender needs to come help with. I've never had to put this plan into action before, probably because I was engaged when we conceived of it. It was really more for Petra's benefit, since she was the one going out with different guys almost every night. But now I feel like I might end up being the first one to put it into play.

From the moment we got in his car, Jared gave me a slimy vibe—it's like he's a different person tonight than he was when I met him last weekend. That whole text exchange in my entryway, the way he ran a lock of my hair through his fingers, and told me he wanted more time with me. My stupid heart held out just an ounce of hope that he was a good guy, that this date would be surprisingly good, even though I wasn't exactly looking forward to it.

Instead, I feel like all I've done is listen to him name-drop all night. I didn't know he was a snowboarder, but apparently he is and he's in awe of me living with Beau right now and keeps talking about snowboarding and how good Beau is, and what other pro snowboarders he knows. There's so much name-dropping going on that I don't even want to mention what I do for work because he'll probably pepper me with a bunch of questions about the athletes, or he'll continue with the one-upmanship he's currently engaged in.

Of course, he's also completely talking to my chest. I don't think he's taken his eyes off the goods since we sat down. I know this dress is low-cut, so a glance here and there wouldn't be unexpected. But honestly, this is ridiculous. He needs to learn a little self-control, like the kind I have to show when Beau walks around in nothing but gray sweats. I don't stand there with my eyes focused on the outline of his junk, no matter how hard it is to tear my eyes away.

"You're awfully quiet tonight," Jared says as he sets down his glass and finally looks up at my face. He's now finished his third scotch. He's comfortably relaxed, while I feel high-strung and edgy, like a live wire about to snap.

I give him a small, close-lipped smile. "Sorry, I think I'm

just tired. The puppy got me up at the crack of dawn today, and I'm really *not* a morning person."

"Ahh," he says, as if that explains everything. "The trick to getting up early . . ." he says, then lectures me about a variety of ways to embrace being a morning person. I half listen to him drone on, hoping I'm nodding and "uh-huh-ing" in the right places, while I think about how to best get my phone out of my purse and discreetly send Petra a text.

I'm afraid that if I pull out my phone and send a text, then immediately get a phone call, he'll be suspicious. *Who cares what he thinks? Just get up and walk out,* I can practically hear Petra's voice telling me. *Slap some money on the table to cover your food and your drink, and leave.*

And even though I know that's probably the best thing to do, I can't quite bring myself to do it. I don't think of myself as a people pleaser, per se, but I hate to offend people. It'd be so much easier for both of us if I got called away from our date because of some emergency Petra needed my help with, and I pretended like I was sorry to go. I want to go home and curl up on my couch in my pajamas and have one of those brownies I made before I left, but I don't want to have to endure a horribly awkward scene to get there.

I reach my hand down into the purse that's hanging from the back of my chair and fish around for the pocket holding my phone while pretending to be hanging on Jared's every word. But then my phone starts buzzing angrily and I pull it out with the tips of my fingers. Beau's name flashes on the screen.

"I'm so sorry," I tell Jared, "I have to take this." I slip out of my seat and rush toward the side of the restaurant where I saw the hallway to the bathrooms.

"Hey." I sigh as I answer. I'm about to tell him he's my hero for his well-timed call, but he starts talking a mile a minute. "Slow down," I say. He's in a car and with the road noise and the speed at which words are flying out of his mouth, the only thing I caught was *Winston*. "I can't understand you. What's going on?"

"Winston got up on the counter and ate the brownies you made," he says. There's real fear in his voice.

"Okay," I say slowly, not understanding why he's so upset.

"Sierra," Beau snaps. "Dogs can't have chocolate." He says that like it's a well-known fact. But I've never had a dog, and I didn't know that.

"Why not?" I ask.

He pauses. "Because it can kill them."

"What?" I shriek, and I can see heads at the tables nearest me turn. I mouth *Sorry* and turn away, my back to the restaurant as I face the bathroom doors.

"Yeah. It's incredibly dangerous. And I don't know how long ago he ate them because I was working out and he wandered away and he must have eaten them when I wasn't looking. Fuck," he growls out. "Red light."

"Where are you?" I ask.

"I took your car and I'm on my way to the emergency vet. When I called, they told me to bring him in as soon as possible." He tells me which one he's headed to, and I tell him I'll get a cab and meet him there.

I'm shaking by the time I get back to the table. "I'm so sorry," I tell Jared as I drop my phone into my purse. "I have to go. My puppy ate a bunch of brownies and is really sick." My hands are so unsteady I almost drop by coat trying to get it on.

"I'll drive you," Jared insists.

"No!" I exclaim. "I mean, that's okay. Beau's on the way to the vet with him and I'm going to meet them there. There's nothing you can do, so I appreciate the offer, but no thank you."

I reach into my purse and grab my wallet, intending to give him some money for my half of dinner, but he holds up his hand. "I've got it," he says, then his eyes slip from my face back down to my chest. "You go take care of your puppy and we'll try for another time."

Oh God, I do not want to leave this open-ended. He clearly has no idea how not-good of a time I've been having. I open my wallet. "I appreciate the offer," I tell him, "but I think one date was enough." I drop a few twenties on the table and rush out the door, my arm already up, looking for a cab and hoping there's one nearby so I don't have to wait for an Uber.

———

When I fly through the glass door of the veterinary clinic fifteen minutes later, I'm surprised to find a totally empty waiting room, save one lone figure sitting hunched over with his elbows on his knees and his head in his hands. He looks up when I approach him, and I'm greeted with hollow eyes and pale skin. Beau couldn't look less like himself if he were in a costume.

I sink into the seat next to him. "So what happened?"

He leads me through the progression of events, ending with finding Winston almost passed out on the counter. "It was some scary shit," he says, lifting his head to look at me. "His eyes were half-closed, and he was panting like he'd just run a mile in five seconds. He couldn't even lift his head up, and his tongue was just hanging out of his mouth. When I put my hand on his chest to feel his heartbeat, it was so fast I was afraid it was just going to burst or something."

I can't help the squeak that escapes my lips at the thought. Beau looks over at me right as my eyelids lose their battle with the tears I've been trying to hold in.

"Hey," he says, his voice deep and soothing. He wraps an arm around me and pulls me to his side. My cheek is pressed up against the zipper of his open jacket, but I don't even care.

"I'm so sorry," I say as I wipe the tears from my face with the back of my mitten. "This is all my fault, and I wasn't even there."

He pauses and pulls his head away from where it rests against mine. "Sierra, this wasn't your fault."

"Yes it was," I say, then swallow after my voice breaks. I've had a ten minute cab ride over here to think about what Beau said—Winston ate the brownies that I left out on the counter. "If I knew the first thing about dogs, I would have known not to leave chocolate out on the counter."

He wraps his other arm around me and leans back in his seat, so I'm comfortably cradled in his arms. I feel his chin when it meets the pom on top of my winter hat. "You left them *on a counter*," he emphasizes. "Three feet off the floor. Hell, I watched you do it and would have done the same, even though I know dogs are allergic to chocolate. Why would any reasonable person think Winston could get up on the counter?"

I pull away and look at him. "Wait, how *did* he get up there?"

"Barstool. But the point is, this didn't happen because

you did something careless. It just happened." He reaches over and wipes more tears from my cheeks, and as I glance up at him, I'm struck by what I see. The compassion. The concern. The fact that he's even here in the first place, taking care of Winston. He's taking care of me. There are probably a hundred other places he could be—maybe would *rather* be—but he's here. I thought he was an unreliable asshole; he's slowly but surely proving me wrong without even trying.

As I look into his eyes, those deep ebony pools I was so struck by that night at the cocktail party, I wonder if they can show me who Beau Shanahan really is. "Beau—" I say when his eyes track down to my lips.

"You two must be Winston's parents," a booming voice says, and I tear my gaze away from Beau to find the vet in his scrubs standing about six feet from us.

We both scramble to our feet so quickly that he smiles. "Don't worry, he's going to be fine. It's a good thing you got him here so quickly. I was able to induce vomiting and there was a lot of chocolate in that stomach of his. I'm surprised he didn't throw it up himself. That usually happens before the other symptoms you described," he says to Beau, "like the panting and racing heart."

"Thank you so much," I gush as I cling to Beau with one arm and clutch the other over my heart. I've never been so relieved in my life.

"Do you know what kind of chocolate was in those brownies?" he asks.

"It was Baker's chocolate," I tell him. "Plus mini peanut butter cups that had milk chocolate."

"That explains why he had such a quick reaction. Baking

chocolate is particularly high in theobromine, which is toxic for dogs."

"Is that why he was so lethargic?" Beau asks.

"Honestly, that was probably just because he ate too much. It hadn't been in his system long enough to cause that reaction. I'm surprised he had any symptoms so quickly, actually. But it's good you got him in here when you did, because that much chocolate could have been fatal if his system absorbed it all."

"Can we see him?" I ask, because I just want to give that little face all the kisses after my ignorance almost killed him.

"We need to keep him overnight for observation, to continue monitoring him for symptoms of poisoning. I'm afraid that if you go back there and see him, he'll get all riled up, and we really need to keep him calm right now."

I feel my chest deflate with a silent sigh. "Of course, that makes sense."

We make arrangements with the front desk about checking up on Winston in the morning, and when we walk out the door, Beau puts his arm around my shoulders and guides me down the street to where he parked my car.

"Want me to drive?" he asks as he unlocks the car.

"Sure," I say, relieved to not have to focus on anything other than my immense gratitude that I didn't kill the world's cutest and most rambunctious puppy.

He opens my door for me and when he plops himself into the driver's seat, I ask, "So, how exactly do you have my car?"

"Your keys were still hanging in the entryway. I didn't know what else to do but take it." He starts the car and cranks the heat, then glances at me. "I hope you don't mind."

"Of course I don't."

Beau pulls out of the parking space and we glide along the road, which is coated with the slush that's left behind after many cars have driven over salted, sanded snow.

I pull out my phone and open Winston's Instagram profile, wanting to see his adorable face and remember a time when he wasn't lying in a crate in a vet's office being carefully monitored for a toxic overdose of theobromine, a chemical I didn't even know existed before tonight.

"Holy shit," I say when the app opens.

"What's wrong?" Beau's voice has an edge of panic to it as his eyes fly toward me.

"Nothing," I say, "eyes on the road. It's just . . ." I pause as I hit the appropriate icon to find out why I have so many notifications. "Thousands of people have liked Winston photos today. I checked this morning, and we had a little over one hundred followers. Now we're almost at ten thousand."

"What the hell?" Beau mutters as he turns onto the main street that will take us back home.

"Oh my God," I squeal. "It's the photo I took of you and Winston this morning."

"What?"

"That's what's gotten all these likes." I click over to the photo and start scrolling through the comments. "About a quarter of the comments are about how cute Winston is. The other three-quarters are about you."

"Right," Beau says, obvious disbelief in his voice.

"And I quote *'I'll adopt that puppy if the hottie comes with him . . . Hopping on the next flight to Park City . . . I'd switch places with that puppy in a heartbeat.'*"

"What the hell? I don't remember the photo being anything special," he says.

"You doubt my photography skills?" I say, pretending to be offended. As far as photos go, it really wasn't anything special. The reason I snapped it, and the reason I posted it, was because of how much love I could see in the way Beau was holding and looking at Winston. I get the sense that Beau's never really had to think about anyone except himself, and Winston is giving him a chance to be a better version of himself.

"I mean, I could teach you a thing or two," he says, and I can see the half smile curl up one side of his lips. He's fucking with me. Or does he really think he's a better photographer than I am? The photos I saw of his the other night were great, but they were heavily edited. When it comes down to it, I bet I could still take a better raw photo than he can.

"I've forgotten more than you'll ever know about photography." I'm joking because given the age difference, I have more years of experience than he does. But he bristles at my words—I can see it in the sudden tensing and then the forced relaxation of his shoulders, in the hard edge of his rigid jaw.

"Want to put a little wager on that?" he asks.

I'm the opposite of a betting person, the kind of girl who always takes the sure thing over what could be. Give me double or nothing odds and, even if I think I could win, I'd always stick with what I have. The safe bet. Because there's certainty in the known quantity, especially when there's more to be lost than gained.

"How could I agree to a wager when I don't even know exactly what we're betting on?"

"On who's the better photographer, obviously." He shrugs one shoulder as he turns down our street.

"As determined by . . . ?"

"We could use Winston's account as a testing site. Whoever posts the photo that gets the single highest number of likes wins."

"And if you win?" I ask Beau.

"You have to learn to snowboard."

I let out a laugh that sounds practically victorious. He doesn't need to know that I already know how to snowboard. I just prefer skiing. "And if I win?"

Beau looks at me as we sit waiting for the garage door to the parking area for our building to roll open. "If you win, what is it you want?"

That feels like a loaded question as he sits there, letting his eyes slide over me like he has all the time in the world and nothing to do but look at me. Why couldn't my date have looked at me like that tonight?

"If I win, you have to be fully clothed at all times while in our condo."

He glances forward, then slowly presses the gas so we pass into the darkened garage. With far fewer lights than outside on the street, he is a study in contrasts: the distinct lines of the straight, flat bridge of his nose; the sharp angle of his cheekbone; his strong chin barely visible under his facial hair; the thick column of corded muscles in his neck. Hell, he looks like one of those marble statues carved by the Renaissance masters, standing in a museum in Italy. But better. I could take a spectacular black-and-white photo of him in this light.

Then he turns toward me, and says, "You'd win and then punish yourself like that? That's savage."

I'm so focused on the black-and-white photo I'm envisioning that for a minute I don't realize he means that him being fully clothed would be a punishment for *me*.

"You're such an ass," I say as I slap his shoulder. He doesn't even flinch, he just turns my car into my parking spot like he does it all the time.

"It's okay," he says, turning toward me. "Maybe you can't be honest with yourself, so I'll level with you. You don't mind when I don't wear a shirt. In fact, I think you'd mind it a whole lot more if you didn't get to look at me half-naked all the time."

"First of all, ew," I say, and roll my eyes, hoping that he can't see how my cheeks are on fire. I thought I was being discreet checking him out. I mean, it's simple biology that my body would find him attractive. Snowboarding uses literally every muscle, and his body is a testament to how good he is at it. Rock-hard everything—every single muscle is individually cut. It's impossible not to look when a specimen of physical perfection is standing in front of you. "And second, I spent the first thirty years of my life not having someone with a perfect body flaunting it in front of me all the time, and I survived just fine. I suspect it'll be a relief when you leave and I don't have to walk in on you half-clothed."

"Keep telling yourself that," he says, and smirks. Like literally freaking smirks. I am not a violent person, but I want to smack that look right off his face so badly my hand twitches.

He pulls the handle of his door and the interior lights come on. I look away quickly because I don't want him to see how much I'm blushing. Instead, I get out of the car too, the words I just said running through my mind. *It'll be a relief when you leave and I don't have to walk in on you half-clothed*. I said too much, because why would it be a relief except if I was attracted to him and trying hard to resist? I wish I could take those words back.

I keep my face turned down as we walk through the underground parking garage, hoping that the cool air will eliminate my flush. Beau uses the keypad to unlock the glass door, and we step into the lighted vestibule where I continue to keep my face turned away from him.

"Hey," he says, the taunting tone is gone and nothing but gentleness remains. When I don't look at him, he reaches over and tilts my chin toward him. "I'm sorry if I made you uncomfortable."

"Beau, you're my best friend's younger brother. And yes, you've grown up quite a bit and you obviously like showing off your amazing body. But when you try to make it sound like I'm attracted to you, it makes me feel like a lecherous creep."

I watch his face move through a variety of emotions—none of which stay put long enough for me to decipher them—before he settles on what is most likely his sheepish "don't be mad at me" face. "That's just how I talk to women"—he shrugs—"sorry. I'll try not to do that to you."

"So what you're telling me," I say as the elevator door opens and we step in, "is that you basically go into every conversation with any woman assuming that she wants to sleep with you?"

"Not to sound conceited or anything, but I'm rarely wrong."

"Oh my God." I laugh and look up at the ceiling like I'm praying for patience. Which, in a way, I am. "You are too much."

"Nah, trust me." He shakes his head. "I'm just right."

"You can't even help it, can you?"

"Help what?"

"The flirting. It's like . . . your natural state, isn't it?" I can't hide how amused I am. But also, I can't help but wonder why he flirts with anyone who has a set of boobs. Does he really need the constant validation?

"Yeah," he says, rubbing the back of his neck. "I guess it is." It sounds like maybe he's never stopped and thought about this before. I resist the urge to psychoanalyze the situation with him, because maybe he just needs to stop and think about it himself first.

The elevator dings and the door opens as we arrive on our floor. I'm still focused on our conversation and wondering what would cause Beau to need this constant validation from women when he opens our door and we step inside.

The very first thing that happens is that my eyes track to Winston's crate, expecting to see him there. It's only been a few days and I'm already looking for him the moment I walk in the door.

"Oh no," Beau says, his voice tinged with fear. "What's wrong?"

I must be grimacing because he's looking at me like I'm in pain and he's worried.

"I . . . I expected to see Winston when we walked in." I can feel my lower lip trembling, so I suck it under my front teeth and hold it steady. I will *not* cry over a dog who the vet insisted is going to be fine.

"I know," Beau says, then sighs. "Me too."

I glance over at him and he seems unusually serious. Melancholy even.

"He's going to be fine," I say as I hang my coat on the hook and walk into the apartment. Then I make the mistake of looking over at the peninsula separating the kitchen from the dining room and living room. Pieces of the brownies are strewn all over the counter, some sitting in chunks and some smeared across the stone like Winston was trying to lick up every bite he could.

The sob that escapes my lips as I stand at the counter staring at the destruction is unavoidable. I can feel Beau as he steps up behind me. "I can't believe I did this to him," I whisper.

"You didn't do this," he says, putting his hands on my shoulders and giving me a reassuring squeeze. "This is my fault."

"How could it be? You didn't make the brownies, and you didn't feed them to him."

"He was after the peanut butter." Beau's voice is grim. "And I'm the one who introduced him to peanut butter. Every time I have some, I share with him. Of course, when he smelled it, he was going to go after it. And if I'd put him back in his crate while I was working out, he wouldn't have gotten up there."

"That's ridiculous," I say, letting myself sink back against him so my shoulder blades rest on his chest. I feel like he's holding onto me for support right now, just like I'm needing him to support me. "You can't blame yourself for that. Why would you crate him when you're home? You couldn't have known he could climb up on the barstool and get to the brownies."

"I didn't. Any more than you knew he'd try to eat them if you made them. So if I can't hold myself responsible, neither can you." The warmth radiating off his rock-hard chest spreads across my back, warming me in more ways than one. His physical presence and his reassurance are a comfort, but

I'm still not totally able to let go of my guilt. "It was an accident," he insists.

I stay there, with my shoulders resting on Beau's chest, while I work on convincing myself that I'm not at fault, that there was no way to know he could get up there and get to the brownies. When Beau moves his head so his chin nudges the top of my head, I know he's trying to move me along. I've overstayed my welcome, using his strength to bolster my own.

I set about cleaning up the mess, willing myself to hold it together as I envision Winston like Beau described him: laying on the counter amid the wreckage of the brownies, panting, heart racing. I close my eyes, swallow down those images, and then I keep on cleaning.

Beau's already thrown away the rest of the brownies in the pan and washed it out when he comes back over to the peninsula. He rests a hand on mine where I'm clutching paper towels and scrubbing at the counter. "Hey," he says gently, "it's clean."

My eyes track across the stone and he's right. There's not a sign of the chocolate or peanut butter anywhere. My sigh comes out in stuttered breaths. I don't know why I'm unable to let go of the guilt. *Winston will be fine*, I remind myself.

I leave the paper towels sitting on the counter as I walk into the living room, headed for the couch. But as soon as I step between the couch and the coffee table to sit down, my foot collides with one of Winston's dog toys, sending it flying across the rug. Predictably, I crumble onto the couch and dissolve into tears.

Chapter Eleven

BEAU

Her ass flexes against the length of me and I can't help but grow hard against her. It's been absolute torture lying here with her crying in my arms and having to control my physical reaction to her. She's upset, and I'd feel like I was taking advantage if I tried something now. Plus, we are all wrong for each other, even if it feels like it could be right.

She moves against me again and I glance down to see why, right as she unzips that sexy as hell sweater dress she wore on her date tonight. The dress falls open, revealing her creamy, smooth peach skin. My mouth goes dry and my dick aches with how hard it is. She's wearing the sexiest fucking lingerie I've ever seen. Some sort of low-cut black lace bra that barely contains her breasts, which are even bigger than I thought. The pink circles around her nipples peek out from the top of the lace. She's also got a thick band of lace high on her hip and a barely there scrap of black lace between her legs.

Sierra reaches behind her to find my hand where it rests against my own leg, and ever so slowly, she slides it onto her hip. She looks up at me over her shoulder, and her puffy eyes have returned to normal. "Please," she whispers. "I want you so badly."

I don't know what's led to this sudden change, but I'm here for it.

"You sure?" I ask. I need her like I need oxygen, and I have a feeling that the fantasies of us together that I've been jerking off to daily will pale in comparison to the real thing. But she has to know that it's just sex, that I can't give her more than that.

"I'm positive," she says, leading my hand down to her underwear and pushing my fingertips beneath the fabric there.

My hand stills involuntarily. My body is screaming "touch her," and I ache to bury myself inside her. But some part of my brain knows I need to set things straight first. "You know this can't be more than sex, right? I'm leaving in two weeks."

"I know, and it's fine," she says, then arches her back as she stretches up to press her lips against mine.

She has the most kissable lips I've ever tasted. They're soft and thick and perfect. She opens for me the minute my lips touch hers, pulling my lower lip into her mouth and letting out a sexy little groan while she rocks her hips back into my erection and pushes my hand further down into her under-wear. The minute my fingertips come into contact with her slick center, I know there's no turning back.

She's so wet for me, there's no denying how badly she wants me, no trying to convince myself she doesn't mean it. Those silky juices coat my fingers as I drag them down the seam between her legs. Then she really groans into my mouth, her tongue tangling with mine as her hips rise to claim my fingers. But I tease her, running my fingers from her clit to her anus and back again, even as her hips buck wildly beneath my hand.

She pulls her head back and I prop myself up on my elbow so I'm looking down at her. "Don't tease me, Beau. You know what I want."

Who is this brazen woman who knows what she wants and isn't afraid to ask for it?

"Do I?" She's so hot when she's sexually frustrated, so I run my lips across her forehead and down her nose instead of giving her what she's asking for.

She takes my hand, pulls it to her mouth, and sucks two fingers deep inside, then pulls them out and twirls her tongue around the pads of my fingers before guiding them back down to her underwear, which she pulls down her legs with her other hand.

I run those two fingers against her clit, circling a few times until she makes soft panting sounds, and then I delve in. I push my fingers in as far as they'll go and those soft, wet muscles move to accommodate me but I don't bottom out, which means she'll be able to take all of me when I finally fuck her the way I've literally dreamed about for years.

"Yes," she whispers as she rides my fingers, taking me by surprise as she reaches out and strokes me through my sweats. I like her being the aggressor.

"Fuck," I growl, then lean down over her shoulder and sweep my tongue under the lace cup of her bra, drawing her nipple into my mouth. I suck on it gently, then swirl my tongue around the hard peak, trying to gauge what she likes. If her soft groans of satisfaction are any indication, she likes everything I'm doing. She arches her back, pushing her breast further into my mouth, and murmurs softly, "Yes, Beau. Yessssss."

Her hips move faster and I curl my fingers inside her, stroking the ridge of muscle and nerves I can feel against the tip of my middle finger. She grinds her pubic bone along the heel of my hand and I can feel what that friction against her clit does for her as the muscles inside her start to clench against my fingers.

She dips her hand into my sweats and under the waistband of my boxer briefs and grips my shaft. Her hand is like satin as it slides along my bare skin, and when she sweeps her thumb over my tip, I suck her nipple into my mouth roughly. There is so much need coursing through me right now, I feel like a tightly wound spring ready to go off, but not before I give her the first of the many orgasms I plan on showering her with tonight.

"Beau, yes," Sierra pants, "just like that. I'm so close . . . I'm going to spill brownies everywhere."

What the hell?

My mouth releases her nipple and my head jerks up, and when I open my eyes to see what she's talking about, I realize that a sleeping Sierra is pressed up against me, where I was just asleep behind her on the couch.

My head falls back onto my arm. *Fuck.*

As I lie there trying to slow down my racing heart, I remind myself of all the reasons that it's a good thing that didn't really happen. *My sister's best friend. Older woman who wants to settle down. Nate's warning about ruining my relationship with my family.* I repeat the reasons in my head several times, hoping they'll calm the raging hard-on that's pressed up against Sierra's ass.

And then my dad's voice infiltrates my thoughts. *Not everyone has the mental fortitude to see their commitments through. It's just who you are.* I think he'd meant to be supportive. I was just a teenager, and I'd fucked up badly. I was about to get my first sponsorship and had dreams of going pro with snowboarding. But the sponsor pulled out after someone sent them a video of me in a drunken stupor, trying to board down a handrail on a set of stairs with not enough snow. I'd landed in a heap after dropping off the rail and having the tip of my board get caught on one of the cement steps jutting out of the snow—which I'd have seen if I weren't snowboarding at night, drunk—and I'd ended up with a concussion and a broken arm. *It's just who you are.*

Just who I am . . . someone who is definitely not good enough for her.

Sierra moves in her sleep, and she presses her ass against me, just like in my dream. But unlike in my dream, she's not awake and unzipping that sweater dress. But she does let out a little moan, and her hips flex forward before pushing back against my erection again.

And just like that, I'm picturing her riding my fingers while I suck her perfect breasts into my mouth.

"Yes." She moans, and my hips reflexively push forward as she grinds her ass along my dick.

Oh shit. I scoot back against the back of the couch so there's a sliver of space between us, and Sierra moans again. I hold my breath. Though I can guess *what* she's dreaming about right now, I can't imagine *who* she's picturing. And it makes me feel like such a creep that I was dreaming about getting her off. But it all felt so real, part of me wishes I could have held onto that dream a little longer, just so I could know what it felt like to be buried inside her. To move over her and hear my name wrapped up on her sighs of pleasure.

I have no idea how long my dick has been this hard, but at this point, it's almost painful. And I can feel it jutting out from my body, defying the boxer briefs and sweatpants that should be holding it in place.

Next to me Sierra moans again, followed by several soft sighs released in quick succession.

Every nerve in my body is on high alert, needing to touch Sierra, wanting to pull her back against me and wake her up and show her how badly I want to fuck her. But I'm one hundred percent a full consent kind of guy, and there's no way that waking her up out of this sex dream she's having by rubbing my dick against her equals consent. *Fuck.*

I very slowly pull myself up against the back of the couch, then get up on one knee and swing my leg up over Sierra. I step off the couch as gingerly as I can and manage not to touch her. But as I glance down at her, I notice that the top of her dress is unzipped a bit, and one of her hands is shoved up inside it against her breast. She moans again and I practically run to the bathroom, where I shut the door as quietly as humanly possible, strip off my clothes, and step into the shower.

As the hot water runs over me and I fist my cock into my hand, I can't help but imagine that it's Sierra's hand and we're back on that couch. The visions take over my thoughts as I picture how that whole scene could have played out if it were real life. And despite how hard I am, how badly I need to come, I chase that orgasm for too long before I feel that tingling at the base of my spine. I continue to slide my hand up and down my shaft almost violently as I picture what could have been, what maybe could be, if we weren't such different people who wanted such different things. And when my release finally happens, I feel more pissed off than sated, because sometimes reality is such a fucking disappointment.

―――――

SIERRA

There's an empty aching between my legs when I open my eyes. It takes me a minute to realize where I am: on the couch where I fell asleep in Beau's arms, but now I'm alone. My vagina clenches violently, the need to be filled rushing over me. *What the hell?*

I blink again, taking in the faint rays of light seeping through the wooden blinds on the opposite wall of the living room.

I close my eyes and images of Beau and me on this couch fill my head. The vision of straddling him—riding him hard as he cups my breasts in his hands and sucks my nipple into his mouth—fills my mind so sharply it's like a memory rather than a desire. My core clenches again, and I close my eyes, picturing myself sliding up and down him, the way he looked at me with longing and appreciation as he worshipped my body.

That's the kind of sex I need, not just in my dreams, but in real life, I think to myself as I roll onto my back. That's when I realize that my left hand is cupped around my right breast. And not just because I was sleeping curled up on my side. No, my hand is inside my bra, my nipple is pinched between two fingers and as I go to pull my hand out, my fingers graze the hardened peak and I feel that tingling in my belly and that aching in my core.

I hope that I didn't have my hand in my bra when Beau woke up and went to bed, because what kind of a freak would he think I was if he knew I was touching myself in my sleep. At least he wouldn't know it was because I was dreaming of him.

My core clenches and my hips contract as my body reminds me that in my dreams I was in the middle of having the best sex of my life. The kind where I knew what I wanted and my partner knew exactly how to give it to me. The need to touch myself, to take this edge off and give myself as much pleasure as I can, overwhelms me. I reach down and start to hike my dress up toward my hips, then I realize I'm on the couch and Beau could wake up and come out here at any minute. I would die of mortification.

So I push myself up off the couch and head to the hallway, planning a date with my vibrator and thanking past Sierra for upgrading to a better model when Peter started traveling so much for work. Or maybe traveling a lot to fuck his admin, as it turns out. Whatever. My vibrator gives me far better orgasms than he ever managed to.

Once I hit the hallway, I realize that there is running water coming from the bathroom. Is there some sort of water leak or is Beau taking a shower at—I glance at my watch—five in the morning? I pause at the door, wondering if I should knock just to double-check that he's in there and not that the water was left on in the sink or something. But the door is fully shut and the light is on, so all signs point to him being in there.

My still-hard nipples tingle as they press against the lace demi bra I'm wearing, reminding me that I was on my way

165

toward my bedroom for a little self-care. I take one step away from the bathroom door when I hear it—an unmistakable sexual growl. *Oh my God, am I listening to Beau jerk off? And why is it the sexiest sound I've ever heard?*

Another low sound emanates from the back of his throat and the only thing I can imagine that would cause that sound is his hand sliding over the hard length of himself.

My body reacts to the mental image accordingly: my underwear is so damp I can feel the moisture on the top of my thighs; there's a pulling sensation in my core like those muscles are connected to my nipples, which now ache to be touched, licked, sucked; a tremor runs through my whole body, leaving goose bumps in its wake. I'm fairly certain that if I were to slip my hand into my underwear right now, I would orgasm the second I touch myself.

I eye the door again, wondering who Beau's thinking about in there. I briefly entertain the idea of going in and finding out, but that would be a huge violation of trust and of our "don't be an asshole" roommate agreement. Because if the situation were reversed and he intentionally walked in on me masturbating in the shower, I'd be livid.

Or would I?

And then there's another growl, followed by a grunt. If a sound could be part pain and part pleasure, this would be it. I give into my aching need and slip my fingers into my under-wear, only to find I'm even wetter than I anticipated. My fingers slide through my folds and bring the moisture up to my clit, circling it once as Beau grunts again.

And right as my orgasm is about to crash over me, Beau knocks something over in the shower and the sound has my whole body going stock-still at the sudden realization of exactly what I'm doing.

I turn away quickly and rush down the hall to my room, wishing my feelings toward Beau weren't so confusing. He's everything I'm not looking for, and yet I'm stupidly attracted to him. At first it was only sexual attraction, but it feels like it might be morphing into more. And that's a path we can't go down. Even if that's what I wanted with him, it would be impossible.

The best thing to do, I remind myself as I crawl into my bed and reach over to my nightstand drawer to grab my vibrator, *is to not want what you can't have.*

Chapter Twelve

BEAU

I tap on her bedroom door a couple of times and am greeted with a sleepy "Come in."

I reach down and turn the knob, then wrap my arms tightly around the wiggly bundle of energy I'm holding. I push the door open with my foot, and the second Winston sees her, he tries to jump out of my arms. Luckily, I have a good hold on him.

"Oh my God, Beau!" she squeals as she sits up in bed so quickly the covers fall away. "How do you have him already?"

I let out a laugh as I set Winston down on her bed and she scrambles to her knees. "It's ten o'clock already, sleepyhead."

"Did you just call me sleepyhead?" she asks, cocking one eyebrow at me before turning all her attention back to Winston, who is already licking her face.

Someone kill me, please. "I'm fucking turning into my mother, aren't I? Is this what being an adult is like? You turn into your parents?" I look at the floor, where the dress she wore last night is in a pile by her nightstand. A bra that looks suspiciously like the one in my dreams lies next to it.

"God, I hope not." She groans and I remember what Jackson said about her having to go visit her mom before the wedding. There's clearly no love lost there.

I glance up at her when Winston starts jumping up on his hind legs, and it's then that I realize she's only wearing a loose cropped cami with the word DREAM across the front—almost like a sports bra without the band across the bottom—and a pair of celestial printed sleep shorts that are so high cut on the sides they might as well be underwear. Winston manages to get his paw caught on the top seam of her cami and it pulls down under the weight of him, so much so that I get an eyeful of cleavage before I turn my head away.

Now the only thing I can think of is how last night in my dream I could barely contain her perfect breast in my hand, and how the hard peak of her nipple felt sliding along the soft pad of my tongue. This vision has my dick stirring, even though I've already taken care of him this morning. *Shit, this is bad.* I can't get those images of her out of my mind. They feel so real, even though they are entirely in my imagination.

Maybe her body isn't half as great as you've imagined it, I tell myself. But when I glance back up, Sierra is leaning forward trying to get Winston calmed down, she reaches her arms out toward him and her cami slips up until I can see the underside of her breasts. Yep, she's stacked like a *Sports Illustrated* swimsuit model. My mind starts running away with all its crazy ideas about exactly what I'd like to do to her body, and now my body is responding and I need to get the fuck out of her room.

"I'm going to get something to eat," I say and turn toward the door. "Maybe put some clothes on before you come out of your room."

Her laugh is vindictive. "What's wrong, Beau," she calls out. "Hate getting a taste of your own medicine?"

I turn around in her doorway, and she's up on her knees, having just picked up a squirming puppy. That scrap of fabric masquerading for a top is barely covering her breasts, and one of Winston's back paws is caught in the waistband of her shorts. "This isn't a game you want to play," I tell her.

"Oh yeah?" She raises an eyebrow at me again. "Why not?"

"Because I *always* win."

———

This isn't how this whole roommate situation was supposed to go. I was going to tempt her, just for the pleasure of turning her down like she did to me when I was seventeen.

It was the winter of my senior year of high school and I thought I was hot shit. Jackson was home for Christmas and Sierra came up from Boston, where she was living at the time, to stay for a couple nights. On her last night there, I ran into her in the kitchen after everyone else was asleep. I'd had a crush on her since I was eleven and I figured now that I was an adult, *why not?* So as we stood there having easy conversation, I leaned in and tried to kiss her. She was all grace and apology, saying she was so sorry if she'd led me on in any way. It was humiliating, not only because I had zero experience being turned down, but because I figured now I'd have to hear about it from my sister forever.

Except, Jackson never said anything to me, which I take to mean that Sierra never told her. It's a kindness I probably didn't deserve at the time.

But now she's in my head. Instead of this being my opportunity to turn the tables and turn her down, I'm thinking about her every minute of every day.

Maybe it's because I haven't had sex since before Jackson's wedding, and two weeks is an extremely long dry spell. I should have gone out last night with Lance and Drew, and taken literally any hot girl home with me. Then, instead of waking up with a raging hard-on next to a sleeping Sierra on the couch, I could have been actually fucking someone who *wanted* me. But Sierra *needed* me last night, and I hesitantly admit to myself that I wouldn't give up being the one to be there for her—especially not to have sex with some random girl I'll never see again.

Who are you? I repeat the question I seem to be asking myself a lot these past few days.

Twenty minutes later when she finally comes out of her room, I'm still pissed off—at myself for being so attracted to her, and at her for being impossible to get out of my head.

She's changed into thin sweater-like joggers and a long-sleeve matching Henley with the top couple buttons undone. It's something that looks super soft, like cashmere maybe?

She walks past me, completely ignoring me as she grabs a box of cereal from the upper cabinet, and I know I owe her an apology for earlier.

"I didn't mean to barge in on you earlier. I just thought you'd want to see Winston." I glance down at the puppy in question, who laid himself down right at my feet the minute he came out of Sierra's room.

"I *did* want to see him," she says, spinning toward me with the cereal box in hand. *And fuuuuuck, she's not wearing a bra.* "What I didn't expect"—she continues, not seeming to notice

that I got an eyeful of her nipples through her thin sweater—
"was you in my room hypocritically telling me to put more
clothes on. You"—she steps up to me and pokes me in the
chest—"who never wears anything but a pair of sweatpants at
home. And no," she says, setting the cereal box down on the
counter so hard the bottom corners collapse a bit, "not just
any sweats, they have to be the gray athletic fitted ones, of
course."

I pause and look at her, trying to figure what she's so
worked up about. And then I can't help but laugh and ask,
"What are you ranting about?"

Sierra lets out a sound that's half guttural groan and half
frustrated yell, her fists clenched at her sides. More than
anything, I want to hear that sound again in a very different
context. "What are you ranting about, he asks!" she says,
rolling her eyes to the ceiling. "Like you don't freaking know."
She narrows her eyes at me.

I reach over and grab the cereal box she left on the
counter, open it, and shake some into my hand. "I don't actually know. Is your problem that I don't have enough clothes
on, or that I'm wearing sweatpants all the time?"

"Both," she says through clenched teeth.

"Would you rather I not wear sweats?" I ask, confused by
her logic. "Because I'm happy to just wear my trusty boxer
briefs."

"Oh my God," she growls as she turns and heads to the
fridge. "You are the most frustrating human being on the
planet."

"I'm not sure what's going on here. What are you upset
about?" I ask, genuinely confused. I know it's never a good

idea to ask a woman this question, but really—how else can I figure out why she's so pissed?

"I'm upset about the obvious double standard," she says as she returns with the milk, swipes the cereal box angrily off the counter, and starts pouring it into her bowl.

Okay, I'd get it if she was talking about the double standard of me walking around shirtless then wanting her to "put some clothes on," which I will admit definitely is a double standard. But it's one I employed intentionally. I wanted to get her all worked up by seeing me shirtless constantly. I *know* what my body looks like, I'm not playing dumb here. But when the tables were flipped, I definitely wasn't prepared to see her with so few clothes on—I wasn't prepared for what it would do to my body, or my mental state.

However, she's not talking about me being shirtless. This is specific to my choice of pants.

"Can you break down the whole sweatpants thing like I'm from another planet, because I'm clearly not getting it."

"Where's your phone?" she asks through a mouthful of cereal. It's totally unlike her, normally so well-mannered, to talk with her mouth full. And it's freaking adorable. Is there anything this woman can't make appealing?

"Right here," I say, sliding it out of the pocket of my—you guessed it—gray sweatpants. Of which I have four pairs that I rotate through, because they are comfortable and go with everything. Unless I am headed to the mountain in my snowboarding gear, or dressed up to go out, I'm pretty much in these all the time.

"Good. Google 'gray sweatpants' and see for yourself."

I follow her directions as she angrily chews on her cereal,

her eyes boring holes in my face. I try to block that out as I peruse the headlines that pop up in my search: *Why the ladies like gray sweatpants; Explained: sweatpants season; Guys, here's why you need to invest in gray sweatpants; Gray sweatpants are lingerie for men.* I click into that last article, which explains how gray sweatpants show the outline of your junk. And the article is accompanied by a slideshow of famous men wearing their gray sweats, and the author's opinion on their dick size. *What the hell?*

I think about this for a second. I see what she's saying—me wearing gray sweats around her is kind of like if she walked around in what she was wearing this morning in bed. Or the shirt she has on now without a bra. I could just admit that she has a point, but what's the fun in that?

"So," I say, drawing the word out. "What you're saying is that basically you can see the outline of my junk when I wear sweats."

"Yep." She eyes me defiantly, even though I can see the heat creeping into her cheeks.

"So it's really not that different than if I was just walking around in my boxer briefs after all."

"Exactly," she says, sounding relieved that I see her point.

"Good, then I'm only wearing boxer briefs at home from now on. So much more comfortable anyway!"

She looks at the ceiling, then back at me. "You have missed the point by a mile!"

"I think I've actually arrived at the perfect solution. I hate to wear clothes at all. And if you can see the outline of my"—I gesture at my crotch and watch her blush even more—"anyway, I might as well have even fewer clothes on."

"Beau." She says my name as a single-word sentence, in the same way my mom said it when she was reprimanding me

174

when I was a kid. "You know that was not my point. It's common courtesy to wear clothing when you have a roommate."

"Really? Because when I'm rooming with Lance and Drew, none of us care when someone walks around in their underwear."

"This. Is. Not. The. Same." She spits every word out as she sets her cereal bowl on the counter. I am laughing so hard inside, but I think I'm doing a pretty good job of appearing serious about this line of thinking. She's so easy to rile up, and honestly, she's pretty sexy when she's pissed off.

"Why not? We're friends, aren't we?"

"Because I'm not a guy, in case you hadn't noticed."

Oh, I noticed. I just shrug. "If you say so."

She steps around the side of the peninsula so only the corner of the stone countertop separates us. "Are you saying you're"—she points her finger right into my chest—"not sure that I'm"—she points her finger back at her sternum—"a girl?"

That fire in her eyes has me leaning in closer, like a moth attracted to a flame. "Of course you're a girl," I say, and my eyes sweep down to her chest even though I didn't give them permission to. "You said I hadn't noticed, and I was disagreeing with that."

"You are infuriating," she says, her eyes locked on mine now that they've found their way back to her face. Her cheeks are flushed, her lips are as thick and kissable up close as I'd imagined them in my dream, and she's so damn close. If we each leaned forward a little bit . . . "I'm going to go get dressed and take Winston for a walk," she says as she pulls back, stepping back into the kitchen to grab her cereal bowl.

"Are you sure you want to do that? It's blustery out there.

The lifts are even on a wind hold," I tell her. And the forecast is that the snow is going to get heavier with the wind continuing to pick up.

She glances out the window for maybe the first time this morning, then squints her eyes at me. "Is that why you're home today? I forgot you should be at the mountain, even though it's a weekend."

"I do try to give myself a day or two off here and there to recover. So with today's forecast, I suspect I'll be home all day."

"Is it going to get worse out there?"

I tell her the forecast, which apparently motivates her to take Winston for a walk now while she still can. I remind her that he's likely to be tired from his big ordeal last night, and encourage her to keep the walk short, then set about determining whether it would totally send her over the edge if she came back from her walk and found me lounging on the couch in my boxer briefs.

If you ask me, it's the best kind of bad idea.

———

I n the end, I decide that whatever satisfaction I'd gain from watching her lose her shit wouldn't be worth the cost. Even I know that there's a thin line between pissing someone off for fun and making them actually hate you, and it's not a line I want to cross, no matter how amusing the journey.

So when she comes back inside with her nose raw and red, her eyes watery, and her hair wet from the snow that got under her hood, I take Winston from her and suggest she take a warm shower instead. She looks at me like I've just offered her a million bucks, and it occurs to me that my small gesture, her adoring look, this feeling blooming in my chest . . . maybe it's better than pissing her off.

Winston is exhausted, so we settle into the living room. I take one of the chairs that sits kitty-corner from the sofa, and he curls up on the rug at my feet. Down the hall, Sierra is singing in the shower as I pull my phone out and open up Winston's social media account. A smile pulls at my lips when I see the number of notifications.

In the early hours of this morning, after my frustrating shower, I took the photo I sent Sierra a few days ago and posted it. I mean, I'm nothing if not competitive, and we did agree that whoever posted the photo with the most likes would win our little bet. I figured that if the photo she took of me and Winston was so popular, this one—the selfie where Winston is cuddled up asleep on my bare stomach—would likely be too. And it paid off because as people woke up this morning, they apparently really liked the puppy curled up sleeping, or they really liked the body he was sleeping on. The caption reads: *Who wouldn't want to snuggle up with this guy?* And in reading the comments section, I realize I should probably have been more clear about which "guy" I was talking about.

I don't know how long I've been browsing the comments before Sierra is asking me what I'm reading so intently. I glance up and my chest hurts. She's too freaking beautiful. She's in the same knit joggers and Henley she was wearing before her walk, her face totally free of makeup, and her wet hair piled in a big, loose bun on her head.

"Don't mind me, I'm just over here kicking your ass in our photography contest."

"What?" she shrieks, her voice joyful. I hold my phone out and she leans forward to see how many likes and comments this morning's photo has already. "Oh my God, Beau. That's awesome. So many people love Winston, he's bound to find a forever home. Let me see," she says as she swipes my phone from my hand and scrolls up.

Her thumb pauses over the screen, her eyes are a little unfocused. I can't read the look on her face, which scares me a bit. "You are unreal."

What is that tone? It's like bitterness and disappointment were mixed together, then sprinkled over her words.

"Our little bet is over," she says. "I can't compete against these types of pictures. You might as well be naked. *That's* what's got so many people liking that photo. Photography skills have zero to do with why this photo is getting so much love."

"Rewind," I say, sitting forward and resting my elbows on my knees as I look up at her. "I am not naked. I am very clearly wearing pants."

"Yeah, gray sweatpants, which I think we *just* established, are . . . revealing. And we can pretty much only see your crotch anyway. All these comments," she says, looking down at the phone as she scrolls through them. "They're about *you*, not about your photography or about Winston."

I've never been so tempted to tell someone about my photography account in my life. I feel like she would understand my passion if I were honest with her, but the alarm bells are going off in my head. *Warning, warning, you shouldn't care about her opinion . . . you'll be gone in two weeks anyway.* I've never cared what anyone thought before. If people don't understand me, screw them, move on. I don't know why that feels so wrong in this situation, but it does.

"You did say that whoever got the most likes on one of their photos would win. Why would you think I wouldn't post a photo that was going to get a lot of attention?"

"I guess I just didn't think you were so . . ." She looks away toward the windows, like she's trying to think of the right way to say this.

I stand, and stepping over Winston where he sleeps on the rug I take a step toward her. When she looks back at me, I'm close enough that we're sharing the same air. "So . . . what?"

She hands me back my phone. "So desperate for attention." Her voice is quiet, like she's ripping the bandage off some sort of wound and isn't sure what the repercussions might be. Will there be an explosion of blood and pus? Or is it an old wound that's healed?

So I do what I always do when someone hits a little too close to home, I redirect. "Not desperate," I say, my words as low and quiet as hers, "just not afraid of attention. Which I think begs the question, why are you so afraid of being *seen*?"

I can feel the air she sucks in as it pulls away from my face. She's breathing in my words, trying to trap them so she doesn't have to face them.

"I know who I am, Sierra, and I'm not afraid of people *seeing* me. I don't need to hide. What are you hiding from?"

"This feels a lot like gaslighting," she says, taking a step back. "Don't try to make me believe I'm imagining your attention-whoring tendencies by redirecting this to be about me."

I look down at her and hope she can't tell that our proximity has my fingers itching to touch her, my mouth trembling to taste her, my arms aching to wrap themselves around her. Instead, I deflect. "Are you denying that you intentionally step out of the spotlight whenever you have the chance?"

"I don't know." She looks at the ground. "I've never really thought about it."

"Well, maybe you should."

"And maybe you should think about why you constantly need to be the center of attention."

"You don't know me well enough to know if that's true or not." Off the top of my head, I can think of a hundred instances it's been true in just the last year. I didn't become a professional snowboarder because I'm attention adverse. But the things I really care about, I keep those close to my heart and out of the public eye.

"And you don't know me well enough to know if, or why, I avoid the spotlight."

That's where she's wrong, but I have a feeling we'll end up fighting about it if I push any further, and that's not how I want to spend this snowy Sunday where we're pretty much going to be trapped here together. "Fair enough," I say.

I go to step back to my seat, but I forget that Winston is lying behind me and I end up with my heel pushing into his side. He jumps up with a yelp and in my attempt to not hurt him, I fall backward into the chair with my knees tucked up so my feet are off the floor. He runs to Sierra, who squats down and cuddles him, rubbing her hands up and down his sides gently while she rubs her nose to his. I have the perfect profile image of them from where I'm sitting, so I snap a couple shots quickly, trying to frame the image just right.

"C'mon, boy," she says to him like she's soothing a crying baby, "let's get you a little treat." She heads to the kitchen with

Winston on her heels and I pull the photo into my favorite editing app.

I know this is a good shot, and I'm going to make it great. Maybe somehow this photo will make her less mad at me. Or maybe it'll get even more attention than the half-naked photo of me so I can win our little contest without her insisting it's because of my body rather than my photography skills.

As I make a few tweaks to the photo to curve the light illuminating them, I hear her banging around in the kitchen talking to Winston. I get up and take a few steps across the living room to peek into the kitchen. Sierra's got a spoonful of peanut butter she's using as an incentive for him to sit. On my phone, I swipe over to my camera and capture a short video of Sierra getting Winston to sit, then holding out the peanut butter for him to lick off the spoon.

I sneak back to my seat on the couch, where I post the photo and video with the caption *Things Winston loves: his foster mom, snuggles, and peanut butter.* I add all the hashtags I've identified to help the post get noticed, and sit back and wait to see how it does.

As I scan through my email, Sierra comes back to the couch and sits at one end, her knees bent and her feet tucked up beside her with her Kindle in her hand. She pulls a blanket over her lap and Winston jumps up on the couch and curls up on the blanket.

What is this tightness in my chest? This banal domestic scene has me feeling things I've never felt. My feet aren't itching to get outside and shred through the trees on my snowboard. I'm not even sure where I'm headed after Aspen because I haven't bothered to plan it, have even put off making plans when Lance and Drew have pressed me. I'm not trying to figure out the quickest way to get laid, or the best place to party. In fact, this weekend is one of the first I can remember where I did neither. And yet . . . I'm content.

And that contentedness scares me. Deep down in my bones I've always had an aching need to move, a restlessness that's never satisfied unless I'm thinking about the next place I'm going to land. And not feeling that—no matter how temporary this might be—has me wondering what is so great about the constant travel, the never-ending rotation of women and parties, and fresh lines through deep snow at new mountains.

Surely the joy of truly knowing and loving someone, of staying in one place long enough for it to become more than just familiar, that could be as fulfilling as the excitement of constant change, no?

I glance over at Sierra and wonder if this isn't some sort of crazy mind meld, where her need for consistency and predictability has somehow seeped into my psyche. Instead of hating the idea of her having taken over my brain, I wonder at the possibility—what would it be like to wake up every day to a woman like Sierra? To have someone to come home to?

She glances up at me, and I don't look away.

"Why are you staring at me?" she asks. "Do I have a big smear of peanut butter on my face or something?" She rubs her cheek with the back of her hand.

"I don't know." I shrug, because that's the most honest response I can give her. I can't tell her that I'm sitting over here imagining a future with her. Aside from the obvious physical attraction, there's no reason to believe she feels anything more than that for me. If anything, I have every indication that she doesn't. That she's repulsed by her attraction to me because she still thinks of me like a little brother.

"Well, stop," she says, setting her Kindle down and picking up her phone. "You're weirding me out."

I don't take my eyes off her, even as she intentionally looks away from me. "Stop it," she says, with a little laugh following the request.

"My eyes have a mind of their own," I say. I'm halfway smiling and even though she isn't looking at me, I think she can hear it in my voice.

She glances up at me, then back down at her phone. She looks like she's swallowing a smile, but it's attempting to escape anyway. Then she gasps and looks at me with wide eyes and a half-open mouth.

"What the hell, Beau? You didn't ask me if you could post these pictures! You didn't even tell me you took them."

It takes me a second to figure out what she's talking about.

"They're really good pictures."

"But you don't just take pictures of someone without them knowing and then post them to an account with over fifteen thousand followers, even if they're good pictures," she says.

"Really?" I shrug. "Because it happens to me all the time." If I had a dollar for every time someone took a picture of me at a mountain or at a bar, then posted it online tagging me in it, I swear I'd probably be a millionaire. I know it goes with the territory, especially when I'm in Europe, where I am even better known for my snowboarding than I am here in the US. It's just a part of my life that I have no control over, and I guess I didn't stop to think about the fact that Sierra's life isn't like that.

"Yeah, but that doesn't make it okay."

"You're right. I'm so used to my entire life being posted online that I didn't stop to think that you might not want that. If it makes you feel any better, I have very intentionally not tagged either one of us in any of the posts. I think it's better if we remain anonymous on Winston's account, don't you?"

"Yes, but just because you didn't tag me as Sierra Lemieux doesn't mean that I want my picture posted. Notice I *asked* you before posting your picture."

"Want me to take them down?" I ask as I swipe over to the app.

She pulls one side of her lower lip between her teeth as she looks at the pictures. "No, I guess it's fine. I mean, engagement is high, so that can only be good for Winston. Just ask next time, okay?"

I hear her, but I can't respond because I'm too busy reading the comments. *Oh shit.* She must see something in my face, because she asks me what's wrong.

"Have you read the comments?" I ask.

"Only one or two."

"Keep going."

We sit there reading with the sound of the wind howling outside and the icy snow lashing against the building as our background music.

Oh wow, your foster mom is as hot as your foster dad. Lucky puppy!

With genes like that, these two should have a baby, not a dog.

Holy shit—he brings the hotness and she brings the sweetness.

The comments about Sierra and me and our couple status and our looks are pretty consistently sprinkled in among comments about Winston being an adorable puppy.

"Well, clearly they don't know we're just roommates," she says, but she isn't looking at me. Are her cheeks flushed?

"I guess I see why everyone is jumping to that conclusion, given that we obviously live together."

"Set them straight," she says, and her eyes meet mine. Yep, her cheeks are distinctly pink, and it's the cutest thing I've seen in a while.

"Why me?" I ask out of curiosity, not because I'm unwilling.

"Because you're the one who created this confusion, not me."

"Fine," I say, and I get up from my chair. I walk over to where Winston is sleeping cuddled up on the couch next to her, and I squat down to get a closeup of his mushy brown puppy face.

"Oh my God," she says, we've gained another thousand followers since I checked last night. "We're actually at sixteen thousand now."

"Because we're hot puppy parents, obviously," I say, looking over at her and winking. She's closer than I realized and I'm flooded with the awareness of her proximity: a tingling sensation moves up my spine, over my shoulders, and across my chest. It's all I can do not to shudder.

I post the picture I took of Winston with the caption *Hello and welcome! I'm Winston, and I'm an eight week old chocolate lab. Since we're all new here, I just want to clarify that these two humans who keep posting pictures of me aren't together, they're just roommates. But they're glad you're following my story and hope that you'll help me find my forever home!*

I hold my phone out to Sierra to read, and she glances up when she's done. I'm pretty sure her eyes are watery, but she says "It's perfect" and looks away so quickly I can't be sure.

"Hey," I say, reaching out and touching her chin with my

185

fingertips, pressing gently to see if she'll willingly turn back to me. "What's wrong?"

She looks over at me and I was right, her eyes are filled with unshed tears. I want to wrap her in my arms and figure out how to make this better.

"Nothing. Honestly. I'm just emotional."

"Does this happen a lot?" I ask.

"Have you really never spent more than forty-eight hours with a woman?" she asks, but she smiles and I feel a little relief at that.

"I mean, forty-eight hours might be a stretch. So educate me. Does this happen a lot?"

Her eyes search my face, like she can impart an understanding with a look. "Beau . . ." she says, but she's cut off my the shrill ringing of her phone. She looks mildly worried when she says, "It's my sister."

I see Sydney's name flashing on her screen. "You better get that then."

For a second she looks torn, eyeing her phone like it might be a bomb before she answers it.

She listens for about half a second, then screeches, "You're doing what?" She stands so abruptly Winston wakes up startled and nips at her foot as she jumps off the couch. She runs to her room and slams the door behind her, and Winston and I look at each other, neither of us quite sure what just happened.

Chapter Thirteen

SIERRA

Sydney takes a deep breath. "Why did you just slam your door?"

"I ran into my room because I didn't want to have this conversation in front of Beau. He doesn't need to know our family is crazy."

"Wait, who's Beau?" she asks.

"Jackson's little brother. You remember him?"

"The snowboarder? Holy shit, Sierra!" she practically yells. Sometimes I forget that he's the same age as my twin sisters. Of course they met at Blackstone Mountain, the same way I met Jackson. "Why is he at your place?"

"He's in town for a few weeks, training for the X Games, so Jackson said he could stay in the spare bedroom. Since I'm staying at her place and she won't even charge me rent, it's not like I have much say who my roommate is."

"Is he as hot as he looks on social media?" she asks, skipping right to the part of the story she's clearly most interested in.

"Unfortunately," I tell her as I pace back and forth in my room. "Why do you even follow him?"

"Because he's a kid I kind of knew when we were in high school and now he's a pretty famous professional snowboarder. Why is it unfortunate that he's as hot as he looks online?"

I drop my voice low. "Have you ever tried living with someone who's ridiculously hot and looks at you like he wants to devour you, but you absolutely *cannot* go there? Sydney, he's my best friend's much younger brother. Nothing can happen."

"First of all, five years isn't that big of a difference now. I mean, you and I are in much more similar places in our lives now than say, when I was fifteen and you were twenty. And the older you get, the less a five-year age difference would matter. I mean, Joe is four years older than me, and we're getting married."

"Yeah, back to that," I say quickly, anxious to get off the topic of me and Beau, and back to the all-important breaking of our family's curse. Which of course isn't real, so it doesn't need breaking—but better safe than sorry, right? "What the hell do you mean you're getting married *next weekend?*"

"Joe proposed last night. And given our family's history with marriage, we don't want a long, drawn out engagement period. Since his only family is his brother, he doesn't want a big wedding and I honestly don't care either way. I just want to actually marry him." I can feel the love in that statement. This isn't about breaking a curse, it's about her wanting to spend the rest of her life with Joe. And it makes me wonder if I sounded the same way talking about marrying Peter. "We thought about doing it here in Boston, but then we'd have to invite people or their feelings would be hurt. And Ma—" She sighs deeply. "—I'm not sure that having her there on my special day would be the best thing for me."

"I completely understand." She doesn't need to explain to me why that's complicated. Sydney and my mom have a similar relationship to me and my mom, but maybe even worse because Ma grew more and more bitter as we girls got older. I think watching her youth and vitality fade as ours grew was way too much for her sociopath brain to handle. She was only happy when she was making us feel less-than.

"So anyway, eloping seems like the best option. We're flying to Vegas next weekend. There's no wait-time for a marriage license and it's a long weekend, so it's perfect. And I want you to be there."

"Of course I'll be there," I squeal. I've never been to Vegas, and I haven't seen Sydney in too long. "I can't believe this is really happening. Are you . . ." I trail off, afraid that me being scared something bad will happen to ruin this for her will actually be what ruins it.

"Scared?" she offers.

"Yeah."

"Hell yes. Part of me wants to just hop on a plane today and get this taken care of. Or apply for a marriage license tomorrow when city hall opens, wait the three days, and get married here on Thursday. But I want you to be there, and Joe wants his brother there. His brother is in LA, and you're in Park City, so Vegas—with its lax marriage laws and its location—just makes sense."

"If it were me, I would probably do both," I admit, even though she's not asking for my advice.

"Really?"

"Would the Vegas wedding be more relaxing and fun if you knew you were technically already married? You'd still get to do the ceremony, and have Joe's brother and me there with you to celebrate, but you wouldn't have to spend this next week worrying that something might happen to stop the wedding."

"I can't stop thinking about Lydia," Sydney says, her voice barely a whisper.

"Me too. But Syd, Lydia's situation was different. They were fighting all the time. She was already pregnant. I think he just cut his losses, but was too chickenshit to tell her."

"I know," she says. This is a conversation we've already had a million times, each assuring the other that it doesn't mean "the curse" is real. "But I'm still scared, even though, logically, I know it makes no sense."

"Think about getting married at city hall before you fly out to Vegas, just so you have the peace of mind and can actually enjoy the ceremony and celebration there."

"I'm also worried about how Lydia will feel about me getting married and inviting you, but not her," Sydney says. She and Lydia are like two sides of the same coin—opposites in every way except DNA, yet intrinsically bound together.

"That's fair. But it's your wedding. If having her there would make it less enjoyable for you, it's not worth it."

"She's just so freaking difficult. I don't want her ruining the excitement or my happiness with her doom and gloom scenarios. I don't want her comparing our lives. She always makes me feel like somehow it's my fault she's living in a trailer park in Blackstone. Like I made her choose to date Anthony and get knocked up when she was nineteen."

"Like Ma, Lydia can hardly stand to see others happy. Her

life *is hard*, and the fact that our lives aren't—that we made different choices and are happier than she is—she just doesn't know how to deal with that."

"I know. But it doesn't make it any easier to deal with her."

"True. Maybe you can wait until midweek and invite her? I mean, the chances of her being able to come on such short notice are low?" I feel like a complete asshole suggesting this, but Lydia's just so exceptionally difficult. Having her there really could ruin the whole experience for Sydney.

"Let me think about it," she says. "But anyway . . . Vegas!" She shares her plans with me, insisting that she and Joe are booking three rooms at the same hotel they're having the ceremony at, and all I have to do is get myself there. "Joe's brother will be there with his wife," she tells me. "Maybe you should think about bringing someone too?"

I stop pacing, coming up short at my mirror. "I literally just broke up with my fiancé, Syd. There *is* no one else." I take a good look at myself and wonder if that will always be the case. Peter was the first guy I dated who really "stuck." My track record before that was full of short-term relationships that just fizzled out.

"What about Beau?" she asks. "Obviously there's some strong attraction, and you know what they say—what happens in Vegas, stays in Vegas. Might be the perfect place for some no-strings fun for the two of you."

My entire body shudders, goose bumps prickling my skin at the thought. At how badly I *want* that option. "No. That's a brilliant but terrible idea. And Jackson would never understand me having a fling with him."

"You know, you don't have to tell her."

The idea of keeping a secret like that from my best friend

is . . . preposterous. Then again, I never told her about that night I turned him down when he was seventeen. And she lied to me about Nate when they first got back together. She had good reasons, and I've forgiven her, but I can't help thinking that this wouldn't be that different.

Yes, it would, I tell myself. *This is her brother.*

"I don't think I could outright lie to her about something that big."

"Are you sure she'd even care? They're not close, right?"

"No, and that's *why* she'd care," I say, making sure to keep my voice low. I end up heading into my bathroom and shutting that door too. This is not a conversation I want Beau to overhear. "She has this picture of who he is, and she doesn't like that person at all. But as I've gotten to know him better, I think her version of him is . . . incomplete."

"Oh, man." Sydney laughs. "You've already thought this through."

"Hard not to when I'm living with someone who walks around half-naked and blatantly undresses me with his eyes. The worst part, Syd, is he's not just some snowboarding sex god, he's actually a good person—and I'm attracted to that aspect of him as well."

Her laugh is low and rumbling. "You are so screwed."

"He's leaving in two weeks," I tell her. "I can get through two more weeks."

"You're a mess after only one week," she reminds me. "I've never heard you like this before. You've never expressed this level of attraction to Peter. Or anyone."

"I know. It's bad." It feels good to admit this out loud, to tell someone else instead of having to hold it inside all the time.

"Where's he going in two weeks?"

"The X Games in Aspen. Then he'll be off to the next competition, or whatever. I think he said maybe Switzerland? He never stays in one place for long. He doesn't even have a home base, just travels all the time. New locations, new girls, that's his lifestyle."

"So in other words, you couldn't be more different."

"Exactly."

"Well," she says slowly. "If he's only there for two weeks and then you'll probably never see him again, why *not* have a little fling?"

The thought of never seeing him again has my chest seizing up painfully. *You've just gotten used to having him around,* I remind myself.

"That could go wrong in so many ways," I insist.

"A no-strings-attached fling with an end date set in stone? It actually sounds like the perfect way to get over Peter, and not get your heart broken in the process."

"Can I tell you something honestly?"

"Always."

"I'm not trying to get over Peter. Like, I think I was over him the minute I saw Jane waltz into his hotel room in lingerie. I've felt nothing but anger and . . . I don't know. I kept thinking that I'd be sad, but honestly, the anger is starting to morph into relief. I just feel lucky that I didn't end up married to that cheating bastard who sucked so bad in bed."

"This is new info," Sydney says.

"To me too."

"You didn't know he sucked in bed?"

"I mean the part about being relieved was new info."

"Sierra," she says, "how were you going to *marry* someone who sucked in bed?"

"I kept thinking he'd get better?"

"Life is way too short to have bad sex, big sis. Beau is sounding like a better and better idea. You said there's a lot of chemistry there?"

"Off the charts." I tell her about waking up on the couch last night, and about hearing Beau in the shower.

"Oh my God," she chants multiple times. "That's so hot. Seriously, Sierra, what are you waiting for?"

"Sydney, I *can't*," I say, glaring at myself in the mirror. My cheeks are pink, my whole body feels flushed from the memories.

"You can," she says. "What are you so scared of?"

"Besides ruining my relationship with my best friend?" I pause. "I'm scared that it'll hurt too much when he leaves."

"He's leaving either way," she says. "You might as well get some mind-blowing orgasms out of it before he goes."

She's right, but I've never been good at compartmentalizing.

"I'm not sure that would be worth it. Because if something did happen between us, his leaving would feel personal. He wouldn't be leaving because that's what he always does, he'd be leaving *me*."

"Nooo," she says, stretching the word out. "He'd be leaving because that was the plan all along."

"Logically I know that," I say. "But I worry that I'd grow even more attached than I already am. And it would feel personal. I don't do sex without feelings. If this was just sexual attraction, it might be easier, but I actually like him."

"Maybe you're right then," she says, but she sounds sad for

me. Which makes sense. *I'm* sad for me too. "It's a shame, because he's stupidly handsome and I bet he knows his way around a clitoris."

"You're getting married. You should *not* be thinking about Beau this way."

"Jealous much, sis?"

"Looking out for Joe, actually," I say.

"Joe doesn't care if I find other guys attractive, as long as it's just looking. But then again, we have a healthy relationship with really good sex, so why would he be jealous?"

I can't say that I know anything about a healthy relationship with really good sex. "I'll have to take your word on that."

"Okay, well, I've got to go, but I will text you the details of the hotel and all that. Plan on flying in on Friday. We can party it up on Saturday, and the ceremony will be Sunday afternoon."

When we hang up, I stand in my new bathroom staring at myself in the mirror. Am I the kind of person who could do this, then walk away, keeping the whole thing a secret that no one but my little sister knows about?

No, you are not, the sensible voice in my head tells me. *But maybe just this once you could be.*

———

"This is out of control," I mumble as I sink into one of the big chairs in the entry of Petra's building. She lives in a huge Victorian that's been converted into several apartments, and her neighbors are some of the most eccentric people I've ever met. Everyone keeps the front door to their apartment open when they're home, and they wander in and out of each other's places like it's a college dorm. Two of her neighbors, a couple in their seventies, let me in on their way to the market after a short discussion about how I didn't look like a serial killer and I'd be good for Petra. I think they thought I was her girlfriend, but whatever, I was just happy to wait inside until she gets home from work.

It's only Wednesday and I'm already exhausted. Between trying to help Sydney get the details of her last minute wedding just right and trying to get all my work done so I can take Friday off to head to Vegas, I feel like I'm running myself ragged. Sydney insists we'll spend lots of time relaxing at the spa to make up for all the hustle getting there.

At least my boss, Heather, offered to take Winston while I'm gone, so I won't have to inconvenience Beau. He's been kind of weird since I told him I was leaving this weekend—distant even when he's physically present.

I glance back at my phone, and at the out-of-control notifications from Winston's social media account. I've never seen numbers this high on anything I've posted, and I've worked in social media management for close to a decade.

When Beau posted the caption, *these two humans who keep posting pictures of me aren't together, they're just roommates*, Winston's followers went crazy. It had the opposite of its intended effect. They became even more committed to the idea that something *should* be going on between us. The comments were bold, insistent, and in most cases overstepping. They took screenshots of the photo of Beau with Winston on his lap and the photo of me loving on Winston, and put them side by side in their stories. They even created a hashtag #ShippingWinstonsParents, which had a stupid number of posts over the past couple of days. Luckily, no one seems to have figured out who we are yet, but I'm worried that it's only a matter of time before Beau is recognized.

I've considered just deleting the account, but haven't because it does seem to be fulfilling its purpose. People are inquiring about how they can meet Winston. The shelter has started processing applications from people they consider possible candidates to adopt him, but they are backlogged right now and told me today that it could be weeks before they're able to get to Winston's case.

I glance at the notifications again. Since I last checked at lunchtime, 175 people have reposted our photos in their Stories and tagged Winston's account. I click over to Winston's account and look at the picture Beau took of that little brown fur ball sleeping on the couch. *God, I'm going to miss that puppy.*

"Why are you looking at pictures of puppies?" Petra's sultry voice booms out from above me.

I turn my phone off quickly and slide it into my jacket pocket, then look up at her. "Because they're cute."

"Meh," she says. "They're a lot of work."

I breathe a sigh of relief that she didn't recognize Jackson's emerald green velvet couch in the background of the photo. "Yeah, they are. But I'm sure it'd be worth it." I stand and we walk toward the huge wooden staircase.

"I'm not so sure," she says. I get where she's coming from. Petra's job has her constantly jetting off to some event she's planned, whether it's a corporate retreat in the British Virgin Islands or a party for potential political donors in LA.

"Hey, I appreciate you fitting me in before you go," I tell her as we crest the top of the stairs to the second floor landing. She's leaving tomorrow for San Francisco. There's some big pharmaceutical conference, and she was hired to plan a ritzy cocktail party Friday night for one of the big pharma companies.

"It's no problem," she says. "My closet is your closet."

I'm here to pick out some things for my Vegas trip because her wardrobe is extensive and her closet is magical—you can always find exactly what you need in it.

The second we're inside her apartment, she offers me a glass of wine, which I happily accept. When Heather came into my office right before I left work to offer to take Winston for me this weekend, she also asked if I'd talked to Beau about not sending me half-naked pictures of himself. I admitted that I hadn't, but that it was a nonissue because he hadn't sent one since.

Of course, I didn't mention that he walks around the apartment like that all the time anyway, or about our whole conversation about gray sweats and just wearing his boxer briefs instead. And now I haven't been able to get those mental images out of my head for the past hour. I'm hoping that hanging with Petra for a bit will get Beau out of my head.

"So, what do you need in terms of clothes?" she asks as we head into her closet. The only reason her apartment is a one-bedroom is because she's converted what could have been a second smaller bedroom into a floor-to-ceiling storage facility for her wardrobe.

"I don't know, I've never been to Vegas," I tell her.

"Oh, you are in for a treat. You want to go in with an open mind. Think of it like Disney World for adults. Anything you want to experience, you can find it somewhere in Vegas."

"I'm sure I'll be pretty busy with Sydney's wedding."

Petra starts pulling semiformal dresses from the racks and

giving them the once-over. "How are you feeling about going to your little sister's wedding? I mean, you and Peter broke it off," she says, which is her gentle way of saying *Your fiancé dumped you for another woman*, "and then you had Jackson's wedding. Now, like two weeks later, you've got your little sister's wedding. Are you doing okay with it?"

"I'm thrilled for her, actually," I tell Petra. Because yes, while I am a little jealous that the one thing I've always wanted for myself seems to be happening for everyone else, I am equally relieved that Sydney's wedding will prove once and for all that there is no family curse. But, of course, I know Petra would think the whole story of the curse was absolutely ridiculous, so I don't mention it.

"Good. I'm glad to see you aren't pining over Peter. He had such a slimy vibe. Like, the way he looked at women was . . ." she shudders.

"Why didn't you ever say anything?" Honestly, maybe if she'd said something sooner, it could have saved me a whole lot of heartache.

"He was hardly ever around," she says. "You came out with us all the time, but it was always just the girls. Even when Josh came with Lauren, you hardly ever brought Peter." She drops a few dresses onto the huge ottoman that takes up the middle of the room. "So I wasn't entirely sure my assessment was right. Did I have enough exposure to him to *really* know?"

"Petra, you pride yourself on being able to sense these types of things. And you're always right."

She drops her voice low when she says, "Well, I wasn't sure you'd be open to hearing it."

Would I have? I ignored warning signs that I shouldn't have. Would one of my best friends telling me my fiancé seemed a bit slimy have changed my mind? Or just strained the friendship?

"Did Jackson and Lauren feel the same way?" I sip my wine but watch her closely. Have they talked about me behind my back?

Petra turns to sort through more clothes, and I have to wonder if it's so I can't see her face when she responds. "I don't know. We never really talked about it. My guess is that they also had reservations. You'd have to ask them, though." She turns back with another set of dresses. "Okay, let's look through these. I picked out some more formal options for the wedding, and these are just for fun. For dinner and going out at night."

We look through the options and weed a couple out. Petra's got about the same size breasts and waist as I do, but I'm also curvy through the hips and thighs where she's less so. Once we've narrowed it down, I start trying dresses on. Petra takes photos of my two favorites for the ceremony and I text them to my sister for her opinion. Then I try on a bunch of fun dresses, all some combination of short, low-cut, and sexy. I pull my three favorites aside, even though I'll likely only have an occasion to wear two of them. I'm not sure why it even matters what I wear, since it's not like I'm bringing a date I'm trying to impress. I'll probably spend the whole weekend feeling like the fifth wheel.

"What's that look?" Petra asks and when I glance up, I realize she's studying me carefully from where I sit, organizing the pile of dresses so I can easily bring them home.

"It's nothing."

"Sure it's not. What's going on?" she asks as she sits down

on the ottoman, her knees turned toward me and her assessing eyes focused on my face.

"Really, nothing's going on. I was just thinking about not having a date to bring to the wedding and how I'm probably going to feel like the odd man out all weekend since I'll be with two other couples."

Petra nods, and I feel like I can see the wheels turning in her mind. I know Petra wouldn't care at all about something like this. She'd see it as an opportunity to meet a new man and "take him for a test drive," as she often refers to her sexual encounters. I wish I had her confidence and her healthy appetite for sex with strangers, I really do. It would make my love life a lot less complicated. But I just can't, mentally or emotionally, get there.

"There's no one you'd want to bring?"

I school my face into a mask of indifference, because if anyone would be able to see through me about this, it's Petra. "I just broke off an engagement and I've had one horrendous date since. Who would I bring?"

Bring Beau, that little voice yells at me. It's ridiculous how much I want him there with me. I know he's the kind of guy who'd make sure I had a good time all weekend. But even though we live together, there's no way I can bring him to this wedding and claim we're *just friends*. It's Vegas. If there were anywhere in the whole world you'd go with the expectation of getting lucky, that's it. There's no way I can invite Beau without him thinking it's an invitation straight into my panties. *So let it be.* I shake my head to get rid of that voice, which usually is so good at reminding me to always make good decisions but has suddenly jumped on the *just sleep with Beau and enjoy it* bandwagon.

"I wish I could hear the conversation going on in your head right now," Petra says with a laugh. "If your facial expressions are any indication, it's a doozy."

"I'm kind of a mess right now." I rest my elbows on my knees and let my head fall into my hands.

"Tell me about it," Petra says. When I don't respond, she adds, "I'm a really good listener. And I can keep a secret. It seems like you might need someone to listen to you without judging, and without sharing your thoughts with anyone else."

I consider this for a moment. Petra knows Jackson well enough to give me advice on this in a way that Sydney can't. I take a deep breath, then explain what's been going on.

Petra's quiet when I'm done, and I instantly regret telling her. "I'm just thinking," she says as she gets up and starts pacing back and forth across her closet. Finally, she says, "On the one hand, he is your best friend's little brother. And you don't know how she'd feel about you sleeping with him." She walks to the other side of the room. "But on the other hand, you're both adults and there's no harm in a short-term fling if you both enter it knowing that it's only going to be a short-term thing." She walks back to the ottoman and sits next to me. "I think you should go for it."

"Wait . . . what?" Did she really just tell me to sleep with Beau?

"I *saw* you two together at Jackson's wedding. There was so much chemistry there. And it sounds like that's only grown since you've been roommates. As long as you aren't going to be heartbroken when he leaves—because we *do* know that he'll leave—why wouldn't you go for this? I bet the sex would be amazing, and you deserve that. You should take him to Vegas with you."

"I don't know if that's a good idea. And I have no idea how I'd ask him something like that, anyway."

"I think it's a great idea," she says. "And you could just say, 'Hey, want to go to Vegas for the weekend?' If he makes excuses and doesn't come, you'll know this wasn't meant to be a thing. But if he does come, well, you'll have a weekend full of great sex."

"And then when we come back? He'll still be my roommate for another week before he leaves."

"You guys will figure it out. But I don't see any reason you need to stop sleeping with him just because you're not in Vegas anymore."

"I feel like that's the tricky part. I really do like him, and if the sex is good, I'm worried I'll start developing feelings for him, and it'll be heartbreaking when he leaves." It's the same thing I said to Sydney a few nights ago, and I wonder if that will change Petra's mind about it like it changed Sydney's.

"You have to go into it knowing that it's only temporary and being okay with that. If you're not okay with it, then you probably need to keep your distance." She reaches over and puts a hand on my shoulder. "There are plenty of fish in the sea."

It's a struggle not to roll my eyes. Yeah, maybe for gorgeous, confident, and uninhibited girls like Petra, there are plenty of fish in the sea.

Chapter Fourteen

BEAU

D rew skids to a stop next to where I'm sitting, my ass in the snow and my board resting on edge perpendicular to the slope. "You've got until Monday to land that quad cork or Mark's going to ream your ass when he gets here," he says.

"Is that your pep talk?" I ask. Talking shit is Drew's way of encouraging me to do better. It's been that way since I met him freshman year of college. But this warning isn't his normal shit-talking campaign, nor is it particularly encouraging.

Lance skids to a stop, raining powder down over where Drew and I sit. "Asshat," Drew mutters.

"I'm going to land it right now, just to get you to shut up," I say to Drew. He's right though, if my coach shows up and sees that I've regressed since this summer, he's going to be pissed.

"Sure you are." I glance over at Drew, and he's got both his eyebrows raised at me. I want to punch him in the face, which is a pretty typical reaction for anyone who's spent time with Drew. He prides himself on being able to get under people's skin.

"This weekend's going to suck," Lance says as he pops his ass in the snow next to us. "The crowds will descend for the holiday. Runs will be crowded, there'll be long lift lines, and you know the terrain park will be overrun by idiots who don't know what they're doing. So you've got today and tomorrow to get the quad cork to stick. Otherwise, Mark's going to show up only to find out you can't do a trick you'd mastered in June. At our age, going backward is not an option."

"Dude, don't give me that *at our age* shit," I say. "Shaun White and Jamie Anderson were still killing it in their thirties."

"Yeah," Lance says, "but Jamie already had back-to-back Olympic gold medals and was one of the most decorated snowboarders in X Games history before she hit thirty. And Shaun's just . . . Shaun. A superhuman, five-time Olympian, freaking legend."

I let out a frustrated sigh and watch it float away as a cloud of ice crystals suspended in the cold air. I'm not trying to become a legend. But it would be nice to get some more wins under my belt before I'm too old to keep doing this. I know that my days in this sport are numbered. I can feel it in the aches and pains I have after particularly grueling days on the slopes. That never used to happen. Mom keeps telling me I should take up yoga like Jackson did after her ski accident, but that's just not my speed.

I pop my earbuds in, crank my music, and stand. It's midweek and only two other people have gone into the terrain park in the past few minutes. I glance behind me. No one else coming. Good, I like to have space, to know that no one is going to be in my landing zone or camped out taking pictures of me.

"See you at the bottom," I say to Lance and Drew, who are now scrambling to get up and join me. But I hop forward, angling my board perpendicular to the mountain. I take off, sailing down through the gates of the park and straight toward the first feature where I do a tailslide 270 spin off the rail and head down to the jump where I land a switchback 720. I approach the last jump committed to landing the quad cork. I push my doubts aside. I've done this before—many times onto the airbag and a couple times on snow—I can do it again.

I'm on the toe-side edge of my board in an athletic stance, prepared to launch off the lip with enough force to propel me through four off-axis flips and five 360 rotations. As soon as I'm airborne, I throw my head and right hand to the left, and grab the heel edge of my board with my front hand. Then I count the sky and the ground four times each before I pull out for the landing. The impact has me going into a deep squat, but I manage to stay upright.

When I skid to the bottom, there are a few people standing around, all of them gawking at me. I used to love that kind of attention, I'd bask in it. Sierra aptly pointed out the other night what I didn't want to see. I really do seek validation in attention from strangers. And I'm not sure why the opinions of people I don't know even matter.

I bend over, putting my hands on my knees and taking a few deep breaths so I don't have to look at them.

"You fucking did it!" Drew whoops as he comes to a stop behind me. "And Lance got it on video."

"No shit?" I say as Lance pulls up next to us. I can't believe I nailed it. There was no fear, it just felt right and I went for it.

"I did," Lance confirms. "I got the whole thing from right

behind you. Wish we'd had someone filming you from below the jump too, but we'll get that another time. This is awesome footage. I'll work on it tonight."

"Sure, but don't post anything yet, okay?"

Lance gives me a look. "You trying to keep expectations low? Head into the competition and surprise the shit out of everyone?"

I shrug because I'm not really sure *why* I don't want him posting the footage. My sponsors expect frequent posting, preferably with closeups that let the viewer see their logo on my helmet or my jacket. Constant photos and videos are what keep me relevant, keep the sponsorships and partnerships rolling in, and allow me to afford to keep Lance and Drew traveling with me. It's not every job that lets you work with your two best friends, and I don't take this for granted. We've come a long way from packing up our boards and road-tripping it to Vermont every winter weekend during college.

"I'm starving, let's grab some food," Drew says. The sun is low, and the sky is streaked with pinks and purples as we head toward the lodge.

"I'm just staying for one drink, then I need to head home," I tell them once we're seated at an outdoor table under the heat lamps.

"What for this time, old man?" Drew asks. "The dog, or the girl?"

"Both, actually. Winston needs a walk, and I told Sierra I'd make dinner."

The two of them stare at me, and finally, Lance laughs. "Oh, how the mighty have fallen."

"What's that supposed to mean?" I ask.

"Dude, you have chicks all over you all the time. And here

we are in Park City, popular tourist destination for the rich and the beautiful, and instead of taking advantage of the *opportunities*"—Lance moves his eyebrows up and down—"you're running home to play house. Either you're lying to us about not sleeping with her, or you're the most pathetic asshole ever."

"Well, I'm not lying about sleeping with her, so . . ."

"What's the deal, then?" Drew asks as he puts his helmet in his bag and pulls on his beanie.

"I just like hanging out with her." I don't know how else to explain it. Given the option between meaningless sex or hanging out with Sierra, I'm pretty sure I'd choose Sierra every time.

"Without sex," he adds, his voice flat. It's not a question, it's a statement tinged with doubt.

It feels like sex between us should be a foregone conclusion. The way she looks at me, the way she's hyper-focused on my gray sweats while pretending to be upset about them, the way she manages to touch me in passing. I know she's thinking about it as much as I am, but I'm equally certain she's not looking for a fling. She wants someone serious, someone to settle down with. Someone who's home at the same time every day and wants a house in the suburbs and kids. That's not me. And I don't think she can move past that, no matter how good the sex would be.

"Without sex," I confirm. "There'll be plenty of time for that once we head to Aspen."

"Did you hit your head? You're like a different person right now," Lance says. "What happened to getting laid as a way of life?"

"Speaking of getting laid," Drew says, perking up, "I heard

from Helen this morning." I snap my head toward him so quickly I might have given myself whiplash. The color drains from his face. "That was a terrible segue," he says, swallowing hard.

"Speaking of sex and your twin sister . . ." I prompt, tipping my beer toward him casually. It's not hard to act like this is fine. I have a lot of practice. "I can't wait to see where this is going."

"You know what, never mind. This story can wait."

"Oh no, we're all ears," I say, glancing at Lance, who looks like he'd rather be anywhere than here. We have an unspoken agreement that we don't talk about Helen. Ever. Last year, Drew flew home for her wedding and didn't even tell me. Just said he had to go to "a family thing."

"I'm going to be an uncle."

I blink and I know I keep my eyelids shut a second too long because when I open them, Lance is silently miming to Drew about what a dick he is.

"Congrats, man. I'm sure you'll be the fun uncle." I drain my beer, then set the empty back on the table. "I gotta go." I've got to get back to my pathetic life where I'm fantasizing about a girl I can never have.

"You sure you don't want to come out with us tonight?" Lance asks. "I think we're going to meet up with those chicks we were talking to at lunch."

"Not tonight," I tell them as I stand and slap some cash down on the table to cover my drink. "But tomorrow, I'm in."

Tomorrow Sierra will be in Las Vegas and I already don't want to think about her going out, meeting some guy. She's not the type for a fling, but if there ever was a place that might change her mind, it's Vegas.

I'm in the kitchen chopping vegetables when I hear her come through the door.

"Okay, calm down," she says, and I assume she's on the phone. Winston bolts from the kitchen and I peek around the wall to make sure she doesn't need anything. She's holding her phone to her ear with one hand and sets a shopping bag on the floor as she bends to give Winston kisses and rub his head. She stands more quickly than he'd like, her attention back on her phone call, and he whimpers at her feet.

"Winston," I call. "Come."

He trots into the kitchen and looks around, expecting a treat for his obedience. Good, he's learning. I reach into the container we keep on the counter and grab one for him. He happily lies on the kitchen floor and chomps on it, and I walk over to the sink to rinse my hands. When the water shuts off, Sierra is saying, "It doesn't mean you're cursed. It's just bad weather and shit luck."

She's shrugged out of her coat and boots and is carrying her shopping bag back to her bedroom when she repeats, "It's not the freaking curse." I miss the next thing she says while she's in her bedroom, but then she comes back down the hall. "But your flight isn't delayed or canceled, right?" There's a pause, and then, "Okay, that's good. So just try to get some sleep tonight. And if you have any delays or anything tomorrow, just call me. If I arrive before you, no big deal." She listens as she comes into the kitchen and winks at me when she grabs a slice of red pepper I've just cut, mouthing *thanks* as she walks away.

As she walks away, hips swaying like they always do, it's

impossible not to focus on her ass in those jeans. I almost don't know what I'm going to do when I don't get to see her every day. *Shit. Where did that thought come from?*

"Okay, text me when you get on the plane in the morning. And just try to relax tonight, okay? Tell Joe I said hi, and that he's right!" She makes big smooching kissing sounds that have me turning away and adjusting myself.

"What's going on?" I ask when she takes a seat on one of the barstools at the peninsula.

"Ugh," she groans. "It's so stupid I don't even want to say."

"Come on, just tell me. It can't be that stupid."

She throws her head back with a laugh. "Oh, it is."

"Let me be the judge." I turn up the heat on the frying pan and throw the chunks of raw chicken onto the hot oil.

"Okay," she says, her voice laced with sarcasm. "So my entire family believes that we're cursed."

"Cursed how?" I ask as I tilt the pan back and forth over the heat to coat the chicken in the oil.

"No woman in my family has been married as far back as anyone can remember."

"But the men have?" I ask.

"There are no men in my family. Lemieux women only have girls, and they never marry."

"But . . ." I stumble after that word because I don't know what should follow it. I glance over at her and she smirks.

"See? Crazy."

"So what you're saying is that, for generations, women in your family have only had daughters and never gotten married?"

"That's correct," she says, her lips settling into a grim line.

"And why is that a curse?"

"Because it hasn't been a choice. In every single instance, the women in my family have gotten pregnant before marriage, and the man has left them. Even Lydia. She was engaged and got pregnant before they got married, and her fiancé disappeared. Like legit just didn't come home one day and she never heard from him again."

"Holy shit. That's terrible. Do you think something happened to him?" I ask as I flip the chicken in the pan, letting it brown on both sides.

"Honestly, Sydney and I think he got tired of Lydia's shit and left. I know that sounds terrible to say, but she's extremely difficult. Nothing he ever did was good enough. She bitched at him all the time. He was a pretty simple guy, I think he just got fed up and was too chickenshit to tell her he was leaving."

"So, what does this have to do with the phone call? Was that Sydney?"

"Yeah. She and Joe were going to get married at the court-house today before they head to Vegas tomorrow. That way, she wouldn't have to worry about something going wrong once they got there, and she'd just be able to enjoy her cere-mony and celebration. It was my idea. And now I feel terrible, because they had a huge blizzard in Boston last night and today everything was shut down. So they couldn't get married, and now she thinks it's the curse and is worried that something's going to happen to derail the Vegas plans." The words tumble out of her mouth at high speed and she pauses to take a deep breath. "Right now her flight tomorrow is still showing up as on time, but given that no planes flew into Logan Airport today, she's worried that there won't be a plane for her flight and they'll have a delay or cancelation."

"As someone who has dealt with their fair share of weather-related travel delays, I can say that while that does sometimes happen, it's more common that they take the planes that were grounded there during the storm and use those so that future travel isn't affected. So there's probably a plane at the airport that maybe was supposed to go to Las Vegas today that'll go tomorrow instead. And it'll go with tomorrow's passengers on it, and they'll rebook today's passengers on new flights."

"Hold on," she says, "let me tell Sydney that." Her thumbs fly over her phone as I toss the vegetables into the pan and add the seasonings, stirring them around so everything's well coated before I add the wine and chicken broth. "Okay," Sierra says. "Sydney says thanks for that info. She seems like she's calmed down a bit."

"I hope I'm right," I tell her. "But even if her flight is delayed, that doesn't mean she won't get to Vegas and get married. It's just an inconvenience. Right?"

"I hope so." Sierra sighs. "But the thing is, even though neither Sydney nor I have ever really believed that this 'curse'" —she uses air quotes with that word—"is real, bad shit does happen to relationships in my family. Sydney's got to be thinking about how Lydia's fiancé left her, mine cheated on me, and now here she is running off to Vegas a few days after getting engaged to try to prevent anything bad from happening and there's this storm that's throwing everything off."

"Wait." The word comes out of my mouth slowly as I think about how I want to say this. "Do you think that Peter cheating on you has something to do with that curse?" I keep my eyes focused on the box of pasta I'm opening so she can't read anything into the look on my face.

"I don't know. It didn't really cross my mind until my mother insisted it was bound to happen because Lemieux women don't get married."

"Your mother justified him cheating on you because of this curse?" Who the hell says something like that to their daughter, especially when she's hurting? And as far as I know, the last time she saw her mom was before Jackson's wedding, only days after Peter cheated on her.

"Yep," she says, and I catch the sadness on her face as she looks down.

I pour the pasta into the pot of boiling water, give it a stir, then walk over to the peninsula. I keep the cabinets between us because I know that if I walked to the other side I'd wrap her in my arms and then there's no telling what would happen. *Do it and find out*, my inner demon yells at me. But I can't. She's hurting, and I don't take advantage of women like that.

"Listen," I say, spreading my arms on the countertop and leaning toward her. "It sounds like the real issue here is that Lemieux women—Sydney excluded, hopefully—have a knack for picking assholes. I'm sorry that Peter hurt you," I say, and I reach across the counter and tilt her chin up so I can see her face. Those big brown eyes are glassy as she stares up at me. "But that has nothing to do with you or how amazing you are. That's on him. And one day, he'll probably regret it. But even if he doesn't, I hope you realize that you're better off without him and that eventually you'll find someone who's right for you."

Her eyes soften as she gives me a small smile. "I hope

you're right." Then she tilts her head to the side and mutters something that sounds a whole lot like, "And hopefully he'll know his way around the female body."

I pull my hand back from her chin, my eyebrows dipping as I take in what I think she's just suggested.

She looks away and mumbles, "Sorry, that's something I've said to my girlfriends, didn't mean for it to slip out just now."

"Why not?"

"Because I don't normally discuss my pathetic sex life with my guy friends."

Well, this is taking an interesting turn. "If he was so bad in bed," I say, and she groans and covers her face with both hands, "why were you going to marry him?"

"Because other than that, he was a good partner. Or at least, I thought he was." She takes her hands away from her face and I move back to the stove to stir the pasta and the chicken and vegetables in the sauce.

"I could be wildly off base here," I say as I start pulling the chicken out of the sauce and putting it on a plate to shred, "but isn't sexual compatibility a prerequisite for a serious relationship?"

She pauses before responding. "Please, share all your wisdom about serious relationships." A deep thread of sarcasm strings the words together.

"Fair point," I say, not looking at her as I start shredding the chicken.

Sierra doesn't know about Helen, she can't understand the heartbreak I felt. Helen's words, in particular, still sting. *How could I ever be serious about a guy who's so decidedly* not *serious?* She let me know that I wasn't the kind of guy you headed toward forever with, and in a way, I guess she did me a favor.

Instead of letting myself fall for anyone else, I've spent my twenties just enjoying life, being exactly the kind of guy she thought I was in the first place.

"Except I have to think that if I were ever to get into a serious relationship"—I glance over at her and she's watching me intently—"the sex would have to be amazing." I string the word "have" out like it's one extraordinarily long syllable.

Her cheeks flush slightly. "What if the girl you fall in love with isn't great in bed?" she asks.

"Then I'd teach her."

Her face reddens dramatically at that statement. "Oh, so you're an expert?"

I lock eyes with her. "Pretty much." I'm not going to deny that I've had enough sex to know how to please my partner. Good sex isn't about me, it's about making the other person feel good, which makes everything about it better for me too.

"You'll have to let me know how that works for you. You know, once you finally meet the right woman to *settle down* with."

I keep my eyes on hers, feeling so many things I've never felt before but being far too chicken to say any of them. "I will." I pick up the plate of meat and dump it back into the sauce and give the pasta another stir. And now her lack of response means it's starting to feel awkward. "So, are you all packed for your flight tomorrow?"

"Just about. I feel like I'm packing way too much for one weekend, but I also feel like I won't know what I need until I'm there."

"Have you been to Las Vegas before?" I ask.

"Never."

"Oh, you're in for an experience."

"Yeah? What's your favorite thing about it?"

"Everything," I say with a low chuckle. "It's like, whatever you want, you can find it there. Vegas was made for guys like me," I tell her. I've said it before and meant it, but it sounds like a lie to me now.

"Guys like you?" she asks, and bites her lower lip. I hate it when she does anything that draws attention to those lips, because it makes me think about how I want them on my body—I want to nibble on her full lower lip, I want to feel her lips trace a path down my abdomen on their way to my sweatpants. And like I'm a teenager again, now I'm hard just thinking about her and those stupid, luscious lips.

"Thrill seeking, pleasure-centric, indulgent assholes." I shrug as I angle my body toward the stove so my back is to her.

"You're not an asshole, Beau." Her words are soft, too kind.

"Not right now. But only because you and Winston have given me something to think about besides myself. Otherwise, I'd be out with Drew and Lance right now, and every night since getting here, raising hell." I grab the pot of pasta and carry it to the sink to drain it. With my back to her, I add, "It's too bad you don't need a date for the wedding, I'd be an amazing Vegas tour guide."

Her pause is a beat too long, before she says, "Yeah, too bad, a tour guide would have been great."

———

The music is so loud I can't distinguish the beat from my own pulse. The bar is packed tonight and bodies are crowded together, pressing in on me, but I'm trying to keep my focus on the hot blonde who's practically attached to the front of me. My left hand is slung over her shoulder as she grinds against my thigh, and the only reason I notice the text message come across my watch is because it lights up right at eye level. I glance over at it and see Sierra's name.

I lean down so the blonde—who has a name, I'm sure, but I didn't retain it—can hear me. Her hair smells like coconut when I want it to smell like strawberries. My nose accidentally brushes along the side of her cheekbone on my mouth's way to her ear, and I see her eyes flutter shut. "I'll be right back."

She glances over at me, eyes wide open now. "Okay," she says, but her smile looks forced, like she can't believe I'm leaving her on the dance floor by herself. She could have had any guy in this bar and she knows it, but she chose me. At one time, that would have made me feel powerful. Instead, I feel slightly guilty that I've snagged a prize I don't really want.

I nod to Lance as I head over toward the floor-to-ceiling windows at the front of the bar, where there's a little more room to breathe. My watch buzzes a second time, and I pull my phone out to see two messages from Sierra.

> **SIERRA**
> I could have used your tour guide-level expertise tonight.
>
> **SIERRA**
> I wish you were here.

The first text is playful and fun, but the second has me wondering if she means it, or if she's just drunk. My finger hovers over her phone number as I look around for the bathroom, because I figure that's the only place in here quiet enough that I'll be able to hear her voice.

Luckily, it's empty when I enter. One ring and she answers. "Beau, hi!"

"Hey, everything okay?" I lean back against the tiled wall by the paper towel dispensers, my knee bent and my foot propped against the wall so nothing but my shoulders are touching it.

"Everything's great," she says, but the enthusiasm sounds forced. In the background I can hear a pop song remixed with a techno beat. "Sydney and Joe, and Luke and Georgia—that's Joe's brother and sister-in-law—are dancing," she yells. "But I've been the fifth wheel all night and my feet are killing me. . ."

"I give great foot massages," I tell her and she groans.

"Now I *really* wish you were here. I can't dance anymore, I'm headed back to my room."

"Whoa," I say, suddenly very alert. "Did you tell your sister you're leaving? You shouldn't be going alone."

"She knows. We're at a club *in* our hotel. I'm just headed out to the lobby and then up to my room. I'm not wandering around Vegas alone."

"I'm staying on the phone with you until I know you're safe in your room," I say. She doesn't sound drunk—no slurred words or inexplicable laughter or lost trains of thought—but I still want to know she arrived there safely.

"Sure." The sound of the music on her end fades, so I assume she's left the club. "I'm stopping and taking my heels off. My feet can't take one more second in these shoes. I wish you were offering that foot message in person. Where are you, anyway?" she asks right as someone pushes the bathroom door opens and music floods the small room. I nod at the guy as he passes me and heads straight to the urinals.

"I'm at a bar downtown with Lance and Drew."

"Why *did* you call?" she asks, sounding both hopeful and curious.

"Just wanted to hear your voice." It's true, and it sounds better than *I wanted to make sure you weren't wishing I was there because you're hammered.*

"I'm glad." She sighs. "I'm so used to seeing you every day."

On her end I can hear the elevator ding, and realize she wasn't kidding about not having far to go to get back to her room. I glance at my watch. It's almost midnight here, which means it's not quite eleven there. "You didn't expect to miss me this much, did you?" I tease.

"I really didn't." Her answer surprises me. "I wish you'd come with me."

"I wish you'd invited me," I say before I can think better of it.

"I should have," she says. She pauses for a second, then tells me, "I didn't want to make it weird."

"Why would it be weird?" I ask, walking away from the sinks as urinal guy washes his hands. It's not that I don't know the answer, I just want to hear her say it. I need the reminder that I'm not the guy for her, because when I'm around her, it's hard to remember that we make no sense together. That she's better off without me—and for the first time ever, I care more about that than about the instant gratification of a night in her bed.

"You know why, Beau," she says. Her voice is low and sensual, and I her to use that voice every time she says my name from now until forever. *Shit, these feelings are too much, and way too soon.* "But I really wish you were here now."

"So you've mentioned." I hope she can hear the smile in my voice.

Through the phone, I hear a door open and shut. "I'm back in my room, by the way."

"Good. What's your hotel room number?"

"Why?" she asks.

"I'm going to have something delivered tomorrow that'll help you have a better weekend."

"Is it a stripper?" She laughs.

"That wasn't the plan, no."

"One of those foot massage chairs? I could use one of those right now."

"Also no."

"Ooh, I know!"

"No"—I chuckle—"you really don't."

"Can't I even guess?" She sounds like she's pouting.

"You can, but I need to get out of this bathroom and as soon as I walk back out into the bar, I won't be able to hear all your ridiculous ideas about this delivery."

"Okay, I'll let you go then. Oh, and my room number is twenty-six fifteen."

"Your weekend will get better," I say, praying I'm right about this. "I promise."

"Thanks. And Beau, for what it's worth, I miss you."

Is that a fucking lump in my throat? I look in the mirror, expecting to see someone else looking back and me. But no, same old Beau. Except this version of him gets choked up when a girl says she misses him. "Miss you too," I say, my throat thick. "Have a good night." I hang up the phone before I do something crazy like make promises I can't keep.

I head out to the bar, find Drew at our table, and tell him I'm leaving. "Minor family emergency," I tell him. It's half true since Sierra is almost more a member of my family than I am. "I'm headed out of town for the weekend."

"What? Is everything okay?" he sits up, leaning away from the girl who's snuggled into his side.

"It will be. Don't worry, nothing major. I'll see you next week." I grab my jacket before he can ask too many questions and head outside. I have a very short window of time to pull this all off. My adrenaline is pumping and I know I need to do this before I have time to stop and question whether it's a good idea.

Because in the back of my mind, I know it's either the best or the worst idea I've ever had. And only Sierra will be able to determine which is right.

Chapter Fifteen

SIERRA

I spit the last of the toothpaste in the sink, still mentally chastising myself for texting Beau last night. I'd been up half the night thinking about how I'd only had two drinks, not enough to blame the texts or what I said during our call on the alcohol. I'd just missed him and wished he were here with literally every fiber of my being—not only because I was the only one going back to my hotel room alone last night, but because I knew that when I woke up in the morning, I wouldn't be starting my day with the friendly banter I'd grown used to. There'd be no Beau in nothing but his gray sweats eating peanut butter toast in my kitchen before heading to the mountain with his snowboard. Or actually, there would be, but I wouldn't be there to see it.

You should have just invited him. Is that Petra's voice or Sydney's in my head? It doesn't matter, the voice is right nonetheless. Or is it? If I had invited him, and something happened between us, how would I deal with that? It's like I told Petra—I don't want to risk my friendship with Jackson or the potential heartbreak when he leaves. After only two weeks of living together, it's already going to be hard enough when he leaves. If something were happening between us, that would only make it harder.

A knock sounds on my door and I set my toothbrush in the glass next to the bathroom sink and wipe my mouth on my towel. Thankfully, breakfast has arrived quickly—I'm starving. I grab the cash for the tip, then unlock and swing open the hotel room door.

Holy hell. "You're not room service," I sputter, wishing I'd changed out of my pajamas after my shower. Beau stands there in well-fitted jeans and a light sweater, his dark hair is combed and styled and a couple days' worth of facial hair neatly trimmed. He's unbelievably hot in sweats with messy hair and scruff, but I'd forgotten how gorgeous he is when he's all cleaned up.

He smiles back at me. "I know you're going to think I'm crazy for showing up like this. But that call last night made me think about how Vegas is always a good idea."

You're always a good idea, I almost say. No. No, no, nooo. Beau is *not* a good idea. He's the antithesis of a good idea. He's a good time. What I need is Mr. Right, but Beau can only be Mr. Right Now.

He's definitely the wrong kind of right.

"You're freaking out right now," he says, his eyes evaluating me closely. "Should I not have come?"

I glance down at his suitcase. "No, I'm glad you did." I let out the smile that's been stifled by my surprise. "I'm glad you're here." I step back to let him in, reminding myself not to make it awkward. But how can this not be awkward, I wonder, as I glance at the king bed in the middle of the room.

"Are you sure?" he asks as he tentatively steps inside.

I place my hand on his chest, then look at it because I'm afraid that if I look at his face I'll kiss him. In my hotel room. And I think we both know where that'll lead. "I'm positive. Surprised . . . but positive."

"Good," he says decisively, and he takes my hand in his and pulls me into the room. "Because not only am I here to make sure you have a good weekend and take full advantage of Vegas, but I also come bearing gifts."

He stops at the foot of the bed, tells me to sit, then reaches down and unzips the outer pocket of his suitcase. "For your feet," he says, handing me a pack of the gel liners that go under the balls of your feet.

"Oh, you are a godsend," I tell him as I take the package and hug it to my chest, thinking about the black peep-toe suede booties I intend to wear this evening. "These will come in handy tonight."

"Also," he says as he reaches into a bag looped over the handle of his suitcase, "I brought the appropriate supplies for a night or two of partying. For hydration," he says as he pulls out four big bottles of Gatorade and lines them up on the dresser. "For hangovers"—he takes out a small bottle of Advil—"for enough energy to get through the night"—he sets a four-pack of energy drinks on the dresser—"and so you don't have bloodshot eyes for the wedding tomorrow," he says as he takes out a small bottle of eye drops.

"So prepared," I murmur. "Like a Boy Scout, but for partying." I glance at the supplies lining the dresser, still too embarrassed to meet his eyes. Did I make him feel like he had to come here and rescue me from being the fifth wheel?

He laughs, and I'm struck by how much his real smile—not the cocky smirk he's always sporting on TV and social media, but the one I see sometimes in private—is like Jackson's. In different ways, I think they both have the outward intensity of their father, and the inner softness of their mother. There was so much love and laughter and fun in their house growing up, something I noticed as an outsider who got to drop in to their family on weekends but that I'm sure was just so normal to them. Now, as adults, they both keep their masks on—each a different form of indifference—but when they let down the facade, it's spectacular. I wonder if they have any idea how alike they are in this way?

"So," Beau says as he pushes his suitcase between the dresser and the wall, "what are your plans for today, and how can I make them more fun?"

"Well, Sydney, Georgia, and I have appointments at the spa at two. I have nothing I need to do until then. Except eat breakfast whenever room service gets here."

"What did you order us?" he winks.

"Oh no, you're going to be like *that*?"

"Teasing," he says. "I've eaten like three times already today. But hey, do you mind if I catch a quick shower and wash off all the travel grime?"

If this is his travel-weary look, we're in trouble. "Of course not."

Once he's ensconced in the bathroom, I grab my phone and shoot Sydney a text.

SIERRA

Holy crap. Beau is IN my hotel room right now.

SYDNEY

You just woke me up with this info and my
brain is not processing it. What???

SIERRA

I talked to him last night after I left the club.
And I may have let it slip that I wish I'd invited
him to come with me. And I may have found
him knocking on my door about five minutes
ago.

SYDNEY

OMG, OMG, OMG! He is right there, and
you're texting with me?

SIERRA

No, he's in the shower.

SYDNEY

Girl, go get naked with him.

SIERRA

LOL. I don't think he's here for that.

I sink onto the chair in front of the window, thinking
about how normal it felt for him to be here with me, after the
initial shock of seeing him at my door wore off. It was
friendly as usual, with even less sexual tension than normal.

SYDNEY

If you think he flew to Vegas to see you with
no hope of sex, you're lying to yourself. And I
happen to know you have a king bed in your
room, so . . . 😉

SIERRA

Things are totally normal between us
right now.

SYDNEY

Yeah, if your 'normal' involves having a hot guy in your hotel room, who came to Vegas just to see you, we're living VERY different lives.

I pause before responding. I mean, it *is* a little above and beyond. But he also loves Vegas, so there's that.

SIERRA

Okay, *maybe* that's not normal.

SYDNEY

Just promise to tell me how good the sex is?

I groan as I read her message, because my and Beau's friendship *cannot* cross that line.

"What's wrong?" Beau asks from across the room. His brow is furrowed as he stands there with a bath towel wrapped around his waist. *Holy shit, I live with the man, how have I not seen this sight before?* His skin glistens, condensed steam like glitter across the defined muscles of his chest. His damp hair is curled forward onto his forehead and his dark eyes look . . . concerned? Consumed with passion? I'm not sure I trust myself to tell the difference at this point.

"N-nothing," I stutter, and watch as he grabs his suitcase, sets it on the end of the bed, unzips it, and grabs a small leather bag along with some new boxers and a clean T-shirt. "Just texting with Sydney."

He glances over. "Everything okay?"

"Yeah, she's just . . . a tiny bit hungover." That sounds believable.

"Maybe we should get her some Gatorade too?"

See, totally just a friendly thing that he showed up and brought you a Vegas survival kit. He even wants to get supplies for your sister. That makes me feel better.

"I'm sure she'd appreciate that," I say.

His eyes lock onto mine and the space starts to feel smaller. It feels like we're being pulled together, even though I'm still seated and his feet are planted in place at the end of the bed. Every cell in my body feels like it's being dragged toward him. Neither one of us blinks, and I swallow to get the lump out of my throat, but it doesn't work. Beau opens his mouth like he's going to say something, but a sharp knock on the door has us both startled out of whatever that was.

"You okay getting that?" he asks as he turns back toward the bathroom.

I clear my throat. "Of course."

Once my food is wheeled over to the chairs by the window and the delivery guy has left, I take a seat, digging into the eggs and bacon like a person who hasn't eaten in days. The coffee is kind of stale, but I need the caffeine badly, so I take a few gulps. I've devoured half my breakfast when Beau walks out of the bathroom in the same dark jeans he was wearing earlier. A thin white T-shirt clings to his chest, and his sweater is draped over his arm. His hair has some sort of product in it that holds it in place, and . . . damn, why does he have to look so good?

My whole body is like *Yes, girl, I'm here for this!* I'm relieved that my short-sleeve pajama top is made out of sweatshirt material, because I can feel my nipples pebbling against the fleece and I'm hoping that he can't see them. Shit, I'm going to have to wear a bra all the time now that he's here.

"How's the coffee?" he asks.

"Mediocre." I cross my arms over my chest, hoping that

hides my body's reaction to him.

"How about I go find us some of the good stuff while you get ready?"

"What am I getting ready for, exactly?"

"Have you ever been to Venice?"

"Nope."

"Well, the Venetian is about as close as you can get without flying to Italy. Let's start there."

"Start?"

"Yeah, your Vegas tour begins in—"he glances at his watch"—half an hour." Then he slides his sweater over his head, shoves his wallet and phone in his pocket, and is out the door.

———

"Well, it's official," Georgia says as she glances up from her phone. "Luke is totally fangirling over Beau right now."

"What?" I laugh as I sling my purse over my shoulder.

"Yeah, apparently he and Joe went to your hotel room and introduced themselves, and they've all been in the casino together while we've been getting pampered."

"That's so nice of them to include him," I say. I had envisioned Beau being bored out of his mind this afternoon while I went with the girls to get a massage and a mani-pedi. Either that, or out creating his own fun without me, which was not something I wanted to spend much time imagining.

"Luke is having a moment right now. He's a huge fan of Beau's."

Between us, Sydney fake coughs as she spits out, "Who

isn't?"

I ignore her and look over to Georgia as we walk out of the spa. "Like, because of snowboarding? Or just because they're having fun together?"

She sweeps her long platinum-blond hair over her shoulder. "Both. I think this is one of those instances of meeting someone you've only ever seen on TV and finding out they're as cool in person as you hoped they'd be."

"Wow, I didn't realize Luke followed snowboarding."

"Oh yeah, we're actually both big snowboarders. We go over to Big Bear all the time in the winter, or up to Mammoth if we have a long weekend. In fact, that's where we would have been this weekend if Sydney and Joe hadn't decided to tie the knot."

"I'm so glad you guys gave up your long weekend to be here. But back to the whole Beau thing . . ." Sydney says and turns toward me.

I really don't want to talk about Beau. I already updated them on our mini-Vegas tour where he took me on a gondola ride at the Venetian, to the botanical garden at the Bellagio, and then on the High Roller observation wheel. By the end of our half hour on the High Roller, I was standing snuggled back against him with his arms wrapped around me and his entire body cradling mine. That sense of closeness—it was intoxicating.

The past few hours at the spa have been exactly what I needed to get some physical distance between us and remind myself that this can't happen.

"Oh," Georgia says as she glances up from her phone, saving me from having to say anything else about Beau. "Luke says they want us to meet them in the casino."

"Well, tell them that we need to shower and get ready first. I mean, I'm not going to the casino covered in oil from the massage!" Sydney insists.

"Okay," Georgia says, "it's almost five. Why don't we go get ready for dinner and plan to meet them downstairs in an hour?"

Ugh. It'll take me half an hour just to dry all this hair and curl it. I hate being rushed. But Sydney and Georgia seem fine with an hour, and I don't want to be the difficult one. So when I get off at my floor, I hurry to my room and take the quickest shower I can manage while still shaving my legs. As always, drying my thick hair is a labor-intensive and hot experience, and I'm relieved that Beau is down in the casino with the guys, so at least I don't have to put a shirt on. I stand there in my lace boy shorts, trying to cool down as I do my makeup in the bathroom mirror, then use my curling wand to make loose curls throughout my hair. I've got some upbeat music playing on my phone to keep me moving at a steady pace, and when I'm done with my hair, I see that I've got less than ten minutes to get dressed and get downstairs. I rush out of the bathroom and turn toward the closet, coming face-to-face with Beau. The hotel room door slams shut right behind him.

For a second we stand there, eyes locked, not moving. Then he flicks his eyes down my body and growls out my name. He sounds incredibly annoyed.

"Oh my God," I breathe the words out as my hands fly to my breasts. He looks away. "I'm sorry. I thought you were down in the casino."

Beau turns away from me and opens the closet door, grabbing one of the terrycloth robes and holding it open in front of me. I turn and slide my arms in, and the second the robe pushes over my shoulders he's stepping as far away from me as possible in the small entryway to our hotel room.

I tie the belt around the robe, both relieved that he's given me something to cover up with and also disappointed that he didn't pull me to him, ready to explore my body. *He doesn't see you that way; you're like a big sister to him.* Except even as I try to convince myself that this is true, it's not consistent with how he looks at me.

"I came up to change," he says, and it's like he's grinding the words out through clenched teeth.

"Looks like we both had the same idea," I say with a level of confidence I certainly don't feel. I turn to face him, look him straight in the eye as I remind myself that there's no reason to be embarrassed. Sure, my superhot roommate just saw my boobs, but I'm guessing he's seen hundreds of pairs of them before. Maybe thousands. Since he's clearly had no reaction to seeing mine, it's obviously no big deal. Except that it is, in the sense that he's one of a handful of people to have ever seen this set.

"Let me grab my dress from the closet," I say when he still hasn't spoken. "I'll get dressed in the bathroom and you can get dressed out here."

"Okay," he says, his voice thick in a way I can't decipher.

I grab the dress on the hanger, slip back into the bathroom, and breathe a sigh of relief when the door is firmly shut between us. After hanging the dress on the door hook, I turn and look at myself in the mirror as I try to quantify what I'm feeling right now. My cheeks are flushed from both the embarrassment and the exhilaration of Beau seeing me practically naked. My underwear is damp and every nerve ending in my skin is humming with anticipation. I give my body an internal talk, reminding it that like so many other decisions in life, just because it *feels* like a good idea doesn't mean it is.

I slip into the black skater dress I borrowed from Petra and reach behind me to pull up the zipper. It's low-cut enough that you get an eyeful of my cleavage, with thin straps that go over my shoulders and cross in the back. The only reason I can wear this dress without a bra is because it's got built-in cups under the fabric and a structured waist that goes up to the chest. The skirt flutters out from my hips and while short, it still covers my upper thighs. I look and feel sexy in this dress, which made it the perfect Vegas dress . . . until Beau arrived. Now I'm half afraid of how he's going to look at me when I walk out of this room.

I crack open the door and ask if he's decent.

"I'm wearing more than just my underwear," he says dryly.

"Hardy har." I step out and find him standing there in dark gray wash jeans and a fitted black short-sleeve shirt. He's wearing black shoes and a black blazer. He's the perfect blend of casual and dressy, and holy shit does he look hot.

He barely looks at me as I walk into the room; he definitely doesn't look like he wants to devour me. I should be relieved, but instead I feel mildly disappointed.

I sit on the bed as I fit the gel pads into my heeled booties, then slip them onto my feet and stand. I love how tall I am in these shoes, the height gives me more confidence. "You ready?" I ask Beau.

"Yep," he responds, looking up at me finally. Nothing. There is nothing in his eyes, just complete indifference—the same way he'd look at a stranger.

Well, okay. That tells me everything I need to know.

I slide on my cropped leather jacket, then turn and grab

the thin card wallet that I've already stuffed with my license, room key, credit card, and cash. "Here," Beau says, "why don't you let me keep that in my front pocket with my wallet so you don't lose it."

"Why would I lose it?" I'm annoyed at the suggestion that I can't take care of myself.

"I assume you aren't going to wear that jacket all night, plus those pockets don't have zippers, which would make it really easy for that wallet to fall out, or someone to take it out."

What he's saying makes a lot of sense, so even though I don't like the idea of having to rely on him every time I need money, I go ahead and hand my wallet over to him with a grumbled "Okay. Thanks."

"Hey," he says gently, grabbing my wrist as I go to pull my hand back, "what's wrong?"

Little flashes of electricity are prickling my skin where his fingers meet my wrist, and the heat is spreading pleasantly through my body. Does he feel it too? "Nothing," I say, looking down at my feet.

He uses his free hand to tilt my chin up so he's looking me in the eye. "Is this because I walked in on you when you were changing? I'm sorry about that. I don't want it to make things awkward between us."

The only thing that's awkward right now is how badly I want him, and how unreciprocated that feeling is.

"It's fine. I'm sure you see girls' boobs all the time."

"Not like that I don't." Before I have a moment to even consider what he means by that, he's putting his hand on my lower back, turning and guiding me toward the door with a mumbled "Let's go."

Chapter Sixteen

BEAU

This. Is. Fucking. Torture.

I didn't think this whole plan through, and this is what I get for flying to Vegas on a whim to stay with someone I'm insanely attracted to, but who is all wrong for me—I get blue balls.

From the moment I walked in on her in that lace underwear a few hours ago, I haven't been able to get that picture out of my mind. Her body is perfect. Soft and curvy in all the right places. And all I want is to touch her, to make her feel good, to worship that body like it deserves to be worshiped.

Except, she made it clear when I showed up at her hotel room door this morning that she only sees us as friends. I had hoped she'd jump into my arms when I showed up at her door (however unlikely I knew that was), but she seems intent on pretending that this is just friendship. A guy doesn't hop on a plane and show up at your hotel room because he's a good friend. But whatever. We can play this game if it's what she needs.

I came here to help her have a better weekend, and even

though sex would *obviously* make this weekend better, she doesn't seem inclined to go there. With the exception of the thirty minutes on the High Roller observation wheel where she curled back into my chest—and only because she's scared of heights—she's been nothing but platonic.

When we made it down to the casino floor and met up with the rest of the group, her sister and Georgia were already there. Joe and Luke gave me a knowing smirk when I arrived with my hand on Sierra's lower back, but I just gave them a small shake of my head. They'd been grilling me all afternoon, insisting that I wouldn't have flown in and surprised her unless something was going on between us. But she'd shown me that wasn't what she wanted, and I thought I'd managed to convince the guys there was nothing but friendship there. But when they saw us arrive together, they weren't buying it. Even though Sierra immediately ditched me to stand next to her sister and Georgia, even though she never once touched me while the guys and I sat there and played Black Jack, not even when I won a really nice payout.

Right now, the six of us are sitting in a big round booth finishing up dinner. Sierra's next to me on the end, and so that she can see and talk to everyone, she has her entire body angled toward me, the knees of her crossed legs resting against my thigh—and she has no idea what it is doing to my body. She's more relaxed now that she's had a couple drinks, and she's close enough that I feel her phone vibrate in the pocket of her jacket.

She pulls her phone out while Georgia tells an animated story about living in Los Angeles, and Sierra's deep sigh has me turning toward her. Without even looking at me, she holds the phone for me to see the photo on her screen. Heather has sent her a picture of Winston chewing on a bone.

"Is it stupid that I miss the little devil?" she whispers.

Her head has made its way to my shoulder, so I rest my cheek against her hair. "Nope. He's pretty damn lovable. But it doesn't mean you shouldn't have a good time while you're here." I don't mention that she also needs to get used to life without him, since eventually he'll get adopted.

The picture on her screen is replaced by a notification that Sydney is sending her a photo. She taps to accept it, and her screen is filled with a picture of us, looking down at the phone. Her head rests on my shoulder and her lower lip protrudes in the sweetest pouty face, and my face is mostly obscured as we look down at her phone.

We both glance over and Sydney, who gives us a wink. Georgia's still telling her story, so I whisper to Sierra, "You should post that. Caption it something about us missing him."

"I feel like that will just inflame our followers even more, make them think something is definitely happening here," she says and I don't know if she even realizes that she's moved her hand to my thigh.

"Then let them think so. If it gets more people paying attention to Winston, who cares?"

I feel a little head nod against my cheek. She opens the app and chooses the photo, then types out the caption *My humans are in Vegas for a wedding. When my dog sitter sends pictures, they sure do miss me!*

I tell her it's perfect and she adds a few of the hashtags we always use before she posts it, then she mumbles about how we'll probably regret it.

The only thing I'm going to regret about this weekend is

not being as close to her as I want to be. Because this super-close friends stage that we've found ourselves at is not nearly enough for me. I don't want her physically—I mean, *I do* want her that way, desperately—I want more. And it's such a foreign desire, I don't even know what "more" means for a guy like me.

————

We are at our third bar since dinner and so far Sierra is holding up her end of the sister-of-the-bride bargain. She's made sure Sydney has a glass of water in between each drink, and she's planned our night so we're basically just having one drink at each bar we go to, then walking and getting fresh air in between. Until now, I'd have described Sydney as sober even though she had a couple drinks with dinner and has had a few since.

"Here's to Lemieux women being able to hold their alcohol," Sydney is saying loudly as she reaches over to clink her drink with Sierra's.

Joe told me that Sydney was a hot mess during the blizzard, and even more so when their flight to Vegas was delayed by three hours, but that by the time they finally arrived, she'd calmed down a little. But she's one hundred percent committed to not getting sick before her wedding, so I'm a tad surprised to see her trying to pound back drinks now.

"Yes," Sierra tells her sister with a huge smile, "but you don't want to be hungover tomorrow. Or sick tonight. So we're going to take a break after this drink."

"What kind of break?" Sydney asks. Next to her, Georgia is sitting on Luke's lap and by the way she's gently moving her hips and the look on his face, I imagine she's whispering some downright dirty shit to him.

"Dancing!" Sierra says, nodding toward the packed dance floor.

"Ohh," Sydney squeals. She sets her drink on the table and grabs Sierra with one hand and pulls Georgia off Luke's lap with the other. "Let's dance now."

Before she's pulled away by her sister, Sierra leans up and asks me to convince Joe to take Sydney back to their room soon. I'm sure she doesn't mean to accidentally capture my earlobe in her lips before she's dragged away by her sister.

"Holy crap, I need to get my wife up to our hotel room soon, or we're going to end up having sex in public," Luke says as he crosses his ankle over his knee and adjusts himself.

"Wouldn't be the first time," Joe says.

"Yeah, but I'm not looking to get arrested tonight. Talk about ruining your wedding. Nope, we're all here to make sure it happens as planned. Which means after this song, I am taking Georgia straight back to the hotel."

"Funny," I say, "Sierra just asked me to have Joe take Sydney back to their room too."

Joe glances over at where Sydney is dancing in her short white dress with her Bride To Be sash falling off her shoulder and her light brown hair flowing around her as she moves to the beat. Another thing about Lemieux women—they can dance.

"I think you just want to get Sierra back to *your* hotel room," Joe says.

He's not wrong. But also, he is. I want to stay out, dance with Sierra, and have time to hang out with her without everyone else watching and trying to figure out what's going on between us. I know that if we headed back to the hotel room now, it'll be awkward, especially with our sleeping arrangement. That bed's big, but not big enough for me to forget we're in it together.

"No, Sierra and I are staying out. But I think you'd be crazy not to take your wife and future wife," I say, nodding to each of them individually, "back to your hotel rooms before they're too drunk."

"You're not just trying to get my future sister-in-law drunk and take advantage of her without us here to stop you, right?" Joe says.

"Dude, *really*? Not only am I *not* trying to take advantage of her, I'm trying to make sure she doesn't make any stupid decisions this weekend either."

Joe nods. "Just had to make sure."

Luke turns and nods toward the girls as the song changes. "I'm going to go get Georgia," he says to Joe. "You coming?"

Joe finishes the last of his beer and then stands. "Take good care of Sierra," he says to me.

"I will," I assure him, then I grab her drink and mine and follow them to the dance floor.

When Sydney and Georgia turn to follow Joe and Luke, Sierra looks at me and nods toward the front of the bar like we're leaving too. I step right in front of her and lean my head down to her. "We're staying," I tell her as I hand her the drink.

"Really?" her eyes light up. "You finally going to dance with me?"

"I didn't know you'd been waiting for me to."

"Only since Jackson's wedding," she says, slinging one hand over my shoulder and taking a sip of her drink with the other.

"I'd hate to disappoint you then," I say, stepping even closer to her.

An hour later, our bodies are connected at the hips. She's a phenomenal dancer and there's no part of her that hasn't rubbed up against some part of me at this point in the night. Her skin glistens with sweat, minuscule beads of it across her chest and over her shoulders and down her spine. I want to dip my head and drag my tongue up her neck.

If she was some girl I'd met at a bar, there'd be no question that she is coming home with me and we are getting naked together. Tonight, the first part is a given. But does the seduction of her dance moves mean she wants to fuck me, or is she just having fun because she sees me as "safe"?

When the song ends, I wrap my arm around her lower back, anchoring her to me. She glances up at my face, and with her heels on, she hardly has to tilt her head back to look me in the eye. She's out of breath, gently panting tiny gasps of air that hit my lips like a caress. Her big brown eyes are so alive with exhilaration and happiness, and as I stare into them, I feel like I'm drowning. She's leaning into me, but I don't want a drunken kiss on the dance floor to ruin our friendship, or whatever this is, so I insist we get some water and I hold her hand as I pull her behind me toward the bar.

There's very little space there, but she wedges herself into an opening between two barstools. The guy to her left looks over at her with open appreciation, so I come up behind her and rest my hands on either side of her body, boxing her in and giving him a "back the fuck off" look.

I lean down to ask her if she wants water or something else, and when I do, she presses her ass back into me. It's innocent enough that it might have been an accident, but then when she feels how hard I am against her, she looks over her shoulder at me, raises an eyebrow, and tilts her hips so her ass runs along the length of me. I groan into her ear as I rest my chest against her shoulder. "You're killing me."

"I highly doubt that," she says, as she brings her hand behind her and to caress my abs through my thin T-shirt, her fingers running lightly over each individual muscle.

My hips press forward into her involuntarily right as the bartender approaches. "Two bottles of water please," I say as I reach into my pocket for my wallet. I slap down a twenty, grab the two bottles in one hand, and wrap my hand around Sierra's lower back as I guide her toward the exit.

"Where are we going?" she asks, leaning into me when we stop at the coat check.

"To our room." I hand her one of the water bottles.

She looks down at it as she twists the cap, and over the music I barely hear her say "We should probably talk about that."

"We can talk when we get there," I tell her.

———

The cool desert air is a welcome relief on our overheated skin. We walk in silence for a block with Sierra tucked under my arm as we take in the lights, but then the cold night air sends shivers over her body and we stop in front of the fountains at the Bellagio to put our jackets on. I've always thought of Vegas as dirty, a little seedy, fun in an ostentatious way. But walking along the crowded streets with all the lights and a little buzz, with Sierra pressed up against me, it feels romantic.

When we get back to our hotel, I toss our empty water bottles in the trash and as we stand waiting for the elevator with my arm wrapped around her shoulders, I start playing with her hair. Her arm's been wrapped around my waist, and now her fingers dip between my T-shirt and jeans to find my skin. She drags her nails lightly across my lower back and over my hip bone before the pads of her fingers run along the waistband of my jeans. Every part of my skin feels electrified, the heat of her touch spreading through me.

We step onto the elevator alone and after pressing the button for our floor, I turn toward her at the same time she turns to me. As her arms encircle my neck, I can't help but respond—even though I said we were going to talk and we certainly haven't yet. Her lips meet mine in an explosion of lust and passion, our mouths opening and her tongue slanting against mine. This is no gentle first kiss, it's the precursor to something much more. I've barely started to explore her mouth when the elevator bell dings to let us know we're at our floor, and she grabs me by my belt buckle and walks backward, pulling me out of the elevator. It's the sexiest and most un-Sierra thing I've ever seen.

In the hallways I kiss her again, gently this time, my lips taking time to get to know hers. They are exactly as kissable as I first imagined. "C'mon," she says, taking my hand and leading me down the hallway.

I laugh and tell her she's going the wrong way, then I lead us to our door. We both stand there and look at it for a second, knowing that when we cross that threshold, things will probably change. Hell, they already have changed.

Sierra glances up at me. "You have both our keys."

I let us in, and the second the door is closed, she's got her arms wrapped around my neck again. I turn us so her back is against the wall and she wraps one of her legs around my waist. I push into her, locking her in place with my hips. She rocks hers against me, clearly enjoying the friction.

I give her a chaste kiss on the nose. "Okay, talk."

"We can talk later," she mumbles, her voice thick with longing as she puts her hand on the back of my head to bring my lips to hers.

I pull my head back, but keep my body pressed up against hers, enjoying the feel of her soft breasts against my chest and the way her hips haven't stopped thrusting against mine. "No, we talk first, so we don't fuck this up. You know how badly I want you, right?"

"I do *now*."

I furrow my eyebrows. "Was there ever any doubt?"

"You're so hot and cold. Half the time, it feels like you're trying to push me away."

"Because I'm not what you want," I say. I think it's important that we establish that now, before this goes any further. I can't be the kind of guy she's looking for.

"Really? Do tell me—what is it I want?" Her voice is teasing and sarcastic at the same time.

"Stability. Companionship. Forever."

"Maybe that's not what I want *right now*. You're only around for another week, Beau. I'm not deluding myself that this will last longer than that."

"And you're okay with that?"

"I'll take what I can get while you're still here," she says, trailing her fingers through my hair and teasing my scalp with her nails.

In any other situation ever, these are the exact words I'd

need to hear before taking a woman to bed. So why do they feel so wrong coming out of Sierra's mouth? She doesn't seem to care if I stay or if I go, and that bothers me.

"What is that look?" she asks.

Shit.

"I'm just worried we're going to mess up our friendship," I say, hoping that's believable.

"Beau, this is already past friendship," she says, and rocks her hips against me again just to prove her point, "at least, for me it is. If you don't feel the same way—"

My mouth crashes into hers, because of course I feel the same way, and I'd be an idiot to let this moment pass. There's no way I could. I've known since we were dancing at the bar that we were leading up to this, and it's what I've fantasized about for weeks.

Her kisses are insistent and when my hands move from her hips down to cup her ass, she uses the leg that's wrapped around my hips to anchor me to her.

"I need this jacket off you," I tell her, and she unwraps her leg from my waist, sliding the jacket off her shoulders. I slide mine off and throw it on the edge of the bed, then reach behind her, capturing her wrists behind her in one of my hands, admiring how her breasts protrude when her shoulders are back like this. I use my teeth to slide the strap of her dress off her shoulder, but the dress is too tight across her chest and doesn't fall away from her breast like I'm hoping.

She senses my frustration because she frees her hands from my grasp and reaches up to pull at the zipper at her back. The entire dress falls to her hips, and with one small tug from her, it pools at her feet. I take a step back to pull my shirt over my head and get a good look at her.

"Holy shit, Sierra," I say on an exhale, one big long sigh. Somehow she's even more gorgeous now than she was when she walked out of the bathroom in nothing but that damn lacy underwear earlier this evening. I let my eyes track down her entire body. It's probably the way her sweat-dampened skin glistens in the low light of the room and the way those damn heels give her at least an extra three inches and make her legs look impossibly long.

I step toward her and she puts her hands on my bare shoulders and fixes her eyes on my lips. But I don't kiss her again, instead I take a moment to appreciate how the stream of light shining through the crack in the curtains illuminates her body, the way her silky hair is highlighted by the light, the way I can see her heart pounding in her chest and her pulse at the base of her neck.

I take my hands and run them along her sides slowly, from her armpits down to her hips, letting the heels of my hands gently skim the sides of her breasts. She shivers and arches her back with a soft grunt, and I can't resist her any longer. I cup my hands under her breasts reverently. "You have the most perfect breasts I've ever seen," I tell her.

"Let's not be thinking about anyone else's breasts right now, huh?" she chides.

"Pretty sure I'll never think about any but yours for the rest of my life."

She lets out a small, throaty laugh, but I'm not joking. Sierra is in my head in a way that no other woman ever has been. I brush my thumbs across her nipples and watch as she arches her back further, pushing her body into mine. I dip my head down, letting my tongue lave over her nipple, then circling it with the tip of my tongue.

My name slips off her lips, and it's part gasp, part sigh. It's a hundred times sexier than the way she said my name last night on the phone and I've changed my mind—*this* is the only way I want her to say my name from here on out. I suck her into my mouth and her hands are at my buckle, fumbling to loosen the belt, then she's got the button and zipper undone and is pushing my jeans to the floor. I toe off my shoes and step out of my pants without letting my mouth or my hands leave her body.

She grips my shaft through my underwear and I about come undone right there. "Bed," I say against her breast and the vibrations give her goose bumps. I sweep her up into my arms and take the few steps into the room until I'm standing at the end of the bed with her. I set her down with her legs hanging off the end, and bend forward to kiss her, pressing her back onto the bed with the weight of my body. I trail kisses from her lips, down her throat, between her breasts, then down to her belly button. I don't stop until I get to her panties.

I kneel in front of her and dip my fingertips into the waistband of these lace boy shorts, visions of which have driven me crazy half the night. I drag them slowly off her, reveling in her beauty, her creamy skin, her smooth legs, the perfectly manicured V of curls above the folds between her legs. When I get the underwear to her ankles and slip them off, I sweep her legs up over my shoulders and bring my face to her center. I gently nip the inside of each thigh, and she sighs my name as I drag my tongue from her clit right down the center of her folds. Her hips piston toward my tongue, and I love how responsive she is.

"Tell me what you need," I say, looking at her across the expanse of her flat stomach and over the curve of her breasts.

"This," she murmurs.

I circle her clit a few more times, then pull back. "Look at me," I insist, and she lifts her upper body and props herself up on her elbows. "Tell me what you need, specifically. What do you like?"

Her eyes flare. "I don't know, Beau. Just keep doing what you're doing."

I fasten my lips around her clit and suck hard, sending her hips flying up again, her fists grabbing the sheets. Then I lift my head and ask, "What do you mean you don't know?"

"I mean, what you're doing is perfect."

"I'm going to make you come, this first time, with my mouth. And I need to know how you like it."

She lets her head fall back to the bed. "I don't know."

How does this woman not know what she prefers when it comes to oral sex? I get up from the floor and slide my body along hers until we're face-to-face. "Sierra, why do you not know what you like?"

She closes her eyes and swallows, a movement that has my eyes hyper-focused on that creamy expanse of her throat.

"Has no one ever done this to you before?" I ask, even though it seems absolutely impossible.

She opens her eyes and looks at me. "Not trying to think about other people right now, Beau," she says dryly. "But no one has done this to me half as well as what you were just doing."

A smile plays on my lips. "That was just the warm-up act."

She swats my shoulder, the sound is a loud crack in our quiet hotel room. "Don't let this go to your head."

"Too late," I say and kiss the tip of her nose. "You can't tell me that I'm doing this better than anyone else you've been with and not expect it to inflate my ego." I reach up and pull two pillows down from the head of the bed, then reach under her back to prop her up on them. "I want you to watch. And I want you to talk to me. Tell me what feels good, tell me what you want me to do."

I can see the heat creeping across her chest and up her neck. So, she's not used to asking for what she wants . . . that's interesting. In my teenage fantasies, Sierra was much more knowledgeable about sex than I was. In my dreams of late, she's always known what she wanted and taken it. It's unsettling to see her so unsure; it's not a turnoff, it's just unexpected.

I slide back down, squatting between her legs and pulling her knees up over my shoulders. Keeping my eyes on her, I set out to give her the best orgasm she's ever had. It takes less than a minute before she's writhing beneath my mouth. "Like this?"

"Yes," she says, and closes her eyes.

I reach two fingers up to her mouth and she pulls them in, alternatively sucking and twirling her tongue around them. It's impossible to describe how much I'm looking forward to having that mouth on my cock.

I bring those fingers down and slide them inside her, her tight walls expanding quickly to accept me. I curl my fingers up toward her abdominal wall, searching for those elusive ridges that will bring most women to orgasm. I know I've found the spot by the guttural moan she lets loose, and when my eyes flick up to hers, she's staring at me in shock. "Right there," she says, "don't stop." I love that she's talking to me about what she likes even though I can tell by her body's response.

A few more swirls of my tongue over her clit while I stroke inside her and she's whispering my name like it's a prayer, her hips moving with the motion of my fingers. "I'm so close, Beau," she says and I increase the pressure inside just the slightest bit, stroking over those ridges as she grunts the sexiest little sounds I've ever heard. Those grunts turn to full-out moaning that has me aching to be inside her, but I'm determined to give her as many orgasms as possible tonight, so I don't stop until I feel her muscles contracting around my fingers over and over, her entire body going stiff, then slackening like she's boneless. Only then do I stop and give her one more wet kiss on her clit, and it sends a shudder through her entire body.

I stand and slide my boxer briefs down before stepping out of them. "Holy hell," she says as she stares at my body.

"That better be a good holy hell," I tell her as I lean down over her, using one knee to brace myself over her.

"Aren't you cute, fishing for compliments."

I lean down and claim her smart mouth. I kiss her like I own her, like I want to possess her. It's a need I've never felt before. This is nothing like the kisses I'm used to, which are only a stepping stone to sex, a means to an end. I could kiss her all night, could keep my lips on some part of her body every minute and never get tired of it.

She loops her leg around my lower back, pulling me down to her, and as my body slides against hers, I know I can't wait any longer to be inside of her.

"I need to be closer to you," she says, reaching her hand

between us and grasping me. Her hand is satin as it glides along my sensitive skin. "I want you inside me."

"You're sure?"

She smiles. "Absolutely."

I reach over to the end of the bed and grab a condom out of the inside pocket of my jacket, then kneeling over her, I sweep her and her pillows up to the head of the bed. She still hasn't stopped stroking me, that tight fist sliding up and down my shaft. "If you don't stop that," I tell her, "there isn't going to be any sex. This is going to be quick as it is; I've been hard since you walked out of that bathroom like seven hours ago."

"Sounds painful," she says, giving me a squeeze that has my eyes rolling back in my head, my eyelids closing, and my hips slamming forward into her fist.

I cover her hand with mine. "You can keep doing that, but if you do, I'm going to come all over you."

She quirks her lip up, not at all turned off by my filthy mouth, and says, "Let's save that for the shower." I like this unexpected side of her.

"Let's," I say as I roll the condom on. "But first, I want to feel you from the inside."

Her legs fall open for me, and I take a moment to enjoy the view before I reach down and cup her breasts. They really are perfect—a work of fucking art.

"Beau," she says, warning and pleading evident in her raspy voice as I drag my thumbs across her nipples. "Inside me, now."

I lean in, planting my elbow next to her, and capture those sweet lips in mine. I'm so lost in the way her lips feel on mine, at the way her tongue feels slanting against mine, at the little sounds of pleasure she's making, that I almost forget what I'm doing until she wraps her ankles around my ass, thrusting her hips off the bed to run herself along the length of my dick. She pulls away from the kiss long enough to pant, "Empty. Without. You."

Three words. Three separate sentences. A perfect description of my life.

I'm empty without her.

I pull my hips back and line myself up with her opening as I stare down at her, our faces so close we're sharing one breath. Slowly, I slide into her, my eyes never leaving hers. She's so tight, and wet, and perfect. We fit together like we were meant to be. I want to remember this feeling—the first time I'm sliding into her—forever.

Once I'm fully sheathed inside her, she whispers, "So much better."

Better doesn't even begin to describe this. It's perfection. I bring my lips back to hers as I begin to move inside her, capturing all her moans and sexy little sounds, trying to memorize every single moment of this because it's a million times better than any of my fantasies led me to believe.

I bring one knee up under her thigh to change the angle, needing to be deeper, closer to her. My body is on fire, humming with the electric desire to give her everything I have, to take everything she'll offer, to make this perfect thing between us a real, living experience.

She pulls away from me and sighs out a "Yes" at the change in position, then puts her hands on my chest and gently pushes me away from her. My body screams *no*, even as she locks eyes with me and says, "I want to see you."

I push myself up with one of my arms, so I'm staring down at her as I slide out and then push back in. The way I can now watch as her eyes roll back in her head and she sighs out another "Yes" makes it worth the physical distance. I will never forget this feeling—the way her inner walls are stroking me, the hungry look in her eyes, the need and satisfaction on her face.

It's too much, and I'm too close. I can tell she's building to something, but she's not as close as I am and there's no way I'm getting off without giving her another orgasm first. "I need you to touch yourself," I tell her.

She brings her middle finger to my mouth, and I circle the pad of her finger with my tongue before she slides her hand between us. As she runs her finger over her clit, I can feel the difference—she brings her other knee up and wraps her foot around my ass, thrusting her hips up to meet mine. She's bucking wildly beneath me when she pants "So close."

I can feel her inner walls contract around me, squeezing me impossibly tighter. I'm barely holding on when she moans, and her mouth falls open. She squeezes her eyes shut, her face contorted into a mask of exquisite torture. Then she opens her eyes and locks them on mine. "Beau . . ." My name on her lips is half chant, half scream, and it unravels the last threads of my self-control.

I lean down, my lips covering hers, my mouth absorbing the sounds of her orgasm as it tears through her and milks everything I have out of me. Over and over, the feel of her tightening around me from the inside has me pouring everything I have into her: every ounce of my orgasm, yes, but also every ounce of my self-control, my dignity, my heart.

I've never felt anything like this, ever.

I still inside her, then lift my face from hers, tracing her nose with my own.

"Holy shit," she pants. "That wasn't an orgasm, that was a religious experience."

A smile plays at my lips, but she's too close to see it. "My thoughts exactly," I tell her.

It felt a lot like my chest cracking open and my heart jumping out. I want to ask her if she felt it too, but I'm distracted by the way she's stroking my face with her fingertips and asking, "How soon can we do that again?"

Chapter Seventeen

SIERRA

ive. That's the number of orgasms this man gave me last night and in the early hours of this morning. Two the first time we had sex, one in the shower, and two more when we made it back to the bed. I doubt I've ever had that many in one week, much less over the course of a few hours.

My body is exhausted, slightly sore, and spent in the best way. I glance at the clock on the bedside table. It's 9:00 a.m. I only slept for five hours, and I should still be asleep, but all that damn water I drank last night has me needing to pee. But at least I'm not hungover, and hopefully Sydney isn't either.

Beau's arm is anchored around me like a steel vice. I gently try to scoot out from under it, but he tightens his grip and pulls me back to his chest, murmuring "You're awake?" into my hair.

"Awake, and about to pee my pants," I say, moving to get up.

"You're not wearing pants," he says, kissing the back of my head and holding me tight.

"Beau, you have to let me go or this is going to get ugly."

"So I shouldn't tickle you right now?" he laughs and I scramble up and off the bed so fast it's like I'm running from a cluster of spiders who've invaded the sheets. He chuckles again as I stand there glaring down at him. "Go pee and then hurry back. I already miss you."

I make it to the bathroom just in time, and after I've relieved myself, I brush out my hair, which is kind of crazy and tangled after the post-shower sex, then wind it into a bun on top of my head. I'm naked as the day I was born, and looking at myself in the mirror, all soft curves where I wish I had flat, hard muscle, I wonder if I should grab a shirt to throw on or something.

"What's taking so long?" Beau calls. "I need you."

I smile to myself and head back into the bedroom. I slide between the sheets next to him, worried for a moment that things will be awkward now that daylight is streaming in between the blackout curtains. It was easy to be wild and free last night in the darkness, when I didn't have to think about all the reasons this shouldn't be happening.

"What is that face?" Beau asks, reaching over and smoothing out my furrowed brow with his thumb. He leaves his palm cupping my jaw, his fingers gently stroking my hairline.

"Nothing," I say, reaching up and giving his wrist a squeeze.

"Don't hide things from me, Sierra," he says as he reaches behind me and pulls me closer so his entire body is flush with mine. He wedges his knee between mine so our bodies are literally entwined, the way he seems to like us best.

"I was just hoping things weren't going to get awkward, and they're not, so it's nothing."

"Things are *not* going to get awkward," he says firmly, "because we're adults. We can handle this, right?" He lifts an eyebrow, daring me to say that I can't handle it.

Of course I can. Because the alternative—falling for this playboy who I *know* is leaving—is ridiculous. But it's exactly why I told Sydney I wouldn't get involved with him in the first place, isn't it? I wish he was just a hot guy who was a provider of multiple orgasms per hour. I wish he wasn't also thoughtful, attentive, and in love with our dog. *No, Winston isn't ours,* I remind myself. He'll be someone else's soon.

"We can handle this." I say the words I know he needs to hear. I need to hear them too. I need the reminder that what we have here, right now—this is all it can be. Really amazing sex.

"Good," he says, as he rubs the length of his erection against my stomach. He's insatiable. He brings his hand to the back of my head and pulls my mouth to his. He nibbles on my lips playfully, but when I lean my hips forward into his, he parts my lips with his tongue and delves in. He claims my mouth, his tongue searching and tangling with mine, over and over in the same rhythm he's now thrusting against me. Beau doesn't just kiss me, he fucks my mouth. There's no other way to explain the possessive, invasive experience that is kissing him.

He wraps his arm around me and rolls to his back with me on top of him. Instinctually, I spread my knees to either side of his hips, rubbing my already wet center along the length of him.

"How are you already so wet for me?" he asks as I rock my hips back and forth slowly, so he slides along my opening. I push myself up so that I'm sitting over him, one hand on his shoulder and the other above him on the headboard. "You are amazingly, impossibly sexy," he tells me, and I can feel my insides melting for him.

"Tell me more," I say, and I'm not sure about this low, throaty voice that comes out of my mouth, because it doesn't even sound like me, and it's not something I'd normally say.

"Do you have any idea what you do to me?" he asks.

I glance down at the hard length of him between my legs, watch how he glistens from my juices as I slide myself along him. Then I look back at him with a half smile and say, "Yeah, I think I do."

"I don't mean now, I mean in an ordinary day," he says, his thumbs stroking my hip bones. It's a touch that's possessive, not erotic, and I don't know what to make of that. "The way your hips sway when you walk down the hall toward your bedroom, how your ass calls to me when you bend over to pet Winston, that dress with the front zipper you wore on your date last weekend . . ."

"I wore that for you," I say and give him a little wink.

"To drive me fucking crazy?" he asks, and I give him a sly nod. "Well, it worked. I dreamed about you unzipping that dress and sharing your body with me. And the next morning, that cropped cami you wore lit my imagination on fire." He reaches up and cups my breasts in his hands again. He's clearly a boob man, which is good, since I'm well-endowed in that area.

When he pinches my nipples gently between his fingers, I throw my head back and sigh. Then with superhuman strength he sits up without using his arms for support, and his lips meet my breasts, kissing them both reverently before he takes one of my nipples in his mouth and does amazing things with his tongue that leave me panting and reaching down to stroke my clitoris with one hand and the head of his cock with the other. He makes a sound in the back of his throat that's an awful lot like a growl. There is nothing more natural than sex, or at least the sex Beau and I are having. It's an intimate connection entirely unlike anything I've ever experienced.

"I want you inside me," I tell him and he mumbles for me to grab a condom. I reach over for his sport coat, but the pocket is empty. He just laughs, telling me we've used both of those. "You only brought two?"

"If we'd used more than two while we were out at a bar last night, that would have been some sort of miracle. There're plenty more in my suitcase, hold on." He sets me on the bed and gets up, walking toward the closet. Our room is so quiet all I can hear is him and me, breathing—the thick sound of anticipation. And then, the silence is pierced by a ringing phone. My phone, with the "Party in the USA" ringtone Sydney had set on it yesterday.

I glance over at Beau. "It's Sydney."

"You should answer it," he says as he tears a condom off a long strip of them. Always so prepared.

I eye the condom in his hand. "I don't want to talk wedding details. I want to finish what we started."

"What if she needs you?" he asks. "What if something is wrong?"

"She'll call Georgia?" My voice is weak. I already know I'll answer the phone, begrudgingly, because she's interrupted my time with Beau. *She's your sister, and it's her wedding day.*

I reach over and grab my phone off the bedside table. "Hey, Syd."

Beau stands there watching me, his massive hard-on jutting out from his body and pointing right at me.

"It's Joe," the voice on the other end says.

I actually hold the phone away from my face and look at it for a second, then bring it back to my ear. "Joe? What's wrong? Where's Sydney?"

"She's here. But she's sick."

"What do you mean, she's sick?" I ask.

Beau reaches into his suitcase and grabs some clothes. He tosses a T-shirt to me and steps into a pair of boxer briefs. I put the phone on speaker and set it on the bed so I can pull the T-shirt over my head, hating that we've detoured so drastically from the direction we were headed.

"Last night we made it as far as our hotel, then Sydney and Georgia insisted on stopping at the bar and doing some celebratory shots." Joe's voice is grim, and I have the sense that he's not feeling so hot either.

"You were supposed to bring her back to the room. You know, have wild and crazy 'we're getting married tomorrow' sex with your fiancée. You weren't supposed to let her get trashed." I wish I could reach through the phone and choke him.

"I didn't think she was trashed," he says, and Beau and I just look at each other.

I glance at the phone laying on the bed. "You had one job, Joe," I say, and Beau smirks.

"I know. I need your help, Sierra. She won't come out of the bathroom. She says there's no way she's getting married today."

My eyes flare and seek out Beau's. I know he sees the

panic, followed by the resolve. "Like hell she isn't," I spit out through gritted teeth. "I'll be there in ten minutes."

I end the call and look at Beau, then down at the phone, then back to Beau. "I am so sorry," I whisper.

"There is absolutely nothing to be sorry about," he says as he moves around the corner of the bed to wrap his arms around me. It's a fortifying hug, which he somehow knows is exactly what I need right now. "You got this."

"I don't want to be the one to get this. I did my part. I made sure she didn't get trashed last night. I was a responsible adult. I deserve to spend this morning with you." I feel some sympathy for toddlers who have temper tantrums when they don't get what they want, as I could easily devolve into one right now.

He pulls back, holding me at arm's length with his hands on my shoulders. "Are you done?"

I drop my head. "Yes. Now I'm going to go clean up Joe's mess."

I get dressed and smooth my hair back into its bun with a little water on my fingertips while I brush my teeth. When I come out of the bathroom, Beau hands me a bag with a couple of those Gatorades we didn't need. "Make sure she drinks at least one of these. But only give her a sip like every five minutes to start or she'll just throw it up. And try to get her to eat something with salt."

"Thanks," I say, standing on my toes to kiss him.

The kiss turns hot and heavy quickly, and he puts his hands on my hips and pushes me away from him, insisting that I go help my sister. I give him my best pouty face, and he chuckles. "Whoever thought that *I'd* be the responsible one?"

"Certainly not me," I say as I head out the door with the Gatorade.

―――――

M y sister is radiant as she stands at our dinner table, clasping Joe's hand in one of hers, and holding her champagne flute with the other. Her engagement ring and wedding band sparkle under the light of the chandelier hanging above us.

"We'd like to thank you guys for being here," Sydney says. "We know we gave you less than a week's notice, and you dropped everything to join us."

I glance over my shoulder at Beau when he leans into me and whispers "I dropped everything to be here for *you*" so quietly I almost can't hear him. A shiver runs down my spine as his breath caresses the nape of my neck. His arm is draped around the back of my chair, and as his fingertips run along my shoulder blade, I have to force myself to refocus on Sydney and Joe—it would be too easy to get lost in Beau's attention.

"I also owe an enormous debt of gratitude to my sister." She looks at me, her blue eyes repentant. "Without you, I'd still be lying on that bathroom floor."

Everyone laughs, even Sydney, and Joe squeezes her hand, telling her, "Eventually, I would have convinced you to get up."

I spent this morning on the bathroom floor with Sydney, giving her tiny sips of Gatorade until she stopped throwing up. I pinched off pieces of a salt bagel I'd sent Joe out to find and fed those to her until her stomach stopped flipping over. I bent over the bathtub washing her hair for her because she felt disgusting but was too weak to take a shower by herself. I made Joe go find greasy hash browns, and salty potato chips, and I got her to eat those this afternoon. I walked her around her hotel suite, bearing most of her weight, until she could manage on her own.

I feel like I've been physically beat up. The lack of sleep combined with caring for someone so hungover has every muscle in my body aching.

"You'd do the same for me," I say, and hold my glass up to clink it with hers.

I barely got her to our hair and makeup appointments on time this afternoon. There, the hairdresser took one look at her, grabbed a clear plastic cup with a lid out of a mini-fridge, stuck a straw in it, handed it to her, and said, "Drink this. You'll feel a thousand times better." It looked like someone had pureed a watermelon and eggplant together—purple and lumpy, grainy and runny at the same time. Sydney was a trooper, she plugged her nose and drank the whole thing, and by the time her hair was done, she was a new person. I have no idea what was in that concoction because the hairdresser declared it a "trade secret" that she kept on hand for brides and bridesmaids who'd indulged too much, but whatever it was, it was a fucking miracle. I would have gotten Sydney to this wedding if it killed me, and it probably would have if it weren't for that miraculous drink.

Joe says a few words about his brother, and about how he wishes their parents could have been there. Watching him and Luke, and the obvious brotherly love they share, I am so happy for Sydney that she found a guy like Joe and is creating her own family.

After she kisses him, they sit down, and Sydney spins around and wraps her arms around me so tight I can hardly breathe. "We did it," she whispers. "Fuck the curse."

I squeeze her back. I can't imagine what it would be like to be the only sane person in a family of ridiculous women who are all convinced they're cursed. Sure, Sydney wasn't pregnant before the wedding like every other Lemieux woman in recent history, but she actually tied the knot nonetheless. That just proves that there is no curse. "You proved them all wrong, and I'm so glad I could be here for it, sis."

We enjoy a relaxing dinner, where the food just keeps coming. Everything feels a little less crazy tonight, which I guess is the difference between Vegas on a Saturday night and a Sunday. We're waiting for dessert and I'm snuggled into Beau, hardly able to keep my eyes open. Last night and today wiped me out.

"Hey," Beau says, when I yawn for the umpteenth time. "Let me go get you something with caffeine."

The minute he's away from the table, Georgia and Sydney are squealing. "So I guess something *did* happen between you two, after all?" Sydney asks.

It never occurred to me to say something about it to her while she was so sick, and it also never occurred to me to try to hide it at their wedding ceremony or since.

I just nod in response, not trusting myself to say anything lest I say too much in front of Joe and Luke. They pry me for details but I'm a vault, and they give up when Beau returns with a Red Bull and vodka. "You're never going to forgive yourself if you sleep through your sister's wedding celebration," he whispers in my ear once he's seated.

I squeeze his thigh and thank him, and then my phone is

buzzing on the table. I pick it up to find another photo of Winston from Heather. "We should take another sad-faced selfie," he suggests, "since last night's was so popular."

"It was?" I'd actually forgotten about that photo amid everything else going on last night and today.

Beau updates me on the photo's stats as of the last time he checked.

"You sure you want to get Winston's followers all worked up again?" I ask.

"Oh, I'm positive. It's even more fun now that something actually is going on." He brushes a kiss across my temple and asks Sydney to take our photo. And even though this one is staged, the sad face I'm making is all too real. Because in a week Beau will be gone, and Winston will probably follow shortly thereafter. Everything that's making me so happy right now has a quickly approaching expiration date.

I t's late when we make it back to the room, and we're both buzzing with anticipation. It feels like it's been forever since Beau was inside me, even though it's barely been nineteen hours. Not that I'm counting, or anything. But the way we were dancing tonight has had my mind solidly on getting him naked, and based on all the dirty things he whispered in my ear while our bodies were pressed together on the dance floor, I know his mind is in the same place.

"Wow," I say when Beau opens the door to our room. Across the room is a spectacular nighttime view of Vegas, like something you'd see on a postcard. "I don't even remember noticing how beautiful this view was last night or the night before." I walk across the room to the wall of windows. During the day this view is nice, but at night with the lights of the nearby hotels, the wide swath of the Bellagio fountains, and the lit up Eiffel Tower, with the High Roller in the distance, it's pretty spectacular.

"The curtains were closed last night," Beau says as he comes up behind me and wraps his arms around my waist. Like every time he's been behind me tonight, I tilt my hips back and rub my ass along his thick erection. Him always being hard for me makes me feel powerful in a way I'm not used to. I look up at him over my shoulder and do it again until he leans down and trails kisses along my jaw.

When I sigh his name and lean back into him, he trails his hands up over my abdomen to my breasts, cupping them in his hands. I can feel my nipples pebble beneath the fabric and I hope he can feel them too. We stay there for a minute, just gazing out at the amazing night time view, with him stroking my breasts and whispering in my ear, nodding toward the High Roller. "Was it really only yesterday afternoon we were on that?" he asks.

"Umm hmm. Feels like we've come a long way since then."

I squeeze my thighs together as he describes all the plans he has for my body tonight, and when I can't take it anymore, I turn toward him and lean up to kiss him, my fingers working the buttons of his dress shirt. I have it off in record time, then I slide his white undershirt up and over his head. My eyes glide over his chest and down his abdomen, and I lick my lips as my gaze lingers. "I'm trying to memorize every muscle." I look up at Beau, hoping he understands what I mean: this thing between us will be too short, and I don't want to forget a single detail.

"They're yours to look at whenever you want," he says.

"For this week, at least," I remind him, my shoulders scrunching up into a shrug, and a frown that I'm powerless to stop turning down the corners of my mouth. He leans down to kiss me, and my lips part willingly, almost desperately, as I lean into the kiss. My fingers work at his belt and the button of his pants, then find his zipper. I push them down his legs where they pool at his feet, so he kicks them off. "I want you naked," I tell him, and he pushes his underwear down and bends to remove them and his socks. On his way back up to standing, he trails the pads of his fingertips up my legs, letting them lightly skim across my skin until I'm practically humming with need, then lets them drift under the hem of my dress. He runs his fingers along my seam, and even through my underwear, I bet his fingers are damp.

"Someone's excited," he murmurs, and I don't shrink away in embarrassment. "Why do you still have so many clothes on?"

"No one has taken them off me yet."

"We'll have to do something about that," he tells me, a primal glint in his eyes. As he steps closer to me, I take a step back. He steps closer again, eyes narrowed on my body like he's stalking his prey—I've never felt so desired. One more tiny step back and I'm against the glass, but when he reaches me, he spins me around to face the windows. My hands come up against the glass, and they're the only thing preventing me from full body contact with the floor-to-ceiling window.

I am breathing heavily, and I'm not sure if it's because I'm scared of heights or because he's brought his hand around to the front of me and is sliding it up to the apex of my thighs.

Beau dips his head so my lips are against her ear. "I'm going to fuck you right here against this glass."

I gasp and look at him over my shoulder. I'm pressed up against a full wall of windows, twenty-six stories above the still bustling streets of Vegas, and with other hotels around us. "Someone will see us."

"In the dark? No, they won't. But we'll have this gorgeous view." He slips his finger inside my underwear, runs it through my folds until it's covered in satiny fluid, then circles my clit a few times before he adds a second finger and delves into me. I can't control how responsive my body is to him as I arch my back and roll my hips so my ass caresses his erection.

With his free hand, he tugs at the zipper that runs along the back of my dress. He gets it about halfway down before the bunched up fabric around my hips prevents it from going any further. He swears, and I laugh, and then both of his hands are pulling the hem of my dress down and unzipping it the rest of the way. He pushes it forward off my shoulders and as I pull it down my arms and toss it on the chair in the corner, I hear him suck in his breath. I assume it's because he's seen my underwear.

I turn toward him, giving him the full frontal view of my sheer skin colored thong and my bra, which has layers of sheer fabric crisscrossing the cups and is held together by satin ribbon lacing it up the front. He brings his mouth down to one breast and sucks my nipple into his mouth through the fabric, which has me leaning up on my toes, pushing more of my breast into his mouth. He does the same to the other breast, and the rough feel of his tongue moving across the wet fabric has my entire core clenching in response. I wrap one leg around his waist, thankful I'm still wearing my nude platform heels, so I'm tall enough for our bodies to meet in just the right place.

"Your lingerie is fucking hot," he says, bringing his face back up to mine. "But it's in my way. I want to feel every inch of your skin." He hooks his thumbs over the straps of the underwear and slides them down my legs, and when I step out of them, he turns me around to face the windows again and unhooks my bra, gently drawing it down my arms and tossing it to the side by my dress. I go to step out of my heels, but he tells me to leave them on. His voice is rough, like he's so turned-on he can hardly speak, and I have no idea how I'm here in this position with a guy like Beau—universally desired, hot as hell, and five years younger than me—but I plan on enjoying every second of it.

I reach behind me and grip him with my hand, stroking up and down his shaft, rolling my thumb over the tip of him every time I come to the top. Suddenly he's frenetic, one of his hands is working my breasts and the other is dipping between my legs again, and he's whispering dirty promises in my ear— he has me almost ready to come just from the anticipation and the way he's expertly stroking the inside of my walls with his talented fingers.

"I need you inside me," I tell him, and I'm not sure I've ever needed anything more. I feel absolutely empty when his hand leaves me, but I glance behind me when I hear a foil packet rip open and I watch him roll the condom on.

I spread my legs a bit further as he steps up behind me, and he teases me by running the head of his cock along my folds and circling my clit. I push my hips back into him with a moan. "Now, Beau," I insist.

"So demanding," he murmurs. "I like that."

He slides into me, inch by glorious inch, until I'm so full I lean forward and put my hands on the glass. I've never had sex like this before, either in this position or in what feels like full view of other people, even though I'm sure he's right that no one can see us with the lights off in our room. Still, the thought of someone seeing us is its own kind of thrill.

He brings both his hands to my hips, pulling me to him each time he thrusts inside, and the push along those ridges of muscles followed by the delicious drag as he pulls out leaves me panting in a matter of minutes. He brings one of his hands up and plants it above mine on the window so his chest cradles my back.

"You are amazing," he says as he pulls out and slams into me again with a grunt. A new description follows every push into me. "A goddess. Spectacular."

He goes on and on, and I want to tell him to be careful. That words like that could lead a girl to believe this is more than just sex. But we know the truth. We established the ground rules. Sex is all this is, and all it can be. So instead, I close my eyes, enjoy his words for what they are—the yearning of a man in the throes of sex. Nothing more.

I find his hand where he holds my hip, lace my fingers into his, and drag his hand to my center. There, I bring his middle finger to my clit.

"No," he says in my ear. "I'm not ready for this to be over."

And then he's pulling out of me, his absence leaving behind a gaping emptiness, and I have a momentary realization that this is what it will feel like when he leaves. But I don't have time to think about that, because he's spinning me around and picking me up. I lock my legs around his hips and my arms around his neck. He holds me in place with one arm wrapped under my ass while the other braces against the steel frame between the two large panes of glass.

And then I'm lost in the moments of raw passion as he slides into me over and over, dragging himself along every single nerve ending that brings me pleasure until I'm panting and moaning and acting without inhibition or fear. I've never felt so lost or so free, and his name is a reverent chant on my lips as I feel that pulsing begin, my muscles tightening around him, quaking with need and sensation. I don't know what I'm saying or doing, only that I need this so badly—this feeling of him inside me, around me, the way my body craves his—and then I'm coming so hard it takes my breath away, white hot pleasure shooting through me, stars behind my closed eyelids, and his name on my lips. Always his name on my lips.

Chapter Eighteen

BEAU

"Are you sure you're okay?" Sierra eyes me skeptically as we walk down the hall, following Winston's lead. His tail waves back and forth enthusiastically, like he's excited to get home after his big weekend away.

"I'm positive," I say, wrapping my arm around her shoulder and kissing the top of her head as I roll our suitcases along beside me. "I just didn't sleep well last night." *Or at all, actually.*

"I slept like the dead." She sighs against my shoulder.

"I know." I watched her all night. But how do you tell someone you couldn't sleep because you couldn't stop gazing at them, afraid that if you closed your eyes, the entire mirage would disappear? That's how this whole thing with Sierra feels—like our future is a hopeful vision flickering in the distance, but ultimately too good to be true.

Because there is no future. Even the voice inside my head is dark and bitter. She told me this could only last until I leave, with no hesitation or remorse that it couldn't be longer. The first time I came inside her, something shifted in me. And last night, in front of that whole wall of windows, that wasn't just the sexiest fucking thing that's ever happened, it was life altering.

But not for her.

She pulls away from me to put the code in the keypad and push our front door open, then turns in the doorway attempting not to get caught up in Winston's leash. She says "I promise not to keep you up *too* late tonight" and gives me a sexy little wink.

I smile because I know that's the appropriate response, but inside, all I can think about is how I want her to keep me up too late *every* night. The thought of walking away from her at the end of this week is . . . I don't know, too painful to think about, I guess. So I don't. Instead, I wheel our suitcases into the entryway and consider how to make the most of the next few days.

"Did you hear Heather when she said maybe *she'd* adopt Winston?" Sierra asks, a dreamy smile on her face as she takes off her coat. "Wouldn't that be amazing? She adores him, and then I could see him whenever I wanted."

"That would be incredible. She really does seem to love him."

"And it sounds like he wasn't that crazy with her. He only ate a pair of her socks, no other mischief."

"He's already calmed down a lot over the last two weeks," I remind her. "I think he just needs consistency, and lots of exercise and attention."

"Yeah, and Heather and her husband don't have kids, so they can give him that. I do think having a couple adopt him is ideal. I couldn't have done this without you." She leans up and brushes her lips against mine, and I consider the implication that we're a couple. I don't think it's what she meant, but it'd be easy to interpret that way. I want to interpret it that way.

We go through the motions that have become second nature for us. I make us dinner while Sierra takes Winston for a walk, I play with him to get some of his energy out while she unpacks her suitcase, she takes him out to pee and plays with him while I edit the photos I took at Sydney's wedding.

It's familiar, but new at the same time because there's a level of intimacy that didn't exist before we left. The way she dangles the bra and underwear she wore last night from her finger as she unpacks it, saying "I should probably wash *this*." The way she wraps her arms around my shoulders and kisses the top of my head as she stands behind my chair looking at Sydney's wedding photos on my laptop. The way she takes my hand after we crate Winston before bed, and leads me to her room.

"You don't actually think you're going to put those on, do you?" I ask when she pulls her pajamas out of the drawer.

"I don't know," she says, and her lip curls up into a smile on one side. That's quickly becoming my favorite look because I know it means she's thinking about us together. "You tell me."

I take them from her hand and set them on top of the dresser, then pull her to me. "Those won't be necessary." I dip my head and part her lips with mine, kissing her deeply as I slide her long dusty pink cardigan from her shoulders. She loops her arms around my neck and I take the hem of the tight sexy white T-shirt she's wearing and pull it up, trailing my fingers along her abdomen and brushing them along the sides of her breasts before pulling it over her head. My fingers unclasp her bra and as I gently pull it off, I take in the sight of

275

a topless Sierra. *I could never get tired of this view.* I swallow those words down, and instead I say, "You're gorgeous."

"You make me *feel* gorgeous," she says. I hear the implication that others have not made her feel this way and there are so many questions on the tip of my tongue, but I hold them in because I know how much she doesn't like talking about past partners while we're intimate. I'll have to ask her later.

"Because you deserve to know how amazing you are," I tell her as she takes my shirt and pulls it over my head.

We make quick work of undressing each other, and once I'm down to my boxer briefs, I tell her I'll be right back. I slip into my bedroom and grab a stash of condoms before returning to her room and dropping them onto her nightstand.

She's waiting for me on the bed, kneeling right at the edge so that when I step up to the side of the bed, her nipples drag along my chest. My hands instinctively go to her hips, which seems to be their natural position of late—always pulling her closer, even though I never feel like she's quite close enough. I dip my head, burying my nose in her hair and inhaling the strawberry scent that will forever remind me of being naked with her. I hate that I'm cataloging away these details, knowing that I'll think about them in the future when I remember a moment in time that couldn't last.

"Did you just sniff me?" She laughs.

"Sure did," I say, my lips already at her ear as I pull her earlobe into my mouth. Her entire body convulses like an electrical current just ran through it.

She dips her chin and sinks her teeth into my neck. The bite is light, but it has me hard for her instantly. I push my hips forward, rubbing myself along her. She sighs and reaches down to push my underwear past my hips, then takes me in her hand, dips her head down, and swirls her tongue around the head of my cock.

I push forward into her mouth without even meaning to, and she takes me willingly. The bed is too high for the angle to be ideal, so she moves from her hands and knees to laying on her stomach, propped up on one elbow as she works me in and out of her mouth. She bends her knees, her feet crossed in the air like she's casually reading a magazine, but the soft moans that are reverberating against my sensitive skin let me know that she's invested. I thought seeing her on her knees in the shower taking me in her mouth was sexy, but this—her ass moving as she subtly tilts her hips into the bed—*this* is next-level.

She lets me slip out of her mouth, but keeps a firm grip on me with her hand as she looks up. "You like this?"

"I love this." Do I mean the blow job she's giving me, or just being with her? I'm not even sure.

She dips her head again, but it's too good and I'm too close, and I want to be inside her. I tell her as much, and as I grab a condom, she repositions herself so she's on her back, with her feet at the edge of the bed and her legs bent up so she's spread wide open for me and I can see how wet and ready she is. I circle her clit with my thumb a few times until she's begging me, and when I push inside her, it feels like coming home. She reaches her hands up to her knees and I lace my fingers with hers. I don't think I've ever held hands with someone while fucking them, and it's strangely intimate, even with the rest of our bodies only connected at the hips.

I glance down, watching myself slide in and out of her. "You like what you see?" she asks. Her voice is rough, raw even, and it's all the more sexy just when I thought she couldn't possibly get any sexier.

"This is amazing," I tell her.

She brings our hands back above her head, pulling me down so our upper bodies are flush. "I want you down here with me," she says, her voice barely above a whisper.

Our lips meet, and our tongues slide along each other's as I kiss her with the same tempo as our bodies meeting each other. It feels like only another minute before she's writhing beneath me, her hips meeting mine as she urges me to increase the pace. I absorb the rhythm of our hips beating against each other, the way our slick bodies glide along each other, the sound of the soft moans that escape her lips as she pants.

She puts her feet on my lower back, saying "Yes, Beau" as she tries to push me even deeper inside her. Not that there's any room for me to go deeper, I'm already bottoming out, but she seems to love the pressure that puts on her. "Oh yes," she pants, her lips centimeters from mine. "Yes!" The word is practically a shout as I feel her muscles clench around me over and over, and even though I try to hold on, I can't. The tingling at the base of my spine is spreading and I feel my balls seize up as I pound into her, chasing my own release.

"Holy crap," she says once our bodies have relaxed, with me still inside her. "How is sex with you always so amazing?"

"It's an *us* thing," I assure her. "It isn't always like this. For me, anyway."

And from the look in her eyes, I feel like maybe I've said too much. Did she think that this kind of connection that we're sharing is always there, every time I have sex with someone? She's already told me it's not like that for her, either. So why is she looking at me like I just crossed some sort of boundary?

"I'm going to go take care of this," I say, gesturing toward my hips as I pull out of her and turn toward her now-refinished bathroom. I can't take another second of that look on her face—part skepticism and part confusion.

When I'm done cleaning myself up, I come back to the bed and find her already under the covers. I'm about to ask if she wants me to stay when she pulls back the covers for me. Thank fuck, because after sharing a bed with her the past two nights, I'm in no hurry to be alone in my own now. *Who even are you?* I ask myself.

"Not that I want to think about my sister right now," I say when slide in beside her and she snuggles into my side, "but how much do you think she'd flip out if she knew I was in this bed with you?"

I feel Sierra stiffen beside me like I've said the wrong thing, again. "Let's not think about that right now. This isn't something Jackson can ever know about."

I stare at the ceiling, absorbing that comment. *So this is what it feels like to be someone's dirty little secret.* My stomach flips over at the thought of Sierra being ashamed to admit that there's something happening here between us, because it could not be more opposite than my own feelings.

When I don't respond, she continues, "Beau, can I ask you something personal?"

"Sure." The word is thick as it slips past the lump in my throat.

This isn't something Jackson can ever know about. Her words run through my head on a loop. It's not that I thought this was something we were going to run and tell my family about. It's the way she used the word "ever." She didn't say that this is something we want to keep to ourselves right now, but rather, something we will not *ever* tell my family about.

Of course it's not. You don't tell your family about any of your other flings, I remind myself. But lumping what's happening here with Sierra, together with the string of meaningless sex I've had over the past few years since I graduated from college, feels wrong on every level.

"Why do you and Jackson have such a bad relationship? I mean, you two got along great as kids."

"Did we?" I ask. "I mean, I guess we did. It's not actually Jackson I don't get along with, it's my dad. And since she's just an extension of him . . ."

"An extension of him?" Sierra says, a hint of challenge in her voice.

"You know what I mean. She follows his lead on everything."

"You think so?"

"I know so," I say.

"So, how would you explain their relationship after she found out he's the reason Nate left? Or once she started dating Nate again?"

My body jerks almost violently as I pull away to look down at her. "What?" I have no idea what she's talking about. I haven't had a meaningful conversation with Jackson in probably seven or eight years. She was always with Dad, always disapproving of everything I did.

Sierra lifts an eyebrow as she looks up at me. "Maybe you don't know her as well as you think?"

Maybe Sierra's right. "All I know is that my dad left me— literally left—at a pivotal time in my life, when I really needed him. And his justification was that Jackson needed him more. That her skiing took precedence over raising his son, over being there for me as I navigated what it meant to become a man."

"Did he actually say that?" she asks. I expect skepticism because I know he was like a father to her growing up, but that's not what I hear in her voice. Just curiosity and concern.

"No, but everything he did and didn't do showed me that. And the one time I told him how I felt, how much I needed him, he essentially told me I was a disappointment and beyond help."

Sierra sucks in a sharp breath. Okay, so *maybe* having that conversation with Dad after I'd just been caught in my car in the high school parking lot about to have sex with my English teacher's daughter wasn't the right time to bring up the fact that if he were around to be a role model, perhaps I wouldn't be doing shit like that.

I'm old enough now to understand that it was a classic cry for help, that I was desperate for my father's attention any way I could get it. And getting in trouble was the only way I found that he paid attention. Making the honor roll freshman and sophomore years barely registered a "good job," but you better believe he was video calling me from Europe the minute I stepped out of line. So it became a game to see just how far I could push the boundaries without actually falling off the cliff. The question is, how did *he* not see that?

"Wow, I never saw it that way," she says, snuggling in closer and wrapping her leg over mine.

"No one did. Everyone looked at it like one parent was just as good as the other when it came to raising me, even though Jackson got both parents for her whole childhood." It's hard to admit that part of my bitterness toward my sister is that she got the childhood I wanted, with two loving parents, and then stole my dad away when I needed him. Have I been more of an asshole to her than necessary because of it? Maybe. But she's never tried to see my side of things either.

"My mom is a saint," I continue, "and I love and adore her. But no one stopped to think that maybe the teen years aren't the best time to separate a dad and his son. There were things I needed my dad for—advice and as a role model—and he wasn't there for that. Not only was he not there, he didn't even seem to care that he was missing out on my life."

"I think he was just so focused on Jackson," Sierra says. "You were always closer to your mom, even as a kid. And he and Jackson were always closer."

"Yeah, but my mom and Jackson are close too. Mom made sure of that. She sent Jackson care packages, they talked on the phone almost every day, Jackson still confided in her, and when she was home in between ski season and summer practices, my mom made sure they did things together. My dad did none of that. Even when he was home, he was focused on Jackson's career or on Blackstone Mountain. I barely registered."

She reaches up and strokes my face, pushing my hair off my forehead. "I'm sorry."

Those two words—the acknowledgment of my experience —crack something open in me. A hardened part of my heart splinters open at feeling heard and seen. I've never really told anyone how much my dad's indifference hurt me, because he and my mom did provide a good life for me and it would just sound like whining. Instead, I stayed as far away as I could, as often as I could.

But the way Sierra sees the hurt and doesn't try to explain it away or defend my dad's actions—because *of course* he wasn't going to let his twenty-year-old daughter go live and race in Europe without a parent—is exactly the understanding that I've always needed.

"Is that why you didn't come home last year when your mom was going through chemo?" The fact that she even asks this question clues me into this being something Jackson must be upset about.

"No. My mom insisted that I not come home. She felt it was overkill that Jackson was moving back because of her, and she didn't want to feel responsible for ruining both of our careers."

"She didn't ruin Jackson's career," Sierra insists.

"I know, but she felt like she did. She kept telling me that she'd never forgive herself or me if I gave up a whole season of snowboarding to sit around and watch her being sick."

"I don't think Jackson knows that," she says quietly.

"She thinks I just ditched my family while my mom was going through chemo?"

I feel her shrug against me. "I think so." The words are almost a whisper.

"Is that what you thought too?"

"I only knew what Jackson's told me, Beau," she murmurs as she squeezes her arms around me tighter. "Thanks for explaining all of this. I know it can't be easy to talk about your past when you have a contentious relationship with your dad and sister."

"I'd say that it's okay, that I'm over it," I say as I turn toward her, wrap my arms around her, and kiss the top of her head, "but obviously that's not true."

She slides her arm around my back and squeezes. "It's okay to have scars, Beau. It just means you went through something tough and survived."

I lie there even after she falls asleep in my arms, thinking about what she said. The two things in life that have cut me deepest—my dad and Helen—don't exactly feel healed over. And it leaves me wondering if what I have are scars, or if they're still open wounds?

———

"All right, I'll keep an eye out for the package and start planning out the promotion. Thanks again for the opportunity," I say. I'm anxious to get off this conference call, which has lasted well over the planned hour. It's another great opportunity for my photography business, but with the X Games coming up, I'm not even sure how I'll fit in the administrative work needed to run this promotion. Lance and Drew are pushing me to solidify our plans after Aspen, and for the first time in my life, I'm not feeling ready to move on to the next place. Honestly, I don't even really feel like going to Aspen because Sierra won't be there.

There are few things in life I know with absolute certainty, but one I'm ready to add to the list is this: I've never felt about anyone the way I feel about Sierra. I need her, in the physical sense, but more than that, my soul craves hers.

And yet, you have to walk away, I remind myself. That was the agreement in Vegas. One week. And there's no indication that she wants more than that. In fact, there's every indication that she doesn't. It would be selfish and wrong to try to get her to come with me when I know it's not what's best for her, when I know I can't offer her the stable life she wants.

If you really care about her, do what's best for her.

I glance at the clock as the phone call ends, wondering how much longer until she's home. Hopefully not more than an hour, though she seems like she's been coming home earlier this week than the first two weeks I was here. As if she's trying to soak up as much time with me, like I am with her before I leave.

So don't leave.

Wait, what? That thought is . . . where did that even come from? Staying would be asinine. There's nothing for me here except Sierra. And there it is, that ache in my chest I've been feeling every time I look at her. The feeling that I don't want to lose her, even though I know that she's not looking for more than a fling with me.

Anyway, I can't stay. I have multiple contracts already signed—with a company releasing a new line of snowboards, with three different ski resorts around the world, with a cruise company adding a new itinerary in Alaska, and with a company releasing a new photography drone. I have a lot of flexibility in when and how I fulfill those contracts, but the reality is I have a lot of travel to fit in between snowboarding competitions over the next year just to shoot all these ads.

And I *want* to do this work. Everything I've worked for over the past few years building this account is finally starting to pay off. Walking away now would be the stupidest thing I've ever done—exactly the kind of passion-driven decision my dad would expect me to make.

Besides, Sierra's never said anything that makes me believe she wishes I'd stay.

I've been with too many women over the past few years, and I've never wanted more than a night or two with any of them. Until Sierra.

I seem to only be capable of falling for the ones who don't want me to stick around.

I open my laptop and busy myself with editing more photos. Currently I'm working on photos I took in Costa Rica two summers ago when I spent a month there surfing. I'm deep into the filters, playing with hue and saturation and white balance for who knows how long when I hear Sierra at the door. Winston bolts from where he's been laying at my feet, running over to the door and putting his front paws up on the frame. His tail wags so fast in his excitement to see Sierra. I know exactly how he feels.

"What are you working on?" she asks as she walks up behind the chair I'm occupying in the living room.

"Just doing some editing." I glance up at her, but don't shut my laptop like I normally would if someone caught me working on a post for my photography business.

"You take really beautiful photos," she says, her voice a happy sigh as she leans down and kisses my cheek, her lips lingering a little longer than necessary, but not as long as I want them to. "Where's this?"

"Costa Rica. Surfing trip last summer."

"You're just editing them now?"

I breathe in deeply, considering how much to tell her. *Fuck it. Why keep hiding it? Especially from someone who will really appreciate what I've created?* "I have a huge backlog of photos to edit and post."

"Post?" she asks, coming around to sit on the leather club

chair next to mine. She drapes her knees over the arm of her chair, her feet resting on the arm of mine.

"Yeah. I have this pet project that's turned into a bit of a business." I explain about my photography account, and how I've monetized it based on sponsored posts and ads.

"What type of sponsors and ads?"

"Usually it's travel related, often for specific destinations." I explain how most of the places I stay when traveling are comped as long as I post a certain number of pictures of the hotel or the excursions or whatever. I tell her about some of the contracts I have coming up.

"So you've monetized the thing you love—photography— and you've used it to fund your snowboarding and travel? That's genius."

"Thanks. Actually, my snowboarding sponsors pay for most of the travel, training, competition fees, all that."

"So, what do you do with the money from the photography business?"

"Invest it back into the business, mostly. Use it to travel in the off season. Donate some of it. Save the rest."

"You just shrugged like it's no big deal that at twenty-five you've got a career as a professional snowboarder *and* a very successful second career as a photographer," she says, sounding equal parts annoyed and proud. "Can I see?"

I bring the site up on my laptop and click over to my profile. "I've never shown anyone this before."

She brings her feet under her and sits on her knees, leaning toward me. "Wait, like *no* one?"

"No one."

The look on her face is surprise, followed by vulnerability —like she's peeling back her armor and baring something sacred. I wonder if she's mirroring my own expression, or if she has secrets to share too?

She glances at my screen, takes in the username, then pulls up the app on her phone. She curls back into her chair and scrolls through the images, stopping at most of them for a closer look. "These are spectacular. And your ads are so clever. They don't even feel like ads, they're such a natural part of the account."

She scrolls some more and I watch the expressions on her face change—the way she zooms in on some, stops and gazes at others, dips her eyebrows as she examines others.

"This is like seeing a whole other side of you," she says, and looks up at me. "Thank you for sharing this with me."

"I don't know why I still keep it a secret," I tell her. "It's gotten big enough that I'm going to have to get help to manage it soon. Like I've got this promotion coming up." I tell her about the camera company that's sending me a new lens to try out and one to give away, and about how I need to manage a giveaway and then send out the other lens. "I'm going to have to schedule it after the X Games and mail it from wherever in the world I am then."

"Why don't you just leave the lens here and I'll mail it for you? It's no trouble to stop by the post office and send it off when you've finished the giveaway."

"Really?" I ask. Even though I always have Lance and Drew with me, I don't normally have someone in my life I can lean on for anything other than snowboarding. *Don't get used to it*, I remind myself. Just because she's happy to drop a package off at the post office for me doesn't mean that I'm the kind of guy she wants to be in a relationship with.

But we're so compatible, being with her is easy, like it's meant to be.

Maybe if I wasn't leaving, we could see where this goes. I *am* leaving, though. I'm heading to Aspen in a few days, then I have to be in Austria in February, and Canada in March. And in between those trips, who knows where we'll wind up? That's what I've always loved about my life—the freedom to do anything, go anywhere. Only now, those trips feel like they're business, and I just want to be home with Sierra.

"Of course," she says, snapping me out of my introspection. "And you should think about getting a virtual assistant. Someone who can handle these administrative tasks for you while you focus on the photography and growing that account."

"I didn't even know virtual assistants were a thing," I admit.

She explains how it works, and how I could find someone to fill that role. It's yet another administrative task I won't really have time for in the coming weeks, but if I could find someone like she's describing, it would save me so much time in the long run.

"Hey, I'm starving," she says. "Want to go out and grab dinner somewhere?"

"Are you asking me out on our first date?" I tease.

"Ha!" She laughs. "I feel like we passed first date status, and then some, in Vegas."

"Okay, so . . ." I say and mentally count off the nights we've spent together, "our fifth date, then."

"Dating someone who is leaving in three days would be insane. Let's just call it dinner." She sets her phone on the coffee table and stands.

"So let's have a date in Aspen too," I say, as I reach out and pull her toward me so she's standing in the space between my knees. The idea has been percolating in the back of my mind for two days now. I can't stay here. If I don't head to Aspen this weekend, I risk losing my sponsorships, not to mention the prize money that's at stake if I'm in the top three in either of my events. But she could come with me.

She smiles, then reaches down and taps my nose with her finger. "You're cute, but don't tease me with things we both know aren't possible." She turns away quickly, so I don't really have time to analyze the look that came over her face when she finished her sentence. "I'm just going to change, then I'll be ready to go." She slips down the hall and into her bedroom while I sit there trying to figure out why we both know her coming to Aspen isn't possible.

Chapter Nineteen

SIERRA

I'm lying in Beau's arms trying to commit every second of this feeling to memory and thinking about all the reasons I wish he wasn't leaving. Two more nights together after tonight. That's all we have.

I want to take the next two days off work and spend every minute with him, but that isn't realistic because he'll be at the mountain practicing. I know his coach has been up his ass since he got back from Vegas, but it sounds like he's finally making the progress he'd been hoping to make. His quad cork for Big Air is solid, and he seems like he's confident about Slopestyle, too, even though he won't know what that course is like until he gets to Aspen.

He hugs me to him, pressing his lips into the hair on the top of my head. "I don't want to leave," he whispers. I pull back and look up at him, shocked at his words. He must see the question on my face because he quickly says, "I have to. But I wish I didn't."

"You probably say that to all the ladies," I tease.

His nostrils flare and his voice is hard when he says, "I've never said that to anyone. I've never even thought it."

I reach up and cup his cheek with my hand. "I was just teasing, Beau. I wish you weren't leaving too, and it's easier to joke about it than to think that in three days you'll be gone." I swallow deeply to push that lump in my throat down. I am not going to cry about this.

"Then come with me," he says.

My lips part, but no sound comes out. "How would that work?" I finally ask.

"I don't know, but I want you in Aspen with me. I know you probably can't come for the whole week, but take a few days off and come over. I'm not ready to let you go yet."

I hear the vulnerability in his voice, and I believe him that this feeling is new for him. The desire to follow someone, no matter where that journey would take me, is totally new to me too. But that's not what he's asking of me. He just wants a few more days in Aspen.

He's not ready to let me go *yet*. That 'yet' speaks volumes, because what he's not saying is that eventually he will be ready to let me go.

The thought of being without him, of not coming home to find him cooking dinner, of not having him here walking around in nothing but his sweats, of not having him to cuddle up to every night, to share secrets and dreams with—it's one hundred times harder than it was when Peter left. But going to Aspen with him would just be prolonging the inevitable, and won't it hurt more in the end if we keep stringing it out like this?

"I have this big work fundraiser next weekend," I tell him.

"I have to be here this week for the planning, and I can't get out of attending the event."

"Oh." Such a simple word, yet it guts me.

"Can I be honest?"

His lips trace my forehead as he whispers, "Always."

"It's going to hurt when you leave Park City. I know we said we'd be adults about this, and we knew there was an expiration date. But I'm still going to miss you when you leave. And even if I didn't have this work thing and I could go to Aspen, Beau, you'd still leave me again after that. I don't know if I could do the leaving part twice."

He'll always be leaving, I remind myself.

He says nothing, just holds me to him. "I understand," he finally says, running his hand down my back and holding me even tighter. "Maybe you're right and that would just make it harder. For both of us."

My lips find his and I try to lose myself in the feeling of being with him. In the here and now, without focusing on the future.

I'd be lying to myself if I said that him leaving isn't going to destroy me. But even though I'm fairly sure it will, I'm not willing to lose a second with him between now and then.

———

"I swear you two are saints," Lauren says as she opens the tall wooden door with the arched top and ushers us out of the cold and into her two-story entryway. The stone floors are heated and melt the snow off our boots as we leave them by the door.

"Nope, just bringing our favorite new mom her favorite

food," Petra says as I hold out the bag of Indian food. The aroma fills the entryway and Lauren sighs with pleasure as she takes the bag and leads us into the kitchen.

"The girls went down okay, I take it?" I ask. It's just about seven at night and her house is silent except for the sound of white noise coming across the baby monitor. I peek at it where it sits on the counter, two angels in fleece sleepers, cozied up next to each other and sound asleep. "Look at those little cherubs," I coo.

"Don't let them fool you. They are beautiful when they're sleeping but holy terrors when they are awake. If they hadn't both napped today, I think I would have lost it!"

"When does Josh get back?" Petra asks.

"Two more days. If I'd had any idea before they were born just how hard this would be, I'd have said no to this trip back when he was planning it." The twins are six months old, so obviously this backcountry ski trip has been in the works for some time. Unfortunately, Lauren's family is in Maine, where she's from, and even though Josh's parents are close by, they aren't the kind of warm, supportive in-laws Lauren needs.

"Where are they?" I ask. "British Columbia?"

"Yeah, they did Whistler yesterday, and Blackcomb today," Lauren says as she unpacks the takeout containers onto her table. "They're headed to somewhere like an hour north of there tomorrow. Then back to Vancouver."

"I love Whistler Blackcomb," Petra says. "I need to get back up there soon."

"Not enough terrain for you at America's largest ski resort?" I tease. Now that Park City Mountain and Canyons are connected, you could ski for days and never do the same run twice.

"I haven't seen you on the mountain recently," she says. Petra runs her own company, so she creates her own schedule. She's generally on the slopes at least a few afternoons a week, but it's almost impossible for me to join her unless I take an afternoon off.

"Work's been busy, and I've only been home one of the last three weekends and the mountain was closed one of those weekend days for high winds. Maybe this coming weekend?"

She nods, and I wish we could invite Lauren to join us, but she really doesn't ski. And keeping up with a former Olympic skier is not for the faint of heart. Despite years on my high school and college race teams, Petra makes me look like a complete novice.

"Speaking of being gone," Lauren chimes in, "you've told us nothing about Vegas. Was it fun?"

We move around each other in the kitchen, grabbing plates and glasses and silverware as we set the table for our dinner. "Yeah. It was way better than I expected it to be."

My eyes flick over to Petra as she sits down at the table, and that was a mistake because she's watching me like she can read my mind. "Oh yeah," she says casually, "what made it better than you expected?"

I'm saved from answering her question by the shrill ring of my phone. I can feel my entire face light up as I tell my friends, "It's Jackson." As the one who brought all three of us together, her absence is felt deeply. "Hey, Jackson, how are you?"

"I'm fine," she says, her words clipped. Clearly, she is not fine. "But I need to talk to you. Is now a good time?"

"Uh, sure," I say. "Give me one second." I mute the phone

and let Petra and Lauren know that I'll be back in a minute and they should start eating without me.

I walk back toward the front of the house and take a seat in the den off the entryway. Jackson sounds mad, and I pray that she and Nate haven't had a fight. Their early twenties were punctuated with consistent ups and downs, fight after fight, always making up and promising each other they wouldn't fight again. It was exhausting. But after a five-year break, they reunited and have been so on the same page about everything since that it's almost eerie.

"Sorry, I'm back. What's going on? Is everything okay?"

"I need to ask you a question that I never in a million years thought I'd be asking you."

My stomach plummets, then slowly I feel the bile seeping into my esophagus, burning its way up my chest until I swallow hard, forcing it back down again. "Okay," I squeak. *She can't know. There's no way she knows.*

"Is something going on with you and Beau?"

"What? Why would you think that?" I don't have to feign the shock. How the hell could she know?

"Kind of a long story, but Nate and I are considering getting a dog once we get through ski season. I was scrolling social media this morning, searching through all the dog-related hashtags and, in multiple instances, I came across this beautiful chocolate lab named Winston."

I had no idea it was possible for my heart to beat so hard and fast that it could feel like it might break my ribcage. I don't trust myself to speak, so I just wait to see what she'll say next.

"In one of the pictures I was like 'wow, that girl playing with him looks like Sierra.' And that's when I looked a bit closer and realized that it was you, playing with him, in my living room."

I don't know what to say, so I focus on the dog, hoping she'll forget about Beau. "I'm so sorry I didn't ask you if it was okay to have a dog at your place."

I tell her about how I ended up fostering him unexpectedly, and she laughs and says, "Only you, Sierra. But I don't care about the dog, as long as he's not ruining my furniture or peeing on my rugs?"

"Nope, he's obsessed with shoes, but furniture is safe. Besides, we crate him during the day when we're not home."

"We?"

Shit.

"See," she says. "That's what I was worried about. The way you describe you and Beau as 'Winston's humans,' and those photos of you two in Vegas, and the half-hearted attempts to quiet your followers' insistence that you two should be together. Sierra, are you sleeping with my brother?"

"Jackson, be real. It's Beau." I feel guilty as I say it, like I'm devaluing him and betraying him. But we agreed that Jackson could never know about this, and I can't betray Beau by telling her. Besides, it's not a long-term thing, so it's not worth going to battle with my best friend over it. Over him.

"Okay," she says tentatively. "So why was he at Sydney's wedding with you?"

"She needed a photographer on short notice, and he was free that weekend so he came to Vegas." Sydney didn't ask him to photograph her wedding, he just showed up with his camera and did it because he was there and wanted her to have good photos. But it's the only logical reason I can give her for why he'd be there, because the only other option is the truth—he was there for me.

"Beau is a photographer?"

It occurs to me that she really doesn't know him. Not the adult version of him anyway. He was thirteen when she went to college and fifteen when she left college to start racing professionally. She spent half of her early twenties traveling the globe for ski racing, and then once she was injured, she went to grad school in Utah and got a job in Park City. It makes me realize she didn't put in much of an effort to keep in touch with him. Which resonates with what he said the other night. I don't know why I never noticed it before.

"As a hobby," I say, because I know that he doesn't want his family to know about the business he's building, even though I don't really understand why.

"So there's really nothing going on?"

I can't say no, because that would feel like an outright lie. *You are lying*, that annoyingly honest voice in my head says. So instead I say, "Jackson, he's your little brother. He's five years younger than me. And I'm only interested in serious relationships."

All the reasons that nothing should have happened between us. But I let it happen anyway and now he's about to leave. We only have one night left together, and it's breaking my freaking heart.

She lets out a little laugh. "Yeah, it did seem a bit too far-fetched. But you just looked so comfortable with each other, like you'd only be that comfortable with someone you were dating."

"Or someone you were living with," I remind her.

"All right," she concedes. "Thanks for talking me off the ledge. I'm sorry I jumped to conclusions."

The guilt twists like a knife in my stomach. But I know how she feels about Beau, and I can guess what this would do to that already strained relationship. Even if I was willing to take her wrath, or her disappointment, or whatever it would be, I'm not willing to subject him to that.

"You are hardly the only one," I remind her. "Half the internet thinks we're dating or that we should be."

"Yeah, they're going to be disappointed when he leaves." Her words hit me like a sucker punch. Even though I've been preparing myself for the reality of him leaving, hearing her say it so casually hurts. And it hurts even more to know that I won't be able to turn to my lifelong best friend for comfort when he's gone.

"They'll get over it," I say. *Just like I'll have to.*

We say our goodbyes and hang up.

I didn't even realize that I was sitting there ramrod straight, my whole body tensed like I was ready for battle until I collapse back into the chair and feel the relief wash over me. I lie there with my head against the back of the chair and my eyes closed, taking deep breaths, and trying to calm my racing heart. After a minute or two, I realize that I need to get back to Petra and Lauren before they realize something's wrong. I sit up and open my eyes and find them both standing in the doorway.

"You have so much explaining to do," Petra says as she levels me with her best serious glare.

"Did Beau really come to Vegas with you?" Lauren asks. "Are you guys together?"

I can feel the heat creeping up my chest and across my

neck and over my face. I'm dying inside. It's one thing to evade Jackson's questions over the phone, but entirely another to lie to my friends, face-to-face.

"It's a really long story." I shrug.

"Thankfully, we have all night," Petra says.

But we don't have all night. This is my last night with Beau, and even though I want to be here to support Lauren while her husband is off on a backcountry ski trip and she's alone with their twins, I also don't want to miss out on more time with Beau than I have to. In less than twenty-four hours, I'll be able to devote all my extra time to my friends.

"Let's eat," I suggest, "before the food gets cold. I can explain over dinner."

By the time we're done with dinner, I've told them the whole story, and now they are both silent, looking at me like they don't know what to say.

"Your silence is scaring me." I tear off a piece of naan bread and scoop the last of my chicken tikka masala from my plate.

"I'm never speechless," Petra says. "But I don't know what to say."

"You were the one who suggested I invite him to Vegas and told me a little fling wouldn't hurt anything. If I remember correctly, I think you said it was a 'great idea.'"

Lauren's head swivels and she looks at Petra with alarm. "Did you really?"

"Obviously, the girl needed to have some rebound sex to help her get over Peter."

"I was over Peter the minute I saw him with his administrative assistant," I insist. "I was angry, not sad. This thing with Beau was *not* about getting over Peter, and I don't want it tainted by the assumption that it was." I look down at my plate when I tell them, "And now what I feared most is actually happening. I've caught feelings for him, but he's leaving anyway."

"You knew he was leaving when this started," Petra reminds me.

"Which is why I wasn't going to let anything happen," I say. "But the attraction was so strong, and since I've never had no-strings-attached sex, I thought 'why not?' And of course my feelings got involved, like they always do."

"He did ask you to come to Aspen, though," Lauren adds hopefully.

"Let's say I went there next week. We'd have a few more days together. Maybe even grow closer, and my feelings would get even stronger. And then he's *still* going to leave. Most of the time, we don't even live on the same continent. How could this ever work?"

"Would you ever consider going with him? You know, beyond Aspen? Like for the full snowboarding season?" Petra asks.

My food suddenly feels like a rock in my stomach. "He hasn't asked. And I don't know how that would even work. I need a job, I'm still paying off my student loans. Plus, traveling is expensive and, unlike Beau, I don't have sponsors to pay for it. And I'm too old to be following some twenty-five-year-old around the globe."

They both sigh, like they've finally recognized the hopelessness of the situation. "Your best bet," Petra says, "is probably to let this die once he leaves Park City, then."

"I know," I say, my eyes filling with tears. "And I hate that. Why did the guy who is perfect for me have to be *him?* A wanderer. He'll probably move on to another woman in the next country he's in, and I'll be here nursing a broken heart." The tears spill over my eyelids and stream down my face. "How did I let this happen?"

"Just because it's not turning out how you hoped doesn't mean it was a mistake," Lauren says. "Now you know what you're looking for in a guy, and you know how good a relationship can be. You can use that moving forward."

I don't want to move forward with anyone but Beau. The thought has the tears falling even faster, because what I want isn't possible. Even if it was what he wanted too, our lives are moving in opposite directions and there's no way to ignore that truth.

Chapter Twenty

BEAU

"Can I get you guys anything else?" the waitress asks. I pretend like I don't notice the way her eyes skim over me, just like they have every time she's come to our table. In another place, and another circumstance, I'd flirt her right out of her panties.

"Just the check," I say. She sets the billfold on the table and heads off with a wistful glance over her shoulder.

"Okay, so we're definite on Laax, right?" Lance asks for what feels like the twentieth time during this meal. I've already said we're heading to Switzerland after Aspen, I don't know why he's hounding me like an old nag.

"I said yes." I know I'm being testy, even though I can't pinpoint why.

"Well, you've been so fucking wishy-washy, you can't blame the guy for wanting to make sure," Drew says as he takes his napkin from his lap, balls it up, and drops it on the table.

"What?" My voice is ragged; it sounds like I'm looking for

a fight. I have no interest in fighting my best friends, but why are they pissing me off so much?

"Hey," Lance says, and he might as well be saying *Chill, dude* with that tone. He's right, I do need to chill. He looks straight at me. "For some reason you're a little high-strung right now"—and then holds both his hands up in a surrendering gesture, then turns to Drew—"and you're being a dick, so stop."

Drew looks at me and smirks. "Now look what you've done, you've made Mom mad."

I can't help but laugh. We all have our roles in our little group.

Lance takes a drink, finishing his beer. "Okay, I'm going to start making our travel plans," Lance says, his voice placating like he's giving me one last out. And it's taking everything I have not to take it. Because all I really want to do after Aspen is head back to Park City and be with Sierra. But while she mentions me leaving all the time, she never asks me to stay. And she won't come to Aspen, either. Why do I continue to cling to some ridiculous hope that she wants me as much as I want her, even when everything points to that not being the case?

"Go for it," I tell Lance, because there's no sense in hanging around where I'm not wanted. I slap enough money on the table to cover my part of dinner, and then I'm pulling my jacket on.

"You literally can't wait to get back to her, can you?" Drew asks.

"What are you talking about?" I ask. I haven't told my friends about Sierra and me, so this is pure speculation on his part.

He just laughs. "It's written all over your face, man. You're so whipped it's pathetic."

"I need to get back and walk the dog, idiot. Sierra is at her friend Lauren's tonight, some female emergency friend session or something. She's not even home."

Drew's chest shakes with laughter even though it doesn't leave his lips. *Asshole.*

I turn and stalk out of the restaurant, welcoming the cold wind as it hits me. I grab my snowboard from the rack outside and head down historic Main Street. I need to chill the fuck out, so I decide to walk home. It's not that far of a walk from here, but I normally take the shuttle because it's an ass pain to carry my snowboard on a crowded sidewalk. But it's a weeknight so there aren't many people out, and I need the exercise and the time to wind myself down.

Sierra's not home when I get back, so I grab Winston's leash and take him out for a walk, hoping that'll give us more time together when she does get home. This is my last night here, a fact I've refused to think about because I don't want to consider what it'll be like to leave her. How do you walk away from someone who you literally can't wait to be with?

The brisk walk with Winston helps calm me down, and by the time I'm heading back toward the condo, I feel centered again. I can do this. We had an agreement, and I just need to stick to it and stop thinking about something beyond what we said this would be.

I can enjoy tonight, and then tomorrow I can leave as planned. Sure it may hurt, but I'll get over it. I've gotten over it before. *Helen was child's play compared to this*, my inner asshole reminds me because apparently he wants me to suffer. And sure, maybe what I had with Helen felt real at the time, but the way I crave Sierra's company, her advice, her body, the connection we have in bed and out . . . that's new. Is this what it feels like to truly be in love?

I'm about a block from home when my phone rings, and I slip it from my pocket, hoping it's Sierra. Instead, Nate's name flashes on my screen. I consider sending the call to voice mail, but he so rarely calls I'm worried that maybe something's wrong.

"What's up?" I answer.

"I told you she was off-limits, didn't I? You seriously couldn't find *anyone* else in Park City, it had to be Sierra?" Nate says, his voice is low and hard and pissed.

"What are you talking about?" I ask. *How does he know?*

"Jackson found the dog's social media account. She saw the pictures of you and Sierra. She read the comments from all your followers. I know you guys said you're just roommates, but dude, I also know *you*."

Okay, so he doesn't know anything yet, he's just speculating. I let out the breath I was holding. "They're just pictures, Nate. To drum up attention and interest so that someone will adopt Winston."

What I'm really wondering is, has Jackson talked to Sierra? Did Sierra tell her the truth?

"You are not fooling me, Beau. You have a steady stream of women in and out of your life on a near-daily basis. Which is fine, I'm not judging. But no one wants that for Sierra, and you sure as hell know that Sierra doesn't want to be that person. She's a long-term relationship kind of girl."

Ha! If only he knew that she's *the one who's kept an end date on this.*

"And now," Nate continues as I let myself into the building and head for the elevator, "Jackson's on the phone with Sierra and she's upset, and you know how I feel about my wife being upset." I'm sure Nate intends his voice to instill fear, but he's not fucking intimidating me from across the country.

"For once in her life, can Jackson get it through her head that this isn't about her?" I spit out. Why does she think that everyone's decisions hinge on what she wants or how she feels? This isn't her fucking life, it's mine.

"She's concerned about you hurting her best friend."

"Too bad she's not concerned about her brother," I say quickly, then regret it.

"Why?" Nate asks. "Are *you* the one in danger of getting hurt here?"

I don't say anything in response. I just step into the elevator and hope the call will get disconnected. But somehow it doesn't, and by the time I get to our floor he says, "Are you going to answer me?"

"There's nothing to say, Nate. Even if something were going on between us, I leave tomorrow." I unlock the door and hold the phone between my shoulder and my ear as I squat down to let Winston off his leash.

"That doesn't answer my question," he says.

No shit. "Everything's fine. No one is going to get hurt," I tell him.

"You better be right," Nate says.

"I'm always right about stuff like this."

"I think what you mean is, you always leave."

"What the fuck, Nate?" I pause and he doesn't say anything. "I am always one hundred percent transparent about my intentions. I'm not trying to hurt anyone and I don't need to lie to find girls willing to have sex with someone they know isn't going to stick around."

"We both know Sierra isn't that kind of girl." His words are clipped. I suspect he and Sierra have had their share of ups and downs. She's a tenacious friend, and I'm sure she didn't take his leaving Jackson, or his returning five years later, lying down. She'd have tried to protect her best friend. And in turn, Nate's trying to protect her now, because she's Jackson's person.

Even though I'm leaving, and even though I'm jealous as hell that any man besides me is looking out for her, I'm glad she's got people like Nate to support her.

"If you're worried about me hurting Sierra," I tell him, "you are literally wasting your time."

"You'd better be right," he says.

The *or what* hangs off the tip of my tongue, but I catch it in my teeth so it doesn't slip out. "I am. And I've got to go. Tell Jackson I say 'hi.'" The last sentence comes out just as snarky as I intend it to, but before Nate can respond, I disconnect the call.

Well, fuck.

―――――

I can tell she's been crying the minute she walks in the door. Her eyes are puffy and ringed in red. I sweep her into my arms before she even has the chance to take off her jacket. She curls into me and I love that I can make her feel safe, protected.

"Tough conversation with Jackson?" I ask, my head resting

against her knit hat.

"How'd you know?" she mumbles into my chest.

"Nate called me."

"Ah, so we got tag teamed. Did you tell Nate what's going on?" she asks.

"No."

"I didn't tell Jackson either. I hated lying to her."

"I know," I say, and squeeze her a little tighter. "You could have told her, if you'd wanted to."

"I didn't want to make things between you and her worse," she says.

While I appreciate that she wants to protect me, the reminder that my sister would be upset about our relationship stings. I'm not the kind of guy the people who love Sierra want to see her with, as Nate made perfectly clear.

I don't know what to say in response, so I just hold her. We stay like that, standing in the entryway, until she tells me she's going to get heat stroke unless she gets her hat and jacket off. As those come off, I find myself peeling the rest of her clothes off too, until she's standing there in nothing but her bra and thong, looking at me like I'm the only thing holding her together. I pull her back to me and when her lips part for me, I kiss her like I'm branding her, making her mine. Like I want her to think of me every single time any other person kisses her for the rest of her life.

The thought of her with someone else spurs something deep inside me, an ache and a need combined into one. I pick her up and she wraps her legs around me, and I manage to get us to her bed without running into anything, even though our lips never leave each other's body.

It's frantic, the way we claw at each other with desperate

need. There is no foreplay, my pants come off and so do her bra and underwear. I'm inside her the minute her back hits the bed. I move my hips slowly, dragging out and pushing back in, feeling the slick heat of her body and the way it forms to my own. I try to memorize it all: the way her lips feel, how her skin slides across mine, the way her breasts fill my hands, the sound of those sweet little pants that turn to moans as she gets closer to her release.

I want to remember every moment with her, no matter how much it hurts in the end. In those moments I'm alone, I want to be able to remember this, the sound and feel of our bodies together wrapped in nothing but the darkness.

"More, Beau," she pleads, and I bring one arm under her leg, lifting it enough to fit my knee under it. The angle is deeper, the need is stronger, the feel of her squeezing me is exquisite torture. I increase my speed and she meets me thrust for thrust until she's chanting "Yes" over and over again. I can feel my own orgasm coming on as I watch her chase hers, and when she shouts "Yes," I clamp my mouth over hers, stroking her tongue with mine. And as I come, the only word running through my head is *mine, mine, mine*, over and over. I want to tell her all the things I'm feeling. That I want her in my life beyond tomorrow morning, that I can't imagine being without her, that I think I'm in love with her.

But I don't say any of that. Instead, I kiss her long after our bodies have come to rest with me still inside her, hoping that she can feel the love I'm trying to pour into her, that even though she doesn't want more than this, she'll at least remember how special I made her feel.

When I finally get up to take care of the condom, I return to a sleeping Sierra. I climb into bed next to her and watch her sleep until the darkness overtakes me too.

And when I wake up at the first light of dawn, she's gone.

Chapter Twenty-One

SIERRA

I send the call to voice mail, just like I've done every other time he's called this week.

I know it was wrong of me to chicken out and not say goodbye to him the morning he left, but I didn't want him to see me break down. I agreed to our arrangement, and its end date, and it wouldn't have been fair of me to make it harder on either one of us. A clean break, that's what we both needed. That's what I tried to give him, but instead it's had the opposite effect—he hasn't stopped calling me for five days. At this point my voice mail box is full of messages that I haven't listened to but can't bring myself to delete.

A sudden, sharp knock at my door has me sitting up on the couch, and Winston's head popping up from where he's laid snuggled next to me. I glance back at my phone. It couldn't be Beau, could it? Could he have come back? My hopeful heart beats erratically until I realize that Beau has the keypad code to the door, he wouldn't need to knock. I set my phone back on the coffee table and move my Kindle off my lap. Sliding my legs out from under the blanket, I pad across the living room with Winston on my heels. I stop at the front door to peek through the door viewer.

Petra stands outside my door looking annoyed, and I can tell that our height-challenged friend Lauren is with her because I can see the red hair piled into a messy bun on top of her head. I step back, wondering if I want to answer the door or get back to my romance novel. The hero and heroine are about to have sex for the first time, and I'm here for it and for their inevitable happily ever after. If only real life was like that.

"I can see you in there," Petra yells, and Winston barks in reply. "Open the door, Sierra."

I crack the door open reluctantly, but Winston still manages to worm his way through the opening and is jumping up on Lauren. "How could you see me through a solid wood door?" I ask.

"When you stick your face up to that peep hole thing," she says, gesturing at the small glass hole in the door, "your head blocks the light. The glass goes from light to dark."

"I'm not feeling great," I tell them, hoping I can get rid of them quickly. I prefer to mope in peace.

"Is that why you're not answering your phone?" Petra growls in her husky voice. "And why your voice mail is full?"

From where she's kneeling on the floor, petting Winston in an attempt to calm him, Lauren reaches up and puts a hand on Petra's forearm—a silent indication for Petra to calm down. "We're worried about you," Lauren says. "We haven't heard from you since dinner last week. You didn't answer our calls over the weekend when we wanted to see how the goodbye went, and you haven't returned our calls since. We just want to make sure you're okay."

"There was no goodbye," I tell them, "and I'm about as good as you could expect."

Petra reaches over next to me and pushes the door open, and she and Lauren bring Winston in along with a canvas bag with four bottles of wine sitting in the divided compartments. Are they planning to put me out of my misery with alcohol poisoning?

"What do you mean there was no goodbye?" Lauren asks once we're all inside, each of them perched on a barstool and me standing, facing them across the peninsula.

"I woke up before him the morning he was leaving, and I snuck out," I say as I fish through the drawer for a corkscrew. "I went to the coffee shop down the street and hung out there for a while, then went shopping and stayed out all day."

When I glance up, they are looking at me like I just told them I torture small children for fun.

Petra takes the corkscrew from my hand and asks, "Why in the world would you do *that*? The night before, you were telling us that you had feelings for him. Is that how you treat people you care about?"

"I know." I sigh. "I just couldn't do it. I knew that if I had to say goodbye to him, I'd be a sobbing mess and probably beg him not to go, or I'd agree to go with him to Aspen. The former would be totally against what we agreed to. The latter would just result in it hurting more when he had to leave. It was a lose-lose situation."

"How do you think it made him feel that you didn't even say goodbye?" Lauren asks.

"I doubt he cared." I shrug. "He's so used to leaving, it was probably a relief to not have to say goodbye."

"Do you really believe that?" Lauren asks, and I shrug my

shoulders. I can't pretend to know what was going on inside of Beau's mind. He didn't share anything about his feelings for me. Except, he did say that the connection we had during sex was an "us thing," and he did ask me to come to Aspen—twice. "Well, how would you have felt if you woke up Saturday morning and he was just gone without saying goodbye to you?"

The question is a punch in the gut because I know exactly how I'd have felt: betrayed, irrelevant, meaningless. But I wasn't the one doing the leaving, he was.

"I think we know the answer based on the look on her face," Petra says to Lauren when I don't respond. "Have you talked to him since?" she asks me as she points toward the wineglasses on the shelf.

I take three down and slide them across the countertop. "No, I haven't."

"He hasn't called or texted or anything?" Lauren asks.

"He's called a bunch of times, but I haven't answered," I admit, and I realize I sound like a complete asshole. "I can't do it." I rush on as I focus my eyes on the wine Petra is pouring. "I can't talk to him and miss him and wish things were different than they are. I just need to have a clean break and move on."

"Don't you think he deserves to know that's what you're doing?" Lauren asks. "He's probably trying to figure out why you disappeared, or wanting to make sure you're okay. Doesn't he at least deserve a response?"

I take a sip from the wineglass Petra hands me. "It's not about what he deserves, it's about what I'm capable of. And I can't do it. I can't talk to him, apologize, or work things out so we can still be friends, because it will hurt even more." I take another sip.

"So it doesn't matter to you that you may be hurting him too?" Lauren asks. She says it gently, like her sympathetic tone will soften the harshness of the words' meaning.

"Trust me," I assure them. "Beau will get over this much faster than me. And I don't need to hear him yelling at me over the phone—I already know what I did was wrong and weak. I don't need him telling me, too."

"But that might not be why he's calling," Petra says. "Has he left you any voice mails or anything? Sent any texts?"

"The reason my voice mail box is full is because of how many he's left." I take another sip of wine, then another. I wish I could mainline the alcohol into my bloodstream until I got that feeling of being comfortably numb, my emotions dulled enough that this wouldn't hurt so bad anymore.

"What did they say?" Petra asks, and when I shrug, her eyes widen. "You didn't listen to them?"

"Too painful," I say.

"This is not happening," Lauren says and shakes her head. "You're so empathetic . . . how are *these* the choices you are making?"

I'm the altruistic one, the caretaker. I know this isn't like me, but I've learned a new truth along the way—this could break me.

"Yeah," Petra adds. "I'd expect this of Jackson, not you. This is like watching her make the same mistakes all over again."

I think back to last winter, when poor communication over an unfortunate mix-up had her leaving Nate, when the whole situation could have been rectified if they'd have just talked. "This is different," I tell Petra. "Because Beau and I both know there is no future in this."

"Do you really know that?" Lauren asks. "Have you talked

to him about what he wants? Have you suggested trying to make it work?"

I hang my head. "No, we haven't talked about it. We had an agreement, and I don't want to be the one desperately begging him to hold on to what we have when he's already intent on walking away."

"If you haven't talked about it, you don't know where his head is. Maybe he feels the exact same way," Lauren suggests. "Maybe he wants to make it work and thinks you don't?"

That idea is utterly ridiculous and brilliantly hopeful at the same time. "I guess I *don't* know what he's thinking. I assumed that his head was still in the same place as when we agreed that this would only last for a week. I never imagined he'd change his mind."

"But you don't know that he didn't," Petra says. "Any more than he knows that you changed yours."

"Touché," I acknowledge the truth of her point. "Fine, I'll listen to the voice mails later."

"Good," they both say, and Lauren smiles and raises her glass. I clink mine together with theirs because it feels like it's what I'm supposed to do, not because I feel like we actually solved the problem.

"So, I have this fundraiser tomorrow night," I say, attempting to change the subject. "It's for work. Want to help me pick out something to wear while you're here?"

We head toward my closet while I explain that the fundraiser is to raise money for a foundation that helps up-and-coming alpine skiers fund their training and travel before they make the national team. They're impressed when I rattle off the list of some of the retired athletes that are going to be there. Since it's happening in-season, all our current athletes are traveling for races.

Petra's flipping through the section of my closet that has what I consider my "fancy attire," when she asks in what capacity I'm attending. "Like, are you working, or there as a guest?"

"I'm working. I'll be taking photos, mostly. But also, it'll be social as well, since I know most of these athletes from when they were on the team."

"Jackson's not going to be there?" Lauren asked.

"She was invited," I say, "but couldn't come because they're still in grand opening mode at the hotel."

Petra flips back a few hangers to some item of clothing she passed before. "I think this is perfect, then," she says, holding up a black jumpsuit that I forgot I even had. It's something Jackson had given to me years ago because it was a too short on her. The front has a relatively low V and the back is mostly open, with wide swaths of fabric that crisscross over my shoulder blades. I remember trying it on and thinking it was perfect, easy to move in and flattering.

"I forgot I even had that," I tell them. "You're right, it's perfect!"

And suddenly I'm looking forward to tomorrow night, because honestly, the perfect outfit can make you feel better about having to work on a Friday night.

―――――

"Wow, don't you look phenomenal tonight?" Heather says when I pop my head into her office shortly before the event is set to begin.

"Thanks. When you said you wanted me to interview some of the athletes about their careers"—a fact she only mentioned to me late this afternoon, despite knowing how much I prefer being behind the camera instead of in front of it—"it kind of put the pressure on me to up my game."

"Well, you are going to not only do a great job, but look great doing it. Hey," she says, her eyes lighting up, "how's Winston? Is he home with Beau tonight?"

I plaster a fake smile on my face and by the way she looks at me, I wonder if she can tell how forced it is. "Winston's great. He's home alone. Beau left for Aspen last weekend. The X Games start tomorrow, you know."

"Oh, I didn't realize he was competing. How's he feeling about his chances there?"

"I—I don't know. I haven't talked to him since he left."

Heather's eyebrows dip and she tilts her head. "Really?" I nod in reply. "I guess I misinterpreted things," she says. "When you guys picked Winston up after getting back from Vegas, it seemed like there was something there between you two."

"Beau and I were just roommates. We got along really well, though." My voice sounds falsely bright.

"Hmm," she says, and I can't even interpret what that means.

But I can say with certainty that in Beau's mind, at least, we were just roommates with benefits. I listened to all his voice mails last night after Petra and Lauren left, hoping to hear something that just wasn't there. His messages were a sad assortment of "Call me back," or "Sierra, what happened? Why'd you disappear?" or "Why are you doing this?"

The last question, which was also the last voice mail he left before my mailbox filled up, is the only one that I could potentially read anything into. And only because his voice cracked slightly when he asked why I was doing this? What did he even mean by *this*? Not calling him back? *Because the end hurts too fucking much, that's why!* I screamed in my head in response.

Heather and I head toward the part of the Elite Training Center that's set up for the event, and I easily slip into work mode as people start arriving. There are photographs to be taken, and I'm the girl to do it. A lot of times, the people photographing these types of events get groups of people together to pose. That's not my style. I like to zoom in on an animated conversation, capture the looks on people's faces as they converse, document the sweet moment when someone brings their grandmother a plate of appetizers or when two athletes clink their glasses together, toasting an old friendship. When I post these pictures, I want our fans to feel like they were here. Like they were part of this event, not like they are looking at posed photos.

I'm squatting down, my butt resting on one heel and my elbow resting on my upright knee, while filming one of our retired athletes dancing with his three-year-old daughter. They're holding hands and she's standing on his feet as he shuffles her around to the instrumentals of the jazz quartet playing in the corner of the room. It's the most heartwarming thing I've seen in a while and I'm so absorbed watching them on the screen of my DSLR camera that I barely register the tap on my shoulder. But then it's followed by my name.

I know that voice. I stand slowly and turn around. "What are you doing here?"

"I come to this event every year," he says. "It's where we met, four years ago."

As if I could forget that.

"But, Peter, why are you here *this year*? This is where I work. You knew I'd be here. Couldn't you have skipped it? Or at least given me a heads-up that you'd be here?" Never once did I imagine he'd attend this event after the way he broke up with me.

He lets his eyes wander up and down my body as I ask my questions, and instead of answering them, he says, "You look gorgeous. I forgot how beautiful you are."

"Yeah, you forgot a lot of things when it came to me," I spit out. "Like how to remain faithful."

"I didn't mean to hurt you," he says, and reaches over to run his hand along my bicep.

"Do. Not. Touch. Me." I enunciate every word clearly so there can be no misunderstanding or misinterpretation of my intentions.

"Don't be like that, babe," he says and I swear I see red.

"Babe?"

"C'mon, Sierra, you know we were so good together. I did something stupid and messed it all up, but I'm willing to apologize and I'm hoping I can count on your forgiveness."

He sounds like he's talking to a fucking business partner, trying to close a deal.

"You're hoping you can count on my forgiveness?" I say, a small laugh escaping with the last word. I lower my voice to make sure no one around us can hear me. "You were fucking your administrative assistant while we were engaged. Speaking of which, where is she?"

I glance around but don't see Jane anywhere, which is a relief.

"I came to see *you*," he says. "I made a very big, very stupid mistake. I need to know what I can do to get you to forgive me."

"Why should my forgiveness matter to you now, when *I* mattered so little to you then?" I ask.

"Sierra, you were always the one for me. Jane was an accident—"

"An accident? Like what, your dick slipped and accidentally landed in her? Then you accidentally asked me to move out?" I'm trying to keep my voice low, because work is not the place to be having this conversation. But these are not things that I can wait to say to him because after tonight I hope to never see him again.

"We were so good together. I lost sight of that, lost track of what was important. The life we were building together, that's what I really want." He's groveling and it's not helping his case, it just makes him look weak and pathetic. "You wanted that life too, didn't you?"

"I thought that's what I wanted. But in the last month, I feel like I've gotten to know myself better, to know what I need in a relationship. I need someone who goes out of his way to do things that he thinks will make me happy, someone who makes me feel safe. I need a guy who looks forward to seeing me when I get home at the end of the day, who is equally happy chilling at home on the couch or going out and dancing all night. I need a man who knows how to worship my body, and who trusts me with his deepest secrets. And you failed at all of those, but especially the last two."

"But Sierra, what we had together—"

"Was pathetic," I finish for him. "I haven't missed you. And if you've missed me, then I'm sorry things didn't turn out the way you'd hoped with Jane. But that doesn't mean that you and I belong together."

"So you'd rather wait for this perfect mystery man to show up? The one who's going to meet your extensive list of ridiculous criteria?"

He's mocking me, so I take a small step away from him, square my shoulders, and level him with the truth. "Newsflash, asshole. I've already met him."

This truth spurs a new realization—*Now I just need to figure out how to get him back.*

————

I pull open the door and step into the lodge. It's absolutely packed, and I have no idea how I thought I'd ever find Beau at this mountain and surprise him. Buttermilk is the smallest resort in the Aspen Snowmass family, but it's packed to the gills with fans here to see the X Games debut tonight.

I glance around and it's wall-to-wall people. I weave my way into the restaurant, thinking that since it's lunchtime, maybe I can find him there. But every table is packed, every seat is taken, and there's barely even passing room between the tables. The big windows and high ceilings, which normally help ski lodges feel less crowded, don't seem to be doing their job today.

I take off my hat and sigh in frustration as I reach into the pocket of my jacket for my phone. I'm going to have to call him. So much for the surprise effect.

"Sierra?" I hear from behind me, and a river of ice flows down my spine. That is not a voice I expected to hear this weekend.

I turn and find Jackson seated and staring up at me, her dark eyebrows knit together in confusion. I know I should be thrilled to see my best friend, I should be wrapping her up in a hug, but I can't. I'm frozen in place.

She pulls her long dark hair away from her face and asks, "What are you doing here?" I wonder if, in her mind, she's trying to figure out if there's any reason I could possibly be here *except* to see Beau.

I'm saved from answering when her dad, Rory, stands from the other side of the table and in his booming Irish accent half yells, "Sierra!" He's nothing if not theatrical, always has been. And he's happier to see me than his daughter is, which means Jackson hasn't shared her suspicions with him.

I give both of Beau's parents a hug, and Jackson removes her ski bag from the chair next to her, gesturing for me to join them. She was clearly saving the seat, so I assume Nate must be around somewhere.

"What are you all doing here?" I ask.

"We decided to surprise Beau," his mom says. "It was so nice to have him home for Jackson's wedding, we decided we needed to see more of him."

I look at Jackson, silently wondering why she didn't mention that she was coming to Aspen, and she shrugs. "I didn't think I'd be able to come so close to the opening of the hotel, but Nate insisted he had it well under control and somehow it all worked out."

So that seat isn't for Nate, which means it's probably for Beau and I just intruded on some sort of family reunion. I'm trying to figure out how I can back away gracefully, maybe make them forget they ever saw me here, when Rory asks, "So, what are you doing here?"

I could lie and say I'm here for work. I don't normally cover social media for snowboarding, but they'd probably believe me. *Jackson would know, though.*

"I came to see Beau. I also thought I'd surprise him. I didn't realize he'd have a whole cheering section."

"So the roommate situation worked out, then?" Catarina asks, her voice warm and friendly, trying to smooth over whatever tensions she's sensing from her daughter. Beside me, Jackson stiffens.

"Beau's been a great roommate. Coming here to support him was the least I could do." There we go, that sounds believable enough without sounding like I was having the most amazing sex of my life with her son.

"I really hope he deserves your support," Jackson says.

"What's that supposed to mean?" The words are out of my mouth before I can think better of it. I want to pull them back in immediately, but it's too late. The hostile tone and the question are both already out there.

"It means that I'm not sure what spell he's cast on you, but you're too good of a person to get sucked into caring for someone so wholly self-centered."

His parents' eyebrows both shoot up as they look at each other, then back to us.

"Maybe you just don't know him that well," I tell Jackson, turning to face her.

"Or maybe he has you totally fooled. He's an aimless wanderer and will always be. Ask him about Helen sometime if you don't believe me." She looks at me with pleading eyes. "Please don't set yourself up to get hurt by him."

Some of her assertions may be based on facts I don't know, but they feel stale and irrelevant. I know who Beau is *now*, and

I have to wonder how long it's been since she's really known her brother. Before I can stop myself, I'm defending Beau like it's my job.

"Beau doesn't go around hurting people, Jackson. But he does retreat when *he's* been hurt. Have you ever wondered why he doesn't come home anymore?" I glance from her to Rory, then back to her again. "And he isn't aimlessly wandering, he's actively building a business that both allows and requires him to travel. Look," I say as I reach into my pocket for my phone and pull up his photography social media account. "He's an amazing photographer, and he's making it into a career."

Jackson looks from my phone where I've held it out, up to my face. Her eyes are wide and her voice is quiet when she says, "I love that account. I've followed it for years."

"And he's not undependable, either. He's been there for me when I needed him these past couple weeks. I wish you could see how much he cares about and helps other people."

"Maybe when he's getting something out of it," Jackson says, and her mom lays a hand on her arm like she's trying to calm her down. "If he was actually dependable, he'd have come home when Mom was going through chemo."

I look over at Catarina, who looks surprised by Jackson's statement. Then I notice that Rory, who is sitting across from me, is looking up above my head and his expression is unreadable. That's when I glance over my shoulder and Beau is standing there, a hardened look I've never seen frozen on his face. He looks down at me. "Sierra, a word?" With his chin, he gestures toward the doors, then turns and walks outside.

I glance back at the table, at the stunned faces of his family.

"I . . . I'll be right back," I say as I stand, throw my hat and mittens back on, and rush outside to find him.

He's standing with his back against a railing, his sunglasses covering his eyes so I can't tell what he's feeling. He looks so good and it feels like I haven't touched him in forever. My body wants to rush up and wrap itself around him, but the hard line of his lips and his arms folded over his chest feel like a protective shield holding me at a distance.

"What was that all about?" he asks the second I'm close enough for conversation. And then before I can respond he continues, "If you thought for one second that talking to my family about me—telling them my secrets—was going to be okay, then you don't know me as well as I thought you did."

"Beau, I'm sorry. I didn't mean to break a confidence. But Jackson just started saying stuff and I *couldn't* not defend you. Why don't you just tell them the truth?"

"And what is the truth, Sierra?"

"That you're not a total fuckup." I throw my hands in the air because how does he not get this? By keeping them in the dark about how he spends his time and what's important to him, he's allowing them to believe a lot of things that aren't true. Maybe he even believes those things about himself. "That you *don't* just travel around the world like a nomad because you're too immature to settle down. That you *don't* sleep with every girl you come across, then leave her heartbroken, just because you can. That you *do* have a purpose and a plan for your future. That you *are* capable of being a responsible adult."

He slides his sunglasses up into his hair and levels me with a glare so flat and void of emotion it's like I'm looking at a sculpture of him in a wax museum, not the living, breathing

Beau that I've come to love. *Wait . . . love?* The realization dawns on me like a sunrise—so gradual you hardly notice how light it's getting until *boom*, you're blinded by the white hot glow of a sun that wasn't there moments before. Except, that look on his face reflects the storm clouds rolling in—big, black, angry ones—and they're chasing my sunlight away.

I fold my arms across my chest. *Why is he not saying anything?* I lift my eyebrow, but still there's no response from him. "Do you not have anything to say?"

"I'm—" he fumbles and shakes his head like he's trying to clear his thoughts. "I'm still absorbing how eloquently you've let me know what my family thinks of me and, by extension, what you think of me."

"That's not what I think of you," I say. "I feel like I've gotten to know the real you, and it frustrates me that you let your family believe you're this asshole with Peter Pan syndrome."

"Jeez, Sierra, don't hold back." He says it like I'm telling him something he didn't already know.

I give him my best, *you're not fooling me* look—the same one I gave my sisters when they were little and trying to pull something over on me while I was in charge of them. Except, the look on his face is the first real, unguarded expression I've seen since he walked up to me and Jackson a few minutes ago. And unfortunately, he looks hurt. No, strike that. He looks mad.

"Beau, all I did was defend you. I tried to clear up some misconceptions. I don't understand why you're mad at *me* about that."

"I told you that I'd never told anyone about my photography business. You know I don't talk about my relationship with my dad. Those things were *private*, Sierra. Don't you think if I'd wanted to have those conversations with my family, I would have already had them?" His voice is a few decibels too loud, and people are starting to glance over at us, which makes me intensely uncomfortable.

"What's wrong," he asks, his voice mocking me as he looks at my face, then glances around, "you afraid people are watching you?" I know he's zeroing in on how much I hate being in the spotlight, and it's like he's rubbing at a persistent sore that's achy and vulnerable. "That maybe now they know something about you that you're not ready to share? How's *that* feel? These people are fucking strangers, Sierra"—his words are venom—"and you're worried about what they might think about you. Imagine how I feel. You just shared my most intimate secrets with my family."

"To portray you in a better and more authentic light!" I practically yell in his face. "Because you're not who they think you are, and I want them to know they're wrong."

"That's what this is really about, isn't it? You couldn't bear to have them know something was going on between us unless you also convinced them that I'm not who they thought. Because you'd be embarrassed to be with the guy they think I am."

"That's not—" I stumble over my own words. "That's not true."

"Isn't it?" he asks, casually taking a step away from me and shoving his hands in his jacket pockets with an air of ease that he clearly doesn't feel. He's like a tightly wound spring. "You only fall for stable, dependable guys. Pretty much the opposite of me."

"I fell for *you*, Beau," I say, and reach out to put my hand on his shoulder, but he leans back so I miss his arm and my hand falls back to my side.

"No, you enjoyed having me as your dirty little secret. The one no one but Sydney could know about. And then when you came here and my family put two and two together, you shared my secrets so they wouldn't look down on you, wouldn't think you fell for a womanizing asshole with commitment issues."

I don't know where to start with his interpretation of events, so when my jaw falls open and no words tumble out, he assumes it's because he's nailed the situation down cleanly.

"Admit it, Sierra. This was never going to work because I don't fit neatly into the box of requirements you built for the guy you'd end up with. Luckily," he continues when I still haven't found my words, "it doesn't matter, because whatever I wanted this to be is dead. I could never be with someone I can't trust. And I certainly can't trust you."

He steps around me and walks back into the lodge, and the tears start falling immediately. I turn and rush through the crowds of people, making my way back to the parking lot where I climb into my car and hope no one walking by sees me sobbing.

Whatever I wanted this to be is dead. Those words will haunt me.

How did I get this so wrong? In the six hours of daydreaming I did on the drive here, imagining what our reunion would be like, I never could have imagined this. Running into his family, defending him only to have him turn on me.

The texts start coming through immediately, interrupting

my thoughts and preventing me from processing what just happened.

> JACKSON
>
> What the hell happened? You didn't leave, did you?
>
> JACKSON
>
> I will kill my brother if he hurt you. He's not saying what happened, and I want to make sure you're okay.
>
> JACKSON
>
> See, this is what Beau does.
>
> JACKSON
>
> Please, Sierra—talk to me.

The need to defend Beau is almost visceral. I'm so tempted to respond that I mute the text thread, figuring that if I don't see her texts, I won't think about replying. I set my phone on the console of my car, noting that while my best friend is texting me nonstop, her brother hasn't sent me even one message.

Without the distraction of my phone, I let the tears fall. All the tears for the life I thought I wanted, and for the love I unexpectedly found with Beau. I don't know how we possibly could have made things work between us, but I wanted to try. *Maybe it's better this way,* I tell myself. *Maybe this ending was inevitable and it's better that it happened before things got any further along.*

Buoyed by the thought that I've saved myself from a lot of future heartache, I dry my tears, take off my jacket and hat, and settle myself in for the long drive home. Alone.

Chapter Twenty-Two

BEAU & SIERRA

BEAU

When I stalk back into the lodge, I find my parents and Jackson huddled around the table with their heads close together in conversation. Mom looks up and sees me first, and her face is such a portrait of confusion that I can't even look her in the eye. Instead, I pull out the seat Sierra had been sitting in and plop myself down with all the pent-up rage that's bubbling up inside me.

"What the hell was that all about?" I say.

"We were hoping you could tell us," my dad says.

I look at him in confusion. "How the hell would I know? I walked in on the middle of that conversation."

I hate myself for how hopeful I'd been in that moment, when saw Sierra sitting there with my family. I'd let myself believe that maybe she cared about me as much as I care about her—enough that she was willing to tell my family about us. Instead, I found her sharing my secrets with them, trying to convince them that I'm "not a total fuckup," as she so eloquently put it.

"Are you and Sierra . . ." my mom starts, but can't seem to find the words, so Jackson finishes for her: "together?"

"No, we're not." How can I feel simultaneously devastated that it's the truth and relieved that I don't have to lie?

"What just happened, then?" Jackson asks.

"Nothing to concern yourself with."

"Then where'd Sierra go?" she asks.

"I have no idea," I tell her, and she takes out her phone. I can only imagine she's texting Sierra.

"Beau," my mom says, "what's going on?"

"I don't know, Mom. All of a sudden, you three show up to surprise me completely out of the blue. Then Sierra, too, and I find you guys at a table gossiping about me."

"You don't seem very happy that we're here," my dad observes.

When I'd gotten their call last night that they were in Aspen to watch me, it was a little surreal. But I'd agreed to meet them for lunch today, never expecting to walk in on the scene I did.

The last time Mom was at one of my competitions was in high school, and neither Dad nor Jackson have ever shown up before. "I've been doing this professionally for almost a decade, and suddenly you're interested in supporting me? Why now?"

Dad sits back in his chair with his thinking face on, his hands folded on the table in front of him. "We didn't know you wanted us here. Is this what Sierra meant when she said you've been hurt?" my dad asks. Surprisingly, I don't hear any condescension in his voice. It honestly sounds like he wants to understand my take on things.

"I don't know what she meant, or why she said that." I shrug. This is not a conversation I want to get into in the middle of a ski lodge.

"She was defending you," Jackson says, her voice softening. She glances down at her phone quickly, then says, "Honestly, Beau, you could have any girl you wanted. Why did you have to go after my best friend?"

I glance at my parents and neither of them seems shocked. This is the worst-case scenario, because they'll never believe that I'm not the one to blame here.

"What was between me and Sierra is just between the two of us. It has nothing to do with your friendship with her. This isn't about you, Jackson."

"If Sierra's going to get hurt, it's about me too—I will *never* not protect her. And I'm not going to sit by and watch you hurt her like you hurt everyone who cares about you."

"What the fuck does that mean?" I ask, the words coming out on a low exhale.

"It means that's what you do, Beau. You push the people who love you away. Me and Dad. Helen."

"Don't fucking mention Helen. You have no idea what happened there."

"Don't I?" she says lightly. "Do you mean to tell me that when she got into law school, when she got serious and needed you to commit, you didn't walk away?"

"That isn't what happened at all."

"What did happen, Beau?" my mom asks, her voice firm enough for me to know she expects the truth, and gentle enough for me to know she can handle it.

I press my lips together. I've never told anyone but Drew and Lance what happened with Helen. And even they don't have all the details. But at this point it was years ago, it shouldn't matter. It shouldn't still hurt. And it wouldn't, except that realizing that Sierra was embarrassed to be with me seems to have resurfaced a lot of the same feelings I had when Helen broke up with me.

"Once she got into Law School at Cornell, I suggested that I follow her to New York so we could get a place together," I say, looking over at Jackson, who is looking down at her phone and frowning, "and she laughed at me." That has my sister's head snapping up in surprise. "Said she could never be serious about someone so decidedly unserious."

Jackson's eyes flare, like she wants to punch someone for hurting her little brother. "I'm sorry, Beau, I didn't know."

"That's because you never asked, you just assumed."

"It sounds like maybe there are other things we failed to ask about," my dad says, sounding contrite. "Sierra brought up some fair points. Obviously, we hurt you. Is that why you messed up in high school so much? Were those cries for attention?"

It sounds so pathetic when he says it. "I just wanted what Jackson had growing up—two parents. I wanted you to see me snowboard, too, Dad, just like you were always at every single one of her races. I wanted to believe you cared."

"And I stole that from you," Jackson says, the realization dawning in her voice.

I can't respond, I just look out across the lodge.

"I took Dad with me to Europe," she continues. "I didn't mean to rob you of that. I didn't realize how important it was to you."

"To have an intact family?" I ask, looking back at her. What kid doesn't want that? "I mean this as no disrespect, because Mom has always been the best mom there is. But boys need dads too." Mom reaches across the table to where my hand lays and gives it a reassuring squeeze.

"This isn't your fault, Jackson," Dad says, his brows knit together, making him look older than he is. "I was the adult in that situation, it was my job to see and understand that, and I didn't, even though it seems so obvious now." He turns to me. "I'm sorry if I made you feel like I didn't care."

"You told me I was a disappointment and beyond help," I say flatly.

My mother's sharp gasp looks like it causes my father physical pain. And maybe it does. Maybe in some small way he does love me, if only for her.

"I don't remember saying that, but I believe you that I did. I let my temper get the best of me often when it came to you," he tells me. "But only *because* I cared and felt powerless to do anything to help you. Everything I tried seemed to have the opposite effect."

I want to ask him if by *everything* he means *nothing*, because how does he think he was trying back then? A weekly phone call? Putting all the responsibility of parenting a teenage son on my mom, who'd just survived her first recurrence of cancer?

Everyone is looking at me like they're waiting to see if I'll accept my dad's apology. But it doesn't feel like much has changed, other than he's recognized that he hurt me. And him realizing that doesn't make it any less painful, which I knew it wouldn't, which is why I never brought it up in the past decade.

I don't tell him it's okay, because it's not. Instead, I tell him, "Thanks for acknowledging that."

"I will do better," he says, as he reaches across the table and clasps my shoulder with his strong hand. "I promise, I will."

Inside my chest, a small flicker of hope ignites. Maybe this is the conversation we needed, after all. And right next to that small flame of hope lies a fire hose of guilt, because even though Sierra broke my trust, she might have been right about my relationship with my family.

———

SIERRA

My friends are waiting for me at my place when I get back to Park City. They've got tacos and margaritas and plenty of Kleenex.

I'm sure I violated several parts of the homeowner's agreement by giving them the access code to the condo, but I could not stomach the thought of coming back to the place I'd shared with Beau and finding it empty.

It'll still be empty when they leave, and now you've permanently ruined things with Beau. My inner voice has taken on my mother's tone, and it's a special kind of hell having her inside my head.

"I can't believe how badly I fucked things up." I cry on Lauren's shoulder the minute I walk through the door.

"It can't be that bad," Petra says. She's standing just beyond Lauren, looking amazing in leather leggings and a sweater that matches her eyes, the same silvery-blue color of a frozen lake on a sunny day.

"It's worse. I completely betrayed him, and he saw me do it, and he said he could never trust me again."

I recount the story as closely as I can without specifically mentioning the nature of his past grievances with his dad or the name of his photography and travel account.

"Is there any truth to his allegations?" Petra asks as she refills my margarita glass.

"That I told his family those things because I was embarrassed to be with the man they think he is?" I clarify, and Petra nods. "I've been asking myself the same question on the entire drive home. And the truth is, I don't know. If that was why I told them, it was subconscious. He's just such a better person than they give him credit for, and for reasons I don't understand, I guess he prefers their current perception."

"Did he want to keep your relationship a secret, or was that all you?" Lauren asks.

"He never indicated that he wanted to tell other people. I mean, it was a fling. You don't tell your family about those. And I needed to keep it a secret because I knew Jackson wouldn't approve. I never wanted to hurt her."

"It sounds like maybe you were more worried about her feelings than Beau's, and maybe even more than your own feelings too," Lauren says.

"Maybe," I agree. But that's how it's always been with us. Jackson has all the drive and ambition, and I have all the instincts to support and nurture. I've always let her take the lead while I've played the supporting role in our relationship, and I've never minded it until now.

"Now that she knows you lied to her on the phone the other night, have you talked to her about it?"

"No. She texted me a bunch of times right after I left, but I haven't responded."

"Why not?" Petra asks as she takes the individually wrapped tacos from a bag and sets them on a platter she found in one of the cupboards.

"I've never lied to her before this, and I don't know how to make it right."

"I am not saying that two wrongs make a right," Lauren says cautiously. "But she did lie to you—to all of us—about her relationship with Nate."

"But that was different, she was protecting Marco and trying not to lose her job."

"How is that different from what's happening here?" Lauren asks. "Knowing that something happening between you two might mess up his relationship with his family, weren't you trying to protect Beau?"

"I guess. I wish he saw it that way. He thinks I was just embarrassed to be with him."

"Are you sure there's no truth to that?" Petra asks, and Lauren looks over at her like she wants to throttle her, which is a feeling I'm familiar with. Sometimes Petra's honesty, and her utter lack of a filter, are a bit hard to swallow. "Are you positive you weren't just the tiniest bit ashamed to have fallen for someone so much younger and so different from what you were looking for?"

"If there was any shame, it wasn't about him. It was because I'd let myself fall for someone with whom I couldn't have anything more than a passing fling."

"I'm still not convinced that you couldn't have had more," Lauren says. "The way he kept asking you to come to Aspen with him, and kept calling after he didn't get to say goodbye—

those aren't the actions of someone who's having a fling. He had opportunities to leave the fling in the past, and he wasn't taking that option."

"Well, that's the path he's taking now. And I hate to think that he's out there somewhere thinking that I'm just another person who has disappointed him."

"So make it better," Petra says as she hands Lauren and me each a plate.

I reach for a taco, then decide I need one of each type. I pile all three on my plate as I suck down my second margarita. What is it about tequila that makes you feel like you can accomplish anything? I need some of that right about now.

"And how, exactly, can I make this better? He's the one who said losing his trust was irrevocable."

"So show him he's wrong," Petra says. "Show him he can trust you."

It sounds so simple, yet feels so impossible. I push my glass toward Petra and eye the half-pitcher of margaritas sitting there. "Refill, please? I need more tequila if I'm going to come up with a solution."

"Don't get her drunk," Lauren says as she nurses her glass of water because breastfeeding twins takes precedence over alcohol. "Nothing will be solved if Sierra's drunk."

"But I'm a happy drunk," I insist, already feeling the buzz of my first two margaritas. Petra has a heavy hand when she mixes drinks.

"You are," Lauren says, "but not a creative or productive one. And if you really want to make this better, you're going to need to come up with a fail-safe plan. Something better than driving to Aspen on a whim because you ran into your ex at a fundraiser."

"Hey, that's not fair. I did it because seeing Peter made me realize that Beau was the perfect person for me, and I wanted to tell him that in person. I wanted to see if we could try to make something work. You make it sound like it was half-hearted."

Lauren raises both eyebrows like she's encouraging me to see something right in front of me. She *does* think it was a half-hearted attempt at winning him back.

"It was heartfelt," I argue, "exactly *because* it was spontaneous."

"Sierra, if you want him to believe that you want something real with him, you might need to do more than drive to Aspen to see him for a weekend. How can you possibly make this work long term? *That's* the problem you need to solve."

I take a long sip of my margarita as I consider her point. "Lauren, why are you so damn wise?" I definitely trip over the last word and it comes out more like *wyyyyth.*

"And . . . she's past the point of making plans." Lauren rolls her eyes.

"No way," I say, sitting up and shaking my head to clear it. Lemieux women can hold their alcohol, no way am I letting a third margarita prevent me from crafting a brilliant plan, even if Petra was heavy on the tequila.

"You never do anything without a plan," Petra says. "And Beau probably knows that about you, right?"

"Yeah. Except Winston, I didn't plan on him."

"Where is he, by the way?" Lauren asks. "We expected him jumping all over us when we arrived."

"He's at my boss Heather's house. Thinking I'd be gone overnight, I dropped him off this morning."

"As I was saying," Petra continues. "You never do anything without a plan. So showing up to see him without a plan, that won't inspire confidence that you're really in this."

"I never thought about it like that. I just thought I was being romantic, rushing off to see him because I missed him so much and because I realized that he's perfect for me in all the ways I didn't know I needed him to be."

"That last part is perfect," Lauren says in between bites of her taco. "Store that away for when you see him!"

"The trouble is," I tell my friends, "I don't actually know how we can make this work. He travels all year. I have a job and commitments here in Park City."

"You don't even have a lease," Petra reminds me. "You can keep yourself tied down here because you're scared to go after what you really want, or you can actually go for it."

Her words hit me like an anvil.

"Are you suggesting . . ." I pause, trying to convince my tequila addled brain to work it out, "that I just up and leave everything behind to follow him? After *one week* of being together?"

"I'm not suggesting anything," Petra says, "I just want you to explore all your options, including ones that don't adhere to playing it safe."

"I don't play it safe!" I argue, and both Petra and Lauren burst out laughing.

"Oh, honey, you're the definition of playing it safe," Lauren says. "Peter? I mean, you were going to marry a man that you didn't even have strong chemistry with because you saw him as a partner in the life you wanted to build. A marriage is a partnership, for sure. But it has to be built on more than just shared goals. You also need someone who loves and cherishes you, and Peter didn't do that."

"There's no guarantee that Beau will either," I say, as I stare down into the murky depths of my margarita.

"Based on how you described him to Peter, it sounds like he already does," Lauren assures me.

"Okay," Petra says, clapping her hands together in a distinctly all-business way. "Are we helping you develop this brilliant plan? Or are you going to screw it all up again?"

I can't help but laugh because that's just such a Petra thing to say. And also because three margaritas and two best friends later, the situation only feels ninety percent hopeless instead of one hundred percent.

Chapter Twenty-Three

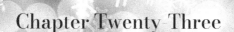

BEAU & SIERRA

BEAU

I'm debating the merits of the omelet and the breakfast burrito while simultaneously wondering how long this breakfast will take. After half a foot of fresh snow last night, Lance and Drew were anxious to get out there and shred this morning, especially since everyone else is packing up and leaving Aspen today. We're not leaving until tomorrow, and it'll feel like we have the mountain to ourselves without the thousands of people that were here for the X Games. I just have to get through this goodbye breakfast with my family and then I can head up the mountain.

The chair across from me pulls out from the table and my dad slides into the seat. Neither my mom nor Jackson are with him.

He flips his coffee cup over and glances around to see if someone is coming by to fill it, then looks up at me. "I want you to know how proud I am of you, son."

I look at my dad, how he leans back in his chair and drops

his hands in his lap. It couldn't be more opposite than my own combative stance with my arms crossed on the table in front of me and my flat bill trucker hat pulled low on my forehead.

Sure, he's proud of me now. I managed a totally unexpected first place finish in Slopestyle and a third place finish in Big Air.

"Yeah, well, now that you've actually seen me snowboard *and* Sierra told you I'm not a total fuckup . . ." It's easy to be proud of your kid once they're already successful. It's the getting there part where you really want the support of people who love you, and he wasn't there for that.

"I'm sorry that you didn't know that before. I always told myself I wouldn't be like my own father, and here I am in his shoes." My dad's father died before Jackson was born, but from what I've gleaned of their relationship, it's always sounded like getting away from his dad was the reason Dad moved from Ireland to America in the first place. "I never wanted to be that kind of father that was so hard on his kids they questioned whether they were loved in the first place."

"You were fifty percent successful. You weren't like that to Jackson."

"If true, that would only make it worse. You have to know that I *was* hard on Jackson. But she fed off that. She took every criticism and disappointment and used it as fuel. I didn't realize that the same strategy wouldn't work with you until it was too late, until the damage was done." Dad pauses while the waitress fills his coffee, then he takes a long sip of it. He's always taken his coffee black and likes it extra-hot. I've never understood how he doesn't burn his lips right off. When I don't reply, he continues, "That's why I meant what I said about trying to do better. I want to catch another competition or two this year."

I stare at him for a second while I process what he's saying. "But Dad, you'd have to leave Mom, and she's still just-barely in remission." One thing I will give him credit for: during her initial cancer treatment and *both* her recurrences, he's been there for her nonstop.

"I can get away for a few days. Besides, now with Jackson and Nate home, it's easier. I'm not doing it all by myself." I don't think he means to imply that I'm not around to help, but I register it anyway. "Plus, now that I'm retired and Nate's basically taken over managing the mountain, I've got time. It shouldn't have taken retirement for me to start taking an interest in your snowboarding, but I won't let my shame over the past stop me from being invested *now*."

Instantly, I wish I could tell Sierra about this conversation. Process it with her, because I'm sure she'd have insights I don't have, and she'd be so happy for me. That knife of guilt twists a little deeper. I wasn't kind and I don't think she deserved for me to hurt her the way I did.

"I'll send you my schedule in the next day or two. Pick one to come to. I'd like that."

Dad asks me about some of the jumps I landed in the competition here in Aspen, and I'm deep in an explanation about the difference between frontside and backside, and explaining some of the other snowboarding terminology that's so ingrained in me I use it without thinking, when Mom and Jackson finally arrive. They claim they were taking too long to pack and Dad didn't want to wait for them, and he gives me a conspiratorial wink that I have to guess means we both know he just wanted to have a private conversation. It feels so . . . natural. Like this is how a functional family really works. And maybe how it has worked all along, just without me, since I was the one who chose to remove myself because I didn't feel wanted.

We make it all the way through breakfast without any snide comments and without anyone asking about Sierra—the topic we've been dancing around since she showed up and then left two days ago. And then, while we're waiting for the waitress to return with Dad's credit card, Jackson has to go and ask, "Have you talked to Sierra yet?"

"No, and I don't expect to." I don't mention how many times in the past couple days my finger has hovered over her number, itching to call her while my mind talked me out of it. She told me that she didn't want my family to know about us, then when they found out anyway, she told them my secrets in an attempt to make our relationship more palatable to them. Hers was the only opinion that mattered to me, and it turns out she didn't think very highly of me after all.

"Beau, can you just tell me what happened? She's not talking to me either." Jackson sounds pained, and while I know it's not like she talked to Sierra every day, I'm sure that calling her nonstop for two days without a single return call is taking its toll. In fact, I know *exactly* how that feels.

I fashion my face into a mask of indifference.

"Don't do that," Jackson says.

"Do what?" I ask, glancing down as I pick up my coffee cup so I don't have to look at those green eyes. When we were kids, Jackson convinced me that her irises were made from shamrocks brought over from Ireland. She had me believing she was half leprechaun, because I was a really gullible five-year-old.

"Don't put on that 'I'm so much better than everyone else' face you like to wear and pretend that nothing bothers you. What did you do to my best friend?"

"I didn't do anything to her." My words are clipped, final. It's my *don't ask me again* voice and I know Jackson recognizes it because it's indistinguishable from my dad's.

"Then what did she do to you?" she asks.

Besides make me long for something I didn't know I wanted, only to show me that I can't ever have it? To give me hope only to extinguish it?

"Nothing." I plant my lips in a firm line.

"The way you were yelling at her out on that deck, either she did something wrong or you're an asshole. I need to know which one of you to be mad at."

"There's nothing to be mad about, Jackson. Just let it go." I wish I could follow my own advice.

The waitress slides the card and receipt back on the table next to Dad and we all push our seats out, anxious to put this conversation that's going nowhere behind us. We make it to the door when Jackson steps in front of me, blocking my exit. "I'll meet you guys outside," she says to our parents. I can see the door just a few steps beyond her. I was almost free.

"I feel like whatever happened between you and Sierra is either directly or indirectly my fault," she says once our parents are outside. "I called her and asked what was going on between you two, so I'm sure she didn't think I approved. And then I got all worked up in the lodge the day she came here, and she got upset and started defending you. If your relationship hadn't put her at odds with me, chances are you'd both be happy right now."

I've rarely heard Jackson apologize. So I want to bask in

this, force her to sit with the guilt for a while. But she's wrong, she's not to blame. And there's no use talking about this, it won't change the outcome.

"It's not your fault, Jackson. Sierra would never have been happy with me. I'm not what she's looking for. I was just a fun fling for her, one she was very clear she wanted to keep hidden."

"I don't know, Beau," she says, her voice dropping low. "She certainly seemed like she cared when she was defending you in the lodge a couple days ago. And she was *right* about all of those things. Why would she have risked her relationship with our whole family if she didn't *care?*"

I push my hands deep into my coat pockets and look off across the restaurant so I don't have to see her eyes as they try to bore holes into me. What she's saying makes sense and I can understand why she's interpreting it that way. But what she's missing is the fact that Sierra told my family those things because it made *her* look better, like she wasn't dumb enough to fall for an immature fuckup. But I don't want to get into that with Jackson, so I just shrug.

"Your default is to push people away instead of just saying what you mean," Jackson says, as if I don't know myself at all. But I do, and it's a defense mechanism that's worked remarkably well for me. *Or has it?* "Did you *tell* her what you were feeling? Try to talk to her about it? Or did you just push her away the minute things got hard, like you do with everyone else?"

I swallow past the lump in my throat, and in a low voice that I hope will broker no discussion, I lay out the truth. "It wouldn't have mattered because I'm not the guy Sierra needs, and I cared about her too much to let her lose sight of her dreams."

I leave Jackson standing with her mouth hanging open in the vestibule of the restaurant, kiss my parents goodbye outside of it, and then head straight for the rack where I stowed my snowboard earlier. I need to feel the snow under my feet and the wind on my face. I need to remember why I do this in the first place, why I can't be tied down, why I'm not the right guy for Sierra.

———

SIERRA

Thirty-one.

I glance at myself in the storefront window as I pass by. I don't look any older. I don't feel any different, except I'm one year further away from the goals I'd set when I was a naive twenty-two-year-old college grad. By thirty I'd be married, own a house, have a family. But all of that daydreaming avoided the obvious issue—the plan is dependent on the people. I was so desperate to do things differently than my own mother did, that I didn't stop to even question whether those were the right milestones, or the right order, for me.

Maybe if I hadn't been wasting time with Beau, I'd have found Mr. Right.

I think about how Beau has chosen to live his life—to really live it. To use his time to pursue the things he loves, visit the places he wants to see, build something he's proud of. And I compare it to my own life. I do like my job and I take pride in how I do it. But if I left tomorrow, they'd replace me with someone else who could do it as well as me. I'm not creating anything that's mine, there's no ability for me to shape my role, and there's no growth potential unless Heather leaves and I get her job. Basically, I feel stuck in a job most people would be thrilled to have.

This is called stability, I remind myself.

Despite my knee-length down jacket, I'm shivering as I pull open the door to the restaurant. I rush inside, only to be assaulted by a blast of hot air that whips my hair around my face where pieces stick to my lipstick and get caught in my eyelashes. I brush them away as I step toward the host stand while also looking for Petra and Lauren. They'd insisted on taking me out to dinner and though I told them I didn't feel like celebrating this year, it's nearly impossible to say no to Petra. So here I am.

I see the two of them waving to me from a high-top table in the bar area so I pivot to head toward them, but someone pushes their chair out and my foot clips the leg of it, sending me straight toward a guy in a wool coat who is moving around the chair pushed in front of his path.

I fall forward toward him and before I can even get my arms out to brace myself for the impact, he's caught me by my shoulders and set me right back on my feet. I look up to see who's saved me. His eyes are the color of the Caribbean Sea, his skin is a creamy gold that I can tell turns gorgeous and bronze in the sun, his jaw is chiseled, and his light brown hair is swept to the side with enough gel to hold it there for good.

"You okay?" His voice is gentle, like he's asking because he actually cares rather than as a formality.

"Yeah. I'm sorry about that, I wasn't looking where I was going."

"Where were you headed in such a hurry?" he asks. A real question with no innuendos. This isn't flirting, this is him actually wanting to converse with me, which makes him the kind of guy I've always imagined being with. A responsible, respectful man—and it doesn't hurt that he's so attractive.

"Meeting my friends," I say and nod my chin toward the table where Petra and Lauren are doing a poor job of not openly staring at us.

"Girls' night?" he asks, and I don't miss the way his eyes track my hand as I brush my hair off my shoulder. *Is he looking for a ring?*

"My birthday, actually."

"Well, happy birthday . . ." He waits for me to fill in my name.

"Sierra."

"Andrew," he says, and holds out his hand. I don't feel sparks when I slip my hand into his, or when he clasps his other hand around our joined fists and says "I hope you have a magical birthday."

"Thank you," I say before walking the rest of the distance across the bar to meet up with my friends.

"What was that?" Lauren squeals when I arrive at the table.

"I'm not sure." I unzip my coat and hang it over the back of the chair, then scoot up onto the barstool to face the two of them across the table. "He was really nice, though."

"Nice? Are you kidding me? He's really cute, and all you can focus on is *nice*?" Petra says.

"Believe me, his looks didn't escape my notice. I was just surprised by now nice he was."

The barstool next to me slides out and I whip my head around halfway, expecting to see Andrew there and I'm pre-embarrassed about him overhearing me talking about him. Instead, my best friend looks back at me, eyebrows raised, like she's challenging me to question why she's here. So I do.

Jackson ignores my question and slides into the seat as Petra says, "You didn't tell us you'd been ignoring her calls for a week."

"Last weekend, it was understandable that you weren't ready to talk," Lauren adds. "But a week later? We don't do that to each other."

Jackson and my friendship goes back twenty years, and never in that time have I gone an entire week without texting with or talking to her.

"I didn't know what to say," I tell Jackson.

"And ignoring me was going to fix the problem?" She shrugs out of her jacket and levels her gaze at me. Jackson's the kind of no-bullshit girl who goes after what she wants. Many people find her intimidating, but I've never felt that way until now.

"There is no way to fix the problem, Jackson. I slept with your brother, he broke my heart like I expected he would, and here we are." My words are more bitter than sad, and the look of shock on her face tells me that was too much, too soon. "Shit. Sorry, I could have . . . I don't know, rolled that out a little slower."

"No, I'd rather just know how you really feel." Her words are a kindness I didn't expect and her face relaxes. I'm not sure how, but I feel like I passed some sort of test. "We have a lot to talk about, but that can wait until tomorrow. Tonight, we're celebrating you!" She pulls me into a hug that's so warm and unexpected it actually brings tears to my eyes, which I guess shouldn't be such a surprise given how much crying I've done over the past week.

I'd felt so hopeful last weekend when Petra and Lauren and I decided all I needed was a plan. But even with the assistance of the margaritas, we couldn't come up with a single solid idea for how I could win Beau back.

You know what you can do, I hear Petra's words from last weekend, but they are as ridiculous now as they were then. I'm not chasing him around the globe while he snowboards. That's not a plan, it's a recipe to end up like my mom—jaded and bitter while my own career stalls, so I can follow him around like a groupie. And besides, I have zero indication that's what he wants, especially now that I've broken his trust.

"What's this?" Petra asks as a waiter arrives at our table with four champagne flutes, each filled with a pale sparkling cocktail.

"It's a French 75 in celebration of the birthday girl," he says, handing me my cocktail first. "From Andrew." He nods toward a table where Andrew sits with two other men, and when we lock eyes, he winks at me. My stomach flips over, but instead of the excited flutter of butterflies, I feel a low sense of dread at knowing I should go talk to him, even though he's not the man I want to be spending my energy on. But Beau is gone, and moving on is the right thing to do.

Thank you, I mouth to Andrew, then turn back to my girl-friends. They raise their glasses in a toast to me, and even Lauren takes a sip.

"Oh God, this is good," she says. "I haven't had a drink in over a year."

"You're okay to drink now?" I ask.

"Josh is giving the girls a bottle before bed. I can pump and dump when I get home."

"I don't even know what that means," Petra says, her voice a low tone of disgust, "but I can imagine, and I appreciate how glamorous you make motherhood seem."

"Motherhood's not always glamorous, and making it seem like it is would be a huge disservice. It's work, but the best kind," Lauren says with a small smile before she takes another sip of her drink.

We chat for a few minutes, mostly catching up on how things have been going for Jackson since it's been over a month since we've seen her in person—except for our disastrously brief meeting in Aspen, which we don't bring up even though we all know it happened. Eventually, I feel like I'm being watched, and a glance over my shoulder confirms that Andrew's looking at me.

I turn back toward my friends and they haven't missed the way my attention strayed. "I feel like I should go talk to Andrew, thank him for sending us drinks and all that."

"Who is he?" Jackson asks.

"Just a guy I bumped into on my way in. He was super nice, and obviously he's cute. I should at least go over and thank him."

"So Beau's been gone for a week and you're already flirting with other guys?" The tone isn't as harsh as I'd expect from such a judgmental question.

"I mean, I need to move on, right?" I say as I push my barstool back and stand. I take a fortifying breath as I wait for Jackson's response, but it doesn't come—she just looks at me like she doesn't know me at all. So I turn and head over to Andrew. He meets me halfway.

"Trust me, you don't want to meet my friends," he says with a half smile, and I'm relieved to talk to him one-on-one rather than in front of other guys.

"Why is that? Afraid I'll like them better than you?" I tease.

"Afraid you'll think less of me after being forced to talk to them."

"I feel like you can learn a lot about a man by the company he keeps."

"Which is why I don't want to be held accountable for these guys. I work with them, they're more like acquaintances than friends." His blue eyes sparkle with amusement.

"I suppose we can't control who we work with." I smile. "So why are you out with them and not your real friends?"

"I just moved here two months ago, I'm still making real friends. But these guys are fun to grab a beer with after work."

"It's a Saturday," I point out.

"And we just finished preparing for an important presentation we're giving on Monday," he clarifies.

Oh great, another workaholic. I feel like I just went down that route with Peter. Then again, he's new to his job, of course he has to put in the extra time to prove himself.

He tells me a bit about the company he works for, and I'm familiar with them because they handle the advertising for one of the biggest sponsors for the National Ski Team. I mention that, and we chat about work for a few minutes before the conversation starts to feel a bit stale. Andrew's cute and he's nice, but after five minutes of conversation, he's also somewhat boring.

I can tell he feels my waning interest because he says, "I don't want to keep you from celebrating with your friends, but I'd love to see you again."

I knew this was coming, but I still stumble over my excuse. "I . . . I just got out of a relationship and I'm not ready to start anything else." His lips turn down and I get the distinct impression that he's disappointed about the idea of not seeing me again, rather than upset at being turned down. He's a good guy, clearly. "Why don't you give me your number, though, in case something changes?" I don't want to give him my number, so instead I open a new contact on my phone and hand it to him to put his info in.

"I'm glad I met you," he says when he hands me back my phone. "I really do hope to hear from you in the future."

"Thanks," I tell him. "And thanks again for the drinks. That was very sweet."

We head our separate directions, and when I get back to the table and update my friends on the conversation, Jackson mutters, "Praise God."

I quirk my eyebrow at her, and she responds with, "You destroyed Beau. I'm just glad to see that you aren't quite as ready to move on as he thinks you are."

"What the hell do you mean, *I* destroyed Beau?" I balk. "He was always going to leave. And then when I came to see him in Aspen, he told me that it didn't matter what he'd wanted us to be because he could never trust me again, anyway. Then he walked away from me and I haven't heard from him since."

"I wish you'd have just called me back any of the hundred times I called you and texted you over the past week." Jackson sighs. "We could have figured this out."

I glance at Petra, whose eyes are wide as she watches this unfold. Then I turn and face Jackson. "Figured what out?"

"Beau's no more over you than you are over him. We can fix this."

It feels like my heart skips a beat, then speeds up erratically to make up for it. A painful, hopeful longing fills my chest. "Are you—" I feel my eyebrows dip as I try to make sense of what she's saying. "Are you serious?"

"Very. And we'll figure this out together. But first you will celebrate your birthday surrounded by your best friends." She reaches out and squeezes my hand.

"See, you just needed to let Jackson in," Lauren says, in case I hadn't come to that realization myself. "All will be right in the world of Sierra and Beau."

"It's the least I can do after you helped me win Nate back," Jackson says.

"So can we celebrate by eating?" Petra asks. "I'm famished."

"I'm glad to see some things never change," Jackson says as we all pick up our menus. For the first time in a week, I find that I have an appetite.

Chapter Twenty Four

BEAU & SIERRA

BEAU

I study the New Year's Eve picture again. Sierra's head is tilted toward mine, her temple resting along my jaw and her smile bright. Her hair cascades over her shoulders in the loose curls she likes to wear when she gets dressed up, and her skin is flushed from all the dancing. My tie is loose, the top button of my shirt is undone, my jacket is long gone, and the sleeves of my shirt are rolled up to my elbows. We look . . . happy. Like two people who are about to embark on the adventure of being roommates, blissfully unaware of the dangers to come.

I click forward to the next photo of her, one I took but never showed her or posted. She's sitting on the couch, leaning forward, rubbing her nose against Winston's. The light coming from the window on the other side of the room illuminates their profiles. It's a phenomenal shot, I couldn't have taken a more perfect picture if I tried.

I flip through the rest of the photos I have of Sierra, all

housed in one album I've entitled *Regret*. As I look at photos of us in Vegas, then back in Park City posing with Winston, the longing to see her and talk to her and just be with her is so strong it's physically painful.

My mom's words from New Year's run through my head, a frequent refrain since I told Sierra to leave. "As long as you love the nomadic life you're living, then do it. But the minute it stops being fulfilling, the minute you want more than all the partying and snowboarding—move away from it . . . I want you to find that thing in life that you can't live without."

Is Sierra the thing in life I can't live without?

I set my laptop on the coffee table of the rental house where Lance, Drew, and I are staying. It's quiet here tonight, the two of them have gone out to visit some of the Laax bars we like to hit up when we're here, which is often. Laax is a snowboarder's paradise, so we treat it like our European home base between competitions and trips for fun or for my photography business. When they left hours ago, I didn't feel like going, but now I think maybe it would have been good for me. How else am I going to move on?

As I glance out the window at the picturesque view of heavy loads of snow on sloped roofs, glowing in the light of the street lamps, I can't help but wonder why I'm here instead of with Sierra. I could be practicing in Park City. Laax has one of the best snow parks in the world, but so does Park City.

I pull my phone from my pocket and scroll through the weeks on my calendar. There are a couple of events—competitions or engagements with my sponsors—that I have to be at per month. But otherwise, my weeks are wide open, like right now. Do I really need to be traveling all the time, or could I use Park City as my home base for training and make it work with Sierra? Would she even want that? Could she forgive me for my hotheaded reaction in Aspen?

There's a huge bang behind me that has my body flying out of the chair. I spin to find Drew face down in the hallway that leads into the living room from the entryway.

"Yeah, total ninja move." Lance groans as he rolls his eyes and nudges Drew with his foot.

"I can be stealthy," Drew says as he pushes himself up to his hands and knees, his words slurring together slightly. "I just wanted to show you how *not* to be a ninja."

Lance laughs and glances over at me. "He thought he could sneak up on you." His eye roll is teenage girl-level. "But apparently this invisible snowboard he left leaning against the wall attacked him."

"You guys are home early."

Lance gives Drew a hand up and they walk past me into the living room. "It was pretty dead tonight."

"It is midweek," I say as I follow them, but when they get to the back of the couch, they stop suddenly.

"What the fuck?" Drew says.

"Is that Sierra?" Lance walks around the couch toward the coffee table where I left my laptop open. On the screen is a gallery view of all my photos of her. "Is this like a shrine to her? You pull your laptop out when we're not here just to look at her?"

"Of course not." I roll my eyes. That's exactly what I was doing. "I was just organizing some photos, and I put these in a folder together."

"Sure," Drew says as he sits and clicks on one of the photos on the screen. A picture of Sierra and me on the night of

Sydney's wedding fills the screen. He clicks to another one, and another.

"Dude, stop going through my shit," I say as I walk around the couch to grab my laptop, but he hands it to Lance before I can reach it.

"Whoa," Lance says, holding the laptop in his arms. "You seriously walked away from this?"

"From what?" My annoyance seeps out in my tone.

"From being happy."

Lance's words are like a slap across the face.

"What are you talking about?"

"Look how happy you look when you're with her." He turns the screen around to show me another photo from Vegas. "And you've been a miserable prick since we left Park City."

"Like even more than normal." Drew smirks.

"If you're so lost without her," Lance continues, "why don't you try to make something work?"

"What makes you think I even want that?" I ask. It's the antithesis of how I live when I'm on the road with them.

"If you don't," Lance says, "then why have you been so miserable for the past two weeks? The whole time we were in Aspen you were pissy, and you haven't been any better since we got here, even though Laax is supposedly one of your favorite places. And you haven't touched a single woman since . . . I don't even know when."

"It doesn't matter what I want"—I shrug and sit back in the chair I was in before they returned—"if she doesn't want the same."

"What makes you think she doesn't?" Drew asks. "Did she say that?" His mind must be filled with memories of Helen and how she broke my heart senior year of college. But that feels like a distant memory at this point.

"She said my family could never find out. But then—" I take a deep breath "—she went and told them anyway. Along with sharing a few other things I'd told her in confidence."

"Why would she do that?" Lance asks.

"Apparently, she was defending me when my sister said some shit in Aspen."

"Sierra came to Aspen?" Drew asks.

I nod in response. "Briefly."

"So what's *your* reasoning why this can't work out?" Lance asks. "Because it sounds like you're basing this on thinking she doesn't want your family to know, but then she told them, so. . . ?"

"She completely broke my trust." I fold my arms across my chest as I lean back against the cushion behind me.

Lance hands the laptop to Drew, who sets it back on the table, then he sits next to him on the couch. "But she broke your trust to try to make things better between you and your family, right?"

"Yeah, but—"

"Let me guess," Lance says. "You were looking for a reason it wouldn't work out, like you always are, and seized on that moment to make sure you were right."

I open my mouth to respond, but his analysis gives me pause. "I wasn't looking for a reason to end things with her."

"You sure about that?" Lance asks again. "You didn't push her away before she could do the same to you?"

"That's not what I do," I insist, but his words are a mirror of Jackson's and maybe they know me well enough to see something I'm not seeing? "Besides, when did you become Dr. Phil?"

"Don't pull this *I'm a guy so I can't talk about feelings* shit," Lance says. "You're being an asshole and making us all miserable. If Sierra makes you happy, go make it work with her."

"What if that means I need to stay in Park City except for events?"

"So stay in Park City," Drew says. "You can train there as well as anywhere else we normally go."

"But what about you guys?" I ask. I've always assumed that they needed me. It's been my sponsors that have made most of our travel possible.

"We'll figure it out," Lance says.

I grab my phone and open the calendar. "The next thing we have is Austria in two weeks, right?"

"Right," Lance confirms. "So in the meantime, go make things right with Sierra."

I glance down at my calendar again. That gives me enough time, but I still don't know if she wants me back, especially if she can only have me about sixty percent of the time. Can I be what she needs if I can't be there day in and day out? Or would the goodbyes in between be too hard? There's only one way to find out.

———

SIERRA

"You are one hundred percent sure this is what you want?" Heather asks.

My stomach feels queasy, like it's tied up in a knot and

trying to push everything out. Jackson assures me that this feeling is how I know I'm doing the right thing, but I know it's because I'm terrified of the unknown. I wouldn't have described myself as risk adverse, but I'm coming to see that it is maybe the single defining characteristic of my personality. Aside from Beau, I've never done anything in life that wasn't carefully planned after an extensive cost-benefit analysis.

I breathe in deeply through my nose as I glance around my office, reminding myself that I can always come back if I need to. I've left the door wide open. To anyone else, this might not seem like a risk, but for me, it's still monumental.

"Yes, I'm very sure."

You're not chasing after him, I remind myself, *you're choosing to go to him.*

The distinction is an important one to me. This isn't a desperate attempt to hold on to something that was never meant to be mine, it's an attempt to build something together.

"You're sure he's worth it?" she asks. Heather knows me well enough to know how out of character this is, and I was honest with her about my reasons for wanting a leave of absence. She also knows Beau's reputation.

"I'm positive."

"Okay, do you want to bring Winston by tomorrow, or do you want me to pick him up?"

"How about if you pick him up after work? I'll have all his stuff ready, and it'll give me time to say goodbye." My throat tightens at the thought of not having Winston with me. He's been an angel this past week and a half since Beau left, like he knows that I couldn't have handled his wild ways given the circumstances. I will miss all the snuggles, but I'm so relieved the shelter is allowing Heather to adopt him. If it can't be me, she will be the perfect dog mom for him.

She pushes the paperwork across my desk. "You are going to be okay," she tells me. "For what it's worth, I think you're doing the right thing. I know leaving Winston behind is going to be hard, but you only meant to foster him in the first place, and you need to spend this time doing what's right for you and Beau."

I glance down at the copy of the Leave of Absence request form I'd filled out a couple days earlier, now complete with both Heather's signature and that of the HR Director.

"And if you end up back in Park City, there will always be a place for you here," she tells me.

"Thank you," I say, wanting to tell her how much I needed to hear her say those words. I'm positive I'm making the right decision for now, but I'm not sure what the future will hold. Could Beau and I end up back here? It's presumptuous to even consider it, given that I don't really know how he's going to react to me showing up in Laax this weekend. In all of our planning this past week, Jackson was insistent that it won't be like when I showed up in Aspen. Petra and Lauren have reminded me that this is exactly the type of plan that will ensure Beau knows I value our relationship, that I value him. It's the brilliant plan we tried and failed to develop over margaritas nearly two weeks ago—turns out we needed Jackson's help too. And I needed to come to terms with letting go of what I'd built for myself here in Park City.

"You should go home early," Heather says, standing up and brushing a piece of lint off her joggers. "I imagine you need some time to pack."

"I do." I take in the two boxes of my personal belongings

that I packed up earlier today. I'm about to say that I'll need to make a couple trips to get my stuff out to my car when Heather offers to carry a box for me. "I feel like you're trying to get rid of me," I joke.

"Don't be ridiculous. I just want to help."

We walk down the hallway with my boxes, but it's surprisingly empty. Most of the office doors are shut, but there's silence—no one on the phone, or in meetings. Not even the sound of clicking keys on a laptop. Then we round the corner to the reception area, and I'm greeted by a shocking chorus of "Surprise!"

The room is decorated with balloons and a banner that reads "We'll miss you!"

I turn toward Heather. "Go home early, huh?"

"We're not letting you leave without a proper goodbye." She sets her box down and takes mine from me, before I'm swept up in a small crowd of people who have been my work family for years. Leaving them is going to be hard, but knowing I'll be missed makes it a little easier.

———

Two days later, I'm standing in the lobby waiting for the car service that will take me to the airport. Outside, the snow has started falling with flakes so large I can hardly see the other side of the street. I glance down at the large suitcase, the rolling bag with both pairs of my skis, the boot bag filled with all my other ski gear, and my overnight bag. Then I glance back outside and wonder if my plane will actually leave with this storm blowing in.

As of right now, it's still showing an on-time departure for late this afternoon, so I'm still heading to Salt Lake City and hoping for the best. But if I make the trip there with all this gear and my flight is canceled, I'm going to be pissed—not only because it'll mean at least one additional day until I see Beau, but also because I'll be stranded in Salt Lake City and have to get myself to a hotel room with all this luggage.

A big black SUV pulls up to the curb directly in front of the building, and the driver gets out. I push open the glass door and stick my head out.

"Sierra Lemieux?" he asks.

"Yes, and I have kind of a lot of luggage," I say, gesturing to the bags behind me.

"Let's get it loaded and on the road before there's too much snow to go over the mountains."

I roll the big suitcase and the ski bag over to him, and he takes the handles on each and rolls them to the trunk, where the lift gate opens like magic. As he loads those in, I throw my boot bag over one shoulder and pick up my overnight bag. The snow falls in fat flakes around me as I walk toward the back of the car, and the driver meets me halfway.

"Here, miss, I'll get these for you," he says as he takes the boot bag from me.

"I'll hold on to this one." I nod toward the overnight bag in my hand. The purse I picked up for traveling is tucked in the top, ready to access when I need my phone, passport, money, and any other essentials.

I watch him pack my bags into the back of the SUV and things feel more real now than they ever have. My stomach drops every time I stop long enough to think about what I'm doing. That I left my job and am packing up my life to be with Beau, and I still don't know how he'll feel about that. Jackson insists that this was never just a fling for him, and knowing that does make some of his actions and reactions make more sense. But she's been wrong about him before—I pray that she's right this time. Either way, this is the turning point.

New snow is accumulating quickly on the packed snow left over from our last storm a few days ago. The fresh flakes crunch under my snow boots as I walk around the car to the back passenger door. I toss my overnight bag on the seat and am about to step in when another large SUV comes careening toward us, honking and flashing its high beams. I jump back in surprise and the driver rushes from the back of the car around to the side, putting himself between me and the car that's now pulling up behind us.

"What the hell?" the driver mumbles under his breath. The headlights from the other SUV are shining in our faces, and I put my hand up to shield my eyes as the brakes squeal and the back door opens.

"Sierra!"

I gasp at the sound of Beau's voice. *I must be imagining things.*

I look up as Beau springs from the back of the car, and then he's running toward me.

"What are you doing here?" I ask as he skids to a stop in front of me. It's an awkward welcome, but I'm so taken aback by his presence. I'm supposed to be flying to him . . . in Laax.

"Sierra, I'm so sorry," he says, taking both my shoulders in his hands. He leans his head toward mine and rests his forehead against my knit hat. "I owe you such a monumental apology that I don't know where to start. I've spent the last sixteen hours of flying trying to figure out how to explain why I screwed things up between us so badly."

"Beau," I say, tilting my head up to look him in the eye. "I'm the one who owes you an apology. And an explanation."

My driver clears his throat. "I'm sorry, miss. But if we don't get on the road, I may not get you there in time. The snow's going to make travel over the mountains really slow."

I glance from him to Beau.

"Where are you going?" he asks.

"To the airport," I tell him. He raises one eyebrow and I know what he's asking. "I was coming to Laax. To see you."

"I don't think that flight is going anywhere," he says to me, and glances at my driver. "The flight attendants on my flight into Salt Lake City were talking about how we were lucky our flight wasn't getting in a few hours later, because they'll definitely be closing the airport. This storm is supposed to dump two feet of snow."

"So, what do we do now?" I ask him.

"We go inside and figure this all out." He kisses the bridge of my nose and then turns to talk to my driver while I step under the overhang outside the building to get out of the snow.

Ten minutes later, Beau drops the last of our collective luggage in the living room of Jackson's condo and turns to face me.

"Hey," he says as he steps toward me. His fingers take mine and he squeezes my hand while he dips his head and plants another kiss on the top of my hair. His proximity is lighting me on fire. Even though I've taken off all my outerwear, I'm burning up with need for him. I wonder if it will always be like this.

"Hey, yourself," I mumble into his chest as I lean toward him. I circle my arms around his waist and breathe him in.

"I've missed you so much," he says as he wraps his arms around my shoulders and holds me to him.

"Beau, I need to apologize. I need to explain about Aspen."

"Me first," he says, and so I nod, swallowing down my protests.

He toys with the ends of my hair and lets out a shaky breath. "I knew I was pushing you away in Aspen, and I did it on purpose."

Well, *that* wasn't what I was expecting. It's an admission without an apology, so I wait to see what else he'll reveal.

"My senior year of college, my girlfriend, Helen, who I thought I loved and who I thought loved me, broke up with me. She claimed I wasn't serious enough to be serious about. I believed her. Maybe even agreed with her. I mean, that rang true with things I'd heard from my dad growing up, too. And since then, it's been easier to push people away. If I don't let anyone get close, I can't get hurt. But with you I did get close, I did let myself care. And every time I suggested that maybe this could be more than just a one week thing between us, I felt like you were pushing me away, trying to keep us a secret because you were embarrassed about being with me."

I pull away from his embrace, planting my hands on his hips and looking up at him. "The only thing I was embarrassed about, Beau, was that I let myself love you, even though I knew you were going to leave and break my heart."

"You let yourself love me, huh?" he says as he reaches out and brushes the errant piece of my hair back behind my ear where it belongs. Then he cups my cheek in his hand. "I'm relieved I'm not in this alone. I don't know how you did it, Sierra, but you managed to change everything about how I view myself and my world. You make me want to be a better person, you make me want to be the person you think I already am."

I reach up and grip his wrist, bringing his hand to my heart. "You already are that person, Beau. You just do a damn good job at hiding it for some reason."

"The things I care about, I hold close. I hide them to protect them—or more likely, to protect me from losing them."

"Is that why you hid your feelings for me?" I ask him, still clutching his wrist as my heart pounds steadily under his hand. "Were you afraid you were going to lose me?"

"Everything you said reinforced that this was a short-term thing in your mind," he says, and I wince at the pain in his voice. "I felt differently, and sometimes I thought maybe you did too. But you kept insisting that this end when I went to Aspen and you were adamant that my family never find out about it."

"I thought I was upholding our agreement. I didn't want to be that clingy girl begging you not to go. I thought if you wanted more, you'd tell me."

"I did tell you. I asked you to come to Aspen with me."

"Beau, you asked for another weekend together. I didn't realize you wanted more than that. Or at least, I assume that's what you're telling me?"

"I want whatever you're willing to give me, Sierra," he says. He reaches into the pocket of the flannel he's wearing and pulls out a folded envelope, then hands it to me. "Open it."

I lead him over to the couch where we sit down facing each other. Then I do as he asks, sliding out a folded piece of paper, printed double-sided with calendars of the next two months on one side, and the following two months on the other. On it, he's written locations and used an arrow to denote the duration of each trip. In the next three months there are six trips, but every day that's not part of a trip he's highlighted in yellow. On the last month, May, he's blocked out a week that's just labeled as "Surprise."

"What's this?" I ask after I finish reading the calendars.

"It's a calendar of all the places I'm committed to being over the next few months. The days highlighted in yellow are mine to spend however I want. And I want to spend them with you. It'll mean a lot more flying, but I can be here more than half the time." He looks at my face and it looks like he second-guesses himself. "I mean, if you want me to be here."

"Yes, I absolutely want to be with you," I tell him, then pause. I can tell he senses my hesitation by the way his jaw tenses. "But maybe not here."

"Where then?"

I gulp, because in my mind I still had a whole day of travel to figure out exactly what I was going to say to him when I showed up in Laax. "I sort of left my job, and put nearly everything I own in storage. Those suitcases and my skis"—I nod toward the luggage we left on the other side of the couch —"that's everything I was bringing with me to Laax. I wasn't planning on coming back. At least, not for a while."

His jaw hangs open like he can't find the right words.

"You're not saying anything," I say, lowering his hand from my chest. *Oh crap, I haven't read this situation wrong, have I? Maybe he still wants those trips to be a guys-only thing, and he just wants to come home to me in the interim?*

"That's the most un-Sierra-like thing I've ever heard," he says, his voice low and smooth.

"I did have a plan, actually."

"I'm all ears," he tells me, and reaches back up to rest his hand against the side of my neck, stroking my jaw with this thumb. The fact that he can't stop touching me has to be a good sign.

"I know you're still growing your photography account, and I happen to have some experience in social media." I give him a tentative smile. "I thought maybe I could work on helping you grow that account. Not take over the creative piece, but I could work on the more administrative part, at least for the next few months."

"And what happens after a few months? What happens when you get tired of traveling all the time and you want to be settled somewhere?"

"I honestly don't know, Beau. If the traveling is too much for me, maybe we try it your way. We find a place to settle down together—whether it's Park City or somewhere else— and I don't travel with you, or I only go sometimes. I'm okay with not knowing, because I trust that we'll figure it out."

He takes both his hands and slips them along either side of my jaw so that his thumbs are resting on my temples and his fingers curve around the base of my skull. Then he pulls me toward him, meeting me halfway. He brings his lips down over mine and sweeps into my mouth like he owns it—I'm pretty sure at this point that he owns *me*. Every nerve ending in my body is singing as our lips clash together and our tongues meet again. I will never get enough of him.

He pulls away too quickly, but rests his forehead on mine. "Are we crazy?"

"I quit my job to follow you after we'd only been together for a week." My laugh is a low, self-deprecating rumble. "I'm pretty sure that's totally normal."

"I hope we look back on this moment and know that this is when we made the right decision for our future," he says.

"I'm reasonably sure we will. We've done everything backward, Beau. We lived together, then slept together, and now we're choosing to make this a real relationship. Just because things happened in the reverse order doesn't mean it wasn't the right way for it to happen for *us*."

"Brilliant *and* beautiful. Pretty sure I hit the jackpot in Vegas."

With our foreheads still pressed together, I can feel his smile more than I can see it, and I'm fine with that. Because if there's one thing I've learned from Beau, it's that it's okay to do what feels right even if you can't quite see what will happen as a result.

Epilogue

BEAU

Eleven Months Later

"I have a couple things planned for you today, and I need you to take every opportunity to relax and be pampered and accept the surprises as they come your way instead of questioning them. Can you do that for me?"

"It depends," she says, trailing her finger down the center of my chest all the way to where the white hotel sheet covers my hips. "What are you going to do for me?"

"Everything," I say, peppering the ridge of her nose with kisses. "Every day, everything I do is for you."

She cups my face in her hands and looks into my eyes like she's trying to see inside me. Or maybe let me see inside her. "I know," she whispers.

I lift myself onto my elbow to look at the clock on the

other side of the bed, trying to gauge if distracting her with sex will backfire when she's stressed about being late. But it's like she anticipated needing this time when she set the alarm because there's an hour and a half before she has to meet Jackson and I have to meet Nate.

I glance down at where she lays tucked up against my side with the sheet loosely draped over her naked form, and wonder for the 330th day in a row if there will ever come a morning I don't wake up and thank my lucky stars that she's in my bed. I can't even remember what it was like to not have her with me, to wake up after meaningless sex with someone I didn't care about. I didn't realize then that someone else could make me feel whole, but I know it now.

"I can see you thinking," she says fondly as she wraps her hand around the back of my neck and pulls me to her.

"I'm feeling really grateful that we're where we are right now. That you're here with me. That we've gotten to travel and experience so much together in the last year." I could never have imagined that Sierra would adapt so well to life on the road—not just adapt, but thrive. She's not just along for the ride, she's driving the bus. She's taken over planning where we'll go next, and making sure that if there's an excursion, we take it. She babies Lance and whips Drew into line when he needs it. She's been more amazing than I anticipated, both when we're traveling with my friends and when we've gone off on solo trips, just the two of us—something she insisted on and I still thank past-Beau for agreeing to.

"Well, stop thinking about it and *show* me," she says, bringing my lips to hers.

I delve into that kiss with reckless abandon, because when those surprises start coming her way, I need her to remember this. To remember how perfect we are together, how happy we make each other.

It only takes a minute before she pushes me onto my back. She rises above me as she swings her leg across my hip and plants her center right over me, and I'm already rising up and trying to find my way inside her while she hovers just out of reach. Instead, I reach up and cup her perfect breasts in my hands, stroking my thumbs over her nipples in that way I know will drive her right down onto my raging hard-on. Sure enough, she thrusts her hips down, running those slick folds along the length of me and back to the tip. Then she repositions herself and I thrust inside her as she sinks down to take all of me. She hovers there for a moment, giving herself time to adjust to this deep penetration before she uses her thighs to raise and lower herself up and down my shaft.

As I watch her take the lead, I think back to that tentative girl I first had sex with in Vegas who didn't even know what she liked or how she liked it. It only makes me appreciate how she now takes control, making sure I give her exactly what she wants.

With my hand on the back of her neck, I bring her toward me until her breasts bounce near my face. In my mind, her whole body is perfect, but if there's one part of her I can never have my mouth on enough, it's right here. I take my free hand and cup as much of her as will fit in my palm before running the rough pad of my thumb over her hardened nipple.

She doesn't try to hide her groan of pleasure, and she arches her back, pressing her tits toward my face. I take that nipple into my mouth, running my tongue over and around it —which has her clenching her walls around my cock—and then I suck her into my mouth with long pulls that have her sighing my name. I give the same attention to her other nipple and then her hips are moving faster and she's mumbling something along the lines of, "So fucking good."

She reaches forward and grips the top of the headboard above me with one hand, and brings the other to her mouth, swirling her tongue around the tip of her finger before she brings it to her clit. With my hands still on her breasts, I watch her circle that bundle of nerves over and over as she slides up and down the length of me and the sight has me aching to fill her with everything I have. I bring my hands to her hips, quickening the pace as I move her up and down at the tempo that I know will bring about her orgasm. I feel the telltale signs of my own just as she throws her head back and hisses, "Yes." Then her thighs are quaking as the muscles of her internal walls clench around me over and over until I'm pouring myself into her and she's repeating my name on breathy sighs.

She collapses onto me, and I wrap my arms around her. She's sweaty and happy and mine.

"I don't want to get up," she complains after we've lain there basking in the afterglow of amazing morning sex.

"C'mon, let's get showered. And promise me you'll embrace the surprises I mentioned earlier?"

"What do you have planned?" she says, regarding me as if I'm the sneakiest boyfriend she's ever had. *Oh honey, you have no idea.* "This is Jackson and Nate's anniversary. Don't do anything that takes away from them and their ridiculous level of happiness. Promise?"

"Promise," I confirm. Because even though this will over-shadow Jackson and Nate's anniversary that we're allegedly here to celebrate, Jackson is fully on board. I might be the mastermind of this whole endeavor, but she's the one pulling the strings.

———

SIERRA

My nails and toenails are shellacked in the prettiest shell pink, a color that Jackson said she picked out especially for us, and we're lounging in the waiting area of the spa, drinking mimosas as we watch the snow fall outside. Jackson looks out the floor-to-ceiling windows that overlook a courtyard with an enormous stone fountain. Her features are serene, all olive skin and dark hair with those bright green eyes and pouty pale pink lips, but there's something there just under the surface.

"What's wrong?" I ask. I wonder if she wishes we were out skiing again today, but my body is still sore from keeping up with her and Petra yesterday, and I'm relieved we're at the spa instead.

She shakes her head as she looks at me, like she's snapping herself out of some internal conversation. "Nothing's wrong. I'm just thinking how grateful I am for all this"—she gestures to the spa that's part of the hotel and village they built at the base of the new backside of Blackstone Mountain—"and for you ladies. I'm thinking about the past two years, how far we've all come and how much has changed." Her eyes travel from Lauren to Petra to me as she says, "Nate and I finally got married. Lauren's a mom, Petra's a married woman, you're living with my brother. We're all spread out, and I'm just so happy you're all here for this celebration."

"Excuse me ladies," I hear from behind me and we turn to see one of the spa receptionists standing there in her sleek, head-to-toe black clothing. "We're almost ready for your hair appointments. Sierra, you're up first if you want to follow me."

She leads me to the door of the dressing room and tells me to take my shirt off and put on one of the kimonos, then to come out when I'm done. I open the door and walk into a room that's darker than I expect. The only light comes from the dozens of pillar candles on the table in the center of the room, and the same Zen music that plays in the rest of the spa quietly fills this space too. The path from the door to the table is scattered with rose petals, and my heart skips a beat as I think of what Beau said about accepting surprises as they come my way today.

I take a few tentative steps toward the table, and then the glint of candlelight off something sparkly draws me closer. I step up to the table to find a red velvet ring box sitting on a round mirror, an envelope with READ ME FIRST scrawled across it in Beau's handwriting lies next to it. I take a shaky breath because *is this real life?* This can't be happening, it's only been a year—which seems lightning fast for a guy who's never been in a truly long-term relationship until a year ago.

I pull the letter out of the envelope.

Sierra,

I already know what you're thinking: it's only been a year. But when you know, you know. And I've known since we were in Vegas. Before then, even. I knew that the only way I wanted to hear my name again was from a breathy sigh rolling off your lips. I knew that I wanted to come home to you every night, cook you every dinner, take care of your every need. I knew that when I went to sleep at night, I wanted you wrapped in my arms, and when I woke up in the morning, I wanted you beside me.

I'll admit that there was a time when I couldn't imagine settling down, it felt like a trap—that "settling" meant that I'd be giving something up, missing out. I couldn't have known then what I'd be gaining. That in being "settled," I'd be adding everything you bring to my life: your strength, your sense of purpose, your ability to mix adventure and business together, your drive, and most importantly, your love.

I am a better, stronger person because you are in my life. We are better together. Every day I appreciate and love you more, and I want to keep growing and nurturing what we have together for the rest of our lives.

All my love,
Beau

I'm smiling and crying as I finish the letter and set it back on the table. I'm about to reach for the ring box when I hear "That box is empty" from behind me.

Gasping, I spin around and Beau is standing halfway between me and the door. I close the distance in two long strides, and he kneels down at the same time he reaches out and takes my hands in one of his, stopping me before I can throw myself on him.

"Every single day has been better since you walked into my life. You're the only person I've ever felt this connection with, you get me on a level no one ever has, and I want you as my partner on every adventure."

"Yes." I nod. "My answer is yes."

"I haven't even asked you yet." He smiles.

"Then hurry up and ask so I can say yes." My smile is so big I feel like it might break my tearstained face.

"Sierra Anne Lemieux, will you do me the great honor of being my wife?"

"The honor is all mine," I say, as he slips a ring on my left ring finger. I hardly even look at it before I'm pulling him up so he's facing me. "I knew there was something special between us when we met in that bar a year ago. I never could have imagined this life we're leading together, but it's perfect."

He dips his head and brushes his lips across mine. "Speaking of this life we're leading, we have another big decision to make."

I can feel my eyebrows wrinkling in confusion, because I feel like all our big decisions for the next few months are already made, and we rarely plan further in the future than that.

"Today, Nate offered me a job."

"What?" I draw back in surprise. "You already have two jobs. There's no room for anything else."

"Do you want to hear what it is?" He laughs. "Or have you already decided the answer is no?"

I glance down at the ring on my finger, admiring the princess cut diamond surrounded by a border of tiny diamonds. It sits low to my finger and is perfect. "You're telling me about a job offer on the heels of proposing. Whoever claimed you weren't romantic?"

"Maybe I should keep the details to myself, and just decide without consulting you?" he teases, wrapping his arm around my lower back and pulling me to him. He plants a kiss on the top of my head.

"Don't you dare."

"Nate and Jackson are going to open a snowboarding program next winter. Something on par with the ski racing program that's been running here for decades."

I think about what a program like that would have meant for Beau when he was younger. To have had a group of people as passionate about snowboarding as he was, to have had mentors to guide him—something comparable to what Jackson and I had on our ski racing team.

"And they want you to . . .?" I prompt.

"Be the face of it. Run the program, recruit the coaches, organize competitions. They're building a terrain park this summer that will be unlike anything else in this region, on par with the bigger mountains."

"But what about your own competing?" I ask. He's been complaining this season about how much longer it takes him to recover from a botched landing or an unintentional collision with a rail—things he would have bounced back from more easily before. I just joke and call him *Old Man* because that'll never stop being funny, given our age difference. But is he really thinking about giving up his career as a professional snowboarder?

"Like I said, it's a lot to consider. And we have plenty of time to talk about it. I want to do what's going to make us both happy, and what's going to be the best for us in the long term."

I pull back and look him in the eye. "Did Beau Shanahan just say 'long term'? What's next, you going to start talking 401(k)s and babies and college funds?" I ask with a little laugh.

A look I can't quite read flashes quickly in his eyes. "Eventually." He smiles. "Maybe even sooner than later."

"Wow. When do we need to decide?"

"We've got time. We'll talk later. Right now, you have a big party to get ready for."

I think about how Beau was complaining on our flight here from Italy. "It's not enough that we all came to Blackstone *last* New Year's Eve for their wedding, now we have to go celebrate them again?" I'd insisted that New Year's Eve was an awesome day to have your anniversary because you'd always get to celebrate it. Besides, after everything Jackson and Nate went through to be together, they deserve this anniversary celebration and more.

I don't for one second mind coming home to celebrate with them. And even though he'd initially complained, the minute we got here Beau seemed more relaxed, even happier. He's made so much progress with his family over this last year, and the fact that Jackson and Nate *chose* him for the snowboarding program speaks volumes.

"All right, I'll see you later. Will you be back in the hotel room when I'm finished getting my hair done?"

"I have to help Nate with some things for the party tonight. I'm going to go get dressed now, so I'll see you when you get down there." He kisses my forehead. "By the way, I filmed this whole thing." He points to a camera on a mini-tripod set up on the shelf above the hanging kimonos I'm supposed to choose from, and another on the far side of the room.

"Of course you did," I say, but I'm secretly elated. I can't wait to watch, and to show my friends.

He walks around the small room and grabs the cameras and a wireless microphone, collapses the small tripod, and then turns to give me a wink. "I'll see you tonight, future Mrs. Shanahan."

I think my heart melts in that moment, because I'm paralyzed in the same way I'd be if my blood stopped pumping through my body. I can't believe we're really doing this. I mean, I knew we were headed in this direction, and even though I'd have married Beau yesterday, I didn't realize he was already ready for this next step.

The minute Beau is out of the room, my friends are flooding into it, asking to see the ring and making me recount every detail.

The afternoon flies by with celebratory mimosas and getting our hair done, and before I know it, I'm back in my room and finishing up my makeup and looking forward to this New Year's Eve party. I glance down at my ring again, admiring the way it sparkles and thinking about how *this* is the only ring I was ever meant to wear, when my phone rings. I tap the screen to accept Jackson's call.

"Are you dressed yet?" she asks.

"No, I just finished my makeup. I can be dressed in a few minutes." I glance at the clock, seeing that we're supposed to head down in about five minutes. I've gotten distracted looking at my ring too many times, imagining walking down the aisle to Beau, and now I'm going to make her late for her party.

"Okay, don't get dressed yet," she says. "I have a special delivery from Beau that I'm going to bring to your room."

"Okay?" I'm not sure why I shouldn't get dressed before she brings this surprise over. But as soon as I hang up the phone, she's already knocking on the door, and I open it to find all three of my best friends standing there. Jackson's holding a giant garment bag, and as they walk in I notice all three of them are wearing the same formfitting long, backless deep green velvet dresses.

"Are we all matching tonight?" I ask, thinking about the dress I brought specifically for the party. It's not new or nearly as pretty as the dress they're all wearing, which manages to look amazing on all of them even despite their different body styles.

"Something like that," Petra responds while Lauren says, "Sure, honey."

Jackson hangs the garment bag on the curtain rod at the opposite end of the room, and when she unzips it, an involuntary gasp leaves me almost unable to breathe. I think I might hyperventilate. Because inside that garment bag is the exact dress I'd texted to Jackson a couple months before with the message, *I'm not saying we're getting married. I'm just saying that when we do, I want to be wearing this gorgeousness.*

It hangs there in all its lacy glory—the deep V in the front, the champagne satin belt, the mermaid bottom. It's even more gorgeous in person than in the photos.

"What? How?" I ask, still scrambling to put the pieces together. "Why is there a wedding dress in my room right now? How is it the dress I texted you?" I take in all three of them again, with their matching dresses. "Am I . . ."

"Getting married tonight? Yes," Jackson says. "So long as that's what you want. If you're not ready, it doesn't have to happen tonight, but Beau thought with your family history you might not want a long engagement." She's smiling so hard that I realize how much secret planning she and Beau must have done to make this happen. A year ago they couldn't stand each other. We've all come so far.

"But . . . it's your anniversary."

"And now it can be yours too."

My eyes dart back and forth between the three of them. "You all knew this wasn't really an anniversary party?"

"We all knew," Petra says. "Everyone who's here is here for you. Even the people who had to stay hidden so you wouldn't see them and start to suspect."

"Like who?" I ask.

"Sydney and Joe," Lauren says, as she starts ticking names off on her fingers. "Your old boss, Heather, Drew, Lance—"

"I can't believe you guys pulled this off. I had no idea. I was surprised enough by the proposal, but a wedding . . . on the same day . . ." I lose my words as tears fill my eyes.

Jackson quickly reaches over to a box of tissues on the dresser and hands me one. "Nope, no way are you ruining your eye makeup right now."

There's a knock on the door and as Lauren opens it, I hear my sister ask, "So, are we having a wedding tonight, or what?"

I spin around so fast I almost make myself dizzy. Sydney stands in the doorway in the same matching dress my friends wear.

"Yes." I smile. "Yes, we are."

———

BEAU

"So we find ourselves back here exactly one year later," Nate says as he steps up next to me. I'm standing along the side of the room with the wall of windows that look out on the surrounding forest, just like he did minutes before his own wedding a year ago.

"Who would have thought?" I say without taking my eyes off the trees and mountain lit only by the moonlight. There's always something so calming about the mountains.

"My car's in the parking lot if you're having second thoughts," he says, repeating my words from a year ago back to me.

My shoulders shake with my laughter. "It sounds even more douchey when you say it."

"What kind of brother-in-law would I be if I didn't let you know I had your back, even if you were doing something stupid?"

I glance over at him. "I'm pretty sure I'm making the best decision I've ever made."

"I'm pretty sure you're right," he says, reaching over and clasping my shoulder. "At the risk of sounding like a total dick, it's been great watching you grow up over this past year."

"Given that you've never had siblings, I'm not surprised you don't know how to fulfill this brotherly role." I elbow him in the side.

My words are literal bullshit. Nate's been exactly what my family needed—he brings out the best in Jackson, is helpful and supportive with my parents, has turned Blackstone's operations around without making the mountain feel too different, and has offered me an amazing opportunity to be part of it all. It's like he's welcomed me back into my own family and instead of it feeling patronizing, he's been the common ground we all needed.

We stand there for a second when his phone buzzes and he takes it out of this pocket. "They're ready."

I breathe a sigh of relief. I knew Sierra would be game, I just didn't know if she'd insist on talking it through with me first. But like she has for the past year, she continues to surprise me with her willingness to go with things, even if there's only a skeletal itinerary and she didn't have a hand in planning it.

"Are Lance, Drew, and Joe ready too?"

"Yeah, they were just showing people to their seats. Everyone's ready."

"Let's do this, then," I say and turn to walk over to the door that leads into the ceremony room. I pull it open, eager to get to the head of the aisle I'll watch Sierra walk down.

The room is lit only by the glow of the soft white lights strung around the trees that line the perimeter of the room, and the candles along the front. They cast a beautiful glow, but it's going to make this quite difficult to photograph. Luckily, I hired the most sought-after wedding photography duo in the region. Unsurprisingly, I care more about the photos than any other aspect of the event besides the marriage itself.

We line up at the front, and when the pianist starts playing the processional, the doors at the end of the aisle open. I watch Lauren and Petra walk down the aisle one after the other, followed by Jackson and Sydney, who walk down together. I wonder if they've told Sierra yet how each insisted the other be the maid of honor until the only logical conclusion was that they should both hold the title. There are so many details of planning this that I can't wait to share with her.

The doors shut before I can get a glimpse of my bride, and I take that moment to look over at my mom, where she sits next to an empty seat in the front row. She gives me a smile and a nod, and I feel more grounded than I ever have. Somehow, being grounded is a welcome feeling now. Not that I don't still love soaring above the jumps, where the snow and the sky flip over one another while my body twists through the air. But these days, that's a fun distraction instead of my purpose in life, which is partially how I know it's time to consider Nate's offer.

The song changes and the door opens, and Sierra comes walking slowly down the aisle, gripping my dad's arm like it's the only thing holding her up. I can see the tears sparkling in her eyes as she gets closer, but her smile is wider than I've ever seen it.

When they reach me, my dad gives Sierra a kiss on the cheek, takes her hand, and places it in mine. Then he clasps both his hands around ours and says, "Be good for each other."

"Thanks, Rory," Sierra says quietly, which I appreciate because suddenly I'm too choked up to speak.

She turns toward the front of the room and brings me along with her to face the justice of the peace, self-assured in a way I'd only gotten glimpses of last winter. She looks over and winks at me, and I can do nothing but stare at her while the woman in front of us speaks about how marriage is one of the few instances where the whole is greater than the sum of its parts.

"When Beau's father joined his hand with Sierra's," she tells our guests, "he told them to 'be good *for* each other.' Truer words could not have been spoken, as being good *for* each other is the work of a marriage. Honoring and cherishing each other, growing together throughout your life— that is where you go from here. The world will throw its share of difficulties your way, but as long as you weather them together, you can handle what life puts in front of you."

She transitions to our vows, and I turn to face Sierra, taking her hands in mine and repeating the words that I've chosen to bind us together in marriage.

"I, Beau, take you, Sierra, to be my wife. I promise to be true to you in good times and in bad, and to love you and honor you all the days of my life." A single tear slips down her cheek as she listens to my vows, and her voice is thick as she repeats hers.

Then Nate hands me her wedding ring, which I slip on her finger as I tell her, "I give you this ring as a sign of my love. I promise to care for you, to give you my trust, friendship, and support, and to respect and cherish you above all others."

She's amused when Jackson hands her my ring, and smiling when she repeats the words of the ring exchange. And when the justice of the peace tells us I may now kiss my bride, I take her at her word and don't hold back. Sierra wraps herself around me like it's been an eternity since she saw me instead of mere hours. Then she pulls back, locks her eyes on mine, and tells me, "You are the best, most unexpected thing that's ever happened to me."

I can't wipe the smile off my face as we are presented as man and wife, and the way our guests cheer when we walk down the aisle, you'd think they just witnessed the impossible. And in a way, maybe they have. But with Sierra, everything feels possible.

THE END

Not ready to see Sierra and Beau's story end? Get their bonus epilogue so you can see what they're up to in the future.

Scan here for
Sierra & Beau's
Bonus Epilogue

Keep reading for an excerpt from Petra's book, ONE LAST SHOT.

One Last Shot

Aleksandr Ivanov was always my person. We helped each other through the worst of our childhoods. I thought we were meant for each other; then he ghosted me.

That's when I learned that the only person I can count on is me.

Fourteen years later, the NHL superstar reappears in my life with an outrageous request: pretend to be his wife and help him adopt his orphaned niece, Stella. I can't commit to the marriage he's asking for, but when I accidentally screw up his childcare arrangement before he leaves for the Stanley Cup playoffs, I end up as Stella's nanny for a couple weeks.

I shouldn't put my life on hold to help him. I shouldn't fall hard for his precocious niece. And I definitely shouldn't let him into my bed, or more importantly, into my heart. Because if I do those things, I might start wanting things I can't have.

There is no happy ending for us: I've got a company to run, and a contract to start filming a television show in Los Angeles. He can't leave New York, and staying with Aleksandr would mean giving up everything I've worked so hard for.

And most importantly, I can't put my very fragile heart right back into the hands of the one person who already destroyed it.

Read on for a short excerpt from Petra and Aleksandr's book...

––––––––

PETRA

I stand at the window in the living area of the hotel suite, sipping my coffee as I take in the view of the southeast corner of Central Park. I can see across The Pond to the Nature Sanctuary, and beyond that, the buildings of the Upper West Side rising above the opposite edge of Central Park.

When my coffee is half gone, I hear the sound I've been waiting for—the rustling of the sheets. I pick up the second cup of coffee off the windowsill and head back into the hotel bedroom.

He's propped up on one elbow and his muscles bunch up in ripples across his abdomen. Yep, he's as fit as he felt in the dark last night.

"Wow," he says, sleep clinging to his voice as he looks me up and down. I'm in nothing but a T-shirt, and I've spent the past twenty minutes fixing my curls from their post-sex messiness.

"I made you coffee," I tell him as I hold up the to-go cup. "To have on your way home."

"Ouch. I was ready for round two. You kicking me out already?" His voice is teasing, like he thinks I'm going to say *Oh, round two? Yeah, let's go for it.*

"I don't do this whole next-day thing," I say, picking up his dress shirt off the floor and tossing it to him. The only reason I didn't kick him out last night was because I fell asleep, exhausted from a day of travel between Park City and New York, combined with some pretty decent sex. It wasn't a terrible way to end my day, but waking up with a stranger in my bed is never my favorite way to start a new one.

His face is screwed up into a mask of confusion as he catches the shirt, but he slips it on. As his fingers work at the buttons, he says, "Just so you know, usually I'm the one gently ushering someone out the door the next morning."

I hold in my *Not this time* comment, because there's no reason to rub salt in the wound. Instead, I say, "I had fun last night."

"Me too," he says, swiping his pants off the floor at the edge of the bed. He slides his legs into them as he stands and looks at me while he zips and buttons them. "Maybe we can do it again tonight."

"I've already got plans tonight," I lie.

"It was worth a shot," he says. I wait while he gets his socks and shoes on, then I head to the hotel room door, which I hold open for him to indicate it's time to go. I hand him the to-go cup of coffee on his way out, shut the door behind me, and lean against it, relieved to have the space to myself.

I have a lot to do to get ready for this meeting today.

———

"I'm Petra Volkova," I tell the receptionist as I step up to the desk in the lobby of the lawyer's office. "I'm here to see Tom Shepherd."

"Oh, yes," the receptionist says. She stands at the wooden desk she shares with the two other receptionists. I glance behind her where *Callahan, MacDonald, Reardon & Shepherd* is written across the frosted glass wall in gold lettering. "Mr. Shepherd is expecting you. Follow me."

She waits for me to step up next to her before she turns and leads me around the glass wall that separates the reception area and the rest of the office. I tower above her as we walk down the aisle between desks. My goal with high-profile clients is to give off the vibe of professional power, and nothing makes me feel more powerful than a well-fitted dress and sky high heels. Still, I wish I knew who I was meeting with today.

Leaning toward me with a conspiratorial grin, she tells me, "I'm probably not supposed to say this, but I've just been temping here, so whatever," she waves her hand in the air like she's brushing away the stigma around whatever it is she's about to say. "All the girls in the office are in quite a tizzy today. We always are when *he* comes in. We've all been dying to see who he and Mr. Shepherd are meeting with."

This type of inane chatter is exactly why I could never work in an office. And though I'm still not sure who *he* is, I'm guessing that whoever Tom Shepherd called me here to meet is a big deal in his own right.

"I can't say that I see what the big deal is," I shrug, feigning nonchalance while hoping she tells me who I'm meeting with.

She gasps. "Okay, maybe you're not a hockey fan, but you're *clearly* a woman. You can't possibly be immune to a guy that looks like he does."

I'm sure my face conveys exactly how unimpressed I am. I know next to nothing about US hockey and care about it even less. I've never loved the sport, and my ex-best friend ruined it for me like he ruined so many other things.

"Hockey players don't impress me," I tell her as we come to the end of the rows of desks that sit outside the offices lining the wide hallway we just traversed. In front of us is a wall of glass windows looking out over Midtown Manhattan. "There's something very—" I pause as I search for the word. "—brutal about the sport . . . and the men who play it."

I've actively avoided hockey for the past fourteen years so it's not like, even if she'd told me his name, I'd have ever heard of this mystery man.

"Brutal, sure." She shrugs and adds, "But he's hot as hell."

She takes a left and I follow her down a hallway of conference rooms with frosted glass doors. When we come to the end of the hallway, an administrative assistant sits alone at a desk with her back to another bank of windows. Across from her is a small but elegant waiting area with comfortable chairs, a marble table with a variety of magazines, and an elegantly simple chandelier lighting the space. It feels cozy and graceful and not at all like the waiting area of a high-rise office building.

The administrative assistant stands when we approach. Her light brown hair is coiled on top of her head in a loose but tidy bun, and her tortoiseshell glasses are a brand I wouldn't think she could afford on an admin's salary. A smattering of freckles across the tops of her cheeks and the bridge of her nose make her look even younger than she probably is. She nods to the receptionist, dismissing her, then reaches her hand across her desk toward me. "Hello, Ms. Volkova. I'm Avery Parker, Mr. Shepherd's admin."

"Hi, Avery," I say, shaking her hand. "Please, call me Petra."

"Right this way, Petra." She steps around her desk and walks toward the door where the hallway ends. *Thomas Shepherd* is written across that door in modern raised letters reminiscent of the lettering on the glass wall in the reception area. Inside the office, we can hear raised voices.

She glances at me, obviously not expecting arguing behind the door. She knocks twice and there's dead silence in there as she pushes the door open for me.

My stomach gives a small lurch as the door swings in, but I make sure I exude confidence on the outside as I take in the imposing space. Natural light from the two adjoining walls of floor-to-ceiling windows floods the far end of this corner office, with dark finishes everywhere else—navy walls, and a sitting area immediately off to the side.

Past that sits a dark walnut desk, the man behind it is presumably Mr. Shepherd. He stands as I walk toward him, saying, "Ms. Volkova, welcome. Please, have a seat." He gestures to one of the two mid-century modern walnut chairs with leather seats that face his desk. The one that's empty.

The man in the other chair hasn't moved since the door opened. He sits there like a hulking beast, his tall and muscular frame barely fitting in the seat. I can tell by the tense lines of his thick neck that there's raw power beneath an otherwise calm exterior. As I come up behind him, I feel like

I'm approaching an animal who could turn and overpower me with no effort at all. Despite my own stature, I feel uncommonly vulnerable as I step up behind that empty chair.

I pull it out and as I prepare to take my seat, and glance down at the man in question right as he glances up at me. Those eyes, the color of steel. That razor sharp jawline, apparent even under the facial hair. Those cheekbones that run along the top edge of the neatly trimmed beard. The permanent scowl. His dark hair is longer than I've ever seen it and the lines at the corner of his eyes are new, but I'd still recognize him anywhere.

"Sasha?" My voice is full of wonder, because I'm not sure how he is here after all this time. Fourteen years of no contact has that sense of wonder turning to anger in the pit of my stomach.

His deep voice is a husky growl, achingly familiar even as the man who sits in front of me is so different from the boy who left me years ago. "Hello, wife."

Books by Julia Connors

FROZEN HEARTS SERIES

On the Edge

(Jackson & Nate's Story)

Out of Bounds

(Sierra & Beau's Story)

One Last Shot

(Petra & Aleksandr's Story)

One Little Favor

(Avery & Tom's Novella)

On the Line

(Lauren & Jameson's Story)

BOSTON REBELS SERIES

Center Ice

(Audrey & Drew's Story)

Acknowledgments

Sierra and Beau's story was entirely written during the depths of winter, in a year where Covid kept me from skiing. Instead, I buried my head and my heart in this story, which unfolded so naturally and so quickly that this was the easiest book I've ever written. Sierra and Beau clearly wanted their love story told and were stopping at nothing to get me to write it! Getting to immerse myself in their winter love story made a winter without skiing more bearable for me.

I have many people to thank for their support and feedback on this book, but most especially:

Danielle, always. You are my never-ending cheerleader, the one who talks me off the ledge and boosts me up when I need it. Our texts and phone calls, the conversations about writing and cover design and books we love…I can never thank you enough for all of it! Your books are amazing, and your support of my writing has been invaluable to me.

Keri, for all the hours of brainstorming on Zoom, for recognizing plot holes and helping me fix them, and for encouraging me to keep writing even when it was hard. Our writing chats kept me going through Sierra and Beau's book.

Laura, for all of the times we've gotten together to write and talk writing. Your feedback on this book was extremely helpful. I'm so glad we are going through the whole publishing process together!

Anna, for reading everything I write and always giving me your honest opinion!

Melanie Harlow, Elsie Silver, and Gina Azzi, for the invaluable advice you've given me about this industry and your willingness to help a newer author—I am indebted to you and only hope I can pay your kindness and support forward one day!

Cate Lane, for going through all of this before me, and sharing your wisdom along the way!

My readers, your overwhelming support and love for On the Edge kept me going through the highs and lows of releasing my debut book. I appreciate how much you loved my book baby, and how many of you reached out to say you couldn't wait for Sierra and Beau's book. I hope I did them justice in your eyes.

Mr. Connors, as always, for everything. Our love story is *my* favorite.

Afterword

Thank you so much for reading! If you enjoyed the book, please consider leaving an honest review. Reader reviews mean so much to authors, and your time and feedback are appreciated.

Sign up for Julia's newsletter to stay up to date on the latest news and be the first to know about sales, audiobooks, and new releases!

www.juliaconnors.com/newsletter

About the Author

Julia Connors grew up on the warm and sunny West Coast, but her first decision as an adult was to trade her flip-flops for snow boots and move to Boston. She's been enjoying everything that New England has to offer for over two decades, and now that she's acclimated to the snowy winters and finally found all the places to get good sushi and tacos, she has zero regrets. You can usually find her in front of her computer, but when she stops writing she's most likely to be found outdoors, preferably with a pair of skis or snowshoes strapped to her feet in winter, or on a paddleboard in the summer.

amazon.com/author/juliaconnors
facebook.com/juliaconnorsauthor
instagram.com/juliaconnorsauthor
tiktok.com/@juliaconnorsauthor?
pinterest.com/juliaconnorsauthor
goodreads.com/julia_connors

Made in the USA
Las Vegas, NV
23 May 2024